EARTH'S BLOOD FATE'S FOLLY

LINDSEY BROUNSTEIN

Cover design by MiblArt

Map by Cartographybird Maps

Editing by Between the Lines Editorial

First edition 2025

ISBN 978-1-964237-03-9 (paperback)

ISBN 978-1-964237-05-3 (hardcover)

ISBN 978-1-964237-04-6 (ebook)

www.lindseybrounstein.com

CONTENT WARNINGS

Thank you for your interest in *Earth's Blood, Fate's Folly*, book two of the Five Fates series. This is a fantasy novel intended for readers 18 years and older. It contains strong language and violence. Specific content warnings are listed below. If you'd rather not see the content warnings, you can skip this page.

This story includes themes and descriptions of events that may not be suitable for everyone. These include:

- blood and physical violence, including murder

- brief mention of child abuse and neglect

- brief mention of amputation

- suicidal thoughts

- alcohol consumption and abuse

- parental abandonment

- religious extremism (and the deconstruction of)

- grief and loss

- panic attacks and anxiety

- depression and PTSD

If at any point—including right now—you need to put the book down (whether for a little while or forever), please do so. Take care of yourself, friend.

THE KNOWN WORLD
MAPPED IN THE PRESENT AGE
CAPITAL CITIES
MINOR CITIES
NOTABLE TOWNS
SNOWFELD
THE WILDS
LOSTWARD
ARMATHAIN
WHITEHOLLOW
VALDA
CLOUD BAY
AETHERANN'S REACH
PORT MERRICK
THE CRESCENT MOUNTAINS
AETHIR
WESTHOLD
GOETH
THE MISTVALE MOUNTAINS
WERYN
FORDRYN
THE SOUTHERN ISLES
NEOMA

PYRRAH
EMBER DEPTHS
EMBERCLIFF
KIREKWALL
THE MOONTIDE SEA
KYLERIA
BREMMARAN
RAVENSPORT
FALLWOOD
BROOKSHIRE
THE RED FOREST
DRAHKONIA
FINNEGAN'S FORDE
SOUTHREACH
TAERNFANE
SOUTHPORT

Pronunciation Guide

Aetherann: AY-ther-ahn
Aethir: AY-theer
Aethirian: ay-THEER-ee-an
Ainam: EYE-num
Bremmaran: BREM-mer-ahn
Bremmarian: brem-MAR-ee-an
Caelan: KAY-len
Corvin: COR-vin
Drahkon: DRAH-kon
Drahkonia: drah-KOHN-ee-ah
Drystan Serah: DRIS-ten SAIR-uh
Ethriel Zamorra: ETH-ree-el zah-MOR-ah
Gregor Thalesen: GRE-ger THAL-eh-sen
Jaelyn Aleissandra: jay-LIN al-ay-SAHN-drah
Lanara: lah-NAH-rah
Lucien Longshadow: LOO-shin LONG-shad-oh
Pyrannis: pie-RAH-nis
Taerna: TARE-nah
Taernfane: TARE-in-fane
Tanithe: TAN-ith
Tykaras: ty-KAHR-us
Valda: VAHL-dah
Verity Corallan: VAIR-i-tee COR-uh-lahn
Vire: VY-er

A GENTLE REMINDER, DEAR READER

When first our tale begins, two Wardens of the Flame — Verity Corallan and Drystan Serah — and a mercenary by the name of Dare are given a mission from the Valdane Council to infiltrate the kingdom of Westhold and investigate rumors of a powerful weapon. The trio takes a smuggling vessel captained by Isabel Gilmore across Cloud Bay to land on Westhold's shores. In the city of Port Merrick, they encounter an army captain who appears to be in charge of a very secretive mission. Although the situation quickly turns chaotic, they soon learn the captain's name is Corvin Crosse, and that he is in possession of the weapon they seek, with plans to move it out of the city. Verity, Dare, and Drystan then receive updated instructions to find the weapon and destroy it.

Drystan ingratiates himself among the soldiers transporting the weapon while Dare and Verity follow along far behind. The caravan of soldiers stops at a stronghold carved into a tunnel system at the edge of the Mistvale Mountains, and the two Wardens and the mercenary make a plan to locate the weapon within the stronghold. But when they find the only locked and magically secured room, there's only a young man being held prisoner. Dare and Verity rescue the mysterious stranger, and the group returns to Whitehollow.

The stranger — Solace, as Verity names him — has no memory of who he is, nor how he came to be a captive of the Westholden army. After some tests, research, and narrowly escaping another run-in with Captain Crosse — who is the powerful Chosen of Ainam — the group discovers that Solace is somehow bound, body and soul, to a weapon forged by the four slumbering elemental gods. Soon after, an ambush in a snowy mountain pass disrupts any hope of a peaceful solution to their problems. During the ambush, Drystan is killed and

Dare is mortally wounded. Solace, however, is able to use his mysterious divine power to heal Dare, pulling him back from Death's gates.

The assassins were Dare's fellow mercenaries, hired by the Valdane Council's spymaster, Tanithe Ash, but one of them — Finn Garrison — survives and the group brings her along as their prisoner.

Verity and Solace discover that there are places of power within the world that are tied to the gods, acting as conduits for their power. Their plan is simple enough: head to the city of Taernfane where there is a sacred tree thought to be tied to the earth goddess, Taerna, and attempt to separate Solace from the divine weapon.

The journey takes them through Brookshire, where Dare is immediately arrested. Verity, Solace, and Finn soon meet Jae Aleissandra and Lucien Longshadow, who share that Dare is actually Darcy Wilhaven, second son — and now heir — of Duke Wilhaven. Dare, for his part, wants nothing to do with his parents, though he reconnects with Gregor Thalesen, his childhood friend and the head of the duke's household.

Finn joins the group as an ally as they try to figure out a way to help Dare, but Solace is kidnapped by Corvin Crosse. Lucien tracks Corvin and Solace while Jae helps Verity and Finn rescue Dare — by having Verity swear him into the Wardens of the Flame, thereby forsaking all ties to his family's inheritance. Then they set off to find Solace.

They're not far from Brookshire when Tanithe Ash, who they discover is the Chosen of Vire, catches up to them—and she's dragging Gregor along as bait. Lucky for the group, Tanithe and Corvin are forced to battle each other, as well as the monstrous shifters in the Red Forest. The distraction allows Lucien — a shifter, himself — to find Solace and Gregor both.

Although rescued, Solace is unconscious, his power completely locked down by a strong Binding spell. Verity uses Dare as a Channel to draw the amount of power needed to banish the spell, but Dare's nature as a Perceptive — someone who can sense magic — complicates the ritual. During the channeling, Dare sees a pair of massive eyes, with violet sclera and irises swirling with stars, watching him.

Their moment of calm is short-lived. Verity and Gregor must hurry ahead to Taernfane to plead their case to King Dominic of Drahkonia and request his aid, while the others travel as quickly as they can to meet them there. One more encounter with Tanithe speeds the larger group on their way, though Lucien is whisked away with Tanithe and her shadows.

Verity and Gregor meet with King Dominic, only to find Corvin Crosse has beaten them there. Meanwhile Tanithe unleashes chaos in the palace courtyard as the rest of the group make every effort to get Solace to Taerna's sacred tree. During the chaos, Tanithe discovers Dare's Perceptive abilities and tortures him using her powerful magic, but a voice offers to help him — he accepts, and Tanithe is locked out of Dare's mind.

In the courtyard, Corvin fights with Verity and Lucien until Corvin unleashes the weapon bound within Solace. Solace loses all control, becoming nothing more than the living embodiment of divine, elemental power. Verity and Dare have no choice but to drive Verity's broken sword through Solace's heart. His spilled blood finds the roots of Taerna's tree, releasing the divine power bound within him and reawakening the elemental gods.

In the aftermath, Corvin and Tanithe have vanished; and Verity, Jae, Lucien, and Gregor have each been Chosen by one of the elemental gods. Verity uses her new-found power from Pyrannis, the god of fire, to heal Finn, who was grievously wounded in the battle. And Dare discovers that the voice he's been hearing throughout their journey is actually Tykaras, the long-lost god of fate and luck, whose violet eyes encompass the stars.

And so ends our tale, as told in *Fire's Hand, Fate's Heart*, book one of the *Five Fates*.

To those who feel like they are either too much or not enough.
You are perfect, you are loved, and this book is for you.

Prologue

I wake to you shaking me, whispering my name. Tears fill your eyes as you tell me it's time for me to go. Beside the bed we share, our little girl is asleep in the cradle I built. It's not even dawn yet, but I get up and dress, donning the forest green uniform of the Southreach royal army.

I tug on my boots, and your arms wrap around my shoulders as you ask whether I truly have to leave. I do, but it's only for two months, I remind you. You hang onto me a little longer, and it's only when I squeeze your arm that you let me go.

I step onto the gravel path of the cottage we built, on the farmstead we cultivated. Our little girl is in your arms. You wave at me from the doorway, moving her little arm so she waves too. I'll be home again before you can miss me, I tell you.

You say that's impossible because you already do.

My thoughts cling to you as I march with my company across Southreach. It's only a couple of days before the Red Forest looms ahead. Crimson leaves filter the sunlight, casting the whole place in shades of blood red.

We camp at the edge of the forest, planning to skirt west around the southern tip before continuing north. The Red Forest is not somewhere you want to be caught after dark, even in a company of soldiers. These woods belong to the shifters, monsters who used to be men. Once turned, they become savage beasts driven only by rage and bloodlust.

The stories say swords are of little use against them. They say the beasts are unkillable, but I've never believed that. Everything can be killed. Anything can die.

Screams come from the forest, startling me awake. Half the soldiers grab their weapons and prepare to charge into the trees in the predawn light. The other half look as though they want to hunker down and wait it out.

The faint light barely breaches the canopy as we move into the forest. One of the men falls, a shriek tearing from him as something dark and lumbering drags him into the underbrush. I charge the beast and plunge my sword into its side. It roars and turns its yellow eyes on me.

The monster lunges, its massive jaws clamping down. Pain like I've never known rips through my shoulder. I'm weightless for a moment before something hard strikes my back, bones cracking as the beast throws me into a tree like I'm nothing more than a rag doll.

I reach for my sword, but my fingers are cold and numb. Blood spills from my torn shoulder. The world tilts and spins.

The beast towers over me, its yellow eyes like two embers in the darkness. I try to push myself away, but my legs won't move. The monster growls, its hot, foul breath washing across my face. My death is staring at me, but with the last coherent thought I have, I think of you. I hold on to that image of you as the edges of my vision darken and the cold seeps in.

I love you. I may be dying, but my love for you never will.

The beast roars in pain, and something hot and wet covers me. A metallic taste fills my mouth, spilling into my throat, and I cough, choking on the beast's blood. Its looming shadow disappears. Another soldier screams.

I feel nothing but cold. My vision fades, and I take one more look at the memory of you, wishing I could hold you in my arms one more time. Wishing I could hold our little girl.

I don't want to go, but the darkness promises peace.

So I let myself fall.

I open my eyes. My world is agony and rage. Screams echo around me—*my screams*—as every bone and muscle in my body feels like it's being shredded. Somewhere within me I feel, more than hear, a voice urging me onward.

Run.

It's me, and yet it isn't me.

Run, it says. *RUN.*

I run. The forest is a blur. I move through the thick underbrush as though it were an open plain. My paws thunder against the ground.

Paws?

Yes, of course. They've always been there.

Haven't they?

It's hard to think. The thing inside me pushes me on.

Run.

Ahead, something moves. I see red. It starts to run and I give chase. I have no choice. My claws find something warm, and I tear into it with my teeth, the taste of meat coating my tongue, the metallic tang of blood filling my senses. The rush of the kill spikes my already surging adrenaline, my heart hammering in my chest.

More, the presence urges. *MORE.*

I run, but all I find are cold dead things. The dead things anger me. I want something warm and living. I want to kill. I run, burning with rage, until darkness swoops in and I collapse.

I awaken to pain, hunger, and confusion, all in equal measure. I push myself onto my hands and knees.

Hands?

Yes, but . . . but no . . . Something in me bristles at the sight of my human hands, broad and scarred from sword training and farm work. Whatever it is, it wants to see those paws again, the claws covered in blood as it rends the life from something. Anything.

I picture you again, trying to find that moment of peace before I died—before I *should have died*—but the thing within me imagines killing you. It fantasizes about ripping your head from your shoulders before devouring the infant in your arms. The images play through my mind, and nausea turns my stomach. Still doubled over, I vomit into the grass, all blood and I don't know what else. I retch again from the sight of it, heaving until I have nothing left.

Run, it says. *Kill.*

"No," I say aloud, forcing the word through my raw and painful throat.

But this thing doesn't like me talking back. It doesn't like not being the one in control. It roars, the sound tearing from somewhere deep in my chest as it rages against the thread of control I have.

Pain overtakes me again as that thread snaps, my bones bending and breaking, contorting into a massive four-legged monster, all fur and claws and fangs.

Seasons change in the forest. Whenever the beast catches me thinking of you, it dreams up new ways to tear you to pieces. I know these dreams for what they are: a promise.

I can never go back to you.

Not like this.

As far as you know, I died that day with the rest of the soldiers in my company. And I may as well have. What's left of me is different, changed in a way I can't come back from. I wish I could find a way to tell you what happened, to hold you and our little girl in my arms again, but I can't. I know what will happen if I try.

The beast stirs as my thoughts linger on your face, and I shift them away quickly.

I was wrong when I said that anything can die. I know that now. And I'll hold onto that—onto my love for you—for as long as I have a human thought left in my mind.

Run, my beast commands. *Kill.*

So I run.

I kill.

CHAPTER 1

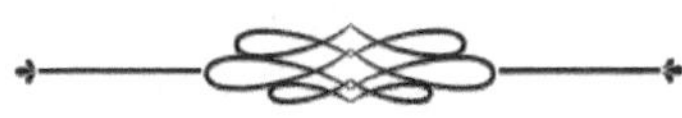

DARE STOOD ON THE battlements overlooking the courtyard. It was something he'd taken to doing often while the six of them had been staying in King Dominic Drahkon's palace as his honored guests. Save for the occasional guard patrol through the dark gardens below, Dare hadn't seen another soul in hours. The full moon illuminated Taerna's tree in all its divine glory, green and vibrant despite the final throes of winter.

It was little wonder why the entire city of Taernfane had been built around this lone tree.

As the nights had turned colder, Dare had found it harder and harder to stand upon the battlements, not for the discomfort of the cold, but for the memory it brought of a snowy mountain pass at the edge of Aethir.

Before his thoughts wandered too far down that worrisome path, Dare focused instead on the night sky, looking to the stars and the god whose eyes they filled.

Or, at least, he'd *thought* it had been a god.

The night Solace died, Tykaras had promised to explain more about what was happening, but the god had disappeared after that. Dare hadn't heard a word from them in months. He must have imagined the whole thing, he'd realized. It made sense. Tanithe had been rummaging around inside his head earlier that day, messing with Vire only knew what; and then with the stress of killing Solace and almost losing everyone else he cared about . . . His mind must have created Tykaras to keep him from spiraling into insanity.

Dare found that explanation far more palatable than the idea that a long-lost deity spoke to him and made him their Chosen. And it was one less thing to worry about, especially considering most of his friends now found themselves the Chosen of the newly reawakened elemental gods.

Yet his heart twisted each time he looked at the stars, so he turned and headed inside. The king had cleared a whole wing of the palace for his six guests. Only six, where once there had been seven and, truthfully, should have had an eighth. Dare rubbed at the knotted scar in the center of his chest that ached in the cold.

The only light in the halls at such a late hour was the moonlight pouring in through the windows. It wasn't much to see by, but it was enough for him. He'd memorized every turn during those first few weeks in the palace.

As Dare reached his door, he slipped the key into the lock and turned it as gently as he could, so the soft *click* was barely audible in the stillness. Gregor would be asleep. He rose with the sun—he always had—and was often asleep well before Dare could ever think of letting the night meander to an end. He turned the latch without a sound and ducked into the room.

It was warm thanks to a fire burning in the fireplace against one wall, which provided plenty of light. A small oil lamp on the bedside table was also lit.

No matter how many times over the last few months Dare told him not to bother, Gregor still kept the lantern lit until Dare got back each night. Always a beacon, leading home.

As he'd expected, Gregor was asleep. His short blond hair was getting a little longer, just long enough for it to get mussed in his sleep, sticking up at odd angles against the pillow.

Dare stripped off his clothes from the day and stepped into the adjoining bathing room. The palace's running water—including a shower—was a luxury Dare had certainly gotten used to over the last several months. After quickly washing up, Dare returned to the bedroom, steam following him as he dried his hair with a plush towel.

As Dare slid under the blankets, Gregor stirred, but didn't wake. He lay on his stomach, tension tightening his face, even in sleep. His hand gripped the edge of the blanket in a tight fist.

Gregor's brow furrowed, mouth twisting as he dreamt whatever troubled dream he'd been having lately. Dare propped his head up on his hand, and his eyes wandered over the rope scar circling Gregor's wrist. Dare could guess the cause of his nightmares.

Gregor had been more distant since they'd been in Taernfane. He'd had his own demons to battle over the last few months, but they'd said they would deal with them together. That first night after the battle, when Dare had awoken panting and soaked in sweat, he'd found Gregor already awake, reading by the firelight, his hands still shaking from his own dreams. They promised each other then that they'd be there for one another, no matter what happened.

Dare set his hand on Gregor's back. He drew slow, deliberate circles with his palm, gentle, soothing. "You're safe," he whispered. "I'm here. You're safe."

After a few moments, Gregor's hand relaxed, and the lines of tension on his face eased. As Dare's head began to droop with sleep at last, Gregor rolled over, settling into the space between them until his back fit snugly against Dare's chest.

Dare smiled, letting his arm drape over Gregor, pulling him in closer so he could pretend that nothing had changed. A sensation akin to a gentle spring breeze thrummed across his skin where he touched Gregor, shattering that brief illusion. Gregor had been Chosen last autumn, just like Verity and Jae and Lucien. As much as Dare wished that nothing had changed, Gregor had the power of Aetherann, the god of air, rushing through him now.

Dare pushed the thought away. Magic or not, it was still *Gregor* in his arms. Dare had spent eleven years thinking he'd never have this again. He wasn't about to let it go now because of a little magic.

As Dare closed his eyes, he belatedly thought of the lamp still burning on the side table.

It'll run out of oil eventually, he decided, resolving not to move from that very spot until morning.

If even then.

❋

Dare woke to the tingle of Gregor's divine power against his face. He groaned into the pillow as Gregor stroked his cheek with the back of his hand.

"You have to get up," he said softly, almost apologetically.

Dare rolled over, blinking hard to clear the sleep from his vision. "I have to do no such thing," he countered. He grabbed Gregor by the wrist and pulled him off-balance. "You have to come back to bed," he said as Gregor toppled down onto him.

"Dare," Gregor began, but Dare kissed him before he could say another word. If Gregor couldn't talk, he couldn't tell Dare he needed to be somewhere else. And he didn't want to be anywhere else. He wanted to be right here.

Gregor pulled back, bracing his forearm against Dare's chest to effectively push himself up while also pinning Dare to the bed. "Dare," he said again. He was trying to be stern, but a smile tugged at the corner of his mouth. "We have training. We're going to be late."

"*You* have training. You and the other god-touched."

The playfulness faded from Gregor's face. "Don't call us that."

"*Chosen*, then? Is that better?"

Gregor's jaw tightened. "Not really."

He hated seeing Gregor so bothered, especially when it seemed like he'd been about to relax. Dare shifted and rolled both of them easily, landing with Gregor on his back and Dare above him, straddling his hips. "The four of you who've been blessed by the elemental gods," he recited like a bored schoolboy.

"Three of us today," Gregor said. "*You* have hand-to-hand training with Verity."

Groaning, Dare collapsed down onto Gregor as though his bones had gone flimsy. "*Today?*"

Gregor tried to shove him off by the shoulders and failed. "Yes, *today.*"

He let his weight sink onto Gregor, making himself impossible to move, like a cat that didn't want to be picked up. "I don't want to," he said, nuzzling Gregor's neck.

"Gods above—" Gregor's breathy laugh surrounded him. "You're like a child."

Gregor's hand drifted up Dare's side, and just as Dare let himself relax into the feeling and the thought of where the morning might lead, Gregor pinched the spot along his ribs—the *one* spot—that made him seize up in helpless laughter.

Gregor chuckled as Dare, now standing a solid six feet away, rubbed at his side. "And *I'm* the child," Dare grumbled.

Gregor pushed himself up and sat on the edge of the bed. He pulled his glasses off and cleaned the lenses with the hem of his shirt. "Get dressed, my dear," he said. "We're going to be late."

Dare's heart skipped a beat, and he did as he was told.

As Dare finished dressing and pulled his hair back into a tail at the nape of his neck, Gregor's voice floated over his shoulder. "Does it bother you?"

"Does what bother me?"

"What happened." Gregor's throat worked as he tried to find the right words. "With the four of us, I mean. Verity, Jae, Lucien, and me. About being Chosen."

A memory of star-filled eyes stirred in his mind, but Dare shrugged it away. It was nothing. Whatever that had been, it hadn't been real. "Why would that bother me?"

"I don't know," Gregor mumbled, smoothing the front of his shirt. "You were there with us, but . . . I don't know. I worry that you might feel . . . left out?"

Dare hadn't yet let himself consider how he felt about it. He'd thought last autumn that he'd heard a god speak to him too. But nothing had come of it, and so Dare had determined it had to have been a hallucination. That realization had come with its own mental whiplash, but Dare was happier knowing he didn't have to bear that burden—that responsibility.

He was.

Wasn't he?

"I don't feel left out," Dare said, trying to mean it. He perched on the arm of the reading chair. "You haven't really told me much about it though." Dare had been trying to let Gregor handle his new abilities as the Chosen of Aetherann in his own way, in his own time.

So far, that had meant keeping Dare in the dark.

Gregor slid his glasses up his nose with his thumb, though he didn't look at Dare. "It's . . ." He sighed, lifting his eyes to study the ceiling. "I don't think I can articulate it."

"How's the training been going?" Dare asked, hoping to shift the conversation before Gregor withdrew too far.

"It's alright, I guess. We've mostly just been trying to figure out what we can do. And more importantly, how to control it." Gregor straightened the sleeves of his shirt, which was loose and casual for training and nothing at all like the clothing he'd always worn in Bremmaran. "We're going to be late."

Dare knew only a little about the sorts of power his friends now possessed. Each of them had some control over their god's respective element, though the degree to which they could manipulate these forces was largely still a mystery to Dare. Verity, at least, could also use Pyrannis's magic to heal and purify injuries, as Solace had done once for Dare. If the others had more powers though, they opted to keep things close to the vest. Dare could respect that. Don't tip your hand until you know what you have. And Gregor was always one to think things through before he acted.

Dare crossed to him, taking Gregor's hands in his own. The breath of divine magic in Gregor tickled his palms. "You know you can talk to me," Dare tried. "About any of it."

Gregor finally met his eyes again. There was such gentleness there, Dare almost forgot how to breathe. "I know," Gregor said. "And I will. I promise. And I know it's been months, I just . . . I'm still trying to wrap my head around all of it."

"I understand," Dare said. And he did. All too well. He smiled, and it was genuine, if somewhat sorrowful. "Let's get to training before Verity comes looking for us."

Dare walked beside Gregor in silence as they headed toward the training yard, though it wasn't too long before his curiosity got the better of him. "Is it the same for each of you?" he asked. "The way it feels—the connection to the gods?"

It is different for each Chosen, answered the voice in the back of Dare's mind—the one he hadn't heard in months.

Dare's steps faltered, though Gregor didn't seem to notice as he said, "I'm not certain, but I get the feeling that it varies."

An expansive presence filled Dare's chest, and he swallowed hard. He tried to keep his face neutral, focusing on putting one foot in front of the other as his mind reeled and rushed to catch up.

. . . Tykaras?

There was a brief pause. *Were you expecting someone else?*

I was expecting no one! Dare shot back silently. He cast a sideways glance at Gregor, who seemed unaware of Dare's mental distraction. He slowed just enough to let Gregor get ahead of him. *Where have you been? I thought I'd lost my fucking mind.*

Dare felt a flicker of amusement run through the back of his mind. *Your faculties seem no more impaired than last we spoke,* Tykaras said. *I didn't realize humans were so impatient.*

Impatient?

I told you I would explain, did I not?

That was five months ago.

The silence that followed went on far longer than Dare anticipated.

Oh, Tykaras said at last.

Dare's lip twitched. *Oh?*

Time dilation, the voice murmured. *I should have accounted for that.*

So, if Dare hadn't been imagining the voice that day on the parapets . . . If it wasn't all some fever dream of his subconscious . . . He tried to form the question. *Am I—*

Dare collided with Gregor, who'd stopped as one of the king's pages approached.

Gregor eyed Dare over his shoulder.

"Sorry," Dare mumbled. He rubbed the back of his neck. "Lost in thought."

We'll speak soon, Tykaras said. *Later in your same day.*

The page bowed to both of them. "Sirs, His Majesty King Dominic requests your presence on the hour."

Chapter 2

Lucien Longshadow enjoyed walking in the palace gardens. He'd always preferred green spaces over cities, even before he'd changed. But ever since he'd been Chosen by Taerna, the garden—and the tree at its center—had been one of his favorite places.

Although the four Chosen of the gods had decided to keep their collective status a secret for the time being, Lucien was not as fortunate when it came to his identity as a shifter. Several members of the palace guard had seen Lucien shift in the courtyard battle last autumn. Word traveled quickly after that. He received a fair number of frightened stares even now, and nearly everyone in the palace still gave him a wide berth. It was one of the reasons Lucien had taken to walking through the gardens in the early mornings. It meant fewer people would cross his path.

The shade of Taerna's tree invited him to sit, and so he did.

Peace was not a word that Lucien had related to. Ever. Before he'd become a shifter, he was a soldier. He'd done fifteen years in the Southreach army before moving to the reserve contingent, which was only called upon when the primary forces needed greater numbers. And after that . . . well . . . peace was an illusion. A dream for other people to follow, not him.

But sitting in this one courtyard in Drahkonia, in the shade of Taerna's sacred tree, Lucien was at peace. The power coursing through the tree, through the very ground of this city, was a balm to the anger that burned in his soul, to the rage that had dominated his heart for the last twenty years.

Lucien set his hand in the grass, not wanting to call attention to himself by crossing the small, perfunctory barrier that surrounded the tree. But he could feel the roots as they ran below the ground, and the power caressed his palm.

Little wolf, said a lovely voice, speaking directly into his heart. It was the sound of spring, of autumn, of mossy woods and towering mountains. It was the voice he'd heard the afternoon Solace had died and the gods had reawakened. And a few times since.

Had Taerna been waiting for him? Was that why he'd been drawn to the shade of the tree this morning?

Did you call for me? he asked.

Somewhere in his mind—or his heart—there was a smile. It was as pleasant and nurturing as a sun shower in spring. *I did.*

Silence stretched between them, but Lucien could still feel the grounded, heavy weight of Taerna's attention wrapping around him like a blanket. Most people he met were uncomfortable with his silence, needing to fill it with their own words. But there was no sense of urgency with the goddess. This was a comfortable silence that could stretch for as long as he needed it to.

Lucien angled his head toward the vibrant leaves. *Do you have need of me?*

Her attention wrapped more snuggly around him. *You are my climbing vines. You reach into the parts of the world where my power no longer extends.*

Whatever she asked of him, if it was in his power to do, he would do it. The serenity he felt in her presence was unlike anything he'd experienced before. Even his beast stilled when the goddess was near. He would serve her until his dying day for that gift alone. *What do you need me to do?*

Lucien felt something like a claw-tipped hand on his head. *The task I have for you is a tangled thicket of brambles. It will take time for the path to become clear—and for you to be ready to walk it.*

I'm ready, he said. He'd been in the palace too long. Even with the tree as a bastion of calm to his anger, he needed to wander.

To run.

It was the only thing he'd ever had in common with his beast. Even now, even with the goddess's presence calming it into a sort of docile submission, it perked up at the thought of leaving Taernfane behind.

Lucien looked deep within himself to where he kept the beast chained. It was the technique he'd always used to keep the monster in him under control. He pictured the monster bound in heavy iron chains with a dozen locks. As he studied the beast now, it was surprisingly subdued—almost reverent—in Taerna's presence. The soft green moss covering the chains and ivy vines threading through the links were both new.

There was another long silence before Taerna said, *I will show you what I can.*

Before Lucien could fully form the question of what she meant by *show* him, the world broke open.

In the darkness between spaces, flashes of light pierced his awareness. When the world resolved again into jagged shades of gray and brown, a group of people stood at the edge of a lake. It almost seemed like a dream.

Or a vision.

You? Lucien managed amid the swirling, pulsing lights in his mind. *It was you?*

The clawed hand tilted his head toward the vision, urging him to watch.

The people held bowls and dipped their fingers into them, spreading some sort of dark paint across their skin, decorating each other with sigils and intricate patterns. They smiled as they worked, helping adorn each other until they were all painted in similar but entirely unique designs of darker gray upon gray. Lucien couldn't hear what they were saying, but it looked as though one of them started a song and the others joined in.

As they celebrated, a dull throb began behind Lucien's eyes. It escalated quickly into a searing, blinding dagger twisting into his head. When one of the people knelt in the sand at the water's edge, the vision shattered as a snarling shifter crashed into his mind, its snapping, slobbering jaws lunging for him. Everything went dark.

It is as I thought, Taerna said gently.

Lucien opened his eyes. He still sat in the shade of the tree, though the sun was much higher in the sky. He blinked and rubbed his face with shaking hands. "What happened?" he asked aloud.

You're not ready.

Frustration pulsed through him. "How do I become ready?"

Explore, she said. Her grace fell over him again, warm and safe.

Lucien tried to form another question, but his mind was sluggish.

Rest, she said. *I will show you more, but not now. Not today. Your mind needs to rest.*

I can—

Rest, little wolf. Her voice grew firmer, insistent. *I will show you what I need, and you will be my champion.*

That strong, comforting weight Lucien had come to associate with Taerna's presence fell away nearly as quickly as it had descended, and he breathed in deeply with the sudden shock of its absence, feeling lighter but also disconnected, like the rope he'd been clinging to had been cut.

Lucien's mind reeled as his mired thoughts struggled to catch up with everything he'd just heard.

And seen.

Another vision. He hadn't had one since he and Jae had met up with the Warden in Brookshire. Had those first visions, which had ended as mysteriously as they'd begun, been sent by Taerna as well? Had he really been meant to be her Chosen from the start?

Thoughts racing, Lucien stood and sprinted back to the castle, running past the scattered visitors in the gardens, though they parted for him without him needing to say a word.

Prey always cleared a path for a beast.

He'd barely made it inside when one of the palace messengers stepped into Lucien's path. "Y-y-your presence is requested," the young man stammered. He was shaking and kept his eyes cast toward the floor. "His Majesty K-King D-D—"

Lucien blew his breath out in a sharp snort, and the boy jumped.

"I-I'm sorry, sir," he said, taking a few steps out of Lucien's way. "Please attend upon His M-Majesty in his study."

"Oh, for fuck's sake." Jae Aleissandra stepped around Lucien, putting herself between him and the stuttering page boy. "Stop making a fool out of yourself and get on with your duties."

Clearly grateful to be dismissed, even so harshly, the young man gave a swift bow and hurried off.

"I know what was wrong with him," Jae said, turning to face Lucien. The tight curls of her hair were pulled back away from her face, held in place by a band of cloth around her head. She took him by the arm and pulled him out of the main foyer. "But what the hells is wrong with you?"

Lucien drew a deep breath. He wanted to tell her everything—for once in his life, he *wanted* to tell her, but—"The king—"

"I know, I know," she said. "Verity, Finn, and I were all summoned too."

"Then what are you doing here?"

"Looking for you," she said, poking his chest. "And don't change the subject. What's going on?"

Jae had always been in tune with Lucien's emotions, but ever since she'd been Chosen by Lanara, the goddess of water, her natural empathy seemed to have been turned up or enhanced somehow. Lucien wasn't sure how it worked, but from what she'd told him, she could sometimes sense the emotions of others.

When he didn't answer right away, she studied him for a moment before lowering her voice. "Are you alright?"

He knew what she was asking with that tone. He hated that she felt the need to ask, but he understood. "I'm fine," he said, casting a quick glance down the expansive hallway. The page was long gone. "It's actually been easier to control since we've been here."

"Makes sense, I suppose," Jae said, angling her head to the side. "Given where we are."

"And what I am now," he added. *Taerna's Chosen.* "I mean, it's still there. It's still fighting. But, the only way I can describe it is that it feels . . . calmer."

Jae blew out a quiet breath. "I'm glad you're getting a chance to rest. You deserve it."

Rest? That wasn't in the cards for him.

"So what has you so on edge?" she pressed.

"The visions, Jae." Lucien started toward the king's study. He needed to move. "The visions that led us to Brookshire. I think that was Taerna."

"Taerna?" Jae hurried to catch up. "But she was asleep with the others. How?"

Lucien shrugged as he walked, his long strides propelling him through the palace. "I don't know. I was just out in the courtyard, at Taerna's tree, and she gave me a vision."

"You had another vision? Of the future?" she asked, brows rising.

He shook his head, dark hair falling into his eyes. "I have no idea. Maybe."

Silence hung between them for only a moment before Jae said, "Well? What was it?"

They passed a few members of the palace staff, who practically flattened themselves against the wall to avoid getting too close to Lucien.

He swallowed the growl that threatened to emerge. "Not now, Jae."

"But if you're having more visions—"

Lucien spun, and Jae nearly barreled into his chest. "Not. Now."

Jae's hand clenched into a fist before she relaxed it, rolling her shoulders.

"We'll talk after," Lucien said, forcing his frustration back down again. "Let's figure out what the king wants first."

Nodding, Jae led the way down the hall toward King Dominic's study. "Alright," she said. "One thing at a time."

Chapter 3

Since training was canceled, Dare had hoped he might swing past the kitchens to grab a pastry or two, but Gregor insisted they head straight to the king's study, despite the half hour before they needed to be there. There was a gleam in his eye that Dare couldn't ignore. He hadn't seen it since they'd both been effectively exiled from Brookshire. If attending upon the king was giving Gregor some pleasant reminder of his old life as a courtier, then who was Dare to interfere? Breakfast could wait.

As could working through the fact that he'd just had another conversation with Tykaras, the god of fate and luck . . . Who was real and apparently *not* a creation of Dare's addled mind. It was probably best if he didn't think too hard about that right now. Later would be good. He'd have time to sort through all of it later. He followed silently behind Gregor, trying desperately to push all thoughts of Tykaras out of his head for now.

By the time they reached King Dominic Drahkon's study, Verity and Finn were already sitting in two of the chairs outside the closed door.

"Warden, Finn," Gregor said, his voice taking on a tone of surprise. "Are you two here to see King Dominic?"

"We are," Verity said. "I take it he summoned both of you as well?"

Gregor nodded. "Were you told what this was about?"

Verity shook her head as Finn muttered, "No clue."

Dare gestured to the study doors. "Is he in there?"

"We were here so early," Finn said, casting an amused glance at Verity. "She wouldn't let me knock yet."

Verity's face reddened even as she gestured at Gregor as though to throw the focus away from herself. "But now that you're here, you could take the lead."

Gregor smiled, and a swell of pride bloomed in Dare's chest. Gregor had been dragged into all the horrors of last autumn and had been wildly out of his depth with the harried cross-country ride to Taernfane, not to mention everything that had happened once they'd arrived in the city.

But when it came to *this*, to matters of the court and nobles and the business of running cities . . . This was Gregor's element.

Before Gregor could respond, the oak door swung inward. King Dominic stood in the doorway. His dark hair, graying slightly at the temples, was pulled back into a loose tail at the base of his neck, and the sleeves of his plain gray shirt were rolled up to his elbows. He looked casual, even by King Dominic's standards. Even the silver circlet that was often the only adornment he wore to signify his status was absent.

Dominic leaned against the door frame as he peered at the group loitering outside his study. "Are you four planning to just sit out here all morning," he inquired, a smile tugging on his lips beneath his beard, "or are you going to come in?"

Gregor's cheeks flushed crimson as he gave a formal bow. "Your Majesty."

The king waved him up before Dare or the others could even begin their own bows. "Enough of that," he said quickly. He turned and moved into the study, leaving the door open in his wake.

The matching expressions of shock on Gregor's and Verity's faces brought Dare a not insignificant amount of amusement.

"As long as we've been here," Dare mused, "and you're still not used to his manner, are you?" He watched with delight as the blush on Gregor's cheeks spread to his ears.

"Not even a little," Gregor said as they followed the king inside.

The study was warm and inviting, and it was clearly used for pleasure reading as much as for business, if not even more so. Aside from the large desk covered in parchments, ink pots, and quills, the room was lined with bookshelves. Several cushioned armchairs were set into corners, and some of the windows had built-in reading nooks. All looked well-used.

Dare hid a smile as first Verity and then Gregor inhaled deeply, pulling in the pervasive scent of books and ink and wax.

King Dominic gestured them toward a cluster of seven chairs of various types surrounding a low table. Verity took one of the hard-backed chairs as Finn sank into the plush chair beside her. Gregor took the armchair on Verity's other side, and Dare perched on its arm.

As they sat, the door opened to admit a young servant boy, probably no older than fourteen, who carried a tray with a tea pot, seven small cups, sugar, cream, and a platter of assorted pastries. He crept into the room, focusing on keeping the load balanced between his hands. The tray landed heavily on the table when he set it down, the cups all clattering.

The boy winced as he glanced at the king out of the corner of his eye. "M-my apologies, Your Majesty."

The king smiled as he took his own seat in one of the plain wooden chairs. "It's alright, Pel," he said gently.

Dare inwardly marveled that the king of Drahkonia knew the name of a young servant in the palace without even having to think about it. And the boy didn't seem surprised.

Pel tucked a stray strand of hair behind his ear and proceeded to set the cups out in front of each of the chairs, pouring tea into them all. "Will there be anything else, Your Majesty?"

"No, thank you," the king replied kindly.

A solid knock sounded on the door before the boy could leave. At a gesture from the king, Pel tucked the empty tray under his arm and opened the door.

Lucien stalked in, followed closely by Jae. The shifter seemed on edge this morning. Even more than usual. Dominic stood, his stance neutral but tense as Lucien moved toward the circle of chairs. Apparently he could sense the difference in the shifter's demeanor as well.

Stepping around Lucien, Jae smiled her usual, cheerful smile, her teeth bright against her deep mahogany skin. "Good morning, Your Majesty," she said. Her tone was pleasant and upbeat, though Dare knew her well enough to see she was forcing it. She was tired. Run down.

Almost as though he took that as his cue, Lucien inhaled deeply and bowed to the king. At least half the tension in the room seemed to dissipate with his exhale. "Your Majesty."

King Dominic's shoulders relaxed as he gestured to the remaining chairs. "Please, sit. Thank you all for coming," he said to the group.

The serving boy left, closing the door behind him.

King Dominic leaned forward in his chair, adding a lump of sugar and a splash of milk to his tea. "Despite everything you've done for Drahkonia, and for the continent, I'm afraid I must request your assistance once more.

"As you know, we've been communicating with Valda regarding the attack their spymaster carried out on our city. I've been trying to reach some sort of an understanding with them, but they remain steadfast that they had no involvement in the attack. They also insist they have no one by the name of Tanithe Ash in their employment." Dominic sighed, cracking his knuckles. "They claim to have no knowledge of any of it, and openly condemn the attack, of course."

"Of course," Dare muttered. "Bastards."

Gregor cleared his throat pointedly as he reached for his tea, but Dominic only snorted his agreement.

"Bastards, indeed," the king said. "Unfortunately, you and your friends are our only witnesses to her involvement."

Gregor's tea cup rattled gently against the saucer, and he set both down on the table. "What do you need us to do, Your Majesty?"

"We've requested a special committee be appointed to investigate the matter," Dominic said, scratching at his chin through his dark beard. "It's taken months to arrange, but the Valdane Council has agreed, provided the committee convenes in a neutral location. I need you all to escort the Crown's emissary to the meeting and testify before the committee about what you witnessed that day in the courtyard." He breathed in deeply through his nose before adding, "I do not wish to ask it of you, but I have no other option. How many of you saw Tanithe Ash in Taernfane?"

Dare considered the events in the palace's courtyard. He'd certainly seen Tanithe there, as had Gregor when she'd attacked him in the palace halls outside the throne room. Lucien and Jae had seen her summon the shadow creatures, she'd shot at both Jae and Finn, and Verity—

"Five," Verity said before Dare finished the thought. "I didn't see her, but the others did."

Dominic nodded thoughtfully. "And how many know about her work for the Valdane Council?"

"All of us," she said.

"Directly? You all have firsthand knowledge of her connection to the Council?"

"I do," Dare said, voice low. "I worked for her there. She gave me jobs on behalf of the Council. Hells, I can tell you what her office in Valda looks like." He nodded across the table to Jae and Lucien. "You worked for her too on occasion, right?" Verity, Finn, and Gregor only knew based on what Dare had told them. "So, three of us."

Jae shook her head, her dark curls bouncing. "We never worked with her as Valda's spymaster," she said. "She was a contact we picked up odd jobs from when we passed through Valda." Jae crossed her arms over her chest. "We thought she worked through one of the local mercenary guilds. We didn't know she had political ties."

"Then the five of you, but you in particular, Warden, will be crucial to ensuring Tanithe Ash takes responsibility for her assault on my city, and that her actions are connected to Valda."

Only when Gregor nudged his knee did Dare realize that the king was referring to him when he said *Warden*. Dare still hadn't gotten used to that yet. "Of course," Dare said, straightening up a little, though he still sat on the arm of Gregor's chair. "I understand."

"Good," Dominic said. "I don't want to put undue pressure on you, Warden, but Tanithe's attack on the city was an act of war. If Valda knew about it, then they've declared war on Drahkonia. If Tanithe acted without their knowledge, then accepting responsibility for their spymaster would go a long way to avoiding more bloodshed."

Dare swallowed thickly. *No undue pressure . . . Sure . . .* It was only the fate of half the fucking continent.

"What of Westhold?" Verity asked.

Dare stifled a groan. Leave it to Verity to voluntarily add in the fate of the *other half* of the continent too.

"Westhold," King Dominic said, "is a different situation entirely. They've been surprisingly receptive to our diplomats. Like Valda, they've openly condemned the attack on the city, but unlike Valda, they acknowledge the part their army's former captain played in the events."

Dare arched a brow. "*Former* captain?"

"According to General Makarn of the Westholden forces, Crosse acted as a rogue agent and a traitor. He's being disciplined accordingly."

"Given the Westholden military," Gregor said quietly, "that's likely to be a very unpleasant fate."

"Good," Jae muttered.

An image flashed in Dare's mind of Solace, blank-faced and slinging elemental magic through the courtyard—the aftereffects of Crosse unleashing the weapon and damning Solace in the process. "It's no worse than he deserves," Dare added.

Gregor stiffened, then set a hand on Dare's leg. "You said the Westholdens have been receptive," he said to Dominic. "Have they allowed your diplomats into the kingdom?"

"They have," Dominic said. "Talks are progressing with Westhold far better than I'd anticipated. Something may yet still come of it that will need to be dealt with, but for now, my focus is on Valda."

"We understand, Your Majesty," Verity said. She cast a quick glance at the others, and at the scattered nods from everyone added, "We'll testify before the committee."

"Thank you." The king leaned back in his chair, crossing his ankle over his knee. "We're finalizing the details for the committee. Once we have all the necessary information, I'll have my secretary make all the arrangements for your travel and provide you with the specifics."

Verity nodded. She seemed eager, though there was a tension in the way she carried herself. She was nervous about leaving Taernfane.

Dare couldn't blame her. He was as well, and he suspected the others felt similarly. They'd all spent months recovering—grieving—and now it was time to get back to their lives. Dare wasn't even sure what that would look like anymore.

Dominic rose and the others rose with him, though Dare remained perched on the arm of the chair. "I'll draw up the notes now," the king said. He looked to Gregor. "Would you bring it by my secretary's office on your way out?"

"Of course, Your Majesty." Gregor clasped his hands behind his back as he waited.

"And if you would attend upon me again tomorrow morning," Dominic continued, still speaking to Gregor. "My sister, Princess Dalarynn, is currently studying at the university in Aetherann's Reach. I need to send her a letter regarding the direction things have taken with Valda, and I could use someone with far more tact than I to aid me in drafting it."

Dare didn't know much about the princess other than that she was much younger than Dominic and that she had a reputation for being much less responsible than her brother. Some of the stories he'd heard reminded Dare more than a little of his relationship with his own brother when he was a teen, though Dalarynn was in her early twenties.

"It would be my pleasure, Your Majesty," Gregor said.

"Wardens, there was one other thing I wanted to talk to you about." Dominic scrawled a quick note and signed it. The rest of the group filed out of his office as he folded the note and handed it to Gregor.

Gregor bowed low and took his leave, casting a quick glance at Dare over his shoulder.

With everyone else out of the room, Dominic turned his full attention to Dare, who stood on reflex.

"When it comes time to testify before the committee, be on your guard. I don't know whether the Valdane Council may try to *discourage* your testimony."

"I understand, Your Majesty," Dare said. Certainly being the only one who could directly tie Tanithe to Valda would put a target on his back. Not that he didn't already have one, considering that Tanithe would definitely want him dead after last autumn, and the Council was very likely furious with him for going against their orders in the first place.

But there were the others to consider as well. Even if their testimony was only that they'd seen Tanithe in Taernfane, the fewer witnesses to her attack, the easier it would be for her to argue that it wasn't her. And it certainly wasn't lost on Dare that this one simple fact put all of his friends in danger.

"I didn't want to say as much in front of everyone," the king said, addressing both Verity and Dare, "but my spy network has been unable to locate Tanithe Ash. Either the Valdane Council is harboring her, or she's in the wind. Either way, we have no way of knowing when or where she might turn up. Watch each others' backs out there."

Verity gave a Warden's salute, her closed fist over her heart. "We'll be careful."

After a gruff gesture from Dominic that they'd learned early on meant *you're dismissed*, Verity and Dare exited the king's study.

The hall outside was empty, the others having scattered.

"So much for training today," Dare said. He couldn't manage to keep the amusement from his voice.

Verity's brows rose. "Oh, you think so?"

Well, he *had*. There were about a dozen things on his mind, especially with the news that they'd all be traveling soon. And with Tanithe running loose who knew where on the continent, how was he supposed to focus on hand-to-hand training?

". . . Yes?"

"Not a chance," Verity said, arms crossing with a metallic *clink*. "I'll round up the others. Meet me in the training yard in half an hour."

Dare sighed. "As you wish, my lady Warden."

Chapter 4

⸻ ❦ ⸻

AFTER THE MEETING IN the king's study, Lucien didn't feel much calmer than he had before, though he tried to muster his control, for Jae's sake. He strode quickly to his chambers where he threw the door open with such force that it slammed into the interior wall.

Jae had barely shut the door behind her when she said, "Alright, now tell me about what happened with Taerna." She watched him with concern in her eyes, but she looked tired and worn.

He could only imagine how exhausting it must be to feel what other people were feeling, and Lucien knew that his emotions, running as strong as they did, were only making things worse. "It was nothing," he said.

"You can't bullshit me, Lucien." She set her hand over her heart, tapping a rhythm that matched his still-speeding heartbeat. "It wasn't *nothing*."

He swallowed. "It can wait 'til tomorrow."

"Maybe it can," Jae said. "But I don't want it to. I can tell this is important to you."

It was. "Fine," he grumbled. "Give me a moment first."

Jae gave a sweeping *do as you please* gesture as Lucien crossed to the washroom that adjoined his quarters. A small hand pump brought warm water straight into a basin, and he splashed some onto his face.

The beast glared at him from the mirror.

Lucien snarled back. After that vision, his control was strained, even here. He wasn't anywhere close to losing it completely, but he wouldn't let it come to that. He needed to regain his composure before things progressed any further.

The beast bared its fangs, daring him to try.

Lucien closed his eyes. The beast was waiting for him there too. It tugged on the chains binding it, growling as it sensed Lucien's attention.

He took a few deep breaths, the chains strengthening as he calmed the simmering rage coursing through him.

When he opened his eyes, it was his own scarred reflection—olive skin and yellow eyes—that stared back at him. He took a few more deep breaths, rolling his shoulders in a vain attempt to unknot muscles that had been knotted for the last twenty years.

Good enough.

Lucien emerged to find Jae lounging in one of the overstuffed armchairs, her legs draped over one of the arms.

"Better?" Her tone was serious, her usual teasing lilt gone. Jae never joked about his beast.

"Better," he agreed.

"Good. Now tell me about this new vision."

The words flowed from Lucien, easier than he'd ever found them before. He paced the room as he spoke, weaving a figure eight across the carpet. He told her of the vision, the people painting their skin in the woods and kneeling by a lake. He told her of the pain and the monster that had cut the vision short, and 'Taerna's words that he wouldn't be ready until he *explored*. Whatever that meant.

When he finished, Jae was sitting upright in the chair, leaning forward until her elbows rested on her knees. "What do you think it means?"

Lucien paced another lap. "I don't know."

"Do you think it's another vision of the future?"

"I don't know."

"And what does she want you to explore? The continent?"

"Jae, I don't know," he growled.

She threw her hands up. "Sorry, I know. It's just . . . ugh. Why can't she be more direct?"

Lucien shot her a glare.

"That was rhetorical," she said quickly. "If there's one thing I've learned in the last few months, it's that gods don't think the same way we do." Jae leaned back in the chair, tapping her finger against her lips. "*Explore . . .* I wonder if she's talking about your power. From being her Chosen."

His pacing didn't slow. "It's not *my* power, Jae. It belongs to her. To Taerna."

"Sure, but you know what I mean. How much have you been practicing?"

His silence was answer enough for Jae.

"Lucien! How are you supposed to—"

"Don't start."

"—figure out what you can do if—"

"Jae . . ."

"—you won't even try?"

Lucien rolled his eyes, but he could feel the smile tugging on his lips. "You are such a—"

"Delight?" Jae finished helpfully.

"Pain in my ass."

She shrugged. "Well apparently someone's gotta be. Come on, what have you figured out so far?"

In truth, Lucien hadn't done much with his newfound abilities from Taerna. He wasn't even sure he'd uncovered them all yet. "You've seen what I've figured out," he grumbled. She'd been at all the same training sessions in the courtyard as he had. "Moving dirt."

Now it was Jae's turn to roll her eyes. "You've got to be kidding me! You haven't tried anything else? You're not even the least bit curious what else you can do?"

He was. But whenever he accessed the power that seemed rooted in the deepest parts of himself, the beast seemed excited—eager. Lucien had learned long ago that anything his beast found enjoyable should be handled with caution, if at all. He'd avoided all but the smallest tests of shifting earth around when training with Verity and the others.

But Lucien wasn't sure how he could explain that in a way Jae could understand, so he simply said, "No."

Jae eyed him like she knew he was full of shit.

He sighed. "It's complicated," he opted for at last.

"That's fair." Her shoulders drooped. "All of this"—she gestured to the air between and around them—"is complicated as all hells. But we'll figure it out. You know that, right?"

"Yeah, I know," he said, but he wasn't so sure. Even though the beast felt easier to control in Taernfane, he couldn't let his guard down. One wrong move, one slip, and he could destroy everything—and every*one*—he cared about. It wasn't a risk Lucien was willing to take. Not twenty years ago. Not ten. And certainly not now.

"What about you?" he asked, moving the conversation into safer territory.

Jae leaned back in the chair again. "I'm good."

Lucien arched a brow. "You're not as good a liar as you think you are."

She chuckled, letting her head fall back against the cushions. "It's *complicated*," she said, sticking her tongue out at him.

He crossed his arms over his broad chest, forcing himself not to smile at her deflection. "Is it the emotions thing?"

"You could say that." She quirked one corner of her lips as she closed her eyes. "And I was up late last night practicing manipulating water."

"Pushing yourself is only going to exhaust you more, Jae," he said.

"Yes, yes," she mumbled. "I hear you."

Lucien resumed pacing. "I'm serious. And what about the . . . What do you call it? Empathy? What about that?" They hadn't discussed it too much beyond some of the basics. "Does it take effort to close it out? Because if it does, then you need to rest, or else everything's just going to get more difficult."

When she didn't answer, Lucien turned back. Her legs were curled up underneath her, and her head listed to the side. Her breathing was slow, steady.

Some of the tension in Lucien's shoulders lessened as he crossed the room and pulled a folded quilt from the end of the bed. He draped it over her, careful not to wake her. Jae was always looking after others. Someone needed to make sure she looked after herself every once in a while too.

CHAPTER 5

VERITY CORALLAN STOOD ALONE in the training yard. She'd been coming here with the others nearly every day for the last couple of months. After Solace's death and the awakening of the elemental gods, they'd all taken time to rest and recover, both physically and mentally, from the events of that autumn. But after some well-deserved quiet, Lucien, Jae, and Gregor—the others who had become Chosen of the old gods—came to her. They asked her to train them. There was power running through them all now. They could feel it, just below the surface.

Solace had been able to do incredible things with the power of the gods he had inside him. And although the magic within each of the Chosen was much diminished by comparison, it was still more divine power than had been seen in the world for centuries. They wanted to discover what they were capable of. And they wanted to learn how to wield it. They looked to Verity to provide structure, and she welcomed the chance to focus on something other than the immense pit of loss in her chest. Without Drystan, without Solace, Verity had been adrift. Having a goal, a routine to pour herself into, was exactly what she needed.

Together, the four of them asked the king for a place to train. He had an interior courtyard cleared the next day and converted into a training area for their sole use. It was surrounded by the strong stone walls of the palace, with two doors providing access. It was open to the sky, with only a few windows overlooking it, and had a large tree off to one side, its budding leaves promising summer shade.

Most days since then, Gregor, Lucien, and Jae met with her in the converted courtyard for training. More recently she had added martial training for Dare, and she'd been considering inviting Finn as well. Finn's recovery had gone quite remarkably, according to Epione, the old healer that worked in the palace, though it had been long and slow—frustratingly so, according to Finn.

When Finn had been injured in the attack on Taernfane, Verity's heart had cracked at seeing her like that, limp and pale. She looked so small being carried in the king's arms. But Pyrannis's fire had sparked within Verity, and she was able to channel that purifying fire to close the wound on Finn's thigh, saving her life. Just as Solace had used the same fire to save Dare when they'd been ambushed in the Crescent Mountains.

Verity let the memory fade away as the door swung open and Dare stepped outside, a full quarter hour later than she'd told him. His eyes swept the empty yard. "Where are the others?"

"It's just us today," Verity said. There was something she'd been meaning to talk to Dare about for a while, but it always felt like there were too many people around. When the opportunity to get him alone finally presented itself, she jumped on it. "I decided to give them the day off. They've earned it."

Dare tossed his hands out to his sides, incredulous. "But not me?"

Verity scoffed. Getting Dare to training at all had been marginally successful at best, and usually only when Gregor was able to drag him. "Not you. Besides, you're late." She easily fell back into the commanding tone she'd used when training the new recruits back at the Wardens' base in Whitehollow. "That's ten laps around the courtyard, Warden."

She was still getting used to the idea of Dare being a Warden, but she did occasionally delight in using her authority against him, if she was being honest with herself. She grinned as Dare's mouth fell open.

He gestured about the empty courtyard. "What about everyone else," he said quickly. "They're not even here!"

"But they would have been if I asked them to. And they would have been on time."

Dare was trying his best to look insulted. "It's not enough you're going to beat on me today, but you're going to make me run laps first? I didn't realize you found torture so amusing." He paused, considering, then widened his eyes as though coming to some dramatic realization. "Or is it that my fighting has come along so well that you're worried I'll best you, and your plan is to tire me out first?"

If he was trying to distract her from training today, it wasn't going to work, although she did find his impotent indignation entertaining.

"I could make it twenty," Verity offered.

"Alright, alright, you win!" He took off at a jog around the outer perimeter of the courtyard.

Verity practiced some of her own meditation exercises while Dare finished his run.

He jogged to her, breathing hard. "Happy now?"

Verity stood, setting her hands on her hips. "I'll be happy when you're on time," she said. "And when you take this seriously."

"Alright, yes, I hear you." He threw his hands up to ward her off. "But really? Hand-to-hand combat?"

She stood her ground.

"Verity, I'm not a fighter."

The image of Dare with a spear through his chest, pinning him to the snow-covered ground, flashed through her mind. "I know," she said sharply. "That's why we're doing this." Verity crossed to the tree and stooped to retrieve some padded gloves she'd left on the ground. She slid them over the steel plates of her hands. Waving Dare over, she planted her feet and held her hands up as targets.

Dare sighed but joined her by the tree, dropping into the stance she'd shown him. He punched the pads as she called out drills. Verity appraised his form, pointing out adjustments as he followed her instructions.

For all of his attitude toward training, Dare was a good student. He was fast and had an excellent understanding of where his body was. He was learning, whether he wanted to or not. And if he was picking this up so quickly, perhaps there was something else she could teach him, at least according to the thoughts she'd been mulling over for the better part of the last month. She'd might as well get to it, since it was the whole reason she'd brought him out here.

"Dare?" She kept her hands up, though his rhythm faltered. "I wanted to talk to you about something."

"Alright," he said tentatively. He continued punching the pads on her hands while she found the right words.

"I'd like to work with you on your magic."

Dare's next punch missed her hands entirely as his eyes landed on hers. "I'm sorry, what?"

Verity took a deep breath. "I'd like to work with you on your magic," she said again.

Dare dropped a hand to his hip while the other pinched the bridge of his nose. "And here I thought I was the only one losing my mind today," he muttered.

"Before . . . before all this"—Verity waved a gloved hand, encompassing the palace—"when I channeled through you to break the Binding spell on Solace, I'd never felt anything like that before."

"Please, don't start."

"Dare, the amount of power, the potential—"

"I've heard enough talk of my *potential* to last a lifetime," he grumbled.

"It would come so easy for you. I can teach you—"

"You sound like my mother."

"I'm not her," Verity snapped. If he would just listen, then maybe he would understand that she was trying to help. "I've trained dozens of Wardens who were natural Channels. And I have some ideas on how I could help with your Perceptive abilities."

Dare's eyes widened, but whether it was from surprise or irritation, she couldn't tell. "Help? What part do you think you could help with, exactly?"

"I could teach you some techniques to help you not let it bother you so much."

"*Let* it bother me?" Dare's voice lowered, but there was an edge to it. Tension rippled through him as he stepped away from her. "It bothers me because it feels horrible. I don't *let* it bother me, Verity."

Her heart clenched. This wasn't going as she'd hoped. "I didn't mean it like that. We still have enemies out there. If they were to find out about you, they could use it against you. Against us."

"So it's tactical?"

"Well, yes," Verity tried. Maybe she could appeal to his reason before this conversation went any further downhill.

"You're worried about me being a liability."

"No—Dare!"

But he was already walking away, heading toward the door leading out of the courtyard. "I think I've had enough training for today," he called over his shoulder. "I'll see you tomorrow." And then he was gone, the door slamming shut behind him.

Well, that went about as poorly as she'd feared. She wanted to help him but had managed to muck things up instead. "Vire's hells."

With her morning blocked off for training and nowhere else she needed to be, Verity decided to train on her own for a while in the hopes of clearing her head.

She ran a few laps herself, then practiced some meditation exercises, as well as her sword forms. While she trained, the sky grew overcast, and after a couple hours, a misting rain fell.

Despite trying to give herself some distance on the subject, her thoughts drifted back to Dare. She'd messed up, and she would need to correct her mistake, but she needed to figure out the best way to approach him again. How could she make him understand?

The spark within her heart, which had been there ever since the aftermath of the courtyard battle five months ago, flickered and winked, flaring to life as she turned her attention toward it.

Hello, Verity Corallan. It was the voice of Pyrannis, the elemental god of fire. The hearth-like warmth of the god's attention filled her.

Hello, she replied.

The flame danced curiously within her. *Why do you stand alone in the rain?* he asked.

Verity chuckled softly to herself. *That's a good question.*

Pyrannis, she had learned over these last few months, had an insatiable curiosity, especially about mortals.

Verity inhaled slowly. *I made an error in judgment, and I'm afraid I may have hurt a friend of mine.*

There was a pause before the god said, *Physically?*

No, Verity replied. *But I brought up painful memories without really thinking through what I was asking of him.*

I see. Pyrannis's fire crackled and flared a little brighter. *And you wish now to purify the injury you caused?*

Verity couldn't help the tired smile that pulled at her lips. *Not in so many words, but yes. I want to apologize.*

Interesting. And this apologizing *is to an emotional wound as cauterizing is to a physical one? It will stop the injury from worsening?*

I hadn't considered it that way, she conceded. *But yes, I suppose so.*

I understand. Please proceed.

She chuckled under her breath. It was amazing how Pyrannis could clearly care so deeply for the humans who inhabited the world, and yet understand so little about them. She doubted it was the five hundred years of slumber that caused the rift in his understanding, though it certainly hadn't helped any. At least he seemed eager to learn. That was more than she could say for many other people she'd known.

Steam wafted from her body as the rain bounced off her shoulders and the steel of her arms. There was one more thing she wanted to work on, but she'd been putting it off for a while now.

Verity focused on her hands, the gears within whirring softly as she flexed her fingers.

She'd spent quite a bit of time over the last few months practicing her control over Pyrannis's element of fire and in that time, she'd become more accustomed to manipulating it. She could increase or decrease a flame's strength, causing it to burn brighter, consume faster, or diminish altogether.

And yet through that practice, she had the nearly overwhelming suspicion that manipulating flames was just the beginning of what she could do with her god's element. She was a Chosen of Pyrannis. A spark of his power glowed inside her. Her own curiosity flared at the question of what else she could do.

The flame of Pyrannis danced with amusement and approval, though he said nothing else.

Verity stared at the fingers of her left hand, slick with rain, though steam still billowed from her as though she were her own furnace. It was all too easy to recall her hand, the one made of flesh and bone, wreathed in fire. Manipulating flame had been cause enough for trepidation, but the thought of creating fire out of nothing . . .

. . . Again.

And yet that little spark glowed within her, flaring, eager to be released. She let the power collect and pool in her chest, and focused on moving it down her arm and into her hand.

A tiny flame appeared in her left palm.

Verity held her breath. It didn't hurt, but then what a foolish thought that was, since the metal of her hands and arms could feel only pressure, not heat nor pain. She watched the flame flicker along the metal of her palm, waiting to see if it extinguished itself or if the plates of her hand would glow from the heat. There was no fuel to sustain it beyond the power from Pyrannis, and yet it continued to burn. When the thought crossed her mind to extinguish the fire, it snuffed itself out, leaving no trace behind.

She remembered to breathe and touched her palm gingerly to the bare skin of her other arm, but the metal felt just as cool as it always did. When she pulled it away again, Verity willed another tiny flame to ignite. This time, however, she willed the fire to move to her fingers, where she let it dance from one fingertip to the next and back again as it hissed in the rain. The movement reminded her of Dare rolling a coin over his knuckles. Verity focused on the flame, and it burned brighter, growing until it encompassed her entire palm.

Her heart beat faster as memories of pain and terror, of screaming soldiers and scraping stone, flooded her mind.

What if she couldn't control it this time either?

The fire curled around her fingers and stretched up her wrist. Her stomach clenched as she swallowed down the fear that threatened to take over. She could do this. She could do this.

But what if she couldn't? What if it tried to consume her? What if it was only her hubris that had her thinking this time could be different?

No, this was Pyrannis's fire. It wouldn't hurt her.

Did she know that for certain? It *wasn't* different. Not really. It was still fire. It would still burn and consume everything in its path.

Including her.

Her breathing was coming in quick gasps as Verity closed her fist and the flame extinguished.

Oh, gods—she couldn't do this. There was a reason she hadn't channeled her magic into heat since that day. She'd thought maybe after so many years she could push the fear from her mind, but it all came rushing back.

I can't do this.

"Verity?"

She spun to find Gregor standing in the palace doorway.

"Are you alright?" The concern on his face brought her focus back to the present.

Verity took a deep breath as her heart continued thundering in her chest. "I-I'm alright," she said. Another breath. "I'm alright." Maybe if she said it enough, it would be true.

Gregor joined her in the courtyard. "I'm sorry. I didn't mean to intrude." He gestured vaguely to the door. "I was passing by and I . . . I heard . . ." He cleared his throat, taking half a step back. "I suppose I did mean to intrude . . ."

She tried to slow her racing heart. Gregor still wasn't in control of his powers from Aetherann, and it seemed the god of air was far less involved in Gregor's instruction than Pyrannis was in her own. Gregor hadn't told anyone else about his new gift, though he'd confided in Verity a couple months ago.

She'd been with him when the voices first started. He'd thought he was losing his mind, but when they'd discovered the truth—that the whispers Gregor sometimes heard were the thoughts of others—Verity had been fascinated, but Gregor had seemed even more troubled.

He must have been in the hall and heard her panicked thoughts.

"You don't need to be embarrassed," she said. "Thank you for checking on me."

He paused in his slow, wilting retreat toward the palace. "I'm sorry," he said again. "You sounded so . . ." His brow furrowed. "Are you sure you're alright, Warden?"

Verity glanced down at her hands again. "I don't know what Dare's told you about my life before the Wardens . . ."

"He hasn't told me anything."

She swallowed hard, forcing herself forward. "Using magic to create fire is how I lost my arms," she said, tapping her fingers against the steel of her forearm. "And with the power from Pyrannis—"

"You were trying to create fire from nothing," Gregor supplied.

"I thought I would be fine. I thought that if I kept my focus, it would be alright."

Gregor moved further into the courtyard, the flecks of rain beading up on his glasses. "I'd imagine that would be terrifying."

Her chest tightened, and the words came out of her in a rush. "When I saw the flames covering my hand, the memory of that night came roaring back. I could see the fire engulfing my whole arm again, and I panicked."

Gregor nodded, like this fear of hers was the most normal thing in the world. Like he'd heard stories like hers hundreds of times. "Would it help to have someone here with you?" he asked, his voice sincere. "I could stay if you want to try it again."

The memory of the College that had been tormenting her was replaced by another that made her eyes sting, though not out of fear or shame, but because she missed her best friend.

Do you want me to stay? Drystan used to ask her that whenever she was having a particularly hard day, especially at the Wardens' camp where they first met. She missed him so much. She could really use his comforting hand on her shoulder right now.

"That's very kind of you," she said, "but I'm sure you have better things to be doing."

He gave a small shrug. "Better than helping a friend who could use support?"

"Than standing out in the rain," she said with a quiet chuckle.

He held his hand out as though gauging the severity of the weather. "This is hardly more than the mist off the falls back home." A small twist of a smile appeared along with a dimple under one eye. "I think my description is the better one." Gregor gestured for her to continue. "If you want to try it again, I'm here."

Verity did want to try again, and she was grateful Gregor was there, even though she was embarrassed. She should be stronger than this.

"As you just told me a moment ago," Gregor said, a gentle blush coloring his face. "It's nothing to be embarrassed about."

So, he'd heard that thought as well.

Gregor winced. "I did, I'm sorry. I, uh, can't turn it off at present. I can go if it—"

"No," Verity said quickly. "No, it doesn't bother me." She drew in a deep breath and blew it out slowly. "I'd like to try again."

"I'll just be right here," he said, moving the last few steps to where Verity stood. "So you know you're not alone."

Verity closed her eyes. *So you know you're not alone.* Within her, the little spark danced at the thought of getting to play again. *I'm not alone.* She let that spark flicker down her arm and into her hand. When she opened her eyes, a flame no larger than a candle glowed on her palm.

"That's amazing," Gregor said, watching the flame.

With the strength of his presence, Verity tried again to make the fire glow brighter, to make it burn hotter. Her heart thundered in her chest as the flames licked up her wrist, brushing against her forearm. She clenched her eyes shut against it, but gods, the vision of the College was there, even behind her eyelids. She tried to force the fear back down. She wasn't at the College, and this wasn't the same fire.

"You're alright, Verity." Gregor set his hand against her right shoulder, squeezing it firmly. "You can do this."

He sounded so calm, so certain. Verity could almost hear Drystan's voice echoed in Gregor's words.

You've got this, Vee.

She willed herself to have as much confidence as Gregor seemed to have in her—as Drystan always had in her.

Verity opened her eyes. The fire still covered her left hand, but it stayed where she willed it, seemingly content with the power she used to fuel it, with no need or drive to devour everything in its path.

The firelight reflected off Gregor's glasses as he watched. "How do you feel?" he asked, his hand still gripping Verity's shoulder.

"Terrified," she admitted. But it wasn't as overwhelming as before, and each small command she gave the fire—each time it responded to her wishes to shrink or grow or move—fed her resolve.

She kept the actions simple. Verity knew enough about training with magic to know not to push herself too far too fast. A new mage trying to do a spell that was too complicated or to channel more magic than they were used to was sure to get themselves into trouble. She focused on keeping it small and manageable. There would be plenty of time to test her limits once she could summon the flames without approaching a panic.

Having Gregor there to tether her, to ground her, was more helpful than she could have guessed. Knowing another person was with her and understood what she was trying to do . . . that someone was there, in case it all went wrong . . .

Verity closed her fist and the fire snuffed itself out, a nervous laugh escaping her in the same moment. Again, she gently touched her palm to her upper arm and found the metal as cold as before. "Incredible," she murmured.

"Do you want to try it again?" Gregor asked.

She did, and so Verity and Gregor stood out in the rain for the better part of an hour as Verity summoned small flames on each of her hands. The first few times, her pulse had quickened again, but Gregor's steady presence and calm tone helped to keep her focused. By the last few, Gregor simply stood by and watched as she summoned and manipulated the flames.

"Thank you," she said as the flame flickered out again. "I couldn't have made so much progress today without your help."

"It's n-nothing," he replied, his teeth chattering.

"Gods, Gregor, you must be freezing." The cold didn't seem to bother her much anymore, as though the spark from Pyrannis kept her warm no matter the temperature outside, but Gregor had no such protection. And although it wasn't particularly cold in the central courtyard, the drizzle certainly added a chill over time.

"It's fine," he said. "Even a bookworm such as myself can handle getting a little soggy."

Verity chuckled.

"Besides," he continued, a small smile spreading across his lips, "the fire was quite toasty while you were practicing."

She gave him a short half bow, taking him at his word. "Let's get inside anyway. I think we've been out here long enough."

CHAPTER 6

INSIDE THE PALACE HALLS, Gregor Thalesen took off his glasses, trying to find a dry patch on his shirt to clean them with. Finding none, he sighed quietly before setting the glasses on the end of his nose.

"Thank you again," Verity said as they walked, passing the ornate tapestries that lined the walls. She hesitated briefly before she added, "How have things been going with your own practice?"

His own practice. Gregor had been training with Verity for several months, along with Jae and Lucien. She'd taught them meditation and exercises designed to calm their minds and focus their thoughts. Gregor had done calisthenics and core strengthening until his muscles burned. But that wasn't the part she was asking about.

Magic wasn't something Gregor had ever had a gift for back home. He wasn't a mage, and he wasn't special. He was gifted with numbers and languages, the structure of both speaking to him in a way that made sense. It was part of why he was good at his job—his former job—as House Secretary to Duke Wilhaven in Bremmaran.

Verity was a skilled mage, one of the best Gregor had ever had the pleasure of encountering, but this was a different set of skills even for her. This was divine magic—elemental magic, the likes of which hadn't been seen on the continent in over five hundred years.

"I feel as though I have a handle on part of it," Gregor said, finally bringing his thoughts around to answering Verity's question. He flexed his fingers, and a tapestry on the wall fluttered in a sudden breeze.

Verity smiled at the small display of elemental control. "And . . . the other part? Have you figured out what triggers it?"

Almost as if on cue, the susurrus that had been plaguing him before he'd joined Verity in the courtyard picked up again, like leaves rustling in the woods.

"Sadly no." The noise in the back of his mind swelled until he could make out whispers among the rustling leaves. He tried to focus on the conversation with Verity, but the more he tried to push the whispers out, the louder they became.

Verity hesitated. "Has Aetherann said anything to you about it?"

He huffed a sullen laugh. He'd tried talking to Aetherann, as the others were able to do with their patrons, seemingly at their discretion, but so far he hadn't been successful. "Not really."

"Does he say anything at all?"

The sounds grew louder still. Voices, words, all vying for his awareness. He paused in the hallway and closed his eyes. Perhaps one of the mindfulness techniques Verity had shown him would help. They hadn't yet, but it was worth trying before the whispers overwhelmed him completely. The voices quieted for only a moment before returning full force, building from a whisper to a dull roar, flooding the back of his mind.

"Gregor?" Verity's voice was muffled. "Are you alright?"

"I'm fine," Gregor said, though it sounded disingenuous even to himself. "It's, um . . ." He took off his glasses and pressed his forefinger and thumb against his eyes. "It's a little loud at the moment."

I wish I knew how to help.

"You are helping, Verity," he said, an instant before he realized he was responding to the words she thought, not the ones she said. Gregor winced. He tried hard to avoid doing that. He'd already intruded on her thoughts when she was in the courtyard, but damn it all to Vire's hells, he just hadn't managed to figure out how to control it yet.

"I'm sorry," Gregor added hastily, opening his eyes. "I didn't mean to do that."

"It's fine," Verity said. "I understand. You'll figure it out, Gregor. I have no doubt."

He rubbed his eyes again. "It feels like I've been thrown off a cliff with the expectation that I'll fly. But I don't know whether I'm supposed to grow wings or turn the world upside down so I never hit the ground." He sighed deeply and slid his glasses back on. "And either way seems equally impossible."

"I wish I knew the answer," Verity said. "I truly do. But I'm willing to help you. And I know the others would want to help you too." Verity searched his face. "Gregor, I think you should tell them."

Dread swelled in Gregor's chest. He'd hoped to have his power under control, at least a little, before he told everyone, but the longer this dragged on . . .

Although this new power had surfaced much later than his ability to manipulate the wind, it had already been two months. Verity had tried to help him, showing him meditation techniques and helping him brainstorm ways to get the voices to quiet once they started up, but nothing had worked.

"What if . . ." He swallowed hard. Finding words for the fear that had been living in his chest proved difficult. "What if they act differently around me if they know that I may accidentally hear their thoughts?" He whispered the words, partially to avoid being overheard and partially because his throat closed up around them. The voices were still rustling through his mind, but they had started to quiet again.

"Do I act differently around you?" she asked.

"No . . . I suppose not."

"Then what makes you think they would? Lucien and Jae are dealing with their own changes; they'll understand better than most. And Dare . . ." Her face softened as she smiled. "I don't think there's anything you could tell him that would change how he feels about you. Gregor, that man would move mountains for you."

Another voice echoed through his mind, though this one was a memory. *For you, he would burn down the world.* Tanithe had told him that. Tanithe, who had her own mind magic that she'd used to wreak havoc on Dare's mind. There was no way Dare wouldn't draw that same connection. The last thing he wanted was for Dare—for any of them—to view him as a monster like Tanithe.

"I . . ." The words stalled. How could he explain this to Dare—to any of them—when he didn't even understand it himself? "I'm sure you're right," he added softly.

Maybe they really wouldn't think any differently of him . . . But Gregor would. This was his power. Aetherann came to him, *Chose* him, for a reason. He needed to figure this out.

"I won't ask you to do anything you're not ready to do," Verity said. "But I will ask that you think about it. I know they'll understand."

The noise around him was fading again, leaving a heavy silence behind. "I'll consider it. Thank you, Verity."

The Warden nodded. "Of course. Whatever I can do to help." Another thought seemed to strike her before she could turn away. "Speaking of Dare, if you see him, can you let him know I need to talk to him?" She started down the hall again, and Gregor followed.

"I'll be happy to. But is everything alright?"

Verity blew out a breath, her metal fingers tapping rhythmically on her arm as she told Gregor about her doomed conversation with Dare from earlier that morning.

"I'm sorry," she said when she finished her story. "I know how magic makes him feel."

Gregor wondered whether Verity truly knew the full extent of it. If she did, he doubted she would have brought it up at all. At least, not without any warning.

But Gregor knew.

"I'm certain you had only the noblest of intentions, Verity, but you have to understand that you've got a lot of"—he chose his next word carefully—"history to get through to reach him."

"I know. I'll talk to him."

"If I see Dare, I'll let him know you're looking for him."

They walked in silence until they reached the hallway that led to their wing of the palace. Gregor hesitated at the intersection, the beginnings of another thought stirring.

Verity motioned toward the suites of rooms. "I'm headed this way. I'll see you later?"

Gregor nodded, his gaze drifting down the other hall. He bid the Warden farewell and headed down one of the back hallways he'd discovered early in their stay at the palace.

Verity always seemed to have good advice; she certainly hadn't steered him wrong yet. But still, the thought of telling anyone about this new power, even Dare—especially Dare—tied his stomach in a knot. Since the events of last autumn, Dare had been struggling with guilt over Solace's death. Gregor couldn't burden him with something he should be capable of figuring out on his own.

He just needed more time. Though part of him wondered whether he truly believed time was the issue.

Perhaps he simply needed a new tactic. A new perspective.

Gregor climbed the back stairwell that led to the outer walls. Careful of his footing in the drizzle, he climbed another set of stairs, then a ladder, until he was on the upper parapets where the watchtowers stood. Although this particular tower was occupied with one of the palace guards, the rest of the upper wall was deserted.

Gregor found a spot away from the guard and leaned against the wall. He was at the tallest part of the palace, which itself was the highest point in the city. This high up, the wind was unimpeded. It rushed around him as he peered down at the city far below, the spray of light rain stinging his face.

Aetherann? Gregor had tried many times, especially in those first few weeks, to speak with his patron, the god whose magic Gregor now possessed. But with the exception of their first encounter that day in the courtyard—the day he became Aetherann's Chosen—he hadn't been able to make contact.

"Aetherann, please speak to me," he said aloud. What answered him wasn't silence exactly, as the wind howled and roared this high up, but an absence of voices, which a part of him actually appreciated. The more people that were around him, he'd learned, the greater the likelihood that his *gift* would activate. The city proper was a nightmare, and he avoided it whenever he could. The palace was hit or miss. But up here, he couldn't hear any thoughts from the people below. He could barely hear his own over the wind.

He thought back to the courtyard that day, when he'd watched Dare and Verity disappear behind a swirling sphere of fire and stone with Solace. Only Jae crouching beside him, her arm broken after her fall from the flying shadow creature, had stopped him from trying to find a way through the maelstrom. And then there had been an explosion of power, a shock wave that had thrown him through the air.

But the air had caught him. And it had spoken to him then. And it had offered him a choice.

"Aetherann," he tried again. He called up the more formal words of an old prayer he'd learned long ago. "Keeper of Air, of Breath. Lord of Mysteries. Please." Gregor's fingers tightened against the stone wall. "I don't understand what I'm supposed to do."

Silence.

"Please, speak to me."

Still there was no answer.

"Lord Aetherann, my breath is yours, but . . . but what am I to *do* with it? How do I control this power you've given me? The voices, I mean. I'm learning how to control the wind." Gregor flexed his hand against the top of the wall. The wind quieted around him, his own little bubble of stillness, but for only a moment before it crashed into him again. It was the first time he'd tried affecting wind that was already so strong, and it was harder than he'd expected.

"Alright, so I could use some more practice with that as well," he muttered, inhaling deeply. "Please, give me guidance. What would you have me do?"

The wind gusted harder, whipping around Gregor, its chill biting through his wet clothes. It surrounded him, roaring past his ears. He closed his eyes, listening, straining to hear anything the wind might be trying to tell him. The gale ended as abruptly as it started, fading to nothing, along with the rain. When Gregor opened his eyes, the storm clouds had moved on, leaving a circle of blue sky above the palace. The air was still. Even the flags that had been snapping in the wind when he arrived drooped to a soft flutter.

"I don't understand," Gregor said, pressing his hands flat against the wall, which scratched at his palms. "I don't understand what you're trying to tell me."

But the wind was quiet. Nothing but the infuriating silence that he'd been faced with since the start. Silence when he wanted words; words when he wanted silence. It was like a cruel joke.

Gregor's hands balled into fists. "Please!" he shouted. "What do I *do*?" He slammed his fist into the wall, a small bite of pain hitting where his skin scraped and split against the rough stone.

"Hey!" The guard from the watchtower took a few steps toward him. "Are you alright?" he called. "Y-you're not gonna jump or anything, are you?"

Gregor relaxed his hands. "Sorry, no, I'm fine!" he called back. "I was just . . ." He looked out over the wall, at the storm clouds beyond. ". . . Talking to myself."

CHAPTER 7

DARE HURRIED THROUGH THE palace halls, heading for the gates. Gregor had let him know the day before that Verity was looking for him. That was the last thing Dare felt like dealing with right now. He wasn't exactly proud of his reaction in the training yard the morning before. He blamed Tykaras and the distraction they'd caused with their sudden reappearance, as well as the meeting with the king and the realization that he was the only one who could tie Tanithe Ash to Valda.

And Tykaras *still* hadn't explained what the hells was going on.

As Dare rounded the next corner, he collided with Jae. She'd been paying more attention than he had, apparently, and grabbed his arm, spinning them both around to redirect the worst of the impact.

"Where the hells are you headed in such a hurry?" she asked.

"Nowhere, I . . ." The scent of jasmine and sage surrounded him, and a little rush of power, like a brook trickling over river stones, tickled his skin where her hand lingered on his elbow. "Sorry, I didn't see you," he muttered.

"Obviously." Her dark eyes narrowed. "What's going on?"

Gods, she always could read him like a book. "Just lost in thought."

Jae withdrew her hand and set it on her hip. "You're worried about testifying against Tanithe?"

Dare's jaw tightened, but he gestured for her to walk with him. He didn't need Verity finding him. "Yeah, you could say that," he admitted. "You really didn't know she worked for the Valdane Council?"

"No idea."

"Well, fuck."

Jae grabbed his arm again, pausing them in the middle of the hall. "Do you think she'll come after you?" Worry tightened the lines of her mouth.

Absolutely. There was no way someone like Tanithe was going to leave a loose end like him just walking around. But he couldn't stand the idea of Jae worrying about him, so he said, "It's possible."

"You should talk to the king again," Jae went on. "If you explain more about what she's likely to do, maybe he'll send some extra guards with us." Before he could respond, she asked, "Do you know when we're leaving? Or where we're going?"

"Gregor's working with the king's secretary on the details now. He knows more than I do."

Jae smiled a sly, wicked grin. "Isn't that always the case?"

He'd certainly walked straight into that one. "If we've devolved into hurling insults," Dare said, "I'll just be on my way." Though in truth there were few things he enjoyed more in life than bantering with Jae.

"Suit yourself," she said, brushing past him. "Don't be an idiot," she called over her shoulder. "Talk to King Dominic about some guards." And then she was around the corner and gone.

Would talking to Dominic help anything beyond giving them a larger entourage and drawing more attention to themselves? Given who and what Tanithe was, Dare doubted very much that a few extra guards would stop her from killing him if she wanted to. He turned and continued toward the palace gates. If he could just get into the city before—

"Dare!" Verity's voice jostled him out of his thoughts.

Dammit.

He slowed his steps, though he didn't stop. "What can I do for you?" he asked as she came up alongside him.

"Where are you headed?"

"Tumbledown," he said, picking a place at random where he suspected she wouldn't want to follow. It was the grimier part of the city, with shady taverns, brothels, and other places Verity was likely to avoid.

She kept pace. "Can I walk with you?"

". . . Sure," he said, arching a brow. He let the silence linger as they stepped outside into the crisp spring day.

Although the climate in Taernfane was notably warmer at this time of year than in Valda or Whitehollow, a chill still hung in the air, and the wind off the plains could be brutal, even in early spring.

Beyond the palace walls, many of the buildings that had been damaged by Tanithe's shadow creatures had been repaired, though several still bore the marks of the battle that had overtaken parts of the city that autumn afternoon. Dare ignored the cracks in one of the buildings they passed and dropped a couple of coins into a beggar's hat.

"I doubt you're walking with me to Tumbledown to take in the sights," Dare said at last. "What's on your mind, my lady Warden?"

"How are you feeling about the king's request?" Verity asked. "About heading back to our old lives."

Dare couldn't help the bitter laugh that emerged. "My *old life* wants me dead, for more than just one reason now."

"What are you planning to do?"

Dare indicated the road ahead with an upward nod. "I'm going to get a drink, likely several drinks, and put off thinking about it for as long as possible."

Her bootsteps were the only sound between them for a time, until she asked, "Do you want to talk about it?"

"I don't." As the wind picked up, he wished he'd thought to grab his coat. He rolled his sleeves down and stuffed his hands into his pockets. "If it's all the same to you."

"Can we talk about something else then?"

Dare eyed her sidelong. This couldn't be about what happened in the training yard, could it? Maybe it was only Dare's paranoia that had him worried she would track him down about that. If that had been her goal, she would have brought it up by now. Subtlety was not her gift. "Sure," he said slowly.

"About yesterday—"

Shit.

"I'm sorry for the way I handled that. I could have approached the issue at a better time. In a better way."

Dare turned down one of the narrower side streets that led into the heart of Taernfane. "You mean like ambushing me in the palace halls and following me into the city to discuss it in the middle of the street?"

"You've been avoiding me," she said flatly. "I don't feel as though you've given me another option."

That was fair.

"I am sorry for how I handled it," she said again, "but I won't apologize for bringing it up. Dare, I—would you just stop and listen for a minute?" She grabbed his arm and spun him, pressing his back against the alley wall. It wasn't forceful, but it was firm. "I need you to understand."

"I know," he snapped, the tension mounting in his shoulders as she cornered him. "It's a weakness our enemies can exploit. You're worried because it makes me a liability to you."

"Vire's hells, Dare, I'm worried because I *care* about you. You're my friend. I've seen what magic can do to you. If there's something that I can do to help you . . . If I can somehow ease the pain it causes you, then I have to try. If you'll let me."

He shrugged her from his arm, pushing away from the wall. Verity thought she understood the problem—thought she knew better than he did. He'd lived it his whole fucking life. "I've tried! You have to know that I've tried."

"Yes, but I think—"

"It doesn't matter what you fucking think, Verity!" All he could hear was his mother's voice, sweet and falsely sincere, manipulation disguised as caring.

I think it's not as bad as you're making it out to be . . . I think you're not trying hard enough, Darcy . . . I think you're overreacting . . .

A shudder rolled through him. "You haven't lived it. You have no idea what it's like."

"You're right," she said, taking a step back, giving him space. "You're right, I don't know what it's like." His shoulders started to relax a moment before she added, "But—"

Dare ran his fingers through his hair. "Verity, I swear to fucking Pyrannis—"

"But I have an idea," she continued, though her voice softened. "I'm hoping I can convince you to give it a chance. Because if you can control your Perceptive abilities, I think you'd make an incredible mage."

Give it a chance, Darcy . . . You're not even trying . . . You could be a powerful mage one day . . .

Dare straightened, his teeth grinding as his jaw clenched so tight he thought it might snap. "I'm not you," he ground out. "I'm not a mage. I'm a thief and a liar."

"You're more than that."

"I don't want to be more than that!"

"You're a Warden now, too."

Was he?

Technically, yes—Verity had sworn him in as a Warden to break the hold his parents had on him. He was no longer bound to inherit his family's estate thanks to the Wardens' oath. But he wasn't a *real* Warden, not in the way Verity was.

Or in the way Drystan had been.

Though even if only a technicality, the fact that he was a Warden gave Verity power over him. So far she hadn't used it except in jest, but it was there. Dare could feel it pulling him in. Locking him down.

"Are you ordering me, then?"

"No," Verity said quickly. "No, I'm not ordering you. I'm asking you to consider it."

"Then my answer is no." Without waiting for her response, Dare spun and continued toward Tumbledown. "I'll meet you back at the palace later," he called over his shoulder, hoping it would be enough of a hint that Verity wouldn't follow him.

It worked. Verity didn't say anything as he left her in the alley.

Dare shook out his hands, which had balled into fists. A small part of him wondered whether he'd overreacted. That part of him was sure Verity meant well, and that she really did care—that her intentions were coming from a place of truly wanting to help. This was *Verity* after all.

And yet he still bristled at the thought. He'd dealt with being a Perceptive—the fucking curse of it—for as long as he could remember. Most days, back when things were normal, it was hardly an issue. But now . . .

Dare shoved the thought from his mind as the tavern he'd been heading toward came into view.

It was nothing a few hours of day-drinking couldn't fix.

A pleasant warmth spread through Dare's body, and his mind was finally quiet, if a little foggy, by the time he started the trek back to the palace. The sun's slanting rays cast long shadows ahead of him as he rounded the corner into a narrow alley that served as a shortcut out of Tumbledown.

He stopped short. Ahead, at the end of the alley, a woman stood, all curves and shadows, though a few strands of fire-red hair stuck out from beneath her hood. Dare's heart jumped into his throat.

Tanithe Ash. She was in Taernfane? How? King Dominic had the city guards on high alert for even a whisper of her presence in the city. It couldn't be . . .

Could it?

Dare blinked, trying to clear his blurred vision. Tanithe was talking to someone around the corner at the end of the alley. Dare's fingers twitched toward one of his hidden daggers, but Tanithe stepped out of view, following whoever she was talking to.

She hadn't seen him.

This could be his chance.

Dare crept closer. The corner was just ahead. If she was still there, he could end this here and now. His fingers wrapped around the hilt of his blade as he stepped around the corner and came face-to-face with—

—A woman selling flowers.

"A fine evening to you," she said cheerfully. Her bright red hair, like wisps of flame, stuck out from beneath a hooded cloak. She wore dark blues and purples, with a leather belt cinched around her waist.

Dare loosened his grip on his dagger, his hand still behind him. "Evening."

Beyond the woman, a man was walking away with a small bouquet of flowers.

She gestured to the cart behind her, which was laden with blossoms in every color of the rainbow. "Year's first bloom," she said. "What would you like?"

Gods, had he really been so drunk that he mistook this happy woman for *Tanithe Ash* from twenty yards away? Or maybe he was just that paranoid.

A pleasant smile fixed itself into place on his lips as he stuck his hands back in his pockets. "Which is your favorite?"

The woman, probably about the same age as Dare, gave a coy smile and reached toward the other side of her cart. A wide black leather bracelet peeked out from beneath her cloak as she stretched, an eight-pointed star etched into it. When she pulled back her arm, she held a little collection of white and pink flowers with verdant green leaves. The pink blossoms were long and thin, while the white ones had wide, round petals. An ice-blue ribbon tied the bouquet together.

"Honeysuckle and raspberry blossoms," she said, offering them out to Dare. "Smells like a warm spring day."

Dare took the flowers and breathed in their scent. "They're lovely. How much?"

He paid the woman for the flowers and bid her a pleasant evening before heading toward the palace once again.

Dare turned the key in the latch and pushed open the door to his rooms. Gregor sat at the desk in the sitting room, scribbling across some paperwork.

"There you are," Gregor said without looking up.

Dare set the flowers on the table by the door and stepped out of his boots.

"I wanted to go over the plan for . . ." Gregor trailed off as he set down the quill and stood, turning toward Dare. He slid his glasses up the bridge of his nose. "Are you drunk?"

Dare waved him off. "I'm fine," he said, which was true, if an evasion of the actual question. "What did you want to talk about?" He flopped onto the sofa.

Now that he'd stopped moving, the world seemed to continue on without him. The room tilted a little, spinning gently as he tried to focus on Gregor.

"Did something happen?"

Dare ran his hands over his face. "I'm *fine*," he said again. He could talk about what happened with Verity, and Gregor would listen, and he was mostly certain Gregor would understand. But still, Dare worried Gregor would tell him he was being an idiot. And he didn't think he could handle hearing that just now. "What did you want to talk to me about?"

Gregor turned back to the desk and shuffled a few papers around. "I spoke with the royal secretary. His Majesty received the missive from the Valdane Council a couple of hours ago. They've agreed to have the independent committee meeting in Whitehollow with the Wardens as the arbiters. We'll take a ship out of Southport in a few days."

Dare propped himself up on his elbow, trying to blink away the drunken haze. "A ship? Wouldn't that take us a bit out of our way?"

"If we could travel directly to Whitehollow, yes," Gregor said. He leaned his hands on the desk, looking down. "But we can't pass through Brookshire, and the trip around would take even longer."

Tension crept back into Dare's shoulders. "We could skirt around the city," he tried.

"It's not just the city."

Of course it wasn't. It was the whole godsdamned duchy. For the second time that day, Dare heard his mother's voice in his head. *Don't you dare set one foot in this duchy again.*

"The ship will be faster than going around the duchy," Gregor continued, shifting a few more papers around. "And safer. And easier, honestly. I, for one, am fine with not having to be on horseback for weeks."

Dare nodded. It made sense, even if he didn't like it. But then, there wasn't much he liked about any of this in the first place. If he'd just been smarter when they'd had to pass through Brookshire before, this wouldn't be an issue. And Gregor would still be safe in Wilhaven Manor.

Gregor inhaled deeply, his head tilting up. "I should go. Give you a chance to sober up." He still wasn't looking at Dare.

"Why would I want that?" Dare asked, pushing himself up from the sofa. He retrieved the flowers from the table by the door before crossing to Gregor. "Stay. Have a drink with me." Dare wrapped his arms around Gregor, pulling him in close as he brought the honeysuckle and raspberry blossoms in front of him. "I got these for you," he said. "The ribbon matches your eyes."

Dare leaned in to nuzzle a kiss in the groove of Gregor's neck, but Gregor's whole body tensed, and he sidestepped out of Dare's embrace so fast Dare lost his grip on the flowers. They fell onto the desk.

Gregor smoothed out the fabric of his shirt as he practically fled from Dare. "I can't right now," he said. He rubbed his wrist, moving toward the door. "I still need to update Verity about the plan and confirm a few more things with the royal secretary."

"Alright." Dare took a step back toward the couch. He didn't know what he'd done to upset Gregor, but he didn't want him to feel like he had to flee. He only ever wanted Gregor to feel safe with him, the way Dare had always felt safe with Gregor.

Gregor pressed a thumb to his temple for a moment before he turned to the door, throwing it open. "Thank you for the flowers," he mumbled as he hurried into the hall.

Dare couldn't help the step he took to follow after him. "Will you—"

But the door swung closed, silencing him.

CHAPTER 8

THE NIGHT BEFORE THEY were to leave for Whitehollow by way of Southport, Dare was out on the parapets again, staring at the patch of dirt where the grass was just beginning to fill in. He wiped his palm against his pants and tried not to remember the warmth of Solace's blood running over his hand.

I'm sorry, Solace. What Dare and Verity had done to him—what *everyone* had done to him . . . It wasn't right. Solace hadn't deserved the hand he'd been dealt. It wasn't fair.

Things seldom are, Tykaras said.

Dare jumped, and an expansiveness filled his chest. He suspected he had the god's full attention.

We really need to teach you about time, Dare said inwardly.

I'm certain it cannot have been long since we last spoke.

It's been four days.

Oh. The strange, dual voice of Tykaras sounded contrite. *That is surprising.*

Dare inhaled deeply. Between his argument with Verity and whatever had happened with Gregor, he already felt nearly at his wits' end. Gregor had barely spoken to him in the last few days, and Dare had done his best to give him plenty of space. But avoiding both Gregor and Verity had given Dare far too much time to dwell on just how poorly he'd been handling things lately. Not to mention that Verity's suggestion to train him to use magic had been needling the back of his brain with past failures and future *what-ifs*.

Add to that their impending journey to Whitehollow, the looming threat of Tanithe Ash, and now the very real presence of a literal god speaking to him, Dare was fairly certain he was about to go insane for real this time.

And yet a thought flitted through his mind. A question for which the answer still eluded him.

"That night after everything happened," Dare said aloud. "After Solace reawakened the gods . . ."

You asked me if you were now my Chosen, Tykaras said, their tone going gentle. *Yes, you are.*

All the air rushed out of Dare's lungs, and he grabbed the edge of the crenellations to keep himself upright. "I am," he said, half question, half resignation. Despite his attempts at convincing himself that it was all a hallucination, he'd felt the shift. He'd known it was true.

Maybe he just hadn't wanted to believe it.

How would he tell the others? It had been so long since everything had happened—what would they think about him coming to them now? And about a god he doubted any of them had even heard of? They'd probably think he really had gone mad.

Perhaps, Tykaras said slowly, *you could wait a brief time before you share our connection with your friends. It could give you the time to find the right words, and it would allow me to sort through a few lingering issues.*

Lingering issues? Dare asked. *Like what?*

Nothing you need to concern yourself with now, Child. Much has happened while the elemental gods have slept. I need time to prepare.

Tykaras clearly wasn't telling him everything, but he wasn't sure how much more he could handle at the moment. If Tykaras wanted time, then that was one less thing Dare would need to deal with right away. It could wait until a few other things had settled.

"Alright," Dare said, leaning his elbows on the parapets. "That suits me fine for now."

Then we are in agreement.

Dare considered whether to ask his next question, but Tykaras answered it before the thought had even fully formed.

There is nothing else that you need to know. At least, not yet.

And why weren't you asleep with the others? Dare asked. *You were supposed to answer that question too.*

A breath that encompassed stars rushed through the back of Dare's mind. *That,* Tykaras said, *is part of the lingering issues I need to sort out.*

That response did not fill Dare with confidence, but that would be a problem for some future version of himself—one who would hopefully have already found elegant solutions to his current circumstances.

Yes, the version of himself that had his shit together, wasn't seeing Tanithe around every corner, and wasn't driving his friends away . . . *that* Dare could deal with it. *This* Dare, he was certain, would just fuck it up somehow anyway.

Dare couldn't help the feeling of unease that settled around him the next morning. It felt strange to be leaving, even though he never had any delusions about Taernfane being a place he could settle down. Still, while they'd been here, he'd learned his way around the city, learned its ins and outs, its secrets.

He sat to lace his boots, trying without success to let the worries float from his mind. Would he come back here again one day? Would the spot where Solace died be finally filled in with grass? Would he remember where it was if he couldn't see its outline in the dirt?

Gregor stepped behind him and set his hands on Dare's shoulders. His fingers squeezed the knotted muscles there, pulling a quiet groan out of Dare.

"Where did you go just now?" Gregor asked. "You look as though you're a thousand miles away."

Dare touched the scar in the center of his chest. "I'm fine," he said. Fine enough, at least, for a simple journey by boat. "Or, I will be," he added.

Gregor rubbed Dare's shoulders, digging into the tension Dare had been carrying around with him for far too long.

Dare leaned into Gregor as his eyes fluttered closed. "Aren't we going to be late?"

Gregor continued his work. "We can spare a few minutes," he said. "I'm sorry I've been so distant," he added after a moment. "I know I haven't exactly been forthcoming. But I want you to know it's not that I don't want to tell you." He inhaled deeply, his breath ruffling Dare's hair on his exhale. "This whole thing . . . It's proving more difficult to figure out than I'd like. But I will tell you. I promise. When I'm ready, when I've worked it through, I'll tell you everything."

"It's alright," Dare said. "So long as you know I'm here if you change your mind."

"I know," Gregor said softly. "And that thought alone gives me strength." He stopped massaging Dare's shoulders and wrapped his arms around him, hugging him tightly. "And hope."

Dare tilted his head back to bring Gregor into view. From this angle, the shadows under Gregor's eyes were darker than usual against his pale skin. Dare gave his arm a squeeze. "Whatever it is, I know you'll figure it out."

To his surprise, Gregor leaned down and pressed his lips to Dare's, holding Dare to him as though worried he'd float away. Dare melted into him, drinking in everything from the citrus and vanilla scent to the feeling of Gregor's fingers threading through his hair.

When Gregor broke the kiss, all Dare could do was sit there, stunned and blinking.

"We should go before we're late," Gregor said, planting a second, gentler kiss on Dare's forehead.

"I thought you said we could spare a few minutes." Dare was reluctant to let him go, to lose this moment of normalcy that he'd stumbled into. Maybe if he held on tightly enough—

But Gregor stepped back, the cool air rushing in between them. "The king is seeing us off personally," he said. "We can't be late."

The normal moment faded so rapidly, Dare wondered whether it had even been there in the first place, or if it had only been his imagination.

"No," Dare said. "No, I suppose we can't."

By the time they gathered their belongings and made it to the royal stables, the others were already there, as were King Dominic and someone Dare had seen around the palace on occasion but hadn't met yet.

Verity caught Dare's eye, favoring him with a stern look, no doubt for being a single moment late. Dare pointed at Gregor, hoping to indicate that he was the one to blame, but she didn't seem to buy it.

"Blaming Gregor for your tardiness again?" Finn whispered as she sauntered up between them.

Gregor, who had been oblivious to the silent exchange with Verity, turned at Finn's abrupt appearance. "*Again*?"

"It was actually his fault this time!" Dare thrust a finger into Finn's shoulder. "And you need to stop getting me in trouble."

"But you make it so easy," Finn said. Gregor stifled a chuckle.

"Thank you all for taking on this mission for the Crown," King Dominic said, his voice booming through the stables and commanding the attention of everyone present. Even the horses seemed to settle their idle shifting.

Dominic's attention landed on each of them in turn. "When you testify before the hearing committee, I urge you all to speak only the truth of what you saw and experienced here, not what you think I may want or expect from you. I want and expect only justice for my city, and your truthful accounting of the events will provide it.

"My royal guard will escort you south to Port Gryphon. From there, you'll take the ferry across the bay to Southport, where you'll board the ship that will take you to Whitehollow. Once you board the ferry, you'll have only a small retinue of guards for the remainder of the journey."

Gregor stepped forward and gave a quick bow. "Excuse me, Your Majesty?"

"Speak."

"Do we need to meet with the Drahkonian emissary to the committee? When last we'd spoken, you were undecided on who to assign."

"I've selected one of my advisors, Chancellor Caelan Toleth." Dominic indicated the person beside him, who gave a formal bow. "He will serve as our emissary."

"I'm honored to serve our kingdom in this role," Caelan said, most dutifully. The chancellor had warm sepia skin and dark hair that was just long enough to hook behind his ears. His features were soft as he smiled at the assembled group.

As the rest of the discussion veered to the logistics about which soldiers would take them to Southport and which Wardens would serve as the arbiters for the hearing committee, Dare's mind began to wander.

The Wardens of the Flame were based in Whitehollow, and Dare hadn't made the best first impression with High Commander Joseph Cairn, though the feeling had been mutual. What would the Warden commander think of him now, masquerading as one of his honorable Wardens?

Then there was the Crimson Brothers. Perhaps Dare could check in with the Whitehollow chapter of the mercenary guild while he was there, since there was no way he was going back to the Brothers' primary chapter in Valda. Maybe there'd even be a job he could pick up while in the city.

Actually, some small job could be perfect. He'd been far too long playing at being a hero. Getting back to what he was good at—what he *was*—might be just what Dare needed.

"It's settled then," the king announced, jarring Dare back to the present. "Safe travels to you all."

Ignoring the suspicion that he missed something important, Dare took in the people around him: Gregor, Jae, Lucien, Finn, Verity. His friends.

His family.

If he held onto this . . . held onto *them* . . . maybe with a little luck the rest would straighten itself out.

CHAPTER 9

THE JOURNEY OUT OF Taernfane was far less hurried than their original trip to the city on the bluff. Dare might have enjoyed the views of Drahkonia's rolling hills had it not been for what he considered to be the obscene number of royal guards escorting them. Although Gregor assured him that twenty soldiers was extremely small by most royal standards, it still called far too much attention to their group, as far as Dare was concerned.

He also couldn't shake the frustration at having to take the long way back to Whitehollow. Even though everyone agreed that travel by ship would be easier, it bothered him that he was the reason they couldn't take the most direct route.

Dare even mentioned to Verity during one of their stops that they could have snuck around Brookshire under the cover of night, if they didn't have the king's advisor with them. She reminded him, dutifully, that he was a Warden now, and should he be caught ignoring his exile, it would cause all sorts of problems, and not just for him.

That little reminder stung more than he'd expected. It chafed him, as the brand had done that first day's ride out of Brookshire. Dare rubbed at the scar absently.

When they arrived in Port Gryphon a few days later, Dare was pleased to see that most of their royal escort bid them farewell. Only four would be traveling with them. Two soldiers were assigned to keep an eye on the group as a whole and assist wherever needed, and two were directly assigned to the Drahkonian emissary.

Chancellor Caelan, for his part, had spent the trip in rough traveling clothes, looking no more a servant of the throne than any of them. The soldiers, too, had lost their Drahkonian insignia before boarding the ferry. Remarkably, their full contingent looked like a group of travelers who had hired on some muscle to guard against brigands on the road.

By the time the ferry docked in Southport, the southernmost town in the already-very-southerly kingdom of Southreach, the sky was slanting toward twilight. Dare expected to want nothing more than a drink and a bed, all expenses paid for in full by the Crown of Drahkonia, but the thought of sitting still irked him somehow. So instead, he dropped his pack in his room and headed back downstairs. Jae and Lucien sat at the bar, with Lucien looking profoundly uncomfortable. Dare could practically see the shifter's hackles raising every time someone brushed too close to him. Jae was beside him, seemingly unaware, caught up in telling one story or another that Lucien seemed to hardly be paying attention to. Dare passed them by and stepped into the cool evening.

Outside, the sea breeze blew past, reminding him of home. Well, of Valda, in any case. He wasn't sure where he was heading, but their ship wasn't scheduled to leave until the morning. He could stand to get lost for a few hours.

Dare hadn't been in the city long before the hairs along the back of his neck rose. Was someone watching him? His senses were on alert as he casually scanned the streets for anything unusual. Everything appeared as one would expect: shops were closing up for the night, restaurants and taverns were getting busier, and the people in the streets, whether heading home or out, were moving with purpose. He shrugged the unease away, though he kept a watchful eye.

As was his way, Dare managed to find the seedy part of town, where the grimy streets were lined with taverns and gambling dens. A man dressed in clothing far too fine for this part of the city hurried out of a building on the far side of the street. A woman followed, shouting after him about paying what he owed. The gentleman's response was so colorfully worded that the matron's face turned bright red, though it was clearly rage that had caused such a flush to come to her cheeks.

The man nearly knocked over another passerby as he stormed down the street. More rude comments flowed from him in a steady stream. Dare dipped his head and cut a diagonal across the cobbles, right into the rich man's path. The rough collision threatened to knock the man on his ass, though Dare caught him by the elbow of his finely tailored coat, keeping him on his feet.

"Woah, sorry friend," Dare said, his grip tightening briefly on the stranger's arm while his other hand slipped into the inner pocket of the man's coat. Dare pinched the leather satchel deftly in his fingers and pocketed it as he brushed some road dust from the man's arm. It was a move he'd done more times than he could count. "Must have been off in my own world. I swear I'd lose my head if it weren't attached," he added with a laugh.

"Out of my way, filthy bastard!" the man shouted. He shoved through Dare, not at all concerned with where his elbow landed on the way by. Dare had been ready for it though, so the breath he exhaled in a sharp puff was purely to shift any suspicion away from himself. Let the rich asshole think he had the upper hand.

Across the way, the matron returned to her establishment, apparently willing to take the loss of the man's business. Dare followed after her.

The main room smelled strongly of ale, sweat, and several scented smokes that marked various popular street drugs. The matron noticed him almost immediately and smoothed her skirts, plastering a pleasant, if worn, smile on her face.

"Evening, love," she said, waving a hand to encompass the room. "Welcome to Rosebud's. We've got anything and everything to help you relax." Her eyes raked appraisingly over Dare, no doubt trying to discern what he would be in the market for. "Our ladies are sweet and our lads are sweeter, depending on what you fancy.

Dare smiled but shook his head. "No, thank you," he said, even as a beautiful woman on the stairs caught his eyes. She beckoned him with one finger, and there was a longer pause than Dare was proud of before he dragged his attention back to the matron with an apologetic chuckle. "I wanted to inquire after the man outside. The one who seemed to be in dire need of manners."

The shift in the woman's countenance indicated she knew exactly who he was talking about. "What about him?" The warm tone had evaporated. "You a friend of his, then?"

"No, not at all," Dare said quickly. "I wanted to settle his tab." He pulled the man's coin purse from his coat pocket. It clinked cheerfully, and the matron inclined her head. "How much does he owe?"

"Not that I'm complaining," the woman said, her gaze still fixed on the purse in Dare's palm, "but why would you want to be helping him out?"

"Oh, I'm not. He's an asshole. I'd just like to make sure his lack of manners doesn't impact you or your ladies and lads." He gave her the most genuine smile he could muster and jingled the coin purse. "So, what does he owe you?"

With the debt settled, and with a healthy tip for the woman who'd had the pleasure—or lack thereof—of the man's company, Dare exited Rosebud's, though he practically had to pry himself away from the dark-haired woman on the stairs. She apparently wasn't one to give up, but as fun as a distraction sounded right about now, a stranger's bed in a Southport brothel wasn't quite what Dare was after.

The coin purse still had more weight to it than Dare had expected, which tickled him a bit. He hadn't thought to turn a profit, but—

"You'd better get out of here before someone catches you." Finn appeared at his side, a hand on her hip. The hood of her cloak was down around her shoulders and her blond hair was pulled back, though little wisps fell to frame her youthful face.

Dare hid his surprise and arched a brow at her. "Catches me?" He glanced over his shoulder at the brothel. "First of all, I wasn't—"

"Not that," she said. She started down the street, gesturing for him to follow. "I mean the purse you lifted from that rat bastard."

Damn, she was good.

"How fucking long have you been following me?"

"Since you left the inn," she said quietly, a self-satisfied grin dancing across her lips.

No wonder he'd felt as though he were being watched. Finn had been tailing him the whole time. Though now that he was outside again, that uncomfortable sensation at the edge of his awareness returned.

"But it doesn't matter," Finn continued. "If anyone caught you . . ."

"No one's going to catch me," he said. "I haven't been caught pinching something since I was nineteen."

"But what if he had?" Finn turned down an alley and Dare followed. When she was sure there was no one in earshot, she said, "What do you suppose would happen if a Warden gets caught thieving?"

". . . Oh." Fuck it all to Vire's hells, he hadn't thought of that.

"Yeah," Finn said, crossing her arms. "*Oh.*"

This brand on his chest was beginning to feel more and more like a lead weight.

Finn's face softened. "Look, I know swearing that oath wasn't exactly part of your plan, and for what it's worth, I'm sorry."

That snapped Dare out of his self-pity. It had been Finn's plan that had Verity swear him into the Wardens. He couldn't even fathom where he would be if she hadn't come up with it.

"You saved my life, Finn. I'm not going to complain about the details."

Yet the oath was hanging over his head, and everywhere he turned was another reminder that he wasn't in control of his life anymore.

Sure, he wasn't bound to serve at the whims of his family, or forced to do his mother's dirty work anymore either, but the Wardens could order him anywhere on the continent or beyond it. Vire's hells, he couldn't even pick an entitled bastard's pockets anymore!

What the fuck had he gotten himself into?

"I'll just need to be a little more selective in the jobs I take for the Brothers," Dare added with a forced smile.

Finn slugged him in the shoulder. It was a solid hit, but there was no malice there. It was the playful way she'd always interacted with him when they were back in Valda.

"All the same," she said. "At least let me buy you a drink. As the first in what I'm sure will be a long line of me trying to make it up to you."

Dare smiled, even as his arm ached from the punch. It felt like they were back in Valda again, heading to the Raven and Hart. "While I maintain you have nothing to make it up to me about, a drink sounds fucking fantastic right now."

✦

As they made their way across the city toward the inn where their group was staying, movement caught the edge of Dare's perception. It was nothing more than a flicker of shadow, but his breath snagged in his throat. Finn stopped short as Dare turned, one hand reaching for his dagger.

An old beggar stepped out from the darkened alley and settled against the building, setting a tin bowl on the ground.

Dare's hand relaxed. Damn, he was getting paranoid. First the flower woman in Taernfane and now this beggar? His mind was playing tricks on him, seeing Tanithe around every corner.

Dare crossed the street, Finn just behind him, and dropped a coin into the man's bowl.

"Gods bless you," the old man said. "For another, I'll tell your fortune."

"My fortune, huh?" Dare glanced at Finn, who chuckled, tucking her hands into her pockets. "Alright, I'll bite." He tossed another coin into the bowl.

The man motioned him closer. "Come down here, lad. Let me see your hand."

Dare crouched and extended his hand toward the old beggar.

Leaning forward, the man made a show of examining Dare's palm. "Hmm, I see," he muttered. "Was it fate or luck, do you s'pose?"

Dare went still. "What did you say?"

The man peered up at him through scraggly graying hair. "Was it fate or luck?"

"... There's often only a faint line between the two." It was the answer Tykaras had given him when Dare had asked that same question five months ago on the parapets in Taernfane.

The old beggar smiled, all crooked teeth. "Indeed there is." He studied Dare's palm again. "Shadows follow you." The smile fell from his face. "Shadows and ash. Darkness watches, waiting to claim what's rightfully theirs."

Dare swallowed thickly. He tried to pull his hand away, but the man tightened his grip.

"It isn't yours," the beggar continued. "This life you lead, it isn't yours. You stole it."

Finn grabbed Dare's wrist and tore his hand out of the man's grasp. The beggar's fingernails scratched the back of Dare's hand as he still tried to hold on.

"Crazy old codger!" Finn shouted as the old beggar cackled like a madman. She pulled Dare up and away. "Shit, are you alright?"

"Shadows and ash," the beggar repeated as Dare and Finn withdrew across the street. "Shadows and ash!"

Dare's hands were shaking, the old beggar's words echoing in his ears as Finn led him onto one of the busier thoroughfares full of taverns and restaurants. "I'm fine," he said, trying to convince himself almost as much as he was trying to convince Finn. He eyed the red line down the back of his hand where the man's nails had drawn blood. How could the old man have known about any of it?

Finn pulled him under one of the street lanterns. "Let me see."

"It's nothing." Dare shoved his hands in his pockets. He couldn't stand the look of worry on Finn's face, so he plastered on a lopsided grin. "Though I could really use that drink now."

Finn looped her arm through Dare's and continued tugging him toward the inn where they were staying. "Consider it done."

✺

Back at the inn, they found seats at the bar and Finn ordered them both a drink.

"So you want to keep running jobs for the Brothers?" Finn asked, spinning the glass in her hands. "When this is all over?"

When this is all over. Whenever the hells *that* was likely to be. "Well . . . Yeah." Dare wiped at the now-dried smear of blood on the back of his hand. The jobs he worked for the Crimson Brothers—it was what he was good at. It was who he was. Warden or not, he was a Brother first. Even if it would take some juggling, he'd make it work. Somehow. "What about you?" Dare asked, hoping to steer her away from too many prying questions. "After all that shit with Caleb, are you planning on going back?"

Finn watched the whiskey in her glass swirl as she continued turning it. Caleb had been Finn's old commander. He'd kept Finn from becoming a full member of the Brothers unless she let him take advantage of her. And he'd dragged her out to that godsdamned mountain pass at the edge of Aethir.

The mountain pass . . . where . . .

This life you lead, the old beggar had said. *It isn't yours. You stole it.*

Drystan had died in that pass instead of Dare. And now Dare was masquerading as a Warden, pretending he was half the man—

"I want to," Finn said, tearing Dare out of his spiraling thoughts. "But I don't know what the captain will say about what happened."

"What happened was Caleb's doing," Dare said into his glass. He downed the liquor, savoring the burn as it slid down his throat. "Not yours."

"I went along with him," Finn muttered. "I followed him on an unsanctioned job, and I was the only one to come back." She finally looked up at him. "You have to admit, it doesn't look great."

"By his own admission, Caleb took a job direct from the Valdane Council. Trust me when I say, the captain's been around long enough to know where the fault lies. You'll see when we talk to her."

The corner of Finn's mouth twitched. "We?"

Dare signaled the bartender for another drink. "Yeah." A smile tugged at his lips. "We."

Finn smiled and finished her own drink. "Is Gregor alright?" Dare sucked in a sharp breath, and she rushed to fill the silence. "I know they're all dealing with all of that . . ." She waved her hand in the air, encompassing everything and nothing at the same time. ". . . And I know you and I are the normal ones, but Gregor just seems . . ." She slid her glass toward the bartender, who added another shot to it as he refilled Dare's as well. "I don't know. I guess I'm worried about him."

Dare had been spending so much time trying to pretend things were normal . . . had he missed how *not* alright Gregor really was? "I don't know, to be honest. He hasn't said anything to you, has he?"

Finn shook her head. "Not really. I've gathered that it has something to do with the whole"—Finn gave a furtive glance around the bar—"you know. I thought he might've told you about it. But I guess maybe he doesn't feel comfortable talking to us, considering."

Considering Finn wasn't a Chosen. And as far as anyone else knew, neither was Dare. "Does he talk to Verity about it?" he asked.

"I think so. Maybe? I think she's trying to help him with whatever it is."

Dare took a long swallow of his own whiskey. He tried to convince himself he wasn't bothered that Gregor trusted Verity with his secret but not him.

But you are, Tykaras's voice chimed into his thoughts.

Dare choked on his drink at the sudden mental intrusion, drawing a curious look from Finn. "Swallowed wrong," he managed between coughs.

Is that a thing humans can do? Tykaras asked. *Can you swallow liquid incorrectly?* Although the god's tone had been very even, almost flat during their previous interactions, it had a lilt to it now. Either concern or amusement. Definitely one of the two. Dare was getting the feeling that Tykaras's emotions would be hard to gauge.

Dare sighed into his drink. *What, are you listening into my thoughts now?*

I can't help it if you're shouting your thoughts out to anyone who can listen.

What? Dare blinked. *Was I—*

"So he hasn't told you anything about it either?" Finn asked.

Dare forced his attention back to her. "Not really . . . I think he doesn't want to burden me with it." He finished the rest of his whiskey quickly and tapped the glass against the top of the bar. It seemed he still didn't feel much like sitting around. "I'm going to head upstairs," he said. He patted Finn's shoulder as he slid off the stool. "Thanks for the drink."

Finn's voice stopped him in mid-turn. "Just like back in Valda, huh?"

"Yeah," he said quietly. "Just like Valda." Dare headed up the stairs, taking them two at a time.

The Crown had paid for them each to have their own room, and Dare stopped on the threshold of his. Finn's words clung to his thoughts, overpowering the old beggar's, at least for the time being. Dare had been trying to give Gregor enough space for everything to work out on its own. But if Finn was worried about him too . . .

Dare closed his door and crossed instead to the room that had been assigned to Gregor. He tried the handle and found it unlocked.

Gregor was reclining on the bed, legs crossed at the ankles, one hand cushioning his head while the other was open in front of him. A small piece of ribbon hovered above his open palm. It flipped this way and that, but only occasionally strayed toward the edges of his hand, where some invisible boundary seemed to push it back toward the center. Gregor was focused on the ribbon, watching it dance back and forth. He was so focused, in fact, that he apparently didn't hear Dare enter.

Dare leaned his shoulder against the doorjamb and watched the fluttering ribbon, mesmerized. Gregor hadn't been too keen on practicing his elemental control in front of Dare, so the only glimpses he got were during the group training sessions Verity led.

It was incredible to think that Gregor could control the flow of air just by thinking about it. Dare had known him his whole life and, thankfully, magic had never been something that Gregor was gifted in. He'd been Dare's safe haven whenever his mother's magic had been too overwhelming. This new power of Gregor's was entirely different, though. This magic even felt pleasant to Dare, but it was still new. Yet another change that he was still getting used to.

"You really should lock your door," Dare said. "You never know what kind of unsavory types might wander in."

Gregor startled, bolting half upright in a sudden jerk of movement. The ribbon fell to the floor.

"Sorry," Dare said, moving to sit on the edge of the bed. "I didn't mean to scare you."

"I just didn't hear you come in," Gregor said, propped up on his elbows. "I was just . . . practicing, I guess."

"You guess?"

Gregor sighed and flopped back down on the bed. "I don't know." He rubbed his hands across his face, pushing his glasses up onto his forehead.

Dare brushed a stray lock of Gregor's pale blond hair back into place. Dare was pretty sure it was longer than he'd ever seen it.

"Can I see?"

Gregor dropped his hands. "It's not much," he said.

"I'm going to assume you're being the overachiever you always are and that it's actually quite a bit more than you think it is." He smiled down at Gregor. "Let me see."

Gregor pushed himself up to sit beside Dare. He hesitated before holding his palm open in front of him. After a moment of focus, he took his other and passed it through the space above his open palm. "Here," he said.

Dare moved his hand over Gregor's, through the gust of wind he'd created there. It wasn't strong, but it was distinct. The air felt cool and had a small, pleasant tingle to it that Dare had come to associate with the undercurrent of Gregor's newfound magic. He let the wind blow over his fingertips and tickle his palm, sending a shiver through his body.

"Gregor, that's incredible," he said, breathless.

"It's not much. You should see what Jae's been able to—"

"You're not Jae," Dare said quickly. "This is *incredible*. Have you practiced changing the strength of it, or just control?"

When he looked up, Gregor was smiling, the little dimple beneath his eye appearing for the first time in a while. "A bit of both. Verity said it's important to practice power and precision."

"Verity's a smart woman," Dare conceded, ignoring the pang of jealousy. "Don't tell her I said that though. I'll never live it down."

Gregor laughed. "I won't."

Dare watched him. "Well? Let's see it."

"What, here?"

"Why not?"

"We're inside, Dare."

"And?" Dare glanced around the small room. "There's nothing here to knock over or break. Come on! It's been a long day, and I'm bored."

Gregor chuckled quietly and flexed his hand, splaying his fingers. Across the room, the curtains flapped sharply, like a flag snapping in the wind.

It was impressive, certainly, but Dare's curiosity was only growing. What else could Gregor do?

"Is that as strong as you can make it?"

The curtains fell straight as the gust suddenly died. "Well . . . no," Gregor said, gaze shifting to the floor.

Dare elbowed him gently in the ribs. "Let me see!"

Gregor didn't look up, though his thumb brushed back and forth against one of the scars on his wrist. It was a new nervous tic he'd picked up, courtesy of Tanithe Ash.

Dare captured Gregor's hand before it made more than a couple of passes, gripping it tightly with both of his. "Gregor, this power . . . whatever it is, however it works, it's a part of you now. I'm not going to hide from it, and for what it's worth, I don't think you should either. I'm here. And . . . and I'm not running away again."

"You escaped," Gregor said, frowning. "There's a difference."

"Whatever you want to call it, I'm here." Dare squeezed his hand. "I'm *here*, Gregor. For all of it."

Gregor took a long, deep breath, during which Dare held his. Dare should have said all of this months ago, but he'd thought things between them would get back to normal on their own. But eleven years had passed since they'd been together before everything had happened with Solace and the weapon—what was *normal* anymore anyway?

After an eternity of stillness and silence, Gregor brought Dare's hand to his lips. "Thank you," he whispered against the back of his hand.

Before Dare could say anything else, Gregor slipped his hand from Dare's and twisted it in a small, circular motion. A strong blast of wind swirled around Dare. It rushed past his ears, whipping through his hair and ruffling his clothes. It was far stronger than anything Dare had expected, and the rush of divine magic was exhilarating.

Dare laughed within the small cyclone. "I take back what I said earlier!" he shouted over the roar of the wind. "*This* is incredible!"

Gregor blushed, but before he could say anything disparaging or argue about it, Dare set his hands on Gregor's face and kissed him. The wind stopped as abruptly as it had started, and the same little leaf-dancing tingle of magic rushed across Dare's palms and over his lips. Gregor relaxed into the kiss, wrapping his arms around Dare and pulling him closer.

Now this was just the type of distraction that Dare was after.

CHAPTER 10

LUCIEN SAT IN THE shade of a massive willow tree, its long tendril-like branches reaching nearly to the ground. A gust of wind blew, and one or two of them brushed along the length of his arm. As they did, the feeling of being grounded, of being connected to the earth beneath him, settled into him.

My little wolf, Taerna said, the words like the scatter of pebbles on a hillside. *You travel far.*

Lucien leaned his head against the tree. The sun flickered through the branches as they swayed and bounced in the breeze. "My friends and I have a task for Taernfane. We leave for Whitehollow soon."

The world around him faded. All but the tree, which remained solid, though its branches stilled.

Lucien stood and set one hand on the trunk for balance, for even the ground had disappeared and he seemed to be standing on nothing but emptiness. Beneath the tree, among the tangle of roots, a cavern opened. It gaped and yawned, beckoning him forward. Lucien crouched before the darkened opening. A presence, unseen but felt deep in his core, called to him from within the cavern.

He crawled inside.

The darkness within the tree was all-encompassing. The ground was wet and slick, and the small, flexible roots brushed against his head and his back, trailing something wet behind. A soft light glowed ahead, and Lucien moved toward it until he emerged from the darkness into somewhere else. When he stepped into the light, the world had faded to shades of gray.

The tree was gone, but so was the blackness. Instead, Lucien stood at the top of a bluff surrounded by rolling hills. He was covered in the sap from the tree. It dripped from his fur and coated his muzzle. There was a copper tang in his snout and on his tongue.

Lucien was in his monstrous shape, though he had no memory of shifting. He looked inward and the beast, in its moss-and-ivy covered bonds, stared back. It didn't struggle or wrench against the chains. The beast lowered its head, resting its chin on its paws. Lucien had never felt it so calm. As he considered the beast, its tail thumped lightly.

Do you see? asked the voice of Taerna.

No, Lucien said. He searched the empty landscape. The only thing around him was the sap.

My blood, Taerna corrected. *From the center of my heart.*

Lucien thought hard. Verity had explained how each of the elemental gods had a place in the mortal world where their power was strongest—where it flowed more easily. Taernfane was the seat of Taerna's power. *Your tree?* he asked. *In Taernfane?*

That tree is a part of me, but I am not that tree.

In the distance, a massive wolf dashed across the plains, heading toward the hill on which Lucien stood. The wolf climbed to the top, though it didn't pay Lucien any attention. The wolf slowly— gracefully—became a man, clad in fine leather armor with a dragon emblazoned on the chest piece. It wasn't a shifter—the change from animal to man was far too fluid and painless, and the beast shape was clearly a large wolf rather than a monstrous, bloodthirsty creature.

Humans built cities, Taerna's voice continued. *But before the cities stood . . .*

The man crouched at the very top of the hill and removed a pouch from his side. From within the pouch he pulled a tiny sapling.

When humans were but a thought and a dream, my Heart stood. My roots. It is the place from which the world spawned, from which the creatures crawled.

The man planted the sapling in the center of the hilltop. And as the sun and moon rose and fell, rose and fell, rose and fell, from the sapling grew an enormous, towering tree. Taerna's tree.

My Heart is the oldest and truest place in the world. The trees are my heart, and the sap my blood. The task I have for you, my little wolf, my climbing vines, lies there.

As Lucien studied the vision of Taerna's sacred tree—of the birth of Taernfane—an enormous shifter bounded over the hill. The sky's shades of gray seemed to darken with its presence. The man at the tree paid the shifter no attention. The beast was easily twice Lucien's size, and unlike the muted grays of the vision, its fur was a deep sable that blended to sepia and then finally a striking pale silver.

Pressure built behind Lucien's eyes. He felt a tug from Taerna, pulling him away from the vision. But no, this was the shifter whose snapping jaws had interrupted the vision in the palace courtyard. Lucien didn't want to run from it, so he dug his claws into the ground, resisting Taerna's gentle pull. He growled at the beast.

No! The goddess's voice was urgent. *You mustn't—*

The monster's attention snapped to Lucien, and the pressure in his head morphed into a blinding pain as his heart felt as though it were set ablaze. Rage burned through Lucien, swift and sudden, clawing its way up from some deep, dark part of himself.

The beast lunged, but Taerna's power wrapped around Lucien like a chrysalis. The monster bounced off the hardened shell, and the ground seemed to tremble with the impact. Through Taerna's encasement, the massive shifter snarled at Lucien, its eyes glowing a baleful green.

Lucien's claws dug deeper into the earth, and the world turned a violent crimson.

No! Taerna said again, but it was from somewhere far away, at the edge of Lucien's perception. There was another tug in his core, sharper this time, like a weed being uprooted.

The vision fell away to darkness. He tried to move, to run, but he was held in place by Taerna's power. He couldn't see anything. The beast inside him roared at being held captive.

Lucien . . .

He could only growl in response.

Lucien, Taerna said again. *I cannot let you go until you regain control.*

Without the monstrous shifter's presence, the rage slowly faded until Lucien could think rationally again. Fury still roiled within him, but he gathered his wits. He hadn't felt rage like that since he'd first turned.

What was that? he asked.

Without warning, the chrysalis around Lucien dissolved, releasing him into the infinite dark.

Lucien woke with a jerk, bolting upright in the narrow inn bed. The linens and mattress beneath him were in tatters, torn to shreds. A cold sweat coated his skin as he rubbed his face and ran his fingers through his dark hair.

What the fuck was going on? Lucien tried to untangle what he'd seen and felt, but it was too knotted up. He stood and dressed, crossing to the door while he was still tugging his shirt on. He needed to talk through this mess with someone who could cut through the bullshit and help him figure out what he needed to do.

Down the hall, Jae opened the door to her room as Lucien raised his hand to knock. "You alright?" she asked. "What's wrong?"

"Dream," he said. "Did I wake you?"

"Yeah, but it's fine." Jae stepped back from the doorway, beckoning him inside, where a lantern cast a soft glow through the space.

"Sorry," he muttered. This was stupid. What was he hoping to accomplish here besides ensuring that Jae also couldn't sleep? "I should let you get back to bed." He turned toward the door.

She caught him by the wrist. "Hey, you don't get to come in here feeling like *that*"—she gestured to all of him—"and then walk away. Whatever's eating at you woke me up even before you came over here."

Of course. Jae's *gift* from Lanara. But he'd been three rooms down the hall. How far did her power extend?

"Now I need you to calm down and tell me what happened. You said it was a dream?"

Lucien nodded, pacing the small room while Jae closed the door.

"Was it another vision?"

He nodded again. "Yeah."

She sat on the edge of the bed, her face softening. "Go on." Her tone was gentle, encouraging.

These visions from Taerna had seemed so real. Much clearer and stronger somehow than the ones he'd had months ago that started him on this whole journey. The goddess being awake now, and Lucien being her Chosen, must be making them stronger than they were before. And this last one . . .

He steadied his breathing, trying to calm his racing heart, and told Jae about the vision he'd just had.

"Holy shit," Jae said when he was finished. "You're not getting on the ship, are you?"

"I'm not getting on the ship," he said at last. "I don't know what she needs me to do, but I know it's somewhere between here and Taernfane. I can't go to Whitehollow with you."

"Not a problem," she said, "'cause I'm going with you."

"You can't."

"Like hells I can't."

"You *can't*, Jae," he snapped. "I'm serious."

"So am I."

Whoever—whatever—that shifter was, it didn't like Lucien poking around. Whether the beast was a vision of the future or a sign that the shifters would try to stop him, he couldn't get Jae involved. "They need you in Whitehollow."

"For what? To say Tanithe attacked Taernfane with shadow monsters? Dare's testimony is the only one that matters there. And if they need anything beyond what he has to say, Gregor and Finn will be there. They don't need me, but you do. And before you give me your tough guy bullshit, your night terror woke me out of a dead sleep, and you were here about to knock on my door, so don't even try to say you don't need me."

"It's not *tough guy bullshit*," Lucien spat. "That shifter in the vision, when it looked at me . . . I lost control. What if the next time that happens, you're on the other side of the campfire?"

Jae stood. Lucien expected her to plant her feet and bring forward the bravado she always stood behind. But she crossed to him slowly, sorrow in her eyes. "But what happens if I'm not? If something like that happens again, do you really want to be alone?"

He'd always thought he would, but now . . .

"I'm not afraid of you, Lucien. But I'm afraid for you. I want to help."

Dammit.

If Lucien ever lost control—*really* lost control—there was no one else he would trust to put him down.

Chapter 11

Dare could hardly fault Lucien and Jae for leaving. Visions from a god were hard to ignore, especially considering the last time Lucien had visions, he and Jae ended up in Brookshire, helping Verity rescue Dare's sorry ass. And Gregor.

And Solace . . .

Jae was on him before the memory could take hold, hugging Dare so tightly he thought for a moment his ribs would crack. "Stay out of trouble," she said, stepping back. "I won't be there to save your ass next time."

Dare held his hand to his heart as though offended, but he knew he would miss having her around. Gods, why did it feel like he was leaving all over again? He hadn't said goodbye to her the first time, but it felt far too final to say it now. So instead he said, "Travel safe. We'll see you soon."

She smiled though one brow raised, and Dare suspected she knew what he was doing. "You too," she said.

Jae hugged Gregor just as long. She whispered something in his ear, and he squeezed her a little tighter before letting her go. She turned next to Verity, and finally Finn, whose whiskey-colored eyes shimmered.

"Don't let him get you into any trouble," Finn said, indicating Lucien with an upward nod. When Lucien turned a mock glare in her direction, she gave him a wink. "And don't let *her* get *you* into any trouble."

Lucien's farewells were far more gruff, even by Lucien's standards. He grumbled a few parting words about everyone staying safe and then encompassed the whole group with a short wave.

As Jae and Lucien left the inn, Dare kept silent for as long as he could stand it before his curiosity got the better of him. "What did she say to you?" he asked Gregor.

The corner of Gregor's mouth quirked up. "Jealous?"

Dare chuckled. If there was ever something he wasn't worried about, that was it. Jae and Gregor had always been best friends, but they had never been interested in one another. "Hardly," he said. "But I am curious."

"You know what they say about curiosity."

"That it's an endearing trait you want to nurture so you'll tell me everything?"

Gregor laughed aloud. "Well how can I argue with that?" His smile turned wistful as he said, "She told me to stay close to you and Verity and Finn. She said to keep myself safe. And that you three would protect me." His cheeks flushed a truly delightful shade of red as he spoke.

"We will," Verity said as she turned toward the stairs. "Though I hardly think you'll need it."

She didn't see Gregor's shoulders draw inward at her words. But Dare was beside him, and he knew all of Gregor's tells. Something was bothering him, but he also knew that Gregor wouldn't want to talk about it. He slipped his hand into Gregor's and squeezed. "They'll be alright," he said, doing his best to summon Verity's confidence. "And so will we."

They boarded the barque out of Southport that afternoon, the four of them plus their Drahkonian contingent.

The first three days of the journey by sea were blessedly uneventful. A pod of whales breaching off the port side of the ship caught Finn's and Gregor's attention, neither of them having seen the magnificent creatures before. Finn's excitement over the discovery was contagious as she yelled for the others to come and see. Gregor had been more subdued, but there was no mistaking the awe in his eyes at the sight. Dare hung back, letting Verity slide between them to lean against the railing, answering Finn's questions and sharing in their joy. A few other passengers took an interest as well, pointing and shouting at each appearance of the massive creatures.

"No interest in the wonders of marine life, Warden?" a pleasant voice called from his left. Caelan, chancellor to King Dominic, sidled up beside Dare, leaning his shoulder against the mast as Dare was, almost mimicking his pose on the opposite side. He was a little shorter than Dare, with soft features, and a few flecks of gray in his dark hair that caught the sunlight.

"Please, Lord Chancellor, call me Dare," he said, using the correction to dodge his question. He liked watching the excitement bubbling from the others, but he wasn't about to explain that to the chancellor.

The chancellor grimaced. "Only if you call me Caelan," he replied. "I see no need for formalities. At least out here."

Dare's eyebrow arched. "That seems to be His Majesty's way with most things, doesn't it?"

Caelan chuckled, a gentle, melodic sound. "Quite. I think His Majesty might actually be allergic to formality. He's much more of a function-over-form sort of man."

Dare kept his attention fixed on the group at the rail. Eventually the whales moved on, and so did the onlookers.

"About twelve years ago," Caelan said, "maybe a little more, I spent a brief time in Brookshire. It was just after I'd been appointed to King Dominic's royal council, and I stayed in Wilhaven Manor for a few weeks, as a guest of the duke and duchess."

Dare's body tensed at the mention of his parents, but he forced his face to remain passive. "Oh?" He gave the chancellor a closer look, searching his memory for a time when they might have met while Dare was still living at his parents' estate. "I'm sorry, I don't remember."

Caelan waved the comment away, dismissing it entirely. "A lot has changed since then, but that's not the point I wanted to make." He took a breath and turned more fully to Dare. "I wanted to say," Caelan began, "and I hope it's not too presumptuous of me—but I wanted to say that for what it's worth, I think you did the right thing by leaving."

Dare slid his hands into his pockets to keep from balling them into fists. "I didn't realize my past had made the rounds all the way to Taernfane," he muttered, turning his attention to the waves again.

"His Majesty pays a lot of people to be kept abreast of political upheaval in any of Drahkonia's neighboring kingdoms."

Dare turned toward Caelan. "A scared kid running away from home is hardly *political upheaval.*"

"A son of the most powerful Bremmarian nobles goes missing?" Caelan arched a slender brow. "What would you call it?"

A snort was the only answer Dare had for him.

"I also wanted to say," Caelan continued, "thank you for your service to Taernfane and the realm. You're a hero, Warden, and the world owes you a great debt."

Bile burned the back of Dare's throat. "I'm no hero, Lord Chancellor." He pushed off from the mast and headed toward the hatch that led below decks. "There's only one person the world owes a debt to, and he died in Taernfane."

Chapter 12

Lucien had found Verity first thing in the morning, before speaking with anyone else. He wanted to make sure she understood why he and Jae wouldn't be continuing on with them to Whitehollow.

"Whatever task Taerna has for you, be careful," Verity said. She dug in her knapsack and pulled out a small piece of parchment, rolled and tied with a length of twine. "This parchment is enchanted with a Sending spell. If you write a message on it and speak the incantation, I'll receive it no matter where I am." She handed it to Lucien. "Let me know when you're finished, and I'll tell you where you can meet up with us."

Lucien took the enchanted paper and Verity taught him the incantation. The others joined them before long, and Verity helpfully gave them an abbreviated explanation of why they had to leave.

He was used to wandering across the continent with Jae, laying their heads down wherever they stopped for the night to make their camp. But beyond her, it had been a long damn time since he'd had anyone he cared about.

Or who cared about him.

But he knew he would see them again once he completed whatever it was Taerna needed him to do.

As hard as it was to leave the others, it was nice to be on the road with Jae again. It felt like home, or the nearest thing he had to one.

"Do you know where we're going yet?" Jae asked once they were about two hours outside of Southport.

They'd been walking north, following the trade road that would take them the long way back to Taernfane. There was a lot of ground to cover between here and there.

"Not yet," Lucien mumbled. He hoped to have more direction from Taerna before long, but these things with the gods—these connections they all had—they were strange and otherworldly in every sense of the phrase. If there was one thing Lucien was coming to understand, it was that the gods couldn't be rushed. They would just have to take their time until his path presented itself.

When they stopped to make their camp for the night, they fell into their old roles as easily as if it hadn't been months since they'd traveled together. As Jae laid out their gear, Lucien took his hatchet and set into the trees to gather firewood.

It had been too long since he'd been in a proper forest. As lovely and peaceful as the green spaces within Taernfane were, the city was on a bluff in the middle of rolling plains and farmland, with scarcely more than a copse of trees nearby. But here in Southreach, there were plenty of forests that stretched on and on for miles.

Lucien remembered many of them well.

But as he walked among the trees, something tugged at him. It pulled him deeper in, and down, toward the trunks of the trees, toward the stones and earth at his feet. The farther he walked into the forest, the quieter it got, and the more things settled. His feet were rooted to the earth, as though the connection to Taerna was almost as strong here as it had been in Taernfane.

Stooping in the underbrush, Lucien set his palm against the ground. Did the pebbles rise to meet his hand, or was that a figment of his imagination?

Every time he explored the power from Taerna, the beast within him tugged at its chains, wanting more. He didn't dare push too hard while he was in the city, surrounded by others, but out here . . . He was far enough from Jae that he'd have time to put more distance between them if he felt his control slipping.

And he couldn't keep denying his own curiosity.

Lucien splayed his fingers, and the earth shifted, the dirt moving away from his hand with the motion.

What *else* could he do? Verity could heal, Jae could read others' emotions . . .
Was there another power that came with Lucien's connection to Taerna that was
still buried, waiting to be uncovered?

Within him, the beast tore at its chains, pulling Lucien forward, urging him
onward.

Lucien's hand jerked back.

More, the beast growled. *More!*

No.

His grip on the hatchet tightened as he stood. What was he thinking? No
distance was far enough when it came to the monster inside him. He didn't know
what it meant that the beast wanted him to delve deeper into Taerna's gifts, but
he knew he didn't want to give that creature any more power over him.

Jae had everything set up when Lucien returned with the firewood, as he knew
she would, and by the time they turned in, they were both exhausted from the
day's travel. Yet Lucien lay awake on his blanket, watching the clouds drift by
overhead.

His mind wandered over the riddle of the visions Taerna had given him. She
wanted him to find her Heart, that much was clear. But he had no idea where to
look. He didn't love the idea of wandering all over the continent trying to find
it. He knew the tree at the center of Taernfane was connected to Taerna, and he
knew from the last vision that it had come from somewhere else. Perhaps heading
back to Drahkonia would be the best place to start.

As Lucien thought through possible routes, something itched at the back of
his mind. Taerna's words repeated over and over again.

The trees are my heart, and the sap my blood.

There was only one place on the continent where the trees held blood-red sap.
It couldn't be that simple, could it?

As soon as that thought crossed Lucien's mind, it clicked into place. It had
been many years since he'd had need to think about it, but now that those
memories had been dredged up, it was obvious. Why hadn't he thought of it
sooner?

"Jae," he called.

On the other side of the fire, Jae stirred. "Hmm?" She sounded nearly asleep.

"I know where we have to go."

Jae sat up, her dark eyes watching him over the flames. "What?"

"I know where Taerna needs me to go. But I still don't know why."

"Alright, that's something," she said through a yawn. "Where?"

Lucien swallowed down the fear building in his chest now that he'd put the pieces together. "The Red Forest."

"Shit." Jae looked northward, toward where the forest stood miles and miles away. "You're sure?"

Lucien's teeth ground together. "I'm sure." For what he was about to tell her, he should damn well be looking her in the eye, so he sat up and faced her. "There's an area in the Red Forest that the shifters hold sacred. They call it the Heart."

Jae's brow furrowed as she processed this new information. "Wait. Hold sacred?" She stared at him over the fire. "Lucien, monsters don't have a sense of things like *sacred*."

"Well, these ones do," he growled.

Jae looked as though she might argue, but instead she asked, "And you still have no idea what she needs you to do once you get there?"

Lucien breathed a heavy sigh. "No."

He was convinced Jae was going to bombard him with questions, but she simply said, "I suppose you have until we get there to figure it out."

They packed up their camp and left at first light. When they stopped the next night, they fell back into their same routine: Jae setting out the gear while Lucien set up a ring for the fire and gathered firewood. When he returned to the camp, he found Jae trying to pry a large rock out of the ground.

"I swear we picked the rockiest spot along the whole damn road," she grumbled. "I can't find a single spot to put my blanket that doesn't have a stone jabbing me somewhere."

Lucien surveyed the area they'd selected for their campsite. There were an awful lot of rocks around, he had to admit. Although he'd avoided exploring much of the power he had from Taerna, he had practiced moving small amounts of earth around while training with Verity and the others. Maybe the rocks would behave similarly . . .

He stretched out his fingers and the stones twitched with the motion. Jae jumped back, but then her eyes darted to him.

"You sure?"

Lucien ignored her, concentrating on the rocks scattered throughout their camp. Now that he was looking for them, he could sense them, even some that were just below the surface. He pushed his hand to the side, and the stones moved too, the ground smoothing out in its wake.

"You know," Jae said, "that would have been a handy skill years ago."

Lucien couldn't help the curl of his lips. It felt good to scratch this particular itch. And she was right. It would have been damn useful.

"If I had a coin for every night I spent with a rock in my ribs," Jae continued, "I'd be rich and wouldn't need to wander all over the damn continent with your grumpy ass."

"Well, if I'd known that . . ." Lucien's deep rumble of a laugh rolled across the campsite.

"Oh please! You wouldn't know what to do with yourself if it weren't for me." Jae busied herself with setting up her blanket near the circle that marked their campfire. "You'd just be wandering the wilderness, all mopey and lonely."

Lucien hadn't expected her words to sting. It was their usual banter, after all. Maybe it was the idea of going back to the Red Forest that had him on edge, or maybe it was that their current route was taking them closer and closer to the one spot in Southreach he'd avoided above all others.

Regardless of the reason, his heart clenched at her words, at the memory they invoked of wandering the forests. Alone.

"Lucien." Jae dropped her blanket as she stood and stepped toward him. "I didn't—"

He held up a hand, bidding her stop, and for once she bit her tongue. "I know," he said, though his voice had lowered to a dangerous timbre. "Just leave it alone. Please. It's fine."

But it wasn't fine, and the look on Jae's face told him that she could feel exactly how not fine it really was. He tried to push the memories away, to lock his emotions down tight, but he couldn't stop himself from picturing her face now. Gods above and below, he missed her.

He missed his wife.

"She lives near here, doesn't she?" Jae asked.

Lucien's muscles tensed. "We had a little farm," he said, glancing toward the east. "Not far from here."

"Gods, Lucien! Why didn't you say something earlier? We should—"

"Don't you say—"

"—go see her!"

"Dammit, Jae." He moved toward the trees.

Jae followed after him. "Where are you going?"

How had she not learned, even after all these years? "Away."

She ran around him, putting herself in his path.

He always hated when she did that, and he bared his teeth.

"Stop," she said. "Wait!"

"Get out of my way," he growled through clenched teeth. He didn't want to have this conversation right now. He didn't want to think of her. Of them. Of the life he'd left behind.

"Don't you want her to know you're still alive? We don't know what we're walking into in the Red Forest. This might be your last chance to see her again, Lucien. Don't you want to take it?"

He did. Fucking hells, he did. If there was a chance he could have closure for this wound he'd carried for the last twenty years . . .

Lucien growled again, but this time it was a guttural, feral sound that caused Jae to step back.

"See her again?" he snarled, and his teeth had elongated into fangs. "So she can see me as a monster? I'd rather she think I were dead."

"You're not going to hurt her," Jae said quickly. "Listen to me. We've been traveling together for years, and you've never hurt me. You're not going to hurt your wife."

Lucien hesitated, though he still stared at her with predatory focus. "You don't know that."

"I do."

Lucien's hands balled into fists. "And if you're wrong? What then? I can't risk it. I won't risk them. I won't be that selfish."

"It's not selfish," Jae said firmly. "This is your wife we're talking about, Lucien. Your daughter. It's not selfish to want to see them."

Wasn't it? Everything he'd done had been to keep them safe. "I *can't* hurt them, Jae," he said. The fangs receded. "I . . . won't be able to survive that."

"It's not going to come to that," Jae said, stepping closer. "But I won't let you hurt them."

"I appreciate that you'd try," Lucien said. The anger that had welled up was dissipating, leaving a deep sorrow in its wake.

"Oh, please!" Jae crossed her arms and thrust out her chin. "I could bring you down without breaking a sweat, old man."

Lucien laughed, though it sounded hollow. "It's been twenty years, Jae. What would I even say to her?"

She seemed to think hard about her answer, dropping the smug act. Only a soft sincerity remained. "Tell her the truth," she offered. "Tell her that you left to protect them. Tell her that you've missed her every day for twenty years. Tell her you love her." Jae closed the distance to him, meeting his eyes. "Lucien, you would never let anything happen to them. Shit, you put yourself through hell just to keep them safe. It'll be alright. You'll see."

His chest ached at the thought of seeing them again. Maybe . . .

"I can't," Lucien said. Monsters didn't get closure. "I won't." He stepped around Jae, heading for the trees. He needed to be alone. "I'm going for a run. Don't follow me."

Chapter 13

Gregor woke in the darkness of his cabin to a violent lurch of the ship and the shouting of the crew. He pushed himself up onto his elbows to get his bearings, and the next pitch of the boat nearly sent him tumbling out of his bunk. Grabbing his glasses and making it to the door of his cabin, he found the narrow hall teeming with passengers. Some were poking their heads out of their doors as he was, while others were frantic in the hallway. A member of the crew pushed through them on his way toward the steps that led up to the deck.

"Everyone stay calm," the crewman said. "Please return to your bunks."

"What's happening?" someone cried. The question was met with shouts from the other passengers, everyone demanding answers.

"There's a ship." The crewman wiped his palms on his shirt. "Coming up fast. Captain's begun evasive maneuvers, but we need everybody to stay in their bunks 'til we give the word."

"Pirates?" someone else shouted. "Is it pirates?"

Panic began to spread through the crowd.

"We don't know anything yet," the crewman said as he reached the stairs, wincing as though regretting saying anything at all. "Just please, return to your bunks." Before he could turn to climb the steps, the ship rocked again and the man steadied himself on the railing. It looked like he paused to speak more quietly with another of the passengers in the hall, and when he continued up the narrow stairs, Dare followed behind.

"Dare!" Gregor called, but the clamoring passengers swallowed his shout. Gregor hurried to get through the crowd and to the stairs. Perhaps he could help somehow. What good was having these gifts—was being the Chosen of a god—if he couldn't help? In any case, he needed to try.

"They're going to tell us to stay out of the way," Finn said softly, startling Gregor as she appeared out of nowhere.

"And I'm not planning on listening," Gregor said, taking the stairs up as quickly as he could. "Are you?"

Finn laughed, even as the ship lurched again. "Fuck no."

On the deck, the crew rushed back and forth, tying off rigging and unfurling sails. Through the darkness, with the sky only just beginning to lighten in the east, another ship with no visible markings or flags was much closer than it had any right to be.

Finn took the last of the steep stairs with a groan and pointed aft. The captain stood near the helm, barking orders, with Verity beside him. She raised her arms toward the sails as Dare and the crewman he'd been following reached the small set of steps leading up to them.

Finn took off at as close to a run as her limping gait would allow, and Gregor hurried after her.

The sails billowed outward as Verity pushed magic into them.

That! Gregor thought as he followed Finn. *I can do that.*

"Pirates in these parts aren't known for taking prisoners," the captain was saying to Verity and Dare. "So if we can't flee, our only chance will be to fight."

"Understood," Dare said sharply, almost militantly. He stood stone still beside Verity, his hands clasped behind his back in a pose Gregor had seen Verity adopt countless times. Dare's ability to shape himself into whatever part he needed to play was incredible.

With Duchess Wilhaven's periapt fixed on the back of her hand, Verity forced more wind into the sails, yet the other ship was closing in. *Still* closing in. Verity's magic wasn't enough, and the pirates were nearly close enough to intercept them.

"Verity!" Finn shouted as she reached the steps leading up to the helm. Gregor was right behind her.

"Get below decks," Dare said to the both of them. "It's not safe."

Verity's eyes darted to Finn, and her lips drew tight, her brow furrowing in worry.

"I can help," Finn and Gregor said together.

Gregor moved closer to Verity. They needed wind. Of the powers he'd been gifted from Aetherann, that was the one thing he felt like he understood.

As he stretched out his hands, almost mirroring Verity's motions, the ship rocked violently, which sent him stumbling into Verity. Her solid arms caught him around the waist and kept him on his feet.

Dare and Finn dashed down the stairs as several grappling hooks clattered onto the deck and caught on the edge of railings. The pirates heaved the ropes, forcibly pulling the two ships closer together.

Finn bolted to one of the hooks. She drew her dagger and began sawing at the thick rope. Dare followed after, narrowly avoiding another hook that swung over. He found a rope to cut as more sailors swarmed the hooks along the starboard side, trying to dislodge the ship.

Once Gregor was steady on his feet again, Verity sprinted after them, joining Dare. His blade couldn't cut through the thick rope fast enough, but as Verity grabbed it with one hand, there was an orange glow, and the rope snapped.

Verity shouted something at Dare, and he hurried toward the hatch and the narrow stairs that led below decks, while she moved on to the next hook connecting the ships.

A crunch of splintering wood sounded, and the ship listed sharply; Gregor had to hold on to the railing to keep to his feet. The attacking ship was flush against their charter, and pirates jumped across the narrow gap.

They clashed with the crew. Gregor stood frozen near the helm. Sending wind into the sails now wouldn't do any good with the two ships attached to each other, but Gregor had neither a weapon nor any other way of helping dislodge their charter from the pirates.

From his spot above the chaos, Gregor spotted Dare as he approached the hatch. No one was near him, but he staggered as though struck. Then he swayed, one hand moving to his head. Nearby, one of the crewmen flew over the ship's railing and into the sea.

There must have been a mage among the pirates, and the surging magic was affecting Dare. He took another step toward the hatch but fell to his knees.

Darcy!

Gregor rushed down the stairs and into the battle, pushing his way to Dare. Through the melee, Gregor could only watch in horror as a huge wall of a man gripped Dare by the front of his shirt and hauled him to his feet. Lantern light glinted off a blade pressed to Dare's throat.

No! Gregor was too far away. He couldn't get there in time.

Dare tore helplessly at where the pirate's meaty hand held him.

But then the man's body jerked to the side before he fell to the deck, the hilt of a dagger jutting out from the side of his head.

Gregor was almost to Dare. Just a little farther. He spared a glance over at Finn, her arm extended after the throw that had saved Dare's life.

Dare was barely on his feet, wavering like he might topple at any moment. When Gregor reached him at last, he grabbed Dare by the shoulders.

"Dare!" Gregor shouted. "Are you—"

A hand grabbed Gregor's collar and yanked him back. He barely caught a glimpse of his attacker before the man threw his fist into Gregor's stomach like a sledgehammer. Every bit of air in his lungs was forced out all at once. He doubled over and collapsed against the deck, coughing and sputtering. Pain erupted in his side as a sharp kick from the pirate sent him rolling.

Gregor tried desperately to breathe, but each gasp sent fire through his side.

Dare shouted and took a wild swing at the pirate, who dodged him easily and returned the attack with a right hook that slammed into Dare's face.

Before Gregor could think, he thrust his hand toward the pirate, his palm open. A gust of wind roared, launching the pirate away from Dare. The man slammed into the port-side railing and flipped over it into the sea.

Gregor stared at his open hand. It was the strongest gust he'd ever summoned. He hadn't realized he could—

"Gregor!" Verity shouted from somewhere nearby. "The ship is free! Get us out of here!"

Yes, he could do this. He could do this. Getting to his feet took all his concentration. His side burned like it was on fire and pain flared with every ragged breath. But he pushed it down and bolted for the upper deck near the helm, where he could get a clear line to the sails.

Verity launched one of the remaining pirates off the side of the ship as Gregor raised his arms, gritted his teeth through the pain, and reached for the wind. It whipped around him and into the sails, but the ship barely moved. He needed more.

Aetherann, Gregor pleaded. *Help me. Please.*

Deep within him, something flickered. Wind swirled in his core, roaring through his veins. He pulled at that surging power with everything he had. The air around him crackled as the wind rushed past him. The ship surged forward, sails billowing and waves crashing against the bow.

Down on the main deck, Finn screamed for Dare. Gregor pushed it out of his mind. The worry, the fear, the uncertainty. He pushed everything out except the wind and the power flowing through him that he didn't understand.

"They're coming around!" someone shouted.

Gregor didn't look back. Ahead of him, some of the crew were holding on to the rigging for balance as the ship plowed through the waves. The few remaining pirates fought for their lives and their prize.

Gregor focused only on the wind, on pushing it into the sails as hard and as fast as he could. Every muscle in his body was taut as he pulled the divine magic into the world.

A voice from the nearby till urged him on. "If you've got anything more," the captain called, his voice strained as he struggled to keep the ship steady, "now would be the time!"

Gregor glanced over his shoulder. Their pursuers were far closer than he'd expected, considering the speed at which he had the ship hurtling forward. They must have had a few mages of their own. Mages could provide a direct application of force.

But Gregor controlled the wind itself.

He stretched one hand toward their attackers, hurling a gust of wind back to slow their pursuit, even as his other hand propelled their own ship faster.

The hurricane in Gregor's blood weakened, the roar of the wind past his ears softening. His muscles trembled. The sails still billowed, but there was some slack to them now. He reached for the swirl of power in his core, but found nothing there but himself and the little wisp of power that was always there—had been there since after the attack on Taernfane.

The rest of it was nearly gone, like a well run dry.

No. Gregor planted his feet and dug within himself again. That couldn't be all there was. He needed to do more. The pirates were still behind them, and though the distance between the ships had increased, they were far from safe. If Verity were there, she could help him, but he didn't know where she was. It was up to him.

Gregor focused on the flicker of power deep within himself. Except for Perceptives, magic wasn't something you felt. But there was no mistaking Aetherann's power for anything other than what it was. It fluttered like a curtain in an open window. Gregor tried to pull on that power, but it wasn't flowing fast enough. It was a gentle breeze where he needed a gale.

"They're gaining again!" the captain shouted. They were out of time.

Gregor pictured that trickle of power like a window, open only a crack. In his mind's eye, he grabbed the window and threw it wide.

Aetherann's power roared into him and through him, a raging storm with no place to go. So Gregor pushed that power out, into the sails of their ship, and against the ship behind them, until the edges of his vision darkened and he wasn't sure where the power ended and his body began. It was so pure and beautiful and perfect that nothing else mattered. He was miles away, watching the ships move through the sea from a great height, held aloft by the wind. Or perhaps he *was* the wind.

It was the only thing he could still feel.

Below, the pirates pursued. Gregor lashed at them with a gust of wind. Their ship turned sideways, listing dangerously in the sudden crosswinds.

Deep within him, that window through which power surged into Gregor slammed shut. He snapped back to himself. His knees buckled, but something hard caught him under his arms before he hit the deck.

Verity's face was tight with concern. "Gregor, can you hear me?" When had she gotten there?

"Yes," he said, though his own voice sounded far away, like an echo coming back to him. "Yes, I can hear you." He got his feet back under himself, and Verity kept him steady as he stood.

"Are you alright?" she asked. "What was that?"

Gregor didn't know the answer to either of her questions. He rubbed his face with his palms and pushed his glasses onto his forehead. "I, uh..." What *was* that? Every worldly sensation came rushing back. His whole body was shaking, but whether it was from the power he'd just wielded or simply trying to keep his feet, he wasn't sure. "Did I . . . Are we safe?" On the main deck, the crew worked diligently, though some stole glances up at Gregor.

"We're safe," Verity said. "But . . ." She squeezed Gregor's arm.

His heart sank into his stomach. "What?"

"Dare's hurt."

Chapter 14

"He's waking up," Finn called from the room down the hall.

Gregor had watched over Dare for the better part of three hours, except when the ship's doctor checked Gregor over and confirmed that one of his ribs was bruised. Finn managed to convince him to take a break about half an hour ago, to go sit and rest himself, but he hadn't managed to get farther than a few steps toward his own bunk. The narrow hall below deck was sparsely lit at all hours, making it difficult to judge the time. Now that the danger and excitement of the attack had passed, most passengers were back in their cabins. With the crew above deck assessing and repairing the damage from the attack, the dim hall was empty now save for Gregor where he slouched against the wall.

How Finn knew he was just around the corner was beyond him.

"Hey," Finn said, presumably speaking to Dare. "How are you feeling?"

As Gregor came into the doorway, Dare lay on the cot in his cabin while Finn stood beside him. She held a cloth to his forehead.

"Gregor," Dare said, though he was looking blearily up at Finn. "Where is he? Is he alright?"

"I'm fine," Gregor said. It sounded hollow even to himself. "You're the one we've all been worried about."

"I'll get Verity so she can take a look at him," Finn said to Gregor. She squeezed past him, handing him the cloth on her way out.

Gregor winced as he twisted to let her pass. He took the few steps to the cot slowly.

"What happened?" Dare asked. His words were as slow as Gregor's steps.

Worry clutched at Gregor's heart as he set the cold, damp cloth on Dare's forehead again. Dare's eyelids fluttered closed in relief. "One of the pirates struck you from behind with a blast of force magic and knocked you down the hatch," Gregor said. "You've been out cold for a few hours."

"I meant to you."

Gregor sighed. Would Dare ever learn to worry about himself for once? "A bruised rib." He set his palm gingerly against his right side. "Nothing a little time won't heal."

Dare's face twisted.

"I know that look," Gregor said. "It's not your fault."

"But I—" Dare levered himself onto his elbows, and the rest of whatever excuse he'd been about to give turned into a hiss of pain.

Gregor pressed his hands against Dare's shoulders, guiding him back down onto the cot. "Lie back. You took a hell of a fall."

"I judge from our lack of being dead that we managed to escape our kidnappers," Dare said.

"Pirates," Gregor said. "Verity, Finn, and the crew drove them back and severed the ropes tethering the ships together. Then I . . ." Gregor shifted his gaze to the floor. He still wasn't sure exactly what had happened. He hadn't had the time to examine it more closely yet. He'd need to talk to Verity, but for now . . . "I called the wind so we could get away."

"Gregor, that's . . ." Dare blinked lazily. But then he set his hand to his forehead and winced. "Wait, go back," he said, gritting his teeth. "What did you say? Just now."

Gregor's brow furrowed, concern washing over him again. Hopefully Verity would arrive soon. "About calling the wind?"

Dare waved his hand. "No, no before that."

"Verity drove the pirates off the ship."

He snapped his fingers as if that had jogged some lost memory. "That one. They weren't pirates. At least not *only* pirates."

A quiet knock sounded against the cabin's sliding door.

"Finn told me you came around," Verity said as she moved to stand beside Gregor. The two of them and Dare's cot took up most of the space in the small room. "How's your head?"

"Pounding," Dare said. "Verity, they weren't pirates."

She held her hand up a short distance in front of his face. "How many fingers do you see?"

"Two. Are you listening to me?"

"What do you mean they weren't pirates?" she asked, though she cast a quick glance at Gregor. He shrugged one shoulder. He wasn't sure what Dare was trying to say.

"One of them grabbed me and put a blade to my throat," Dare explained. "And he . . . there was . . ." His stare grew distant for a moment before something seemed to click in his mind. "Finn! Fuck, I need to thank Finn, but they . . ." He trailed off again, his eyes pinching shut.

Gregor had never seen him have so much trouble finding words.

"He grabbed me," Dare tried again. "And he said . . . Dammit, he . . . It had to be Tanithe." His jaw tightened. "She had to be behind it."

That name twisted Gregor's stomach every time he heard it, and he wrapped his arms around his torso as his thoughts were pulled into a memory of ropes and cold and shadows. It was bad enough that he saw reminders of her everywhere he looked; he didn't need help from anyone else.

Verity bit the inside of her cheek as she thought for a moment. "You should get some rest," she said to Dare. "We can talk about this more later."

"Verity, it was her," Dare insisted.

"Alright," Verity said, holding up her hands to settle him. "I hear you. Let's talk about it when you're not concussed."

"The magic," Dare tried, struggling to sit up. His eyes lost their focus. "Verity, they—"

"Later," she said again. "Rest, Dare." Verity set her hand on his arm. "Take it easy for the rest of the trip, alright?"

Dare groaned, but he was too slow to argue.

She tapped his wrist with her finger. "That's an order."

"I really hate when you do that," he grumbled, relaxing onto the cot.

Gregor couldn't help the little smile that tugged at his lips. He never thought he'd see the day when Dare took an order from anyone.

"I know," Verity said. "And I love that you hate it." With one more tap on his arm, she left the cramped space. "You should rest too," she said to Gregor on her way out.

"I will," he said, though he had to admit it sounded halfhearted at best. He knew he should, but there were too many questions left unanswered.

When the two of them were alone again, Dare levered himself up—slowly this time. "Gregor, I swear, this attack wasn't random." He spoke deliberately, trying hard to get the words out.

Gregor sighed. Dare wasn't going to let this go until someone heard him out. "Because there were some mages?" He'd noticed as well that the pirates had a mage or two on the ship. But that hardly pointed to Tanithe.

"How many did you count?" Dare pressed.

Gregor gave another half shrug but was curious what point Dare was trying to get at. "I don't know. Three?"

"There were half a dozen at least. Tanithe knows I'm a Perceptive. She figured it out on the parapets during the fight in Taernfane. She must have sent them to fuck with me. She wanted me to suffer. To be helpless."

Six mages *was* a lot to have in one place, and Tanithe *did* know about Dare, but attacking them with pirate mages three days out of Southport? How could she have even known where they'd be? It was a stretch. Dare clearly believed it, but in his current state . . .

Gregor cleaned his glasses with the hem of his shirt. "Verity's right. We should talk about this after you've recovered—"

"You believe me, right?"

He wanted to. But he also hoped that Dare was very, very wrong. If Tanithe was hunting them . . . hunting Dare . . . "Let's talk about it later."

Dare swallowed thickly. "Later," he agreed. He blinked hard, his eyes seeming to finally refocus on Gregor. "Are you really alright?"

Gregor favored him with as much of a smile as he could muster. "Just sore," he said, setting his hand on his side again. "And tired. I, um . . ." He lowered his voice. "I'd never tried that before—with the wind. Not on that scale."

"I think you should take Verity's advice, too," Dare said. "I need you at your best. Who's going to look after my sorry ass if you run yourself ragged?"

"I'm sure Finn is more than capable of keeping you out of trouble," Gregor said, trying for a playful tone.

Dare finally settled back onto the cot.

"And for the record, I will," Gregor said, taking a step closer. He smoothed Dare's hair out of his face, letting his hand linger, caressing his cheek. "I just needed to know you were alright first."

"I'm fine," Dare said. "Or, at least, I will be."

Although he was still worried, there was a measure of relief in seeing Dare awake and talking. Gregor leaned down to kiss Dare's forehead but stopped before he got very far as a sharp pain flared in his side.

Dare took Gregor's hand and squeezed it, his expression softening. "Go," he urged.

Gregor nodded as he blew out a slow breath. "I'll ask Finn to come check on you in a little bit." His fingers tightened around Dare's hand, then he left the room and slid the thin wooden door shut.

He started toward his cabin, but something stopped him. The power he'd channeled today—and how it had felt—bothered him. A question itched at the back of his mind. What had happened when he'd thrown the window to Aetherann's power open? Was that normal, or had he somehow done something wrong?

Turning away from his cabin, Gregor moved instead to the deck. Verity was talking with the captain. When she saw Gregor, she excused herself and hurried over to him.

"Is everything alright?" she asked.

"No . . . I mean, yes. But . . ." He searched the horizon, where the clear blue sky met the darker blue of the sea. "I'm not sure," he settled on at last.

Verity took his arm, pulling him aside and out of the way of the sailors working on the deck. "What's wrong?"

Gregor inhaled deeply, though it made his side twinge, before explaining what had happened when he called the wind a few hours ago. How he'd felt so far outside of himself.

And how good it had felt.

"Did you stop on your own?" Verity asked. "Or did something break your concentration?"

He thought back to that moment, to the window in the darkness slamming shut. "I . . . I don't know. It was as though the power stopped flowing on its own."

Verity was silent for a long time as she considered his words. Gregor remained quiet, giving her time to think things through.

"If it stopped on its own," she said slowly, "perhaps Aetherann was trying to help you."

Gregor scoffed quietly. "That would be a first," he said, unable to stop the note of derision from creeping into his voice. At the surprise on Verity's face, he added, "I'm sorry, I'm just tired."

"Get some rest, Gregor," she said, setting her hand on his shoulder. "Thank you for telling me about this. We'll figure out what it means."

He nodded. The adrenaline from the battle had long since worn off, and a bone-deep weariness had settled into its place. "Alright. Thank you, Verity."

Before returning to his cabin, Gregor found Finn and asked her to check on Dare later. It was only after she promised that she'd wake Gregor if there was a problem that he sank onto his cot and fell asleep.

CHAPTER 15

THE NEXT DAY, DARE'S head was still throbbing, but he had even odds on whether it was from the concussion or the remnants of the magic-induced hangover that had settled over him after the battle. On top of it, his back was sore from his tumble down the stairs. Finn had been kind enough to confirm that he had quite a bruise across the small of his back, though her exact words had been, *That looks fucking horrible*. Dare appreciated that he could always count on Finn for a healthy dose of reality.

It was just past midday when he finally felt well enough to let Finn drag him out of his cabin. He stood with her on the bow of the ship, watching in silence as the waves broke against the prow. A memory stirred of a journey by river barge when he was young, when his older brother, Dorian, had convinced him that sirens lived in the Kylerian River. Dare had been too young to know better, and Dorian had assured him he was joking as soon as he'd seen how terrified Dare was of the water.

It had now been more than a year since his brother died. Dare drifted through other old memories. He raced through the unpleasant ones, but he let himself linger for a time in the ones that felt warm and safe, few though they were. They were all from when Dare and his brother were very young. Dorian consoling him after a skinned knee, the two of them playing hide-and-seek in the library, or climbing the apple tree in the garden. Dare had been five perhaps, maybe six, and Dorian would have been about ten.

The following year had marked Dare's parents' discovery of his *arcane gifts*. His memories for the decade that followed were not ones he preferred to focus on. Even his relationship with his brother had been tainted by his parents' greed and ambition.

"There you are." Gregor's voice jarred him out of his thoughts.

Dare turned to lean against the rail as Gregor and Verity moved to stand on either side of him. Finn slid over to make space.

"How's your head?" Verity asked.

He resisted the urge to touch the lump on his forehead. "Far less scrambled than yesterday thankfully."

"That's good," she said. "Though you'll probably be sore as hell for a while. I want you to take it easy for the rest of the trip, understand?"

Dare held up a hand to stop her. "Yeah, I know. You said that yesterday, but—"

"Oh good, you remember.

"Yes, but Verity—"

"No buts." Her voice was firm. There was no room for argument. "I want you resting. Nothing more than a light walk around the decks, alright?"

Not that there was much to do when stuck on a ship for two weeks, but Lanara's shining tits, bed rest was going to have him bored out of his mind within a day or two. He was *already* bored.

"I'm sure you'll find something to keep your mind occupied," Gregor said, intuiting the argument Dare was planning. Damn, Gregor knew him too well.

Dare shot a look to Finn in the vain hope of finding some support, but she only shrugged helplessly. Dare deflated, sinking back against the ship's railing. "Alright, fine."

Gregor and Verity exchanged a look and nodded to each other, apparently satisfied with their teamwork in making an already miserable trip even more so.

"Anything else, my lady Warden?"

"There was one more thing."

Dare braced himself.

"Do you remember," Gregor began, as though they'd rehearsed it, "what you were saying yesterday? About the pirates?"

"Of course." Dare stuffed his hands in his pockets. "I said they weren't only pirates. Tanithe sent them."

Finn's face screwed up, as though she were thinking back to the events of the day before.

Verity set her hands on the railing with a quiet *thunk* of metal striking wood. "What did you see that makes you suspect Tanithe? Did one of them say something?"

Dare shook his head, regretting it as his headache amplified. "Not really. Well, I'm not sure. It's fuzzy," he admitted. "But they were using magic—so much of it that I could barely move. And Tanithe knows. She knows about me. To have that many mages in one place . . . And she must have figured out by now that I'm the only one who can connect her to what happened in Taernfane—come on! It was her."

"The captain said the pirates based in Neoma have all sorts," Verity said. "They attack trading ships and passenger charters, and they don't leave survivors. The attack fits their methods."

"But they weren't trying to kill me," Dare said.

"That's not what I saw," Gregor said quietly, eyes cast toward the deck. "And you said it yourself yesterday: One of them had a knife to your throat, Darcy."

"Yeah, but he was trying to get me onto their ship," Dare said quickly, the recollection slotting back into place. "He wanted to take me, not kill me." None of the others had been near Dare when the man had grabbed him and threatened to gut him if Dare didn't go with him onto their ship. That had been just before Finn's dagger had found the side of the man's head. "That was a hell of a throw, by the way," Dare said, leaning forward to see Finn around Verity. "I should have thanked you sooner."

Finn shrugged like she'd hit a target during training, not struck a man square in the temple while standing on a rocking ship from halfway across the deck. "You'd've done the same for me," she said.

"Well, sure," Dare shot back. "If I could've landed the fucking hit."

"But why?" Verity interrupted. "Why go through all the trouble? The mages, kidnapping you? It doesn't make sense. If it's about your testimony, why wouldn't she just kill you?"

Because she wants me to suffer first. The thought crossed Dare's mind, but he bit it back before he said it aloud.

Beside him, Gregor tensed and crossed his arms over his stomach. "Stranger things have happened, I suppose."

Another look passed between him and Verity.

"I know she likes to toy with you," Finn said, tucking a wisp of her unruly hair behind her ear. "But this seems like a lot of effort, even for her. If she wanted to kidnap you, wouldn't that have been easier before we left port?"

"The southern seas are full of pirates." Verity leaned her elbows on the railing, looking out across the open water. "It could just be a coincidence."

Dare had to concede that it seemed implausible. But he knew what he'd heard, and he knew what he saw. He followed her gaze to the horizon. "After everything that's happened, Verity, do you really still believe in coincidences?"

In my experience, Tykaras said, *there are rarely such things.*

Dare was grateful he was facing away from everyone. He cast around a quick glance to ensure no one had noticed him startle at the god of fate's sudden intrusion. Gregor's head tilted, his brow furrowing, but it seemed as though something behind them had captured his attention.

Verity kept her eyes fixed on the water. "We'll be vigilant until this committee hearing is done and Tanithe faces justice," she said firmly.

"We've got each other's backs." Resolve settled on Finn's youthful features. "That's all we can do until this is over."

Something like pride flashed across Verity's face before she focused again on Dare. "Whatever happens, we'll deal with it together. As a team, the four of us."

Child. Tykaras's voice pushed into this shared moment with his friends yet again. *I need to speak with you when you are alone.*

Dare nodded, though it was as much to Verity and Finn as it was to Tykaras. He kept his face passive.

Gregor pushed his glasses up onto his head, rubbing his face with both hands.

"I'll update Chancellor Caelan and the Drahkonian guards about everything," Verity continued.

Gregor's attention snapped back at the mention of their royal-adjacent companion. "Gods, I'd nearly forgotten," he said. "Is he—"

"He's fine," Verity said quickly. "He stayed below decks during the attack. One of the Drahkonian guards was injured, but the ship's medic said she'll be alright. I promised Caelan a debrief once things had settled down." As Dare opened his mouth, she added, directly to him, "And I'll mention your theory as well."

It didn't give him a strong sense of confidence for her to refer to it as a *theory*, but he'd have to make do for now. "Thank you, my lady Warden."

With one last look to Gregor, Verity headed toward the passengers' quarters. Finn bid Dare farewell with a somewhat gentle punch in the shoulder and followed after her. "Vee, wait up."

Gregor glanced at Dare but then turned to the sea again, leaning on the ship's rail. Dare briefly considered whether he should leave Gregor to his thoughts.

"Would you stay with me for a little while?" Gregor asked, his voice soft.

"I'll stay with you for as long as you'll have me."

Gregor's lips curved into a smile, the dimple appearing under his eye. But it faded just as quickly, there and gone in a blink. "If you're right, and she . . ." His thumb traced the the scar around his wrist. "If Tanithe's trying to stop you from testifying or . . . or if she has some plan for you . . . I . . ." Bowing his head, he sighed. "I need you to keep yourself safe, alright? Don't go doing anything stupid. You're one of the smartest people I know, Dare. I need you to start acting like it."

Dare croaked out a laugh. "I'm not sure whether to be touched or offended."

"You know what I mean," Gregor said sharply. He turned to face Dare, worry evident in the lines of his mouth and the dark circles under his eyes. "Play it safe. Please, Darcy."

It never bothered him that Gregor was the only person in his life to still call him *Darcy* on occasion. Somehow, from Gregor, both names felt like home.

"Don't worry," Dare said, running his hands along the length of Gregor's arms.

Gregor shivered as though from a chill. "Promise me you'll be careful when we get to Whitehollow. Promise me you won't do anything stupid."

"I promise," Dare said, his heart squeezing in his chest.

Gregor studied him for a moment and, seeming satisfied, nodded at last. He leaned in and kissed Dare's cheek before turning and following after Verity and Finn.

Dare watched him walk away, leaning back against the railing. *Tykaras?*

The expansive presence filled his chest. *Yes, Child. I am here.*

Annoyance prickled the back of Dare's neck. *Now you are, sure.*

A slight hesitation, then, *You are bothered?*

We could have used your help yesterday.

The dual voice of Tykaras turned icy. *I do have other demands on my attention, Child.*

A twinge of shame flashed through him as he tried to push back his irritation. *Of course,* he thought, shifting uneasily. But he'd called for Tykaras when the pirates first attacked, and then again in the middle of the fray, when the mages had him locked down. He couldn't help but feel like a little help from the god of luck could have gone a long way. *I called for you. I . . . I thought you could always hear me—my thoughts.*

That is not entirely accurate.

Is that why I couldn't summon any of your power either? Dare asked, forgetting his irritation in favor of curiosity. He'd tried that too, hoping that he could work some divine intervention to help out the ship. The other Chosen had divine magic they could summon at will. *I tried, but nothing happened. Was it because you weren't here?*

You were not able to summon any of my power, Tykaras said, their voice no less tight, *because you do not know what it is you are trying to summon. I told you in the beginning: my realm is a subtler one. Besides . . .* Tykaras's voice softened, and a slow smile appeared in Dare's mind. *My power* was *with you yesterday, as it always is.*

It was?

The smile broadened. *You survived, did you not?*

Dare stiffened, casting a glance at the sky. "That's not funny," he muttered aloud.

It is not a joke, Tykaras replied. *How many close calls did you have yesterday? How many moments where something almost did you in?*

Dare rubbed at the small of his back, which still had a deep ache from the battle the day before. Looking at the stairs this morning, Dare had quietly marveled how lucky he'd been that he hadn't broken his neck when he'd tumbled down them.

My point exactly, Tykaras said, a smugness replacing the icy chill from moments ago. *You are welcome.*

Dare rolled his eyes, though a smile tugged at his lips. *Fine, point taken,* he remarked. *Did you want to talk to me about something, or are you just here to lecture me today?*

Another pause. *Would you prefer a lecture?*

Fucking hells. Dare rubbed at his eyes with his thumb and forefinger. *What did you want to talk to me about?*

It has been a long time since I have had a Chosen, Tykaras mused, *but I recall humans having more reverence.*

Dare sighed, though he couldn't deny the amusement dancing through him.

I wanted to tell you, Tykaras went on, the smugness returning, *that I have taken the requisite steps on my side that were needed ahead of you informing the other Chosen of our connection. You may proceed with telling them about me.*

"Oh." Even attempting to wrap his mind around how to tell the others about Tykaras threatened to make Dare's brain explode. "Thanks. I'll, uh . . . I'll handle it."

We will speak again later. There was a gentle farewell, like a hand gliding down his back, and then Tykaras was gone.

Dare turned his attention back to the waters that would carry him, carry them all, on the next part of their journey.

Later. He'd find a way to tell them about it later. Maybe once the trial was over? It wouldn't do any of them any good for him to spring this on them when there were so many loose ends in Whitehollow to be addressed. He would tell them everything once the trial was behind them.

Chapter 16

Lucien spent the next day asking Taerna for an explanation of what she needed him to do in the Red Forest, or at least another vision, but the goddess remained frustratingly silent. Though, admittedly, he'd found it hard to concentrate on anything after yesterday's conversation with Jae. The nearer they came to the little farm he'd built with Ethriel all those years ago, the more his mind wandered. Did she even still live there? How had the farm changed in the last twenty years? How had *she* changed? If he went back, she would certainly hate him for leaving. Could he handle facing that?

Did he owe it to her to do it anyway?

And what of his daughter? She'd been an infant when he'd walked down their little gravel path for the last time. She wouldn't remember him, of course, but what stories would Ethriel have told her about him? Would she have told her anything at all?

Lucien shook his head. He needed to focus on the task at hand. If Taerna wouldn't give him any further guidance, perhaps his best bet would be to ask the shifters for access to the Heart. Maybe then Taerna would make her intentions clear.

Lucien and Jae stopped early on the last night before they were to reach the Red Forest. Having to enter the Forest again was bad enough; he didn't want to be within its borders come nightfall. Better to approach the shifters in the light of day.

When the sun rose, they packed up their camp in silence. An hour later, they were standing at the line of trees with their dark trunks and blood-red leaves.

"Are you sure you want to do this, Jae?"

The look she shot him was clearly intended to strike him dead. "Don't be an idiot. I'm not letting you do this alone."

"This isn't just some job," Lucien said. "This is the Red Forest."

"I know that."

Lucien rolled his shoulders. He needed to make her understand. "We aren't talking about trying to travel through while dodging shifters. We're talking about walking right into the middle of their territory. We're talking about trying to reason with them."

Jae crossed her arms over her chest. Her notched eyebrow arched as she smirked. "And of the two of us, you think you're most likely to be reasonable?"

He growled deep in his throat. "I'm not joking. You don't know what it's like in there."

"No shit," she snapped, "because you never told me anything about it. But it's too late for that now, so here we are. Here *I* am." Her shoulders sagged as her arms fell to her sides. "Lucien, I can't watch your back from out here. We've always looked out for each other. Don't go trying to be all heroic now. We're in this together." She nodded toward the forest. "I trust you to have my back in there. Trust me to have yours."

Lucien was getting awfully tired of Jae having a point. "Follow my lead," he said.

"Of course."

"I'm serious. They're not going to take kindly to having a human in their territory, and if you start talking back—"

She scoffed. "When do I *ever*—"

"*If you start talking back*," Lucien plowed forward, "they're not going to care about what you're saying." He set his hands on her shoulders. He needed her to understand the danger they were walking into. He needed her to keep herself safe. "Please, Jae. Promise me."

"I promise," she said softly. "I'll follow your lead."

Lucien blew out a breath, trying to release the tension knotted in his back as he turned toward the forest.

Not counting a few months ago when he was looking for Solace, it had been twelve years since he'd set foot in the Red Forest. The leaves dipped low from the branches like fingers reaching toward him. It seemed the forest remembered him.

He hoped the shifters didn't.

✳

Lucien led the way through the trees. Even in his human form, he could smell the shifters' presence, and the deeper they went into the forest, the stronger that presence grew. Jae stayed close to his side, her attention on their rear, guarding their backs. They had always worked well together, trusting each other, which was good because he was going to need Jae to trust him more than she ever had before. But he didn't know how to tell her everything they were walking into.

The birds stopped chirping as Lucien stepped over a raised root, and a bark of warning rang through the silence. Jae froze at Lucien's upraised hand. It was now or never.

Lucien let the beast out.

His bones and joints snapped painfully until he was on all fours, his clothing, his boots, even the gear he carried all melding into his skin, replaced by dark, charcoal gray fur. His massive paws flexed, and his claws dug into the soft earth. He angled himself in front of Jae, his huge bestial form blocking her from sight as he tipped his head back and yowled once, long and low. He followed it with a few short yips as he bowed his head. *Peace. Respect. Talk. Human. Protect.* Lucien was out of practice, but he was fairly certain he conveyed what was needed: He was there peacefully, respectfully, with a human under his protection, and he wanted to talk. The intrinsic form of communication never really faded from memory. Some part of him remembered.

Another howl reverberated through the trees. *Stay put.*

Lucien looked back at Jae, whose dark eyes were wide with what was certainly a thousand questions, but she kept them to herself. For now, at least. He'd get an earful later, he was sure. He wouldn't blame her for it. He'd never told her about the years he'd spent living in the Red Forest—if he could even call it that. *Surviving* was more the truth of it. But he'd never told her about the shifters' way of life here. How could he? And what would it have mattered? The rumors were there for a reason.

The trees rustled ahead of them and two shifters emerged in their monstrous forms, one an icy pale gray and the other a ruddy brown. Their heads were lowered, ears back, teeth bared. Lucien stood his ground, keeping himself angled in front of Jae.

Mine, he yipped again. *Protect.*

The shifter with the pale gray fur pushed onto her hind legs and changed, the fur sliding away until a short, fair-skinned woman stood in its place. Maldren Thorn. She flung her braid over her shoulder, black as night except for the white streak that started at her temple and wove through the braid. She gestured for Lucien to stand, then set her hands on the curve of her hips, waiting for him to shift back into his human form.

"Lucien Longshadow," she said. "As I live and breathe. Never thought I'd see your scruffy face back here."

"Didn't expect to be back," Lucien grumbled when he stood on his own two feet. He rolled his shoulders, the joints popping again with the residual tension of shifting back and forth so quickly.

Maldren gave an upward nod toward Jae. "You going to introduce me to your friend?"

"This is Jae Aleissandra," he said. Lucien didn't take his eyes off Maldren or the other shifter. "Jae, this is Maldren Thorn."

"Lucien," she chided in that singsong way he'd always hated. "You know better." She set her focus on Jae. "Please, call me Mal."

Jae, one hand resting on the sword on her hip, nodded a curt greeting. "Hello."

Maldren flashed a pleasant smile and gestured to the brown-furred shifter a few paces behind her. "Lucien, you remember Ethan Stonefang."

He didn't, but he nodded all the same. The other shifter dipped his head in response.

"I thought I picked up your scent a few months back," Maldren went on. "But I didn't think it was possible. It *was* you then, wasn't it?"

Lucien shifted his weight. The beast within him pulled at the chains, sensing the others. He'd felt it the last time, too. "We're here to see Barrick," he said, ignoring both her question and his inner beast.

Her smile faded. "Barrick's gone," she said, her voice going flat. "Micah's in charge now."

The hairs on the back of Lucien's neck stood on end. Even the beast chained within him growled at the name. Micah Fogrender had been second-in-command to Barrick Stoneclaw, last Lucien knew.

"How long?" he asked.

Maldren shrugged one shoulder. "Three years, give or take."

"What happened?"

She arched a brow. "You care all of a sudden?"

His shoulders tensed. Barrick had been a violent old bastard, but from what Lucien remembered, Micah had been the one behind some of the more egregious, sadistic punishments for humans entering their territory. Lucien was acutely aware of Jae standing silently beside him. "I need to speak with him," he said tightly.

"What for?"

Lucien inhaled, long and deep. "I need access to the Heart."

"The Heart?" Mal's brows rose. "Why?"

He crossed his arms, muscles flexing. "What's it matter? I need to speak with him."

Mal mirrored his pose, standing her ground. "Come on, Lucien. You should know that's not how this works. You can't wander back in here and start making demands. After you've been gone how many—"

"It's urgent."

"Micah will be the judge of whether or not it's urgent," she snapped. "And if you won't tell me what it's about, then I can't help you."

Lucien huffed a sigh. "It's about the shifters," he said. He'd pieced together that much at least, but he was going to need more to go on, and soon. He offered up a silent prayer to Taerna for guidance.

Maldren didn't move. "I'm listening."

"Just tell Micah," he said instead, giving an upward nod toward the trees behind her. "I'm sure he'll be interested to know that I'm here."

"I'll see if he's around." Maldren studied him for a moment. "Wait here. We'll come back within the hour. And don't go getting curious and wandering off." The corner of her mouth ticked up. "You remember the rules, I'm sure." She glanced at Ethan, jerking her head back the way they'd come. "Let's go." She disappeared into the blood-red trees with Ethan padding along behind her.

Lucien blew out his breath in a long hiss and forced his hands to unclench.

Behind him, Jae did the same. "Are you alright?"

He wasn't. He hadn't wanted to come back to this damned forest. Not ever. But that hope had been smashed when he'd been tracking Corvin Crosse and his soldiers after they'd kidnapped Solace. When their trail had entered the Red Forest, Lucien had hesitated, though only briefly. He'd hesitated because the forest *called* to him. It called to the beast within him and made it harder to ignore its angry baying.

Even now, even with whatever blessing Taerna had bestowed on him to make it easier to control the monster, he could feel the moss-covered chains straining with the strength of its thrashing. It wanted to be free. It wanted to run.

It wanted to kill.

"Lucien . . ."

"I don't have answers for you, Jae," he said, his voice rough.

Something in the forest beckoned the beast forward, deeper into the trees, and Lucien had to grit his teeth to stop himself from shifting again.

The snap of a twig behind him had him whirling around, snarling, teeth bared and a clawed hand raised to strike.

Jae jerked back and her hand flew to her sword.

Lucien reined the beast in, staggering a step as he fought the change that threatened to overtake him.

Twice. Only twice in all the years they'd traveled together had Lucien come close to losing control around Jae. And both times she'd had the same expression on her face that she had now—a layer of concern masking a deep, primal fear.

Lucien hated nothing more than seeing fear on the face of someone he cared about.

He backed away from Jae, putting more space between them. "I'm sorry," he ground out as he willed his claws to retract. "This place . . ." The memories of when he was changed were here, that was part of it, but there was a power here too, calling to him.

"I get it," Jae said, though she kept a safe distance. "Are you going to be alright?"

He nodded as he moved a few more steps away from her. He needed some time to focus, to calm his mind and secure his control. "Give me a bit."

Jae relaxed, her hand falling away from the hilt of her sword. "I'll keep an eye out for Maldren," she said, then turned her attention to the forest where the two shifters had disappeared.

Lucien breathed deep, the scents of the forest flowing into him. He settled himself beneath one of the blood-red trees and closed his eyes. He tried to imagine he was sitting beneath the great tree in the center of the palace courtyard in Taernfane. It was the only place he'd ever felt a sense of calm. Of *peace.* He tried to remember how it felt to have that peace settle over him.

In the darkness behind his eyelids, a sensation like a heavy blanket surrounded Lucien, pressing down on him from all sides. He breathed into the stillness, into the silence, letting himself simply feel that calming presence until his heartbeat slowed to a steady rhythm. He hadn't realized how fast it was racing until it settled.

Taerna? Lucien asked the silence.

The sound of grinding stones echoed in his mind. He was beginning to suspect it was the sound of the goddess's laughter. *Yes, little wolf. I am here.*

What is wrong with this place? he asked. *I've been in the forest for barely an hour and I can feel my control slipping.*

The forest is at war with itself, Taerna said. *Much as you are.*

Is that why I'm here? Lucien asked.

Yes.

I . . . don't know if I can do this, he admitted. It was often much easier to express his fears to the goddess than to anyone else he'd ever known, though he wasn't sure why. *What if I lose control? I don't want to hurt Jae.*

The comforting weight of Taerna settled more deeply around him, pressing in tightly, stilling the uncertainty that had taken root.

You are as a stone of the earth, little wolf. Pressure does not break you. It only serves to strengthen you.

The earth tilted, and his vision grew hazy, drawing outward until he was at the edge of a lake. It was the vision Taerna had sent him when he sat beneath her tree in Taernfane. The group of people he'd seen before, adorning their skin with paint, were still there, though now Lucien stood among them. He could see now that the paint was blood red, as were the leaves on the trees that surrounded them. One by one, they knelt at the water's edge, spoke words in a language he couldn't understand, and drank from their cupped hands.

His vision lurched back and then rushed forward, into one of the painted men. They stood now among the trees, no longer near the edge of that crystal-clear lake. Lucien saw through eyes that were not his own and looked down at a body that belonged to someone else, though he could feel their emotions as readily as he could feel his own.

Within this body—*his* body—a beast crouched. It felt oddly similar to his own beast, but it held a curiosity within it, in addition to the raw power pumping through his veins. Those around him were looking at their hands, or feeling their bodies, or looking up at the sky, offering up prayers.

Prayers he could now understand.

"Praise the Mother," one said.

"Glory to Taerna," said another.

And they sprinted into the woods as a group.

As a pack.

Almost as one, they bounded forward, leaping onto the ground on all fours as their bodies changed.

Lucien followed, and the shift took him over, his hands and feet changing into powerful paws, his mouth elongating into a fearsome snout with sharpened fangs. It was familiar and yet entirely new. The beast took over, but Lucien was still there, riding alongside it. And the beast looked inward and saw him. It wagged its tail.

Run? it asked.

Lucien smiled. *Run.*

And they did. They ran through the forest of blood-red trees, the five of them with their beasts, natural and wild and pure. There was no rage or fury or fear. The beast—the *wolf*—was a part of him, and he was a part of it. They were separate and one. And the others who ran with him were his family. His pack.

A sharp pain was building behind Lucien's eyes again, and he clenched his jaw, holding onto the vision before Taerna could pull it away. But it faded into blackness, and the pain with it.

How? Lucien managed. He was grateful he didn't need to speak the words aloud. He didn't trust that he could get them out through the tightness in his throat. *How did they . . . How did we—?*

"Someone's coming," Jae called. "'Bout fucking time."

Taerna's presence dissipated as quickly as it had appeared. Lucien's eyes snapped open, searching the trees for something to focus on, to orient himself after the sudden return to his senses. "Time?" he muttered. "It's only been—"

"It's been two hours," she said, hopping down from a branch she'd been perched on.

Two hours? Lucien stood, marveling briefly at the calm that had settled through him. Wolves . . . The shifters had been wolves once.

Jae came up alongside him, checking the draw on her swords. "You good?"

"Enough," he murmured, turning toward the trees as Maldren's and Ethan's scents reached him.

Maldren stepped through the trees first, Ethan following in his human form this time. He was a little shorter than Lucien, with deep tan skin and dark hair that was pulled into a bun at the crown of his head. He hung back, watching Lucien and Jae as Mal moved a few paces closer.

"Micah's unavailable," she said, crossing her arms over her chest.

"Unavailable?" Lucien snarled.

Maldren shrugged. "I don't know what to tell you, Lucien. He won't be able to meet with you for a while. I don't know how long exactly. Could be a few days. Maybe a week."

Jae scoffed. "A *week*? You can't be serious."

"Those are the terms," Mal said flatly. "Come back in a week or not at all." With a wave to Ethan, the two shifters headed back into the trees. But Maldren stopped after a few steps and turned to look at Lucien over her shoulder. "It's good to see you again, Lucien. Take care of yourself."

He waited until they were safely out of earshot to let out the growl that had been building in his chest. "It's a show of dominance. He wants to make sure we know he's in charge."

Jae rested her hand on the hilt of her sword. "What's our next move?"

"We can't get anywhere near the Heart without Micah's permission." Lucien paced through the low underbrush. "There's no way we can sneak through without the shifters scenting us, and if we even try it, Micah will rip our throats out."

"So we come back in a week?" Jae peered through the trees, back the way they'd come. "Where do we go in the meantime?"

Deeper in the forest, a howl ripped through the silence. Another joined it, and then another, and another.

"Anywhere but here," Lucien said, gesturing Jae closer. "I think we've already overstayed our welcome."

They backtracked through the trees until they stood at the edge of the forest, the rolling plains of Southreach stretching ahead of them.

"Lucien," Jae said when they were safely clear of the forest. "Why didn't you tell me?"

"Tell you what?" He knew what. But the truth was messy. Complicated. The lie of it was prolific, and it was simpler.

"That they're not monsters—"

"We *are* monsters," he snapped between clenched teeth. "Just because we're not slobbering, mindless beasts doesn't make us any less monstrous."

"Was it all a lie? Everything that people say about shifters?"

Lucien sighed. "No," he conceded. "No, there are shifters who are no longer in control of themselves, who lost their minds to the beast. But there are plenty who have simply given in to the rage and who let the beast become a part of them."

Jae brushed past him. "You should have told me."

". . . I'm sorry."

"You're going to make it up to me. We have to find some place where we can lie low for a week, and I happen to know a way we can take care of both at the same time."

123

Chapter 17

Dare sat on the railing of the ship, his back against the rigging, one leg hanging lazily over the edge. The mouth of Cloud Bay loomed ahead, leading them back to where they started. It was dark, and overhead the stars, unimpeded by streetlamps or lanterns, towers or walls, shone brilliant and bright.

The ordered rest he'd been on for most of the trip had the unfortunate side effect of giving Dare plenty of time to think. He'd replayed the attack on the ship over in his mind at least a dozen times in the last two weeks, nitpicking every fucking thing he could have done differently. Wandering down the path of every *what-if*.

So, are you going to sit there and sulk, Child? Tykaras asked from the back of his mind. *Or are you going to do something about it?*

Dare snorted at the god's almost playful tone. *I thought I'd brood a while longer, if it's all the same to you.*

It is not all the same to me, Tykaras replied. *And I have had a long time to observe humans, their interactions and emotions. You are not brooding. You are sulking.*

One of these days you're going to tell me why you weren't asleep with the other gods, Dare mused, *since it seems to have given you so much time to observe humans.*

Do not try to alter the topic of discussion, Tykaras said. *You already know what you need to do. You just don't want to do it. And that dissonance is making you grumpy.*

Grumpy? Dare couldn't help the chuckle that snuck out.

Is that not the correct word for your mood?

Dare leaned his head against the rigging and tilted his face to the sky. *No, that's the right word*, he admitted. *Just not the term I expected from a millennia-old deity.*

You shall have to explain to me, Tykaras said, *why my status as a deity of the realm has any bearing on my word choice.*

Fair enough. I didn't think gods would take such an interest in mortals' lives, he said, deflecting the focus again. *Do all the gods listen in on the thoughts and conversations of their Chosen, or just you?*

A flash of amusement flitted through him. *Only when you wish us to.*

When we wish you to?

Yes. When Dare's thoughts stalled around this concept, Tykaras continued, *The connection between a god and their Chosen is like a channel between two bodies of water. It must be open from both sides for anything to flow between.*

Dare turned the idea over in his mind.

For now, Tykaras continued, *stop running yourself in circles. Go find the Warden.*

Raising his brows, Dare stared out at the water. *Are you telling me this is fated?*

No, the choice is yours, as it always is. But you have already made your decision, and evidently require the nudge. Dare felt a presence caress the length of his back. *Find the Warden, Child.*

Tykaras was right, of course. Dare knew what he had to do. He swung down from the rail.

Small lights illuminated the deck and the stairs leading below. It was very late; Verity was probably in her cabin. He planned to start there, though she appeared on the stairs as soon as he approached the hatch.

Dare gave a sidelong glance to the stars for the near-perfect timing. A grin flashed inside his mind before the expansive presence that was Tykaras dissipated.

Verity paused when she saw Dare out of the corner of her eye. "Evening." She smiled, giving him an appraising look. "You're looking better."

Dare held out his hand to help her up the last couple of steps. She certainly didn't need it, but she took his hand all the same. "I thought you'd be in bed by now," he said. "Aren't we docking in Whitehollow tomorrow?" He paused and glanced at the stars again, this time to gauge the hour. "Today?"

"Valda actually," she said. "The ship stops in Valda before continuing on to Whitehollow."

Dare ran his fingers through his hair. Shit, he hadn't accounted for being back in Valda for any length of time.

"Don't worry," Verity said quickly, setting her hand on his shoulder. "It's just for a few hours. We're not even getting off the ship."

"Right," Dare murmured. Of course. It would be fine. Valda was a huge city with a busy port. It wouldn't be a problem. "Right."

"Anyway, I couldn't sleep," Verity said, gesturing toward the starboard side of the ship. "I thought I'd come listen to the waves for a while. What about you? What are you doing up so late?"

Dare followed her to where he'd been perched earlier and leaned against the rail. "Me? You forget, my lady Warden. I prefer the night." His fingers wrapped around the wooden railing as Verity leaned her elbows against it, peering down over the side. "Besides, I had too many thoughts swirling around in my head tonight to sleep."

Verity turned to him, her brow furrowed with sudden concern. "Do you want to talk about it?"

She cared. She really did care. She had only wanted to help him, and he'd reacted like a petulant child.

"No," he said, a quick shake of his head dismissing her question. "I've been thinking a lot. About what you said . . ." His voice snagged and he cleared his throat. Part of him wondered why this was so difficult, but the other part of him knew the answer. "About teaching me to control my . . ." He gave up on words and gestured vaguely to himself instead.

"Dare—"

"You were right." He turned his back to the water and leaned against the railing. "The kidnappers—pirates—whatever they were, they had more mages in one place than I've ever seen. There was so much damned magic being thrown around, I couldn't do anything. I was locked down. Gregor got hurt trying to help me, and they'd have dragged me away if it weren't for Finn."

He inhaled deeply and finally forced himself to face Verity. "I can't let something like that happen again. I can't be the reason someone I care about gets hurt. So I want you to teach me how to control it. And I . . ."

Dare swallowed hard and wet his lips, trying desperately to force the words out while he still had the resolve. "And I want you to teach me how to channel magic. Nothing crazy," he added as Verity's brows climbed. "Just enough that I can help."

Enough that I won't be a burden.

He took another deep breath and set his hand on hers, the steel cold against his palm even as the warmth of Pyrannis's power mingled with the usual soft thrum of Verity's own magic. "You've helped me through more shit than I care to recall at the moment. And I've got your back, my lady Warden. No matter what. I'd just like to make sure that I actually *can*. I don't want to let you down because I couldn't get my shit together."

Verity placed her other hand on top of his. "Thank you," she said. Her voice was gentle, sincere. "For trusting me with this. Trusting me with you." She squeezed his hand. "I won't pretend to understand what it took for you to come to this decision. So just know that I won't ever hurt you, Dare. And I won't let anything happen to you while we're training." She paused for a long moment. "Do you trust me?"

"I trust you," he said immediately. The words came without thinking. Without question. "Between you and Gregor, there's no one I trust more."

"I'm honored," Verity said quietly.

Dare cleared his throat again, finally releasing her hand and turning his attention toward the bay. "So what do we do when we finally get to Whitehollow?"

"Well, we need to check in with Commander Cairn once we arrive."

Dare hid his wince. "Lovely."

"It'll be fine," Verity said. "You'll see."

He wanted to believe her. He wanted to have as much optimism—as much blind fucking faith in the world—as she had. Gods be damned, he *wanted* to.

They stood on the deck for a long time, watching the barque cut through the water. Finally, Dare straightened. "I'm going to try to get a little sleep before we dock."

"Alright," Verity said. "See you in a few hours."

"Night, my lady Warden."

Below deck, Dare started toward his bunk but stopped in the hall. The long row of passenger cabins was silent. He walked a few cabins past his door until he stood in front of Gregor's. No light came from the gap under the door. Dare hesitated as he reached for the latch. He wanted to tell Gregor about the decision he came to, but Gregor had barely spoken to him since the attack. Dare could hardly blame him. He'd gotten hurt because of Dare. Maybe this would give Dare a chance to make things up to him. To be the one looking out for Gregor for a change.

Retreating back to his own bunk, Dare settled onto his cot and tucked his hands beneath his head. Trepidation settled in his stomach as he considered what he'd just agreed to. He was going to learn magic. And how to control his Perceptive abilities. Could that even happen? It was something that had been so intrinsically a part of him for as long as he could remember. Could it be controlled? And if it could, what then?

Dare couldn't see how it was possible, but he owed it to his friends to try.

A few hours later, Dare found himself back on the deck, watching the port of Valda come into view on the horizon as the sky lightened ahead of them.

Tanithe Ash would be in the city. Dare was certain those pirates were on her payroll, so word of their failure would've surely reached her by now. Valda was a huge, sprawling place, but among the masses of people, somewhere, she was there. And if she found him or any of his friends . . .

It was a good thing, he decided, that they were staying on the boat. More passengers who had chartered travel to Whitehollow would board in the coming hours, and the ship would set sail again by midafternoon. There was nothing to do now but sit and wait.

Dare drummed his fingers against the railing.

And yet . . .

He hadn't wanted to come back to Valda at all, but now that he was here, he couldn't deny the urge to head into the city and disappear into the crowds. He'd been cramped on this ship for two weeks. He needed to stretch his legs. And against his better judgment, the city was calling to him.

It was a terrible idea.

But perhaps he should go, he reasoned. At least for a little while. The ship would be registered with the harbor master, so if Tanithe really wanted to find him, staying on the boat wasn't going to do him any favors. And besides, he should check in with the Crimson Brothers. After all, he'd left on a mission at the behest of the Valdane Council eight months ago. Although he didn't take orders from the Brothers the way Verity took orders from the Wardens, they'd still likely be wondering where he'd gotten off to. And considering a handful of Brothers had also disappeared after following Caleb, perhaps Dare could offer the captain of the Brothers an explanation.

And then, there was the other matter that his absence from Valda had forced him to neglect. He'd only need an hour or so, and he could—

"I know that Valda's the largest city on the continent," Gregor said, coming up beside him. "But somehow I still wasn't prepared."

Dare was momentarily surprised anyone else was awake at this hour, but then again, of course Gregor was awake. He rose with the sun. He was more surprised that Gregor was speaking to him.

"There's really only a small part of the city you can see from the docks," Dare said, gesturing toward the paths leading up the cliff beyond the port. "The rest of the city is up there."

"And this is where you lived after you . . ." Gregor fidgeted with his glasses. "After you left Brookshire?"

"More or less. I spent a few days or a week in a couple other towns along the way, but Valda was the first place that felt . . ."

"Like home?" Gregor offered, his voice somber.

"No. I wasn't looking for a home then. I was looking for somewhere I could get lost and not ever be found."

Gregor leaned against the railing, though when his fingers brushed Dare's, he pulled his hand closer to his body, almost like he flinched.

Dare straightened and pushed off from the railing in a failed attempt to not take the gesture personally. "How long before the ship leaves for Whitehollow?" If anyone knew their itinerary down to the minute, it would be Gregor.

"About six hours," Gregor said. "We're due to dock in Whitehollow by sundown."

Dare nodded, his eyes drifting over the docks and the city beyond. Six hours would give him plenty of time. He wouldn't even need half that to take care of everything he needed to do. He could be there and back before anyone even noticed he was gone. Before Tanithe would even notice he was there.

"Have you seen Verity?" Dare asked.

"Not yet. I was just heading to find her. I thought she might want to know we've docked."

"Good idea," Dare said casually. "I'm sure she'll appreciate that."

Gregor gave him a nod and headed toward the stairs that led below.

"See you in a bit," Dare called, though Gregor's only response was a silent wave over his shoulder.

He tried not to read it as a dismissal, but that was fine even if it was. He needed to head out before Verity saw him. He doubted she'd like his plan very much, and she might insist he stay on the ship. But if she wasn't here to argue with him . . .

Dare dashed back to his cabin just long enough to grab a few things before disembarking with some of the other passengers. He felt the rush of the city around him as he disappeared into the throng.

Dare let his feet carry him through Valda. It felt good to be home . . . *Back? Home*, he decided finally. Even if the city didn't want him anymore, a part of him would always feel like this was where he belonged.

He walked through the streets until he came to a familiar building with a familiar sign out front: a large bird perched on the horns of a stag. *The Raven and Hart.* If it wasn't so early, Dare would be tempted to stop for a drink, but as it was, he knew he shouldn't press his luck. Perhaps if his other errands went smoothly, he'd have time for a quick libation before returning to the ship. That seemed like motivation enough to take care of things quickly.

Dare's first stop was the bank where he kept an account with a modest sum of gold he'd saved over the years. The King of Drahkonia had set each of them up with enough funds in Taernfane to very likely keep them in comfort for the rest of their lives, so Dare wasn't terribly concerned with draining this one nearly to the dregs. Though he left enough to cover his living expenses for a few months, just in case. Next was the market district.

Most of the shops had just opened, and the streets were full of market-goers and vendors. For the first time since he'd left Valda months ago, Dare almost felt like everything was back to normal. He stopped at a few shops, first purchasing a simple canvas knapsack, in which he proceeded to deposit the rest of his purchases: a couple small blankets, a few cloaks rolled up as tightly as he could get them, some bread, apples, cheese, a few other odds and ends, as well as the rest of the coin he'd withdrawn from his account.

When he was done, the pack was stuffed as full as he could manage while still being able to lift the damn thing. Leaving the final shop on his route, he rounded the corner onto one of the main streets of the market. Two more stops and he could enjoy a pint at the Raven and Hart before heading back to the ship.

"There you are!" Verity's stern voice cut through the dull roar of the crowded streets. "What in Vire's hells, Dare?" Verity and Finn crossed the street toward him, and the Warden's face was nearly scarlet. Finn didn't look too thrilled either.

Dare plastered a disarming smile on his face. "Morning, my lady—"

"Don't start," Verity snapped. "What do you think you're doing?"

He hoisted his laden knapsack a little higher on his shoulders. "Errands?"

"Alone?"

"I didn't want to bother anyone," he said, trying to sound contrite.

By the look on Verity's face, she wasn't buying it. "More like you knew we would tell you wandering into Valda alone was the worst possible thing you could do right now, so instead of telling anyone what you were planning, you just did it anyway." She set her hands on her hips, daring him to deny it. "Am I right?"

"Look," Dare said, dodging Verity's point entirely. "I'm nearly done. I have two more stops"—the thought of a cold ale popped into his mind again—"*three* more stops and then I'll be back on the ship with plenty of time to spare."

"It's not about the ship." Verity waved a hand at the city around them. "It's not safe."

Dare was about to point out that he'd been handling himself on the streets of Valda since he was a teenager, but he knew that wasn't what she was referring to. Tanithe was here somewhere. And even in a city the size of Valda, if she wanted to find him—find any of them—she could.

"I know," he conceded—and was rewarded with a look of shock fluttering across the Warden's face. Clearly she hadn't expected him to admit it. "But I needed to take care of a couple of things, not the least of which is checking in with the Crimson Brothers." Maybe appealing to her sense of duty would get him off the hook.

Verity's face softened predictably, though Finn's grew stern. "Without *me*?" she demanded.

Shit. A slight miscalculation. "I . . . don't have a good excuse for that."

Finn slugged him in the shoulder, and Dare caught himself on the corner of the building before the weight of his pack sent him stumbling backward. "You're hopeless," she lamented.

"Since you're here now," Dare tried, his smile broadening, "would you care to join me?"

"Well, we're not about to let you wander off on your own," Verity said before Finn could reply. "Lead the way."

CHAPTER 18

"It must feel nice to be home, even if it's just for a few hours," Verity said as she walked beside Finn through the crowded streets of Valda. Dare was a few feet ahead, hands firmly in his pockets and a heavy knapsack slung over one shoulder.

Finn breathed in the scent of the city, which mixed with the salt air from the bay. "I think so." She sounded far less certain than Verity was expecting.

"You're not sure?" she asked.

Finn shrugged and looked around at the buildings as they passed. "I lived here my whole life," she said. "But now that I've left, I'm honestly not sure this city was ever really my home."

"I need to make a detour," Dare called over his shoulder. "Go on ahead; I'll catch up." He ducked down a side street before either Verity or Finn could comment.

"He can't help himself, can he?" Verity groaned, rolling her eyes.

Finn paused at the corner. "I'm a little curious what he's up to." A smirk played across her lips. "Aren't you?"

Verity returned the grin, amused by the conspiracy of it. "I suppose."

Finn gave her a wink, and Verity's stomach fluttered. Then Finn took her by the hand and pulled her around the corner.

Verity let herself be tugged along as Finn expertly navigated the narrow back alleys of Valda. She kept Dare in sight just ahead and giggled as she pulled Verity to hide behind each corner, as though they were spies tracking their mark. Verity was certain Dare knew precisely where they were, but she was too busy laughing at Finn's over-dramatic stalking to care much about it.

But Finn stopped short as they came around the last corner Dare had taken. "Wait, why is he—"

Dare was heading toward them, back the way he'd come, the knapsack he'd been carrying left behind on the stoop of a large building at the end of the alley. Verity recognized the place. Dare had taken the same *detour* before, when he was supposed to be leading her and Drystan to the port. Dare had dropped a small parcel of the-gods-only-knew-what at the same back door. Verity's chest tightened at the memory, and she couldn't help but picture Drystan beside her.

But they'd only just returned to Valda. How could Dare have picked up a job so fast? She was about to ask Finn what was going on, but—

Finn was staring at Dare like she'd seen a ghost.

Verity touched her arm. "Finn?"

Dare's self-satisfied grin faded as he caught sight of the two women. His steps faltered, and he shot a quick glance over his shoulder, as though worried someone was behind him. "What is it?"

Finn's throat worked as she tried to form words. "Wh-what were you doing?"

Dare tried to sidle past them and back down the alley. "I just needed to take care of some—"

Finn caught him by the elbow as he passed. "What were you doing?" she demanded, her voice shaking.

"Finn, relax," he said. "It's nothing."

"Was it you?" Her hand tightened around the sleeve of his shirt. "Was it you this whole time?"

Dare tried to pull away. "What are you talking about?"

Verity looked between the two of them, then back at the stone building. The door swung open, and an older woman stepped out. She didn't see the three of them standing in the shadows at the other end of the alley, but she spotted the knapsack on the step immediately. She crouched to inspect it, her face alight. Pulling open the top, she gasped as she reached in and removed a small, folded piece of parchment. The old woman unfolded the paper, eyes flicking across the page. A hand rose to her lips as she read the note. Then she stood and heaved the heavy pack inside, closing the door firmly behind her.

Verity turned to Dare, the realization striking her even before she saw the soft look of wonder on the mercenary's face.

Finn released Dare's arm and sprinted down the alley, away from the building. Away from Verity and Dare.

He watched after her before dragging his fingers through his hair. "Verity, what the fuck did I do to piss her off so much?"

"This building, it's an orphanage, isn't it?" Verity asked.

Color flooded his face, but he nodded slowly.

"Dare, how long have you been dropping packages off on this doorstep?"

"Off and on since just after I came to Valda. Verity, what's going on? Is she alright?"

"How long?" she repeated.

"About ten years. A little more."

"I think *you* were her Stranger," she whispered.

"Verity, will you please tell me what in Pyrannis's flaming ass is going on?"

Her lips tightened at the curse, but she said, "I think this is where Finn grew up."

Dare went still.

"When we were in Brookshire, trying to figure out a way to get you out, she told me that she grew up in an orphanage in Valda, and that a stranger would come by and leave packages of food and money for them. Apparently he was quite the hero to the children." She bit her bottom lip, holding in the rest of the tale Finn had told her.

Dare sucked in a sharp breath, rubbing a hand across the back of his neck. "Shit . . ."

Verity started down the empty alley.

"Where are you going?" Dare asked.

"To find her." She had no idea what was going through Finn's mind, but she knew she wanted to be there for her. It's what Finn would do—*had* done—for her.

"Alone? In this city?" He scoffed. "You'll be lost in minutes."

"I need to find her," Verity said, not bothering to pause as she moved toward the main street.

"I'm coming with you." Dare's voice came from just over her shoulder. "I know a few places she could go. And don't forget"—he elbowed her in the side as he fell into step next to her—"none of us should be wandering the streets alone, right?"

Gods, in the walk and the playful way Finn had dragged her along through the streets, Verity had nearly forgotten about Tanithe. Her pace quickened.

If anything were to happen to Finn, Verity wasn't sure who she'd be more angry at: Dare or herself.

They searched Valda for nearly an hour before Dare skidded to a halt on the cobblestones. "I'm an idiot," he muttered, turning around and heading in the opposite direction. "I'll bet you ten gold I know exactly where she is."

Verity hurried after him. "Just find her."

Dare led her through several more alleys and side streets until they emerged at the top of the hill near the port. Verity spotted their ship where it was moored among a dozen or so others. "You think she went back to the ship?"

"Not down there," Dare said. He grabbed Verity by the shoulders and turned her until she was looking along the bluffs. "Up there."

An old lighthouse stood on the edge of the Valdane cliffs, overlooking the bay below and to the west. Its crumbling exterior exposed the rotting wooden skeleton within, and the platform on which the beacon stood listed at a precarious angle. Even the ground beneath the lighthouse leaned awkwardly out over the cliffs.

A solid wall about ten feet high blocked access to both the lighthouse and the cliffs. Verity followed the angle of the tower and, sure enough, a pair of legs stuck out from the edge of the top-most platform, dangling out over nothing.

"She let it slip once that this was *her* place," Dare said. "She said it was the one spot in a city of hundreds of thousands where she could go to be truly alone."

Verity muttered a quiet curse.

"I'll talk to her," Dare said, starting toward the wall.

She grabbed his wrist. "Wait, I could use magic to—"

"Please don't." He gave her a confident smile. "It's fine," he soothed, patting her hand. "No need to cause a scene."

How could he be so calm? "Dare, that whole tower is *leaning*."

"And has been for nearly as long as I've been in Valda. There's even a couple of taverns in the Downs that have a pool going on when the whole thing's finally going to crash down into the bay. My money's on another thirteen years or so."

She glared at him. "That doesn't make me feel better about the fact that the entire lighthouse is leaning over a damned cliff."

"Just let me talk to her. Not that she needs my protection, but I won't let anything happen to her, my lady Warden."

She studied him a moment before releasing his wrist. "Fine. Just be careful. That's an order, Warden."

CHAPTER 19

DARE GAVE VERITY A mock salute, then turned and sprinted toward the wall surrounding the lighthouse. He hit it at full speed, using his momentum to run several more steps up the wall until he could grasp the edge above. He swung himself up and over, landing in a crouch on the other side. Crossing to the lighthouse, he easily found a hole in the base large enough for him to slip inside.

Wood beams and planks traversed the vast, empty space. Some were clearly parts of floors or supports from the original structure, while others were laid out like scaffolding from some abandoned restoration attempt a decade ago or more. Anything resembling actual stairs had broken and fallen away years ago.

The odor of rot and mold accosted his nose, and once inside he tried somewhat in vain to dodge the piles of guano—from bird or bat, Dare wasn't sure—that nearly covered the lighthouse floor.

He craned his neck up . . . and up . . . Light streamed in through holes in the walls and roof.

Tykaras, he prayed silently. *If you could grant me the luck to not break my neck here, I would greatly appreciate it.*

Scaling the inner scaffolding of the old lighthouse was slow going at first, until he got a feel for which beams would bear his weight and which would likely splinter under his touch. About halfway up the tower, as he reached overhead to pull himself to the next platform, the piece of scaffolding he was standing on gave way with a sudden *crack*.

Dare dropped. He tried to catch the edge of a beam, but his fingers slipped over the damp wood. The momentary grasp changed the trajectory of his fall just enough that he caught the next beam to his chest and managed to grip the edge to stop himself from falling any farther. He took a moment, hanging suspended a good thirty feet in the air, to catch the breath that had been so violently forced from his lungs before pulling himself up to straddle the beam and assess his situation. He'd fallen about six feet, from what he could tell, and clearly he'd have to modify his route to avoid the section of scaffolding that had dropped him.

The rest of the climb proved uneventful, and soon Dare stepped out onto the leaning platform surrounding the lighthouse's cracked beacon. Finn still sat on the edge, feet hanging over.

He sat beside her, watching the late morning sun glint off the bay. "It's beautiful up here," he said. "It's easy to forget how loud the city can be until you get out of it."

Finn didn't turn to look at him. "So that was you I heard almost killing yourself just now?"

Dare couldn't help his answering grin. "It was a near thing." He glanced at her sidelong, but she was still staring out at the water.

She asked quietly, "What are you doing here anyway?"

Dare turned his attention to the bay. It really was beautiful. For all the years he'd lived in Valda, he'd spent so long on the ground watching where he was headed, not to mention watching his back, that he'd forgotten to look up. And *out*.

What *was* he doing there? He wasn't sure where to begin, so he began at the beginning. "I started stealing before I left home," he said. "Just trinkets, jewelry from visiting nobles, that kind of shit. Sometimes I'd go into town and swipe something from one of my father's allies—the jewelers or the money-lenders who took advantage of people. I got caught once, but they just looked the other way because of who I was. Because of who my father was."

He took a long breath, letting the salt air fill his lungs. "Then I left home. I made my way to Valda, but by the time I got here, I'd spent all the coin I'd taken with me. It was the winter solstice and the weather had just turned. I had no money, no place to live, nothing left to sell, and I realized I had no fucking idea what I was going to do. I've never told anyone this before, but I almost died that first winter."

Dare flexed his fingers, the memory of the damp, biting cold causing a phantom ache in his joints. "I tried to steal the purse off a noble in the market district. I thought it would be no problem. After all, I'd been good at that back home. This should be easy. But I got caught. Turns out that *noble* was captain of a merchant ship, and let's just say he knew how to deal with thieves. He gave me the worst beating I'd ever had and left me with a few broken ribs. Honestly, I'm lucky he didn't break my hands."

He leaned back and braced his hands against the platform. "I took shelter in an alley in the Downs. I could barely move when this old woman found me. A thousand people had walked past me, huddled and freezing to death in that alley, but she stopped." His breath shuddered on the next exhale, and he paused for a moment to steady himself. "The only reason I'm alive is because she stopped. She helped me. She told me she didn't have any money, but she brought me food, blankets, clean water, whatever she could spare. She came by every day for a week until she was sure I wasn't going to die. Then she started coming by once a week to check on me. To make sure I was alright and that I was eating, she said. One day she stopped coming, but I never forgot what she did for me.

"About a month later, I joined the Crimson Brothers and finally had a place to live and money to keep myself clothed and fed. I wanted to thank the old woman somehow, but I didn't know who she was. So I started to ask around. A few months later I finally found out that she ran an orphanage." His throat tightened as he swallowed hard. "And that she'd died. About a month before I joined the Brothers."

"Matron Eliza," Finn said quietly.

Dare nodded. "I still wanted to repay her for what she'd done for me. So . . . I had an idea. Maybe I could help those she'd spent her life helping. Maybe I could check on *them* and make sure *they* were clothed and fed. I started gathering up what food or coin I could spare . . . and I left it on their doorstep. It wasn't much at first, but I was always a quick study, and the Brothers taught me well. Soon, I really was a good thief, and I had more than enough coin to keep myself comfortable. I made sure to keep some squirreled away in case I needed it, but everything else . . .

"I shouldn't have gone today," he continued. "I shouldn't have taken the chance. But when the Council sent me on this job into Westhold, I was supposed to be gone a couple of weeks, not eight months. It was foolish, but I didn't want to wait any longer than I already had."

"What did it say?"

Dare blinked and looked at Finn. "What?"

A tear slid down her cheek, and she wiped it quickly with the back of her hand. "The note. In the sack you left. What did it say?"

The corner of his mouth twitched slightly. "It said *sorry I'm late.*"

Finn snorted a laugh as she sniffled, rubbing at her nose. "How old were you? When you started leaving those packages?"

Dare tilted his face toward the midafternoon sky. "I turned nineteen that spring." He let the silence hang between them before he asked, "How old were you?"

She snatched a small splinter of wood from the platform and flung it off the cliff. "I'd just turned thirteen that winter."

They sat in silence for a long time. "I'm sorry, Finn," Dare said at last.

She chucked another splinter into the bay far below. "What do you possibly have to be sorry for?"

Dare considered the look on her face when she'd grabbed his arm in the alley behind the orphanage. When he saw the shock and the tears in her eyes as she confronted him, even before he realized what she was confronting him *about*, he knew he'd hurt her. And that knowledge had clawed at him all through his search with Verity.

"I can imagine that finding out it was just me must have been . . . disappointing, to say the least."

Finally, she turned to face him. Her eyes were puffy and red, but her jaw was set as she threw her arms around his neck. He hadn't been expecting that, and she embraced him with such surprising fervor he thought he might topple from the platform.

"Or . . . not . . ." he said hesitantly, though he wrapped his arms around her.

"I was too shocked to even know what to think," she said, her voice muffled against his shoulder. "But I can't think of anything that would be *less* disappointing than finding out my best friend turned out to be the hero I wanted to be like when I was young."

He hadn't known it had meant so much. Dare's face grew hot, and his heart squeezed in his chest. "I'm . . . your best friend?"

Finn pulled back and gave him a playful slug in the shoulder. "Hey, don't let it go to your head," she said with another soft sniffle. "You're still an idiot."

He let out a long laugh. "Understood."

Finn wiped her eyes again and turned toward the bay. "You know, with everything that's happened, and everyone else being blessed by a bunch of gods . . . if I've got to be stuck being one of the *normal* ones, I'm glad I'm stuck with you."

The warm squeeze around Dare's heart turned into a twinge. "Yeah," he said after a moment. "Yeah, me too."

Finn swung her legs, kicking at the empty air. "How'd you even know I was up here?"

He gave a halfhearted shrug, grateful for the change in topic. "You mentioned once that you liked to come up here when you needed space to yourself. I thought you were crazy, but now I can see why you do it."

She eyed him. "And you remembered that?"

"Not right away," he admitted. "But it came back to me eventually." Dare gestured over his shoulder. "Do you want to head down? I don't know if it matters to you, but I think Verity's pretty worried."

Finn's ears flushed red. One hand shifted to rub along her thigh where Dare knew she now had a jagged burn scar. "Why would she be worried?"

Dare tracked the movement but only said, "I think it's because she cares about you."

"She cares about you too, but I bet she's not worried about *you* being up here," she countered, a note of bitterness slipping in. "She trusts you."

"You think she doesn't trust you?"

"She's never let me in on the training you all do," Finn lamented. "And you should have seen the look on her face when she saw me when the pirates attacked the ship."

Dare bit his lower lip. He *had* seen Verity's face. Finn must not have recognized the look, but Dare had. It was the same one that had been plastered on his own face when he'd seen Gregor on the ship's deck too. "I can't speak to her inner mind," he said after a moment. "But if I could hazard a guess, I would say that she's scared. I think she doesn't want anything to happen to you." He gestured to her leg. "Anything else."

"I can take care of myself."

"She knows that. We all know that, Finn." He swung his arm around her shoulder and pulled her close, squeezing her into his side. "But we almost lost you in Taernfane. I think she worries about that happening again. I think she's scared that we won't get so lucky next time. Especially after what happened with . . . in the Crescent Mountains." It had been months and he still struggled to talk about Drystan. Finn had never met him, but she knew all about the loss they'd suffered there.

Finn sighed. "So, is this new wisdom you're spouting a side effect of you joining up with the Wardens? Because I know you weren't so clever before that."

He scoffed. "Oh, come now," he said, adding as much exaggerated sincerity as he thought he could manage without risking her pitching him headlong from the lighthouse. "I've *always* been clever. It's just taken my elevated status for you to notice."

"You are so full of yourself, it's astounding!" Finn said, laughing. She stood with a quiet groan, favoring her right leg with a notable limp as she moved to the hole that led to the inside of the tower.

"Are you alright to climb down?" Dare asked.

"Don't you start too! You're joking, right?"

Dare held up his hands. "I'm only asking. If you say you're fine, I'll trust you. But if you need help, I want to be able to help you." After a moment he added, "I would be very sad if you splattered yourself against the ground, but more than that, I think Verity might literally kill me."

Finn laughed again as she rubbed the muscles of her leg. "If anything is going to be the death of me, I swear it's going to be you two mother hens. I'm fine. It's just stiff from being cramped on that damned boat."

"In that case"—Dare gestured to the hole and bowed with a graceful, courtier's flourish—"after you."

Finn rolled her eyes and disappeared into the shadows of the tower, moving across the scaffolding as naturally as if she was born of it. He followed her path, using her experience to avoid any more unpleasant falls, but he could scarcely keep up. He was barely halfway down when Finn ducked through a hole in the outer wall toward the bottom.

Once he reached the spot himself, Dare realized this exit required scaling down the last twelve or so feet of the lighthouse on the outside, but it deftly avoided the mounds of guano on the floor.

When he landed in the open yard between the lighthouse and the surrounding wall, Finn was waiting for him, her hands on her hips.

"You must be getting slow in your old age."

"Hey!" Dare wasn't sure if he was more offended at being called *slow* or *old*.

"I just call it like I see it." Finn shrugged. "You were born in the spring, you said. Your birthday must be coming up then. Which makes you thirty."

"*Almost* thirty," Dare protested. When did Finn start getting the better of him?

She shrugged again. "Like I said, old."

"Come on," Dare said. Maybe if he ignored her, she'd give up. "Verity's waiting."

He hit the wall at a run and vaulted over it, as he'd done before, though this time, Finn was already waiting for him on the other side.

"How did you—?"

Finn leaned against a plank of wood nailed to the wall, and it swiveled as though on a hinge, revealing a crack large enough for a person to squeeze through. "Work smarter, not harder, old man," she said.

Dare sighed, though his heart danced with amusement as he led Finn back to where Verity was waiting.

Chapter 20

With Verity and Finn in tow, Dare headed toward the Crimson Brothers' chapter house. They still had a few hours before the boat left for Whitehollow, and Verity had agreed that Finn and Dare could check in with the Brothers while they were in the city. They'd been gone for months, and Finn was still a junior member whose commander had gone missing. If Finn ever wanted to work as a mercenary again—whether with the Crimson Brothers or not—it was in her best interest to explain what had happened to Caleb, as well as Almestra and the others. Although the Brothers were based in Valda, their reach was broad. There'd be no outrunning them if she earned their ire.

Dare's shoulders tensed as he unwillingly recalled the ambush in the mountain pass. He rubbed at his chest and the ache that was steadily building beneath the circular scar in the center.

"I'll wait over here," Verity said, gesturing to a small café with good sight-lines to the chapter house across the street.

Dare had a witty retort lined up about not leaving anyone outside alone, but Finn waved Verity off and ushered him toward the door before he could open his mouth.

"You alright?" Dare asked as Finn tugged him toward the building. He'd thought she was calm, but the iron grip she had on his arm had him second-guessing his read on her.

"Of course," she said, pausing in front of the chapter house. "Why wouldn't I be?"

"Seriously? Come on, Finn. You don't need to bullshit with me."

Finn stared at the wood and stone structure. Dare followed her gaze. It was the first home he'd had when he came to Valda. The lantern in the window was perpetually lit—always a beacon for a Brother who might be in need. It meant safety. Home. The sight of it warmed Dare's heart.

"Are you worried they're going to blame you for Caleb's death?" he asked.

The grimace on Finn's face told him everything.

"It wasn't your fault," Dare said. "Vire's hells, I'm the one who killed him. If anyone's going to be blamed for his death, it's me."

Finn crossed her arms. "You were defending yourself."

"And you were coerced. Caleb was moonlighting for Tanithe. He took an unsanctioned job."

"He promised us all commendations when we got back." Finn's shoulders drew inward. "When I still hesitated, he promised to promote me to full member."

"It's alright, Finn," Dare said quickly. "I don't blame you. Hell, I would have jumped at it myself, if I were stuck reporting up to Caleb." Thankfully, Dare's own commander had been a much better mentor when he'd first joined the Brothers. "I don't see how the captain could blame you for any of what happened."

Finn looked up at him. "Really?"

"Really." He pulled open the heavy wooden door. "It'll be alright. You'll see."

"Yeah." Finn hooked a few wisps of her blond hair behind her ears. "Yeah, you're right."

Dare smiled with a little spark of mischief. "I know. Kind of you to say so." He bowed low, sweeping his hand toward the open door. "After you."

He followed her inside. The chapter house was exactly how Dare remembered it: a small waiting area with a few chairs, a desk toward the front for receiving clients, and a hall with several doors leading deeper into the building.

Behind the desk was a young man, one of the junior members, like Finn, though he was newer and younger than she was. He welcomed them with a warm smile as they entered even before his face brightened with recognition.

"Finn! Dare!" He practically jumped out of his chair. "You're back!"

"Morning, Hunter," Dare said, unable to stop himself from returning the boy's infectious smile. Well, he wasn't a boy, Dare was sure, but he was young enough by comparison that it certainly felt that way sometimes. "It's been a while."

"We thought something terrible happened to you after the lot of you went missing," he said. "Are the others with you too?"

"Is Zahra here?" Dare asked, dodging his question and inquisitive stare by looking off down the hall.

"Sure. Captain's in her office."

Dare gave a nod of thanks before heading toward the door. Finn followed close behind with a quiet "Good to see you again."

Dare followed the familiar halls until he landed in front of the office of Zahra Gray, Captain of the Valdane chapter of the Crimson Brothers. He rapped his knuckles against the door.

"Come in," called the pleasant voice from the other side.

Dare reached for the latch, but Finn set her hand on his, stopping him. "Wait, I—"

"Finn, it'll be fine. I've got your back. I promise."

She took a deep breath as he pushed the door open. She was worrying over nothing. Dare wouldn't let Zahra or anyone else try to blame Finn for what happened.

The captain looked up from her desk as they entered, dark eyes widening. "Well, I'll be damned." She steepled her fingers as she leaned her elbows on the desk. "Wasn't expecting to see you two again." The captain frowned at them both, the lines around her mouth and across her brow deepening. Streaks of silver slashed through her dark hair, which was pulled back into a tight bun at the base of her neck. "You ever hear of a letter?"

Dare rubbed a hand along the back of his neck. "Nice to see you too, Zahra."

Her stern expression didn't falter. "Which of you would care to tell me what the hells happened to you two?" She fixed her stare at Finn as she added, "And your commander?"

Dare opened his mouth, but Zahra plowed forward. "I've still got seven missing Brothers, so if either of you have information on that, you'd better start talking."

"Yes, Captain," Finn said quickly. Dare ceded the floor and let Finn tell the story of Caleb's outside job and how he'd pulled Finn and the others into it. And how it all went terribly wrong in the mountain pass in Aethir.

Zahra nodded along with Finn's story, her face betraying nothing of her thoughts. Whenever Dare tried to conjure an image of impartial passivity, all he had to do was think of Zahra. The woman was unreadable. Then again, she'd been doing this since before Dare was born, as she was often fond of pointing out.

She turned her attention to Dare. "And you?"

Dare cleared his throat. "I was part of the group traveling through the pass."

One dark eyebrow arched higher than Dare thought was possible. "Explain."

And so Dare told his story, beginning with his contract with the Valdane Council and ending with the battle in Taernfane and the awakening of the elemental gods. He omitted a few details—namely anything having to do with the Chosen of the gods, as well as his run-in with his parents in Brookshire. It made for an abbreviated tale, but he was certain the important information made it through. Caleb had taken some of Zahra's mercenaries and gotten them and himself killed. Dare and Finn had only made it back by the grace of the gods.

Zahra tapped her fingers together. "You say Caleb knew it was you and still attacked?"

Dare nodded. "He knew from the outset, as far as he told me. He seemed amused at the thought of being paid to kill me." Dare pulled the collar of his shirt down to show the edge of the circular scar on his chest that was courtesy of Caleb's spear. "He nearly succeeded too."

Zahra stood and rounded the desk, her gaze fixed on Dare's chest. She was a few inches taller than Dare, though the power in her movements and her simple presence made her seem eight feet tall. "What is that?"

Dare set his palm over the scar. "That's where I was—"

"No, not that." Zahra grabbed the front of his shirt roughly in one of her wide hands and pulled the collar to the right, exposing the other scar on his chest. The Warden's brand. "What is *that*?"

In leaving out the part about his family in Brookshire, he'd omitted the Warden's oath that had saved him. "Oh." Dare paused to buy himself a moment to think.

She didn't give him the time. "You joined the Wardens?"

"There were some extenuating circumstances," he offered.

Fire sparked in Zahra's eyes. "Extenuating circumstances?"

"It won't be a problem." He wasn't sure how just yet, but he was going to make it work.

Shaking her head in disbelief, she released Dare's shirt. "I thought I trained you better than that, kid."

Kid. Gods, she hadn't called him that in years. Not since the last time he'd seriously fucked up.

"Zahra, what do you—"

But Zahra's face softened—actually *softened*—stopping Dare mid-thought. "I'm sorry," she said.

Dare cringed at how gently she spoke. Zahra Gray was not a gentle person by any definition. And he wasn't sure he'd ever heard her apologize for anything.

Finn inhaled sharply, her whiskey-colored eyes widening as one hand covered her mouth.

What was she picking up on that Dare was missing? The very idea that Dare was *missing* something here raised the hairs on the back of his neck. His stomach knotted.

"Dare, I hereby remove your commission from the guild. You are no longer a member of the Crimson Brothers."

Dare's heart plummeted. It was suddenly very hard to breathe. "You . . . what? No, wait—"

"A Warden's loyalty is to the Wardens and to neutrality," Zahra said. "A Warden may hold no office, inherit no lands or titles, and may swear allegiance to no person or group beyond the Wardens."

The words of the Warden's oath washed over him. He'd been so focused on the first two parts, he'd glossed right over the third.

"But Zahra, I—"

"I'm sorry, Dare," she said, leaning against her desk. "I truly am. I need to discuss a few more things with Finn, but I'll need you to leave."

Leave. Leave the building, and leave the Brothers. She was kicking him out.

"Zahra . . ." He searched for words, for some argument or explanation, but he was coming up blank. This couldn't be happening. "Captain—"

"I'll make sure your account is settled and anything owed to you will be sent within the week."

Dare nodded. What else could he do? There was no use arguing with Zahra. There never was. Without another word to the captain or another glance at Finn, he turned on his heel and left Zahra's office.

The young man, Hunter, was still at his post in the foyer. "See you around," he said cheerfully as Dare passed by.

"Not fucking likely," Dare muttered. He threw open the front door and stepped into the busy streets of Valda.

Dare crossed the street. "I'll meet you back at the ship," he said to Verity as he passed the small outdoor table at the little café where she was waiting for them.

"What's wrong?" Verity asked. "Where's Finn?"

"She has more business to attend to with the Brothers," he said tightly. He didn't stop. He didn't want to talk to her right now. Especially not when she hadn't warned him something like this could happen. "I'll meet you back at the ship," he repeated.

"But Dare—"

"I'm heading there now," he said. He couldn't deal with her questions, her nagging, even if it was coming from a good place. He just couldn't do it.

Dare didn't slow down. He fully intended to head straight to the ship as he'd told Verity, but the problem was that he wasn't paying attention to where his feet were carrying him. He just walked, letting himself get lost in the massive, sprawling cacophony of the city.

He'd been a Brother for a decade, since shortly after he'd arrived in Valda. He'd come here as a cocky boy who thought he knew everything, and he'd realized very quickly that he hadn't known anything. But he'd found a place among the Brothers. Even if he still preferred to go it alone, Zahra had taught him that he could be on his own but still belong somewhere.

He hadn't realized how much that meant to him until it disappeared. Who was he if not a Brother?

A Warden? Dare scoffed at the thought as he kept walking. He was hardly Warden material, and he knew it. Verity knew it too, surely.

Sighing, Dare jammed his hands into his coat pockets. He looked around the street, finally taking a moment to figure out where he'd walked to and where he was heading.

He could head back to Verity, he supposed. He could return to the ship like he was supposed to. Gregor would be there; Dare could talk to him, but . . . but Dare's life as a Crimson Brother was still something he hadn't fully explained to Gregor, and he wasn't sure how to bring it up with him.

And Finn . . . well, Finn was busy at the moment. Briefly he wished that Jae were there. She would've told him to quit feeling sorry for himself at first, a teasing jab to get him to loosen his shoulders. But then she'd listen to what he needed to say—once he figured that out—and she'd offer an ear or a shoulder, whichever he needed. She would empathize.

Empathy would be nice right about now, but seeing as how that was decidedly lacking, alcohol would have to do. Dare turned his feet toward the nearest bar.

It was the seediest bar that Dare knew of without actually venturing into the Downs, and it was exactly what he was looking for: dark and discreet. The musty smell of stale beer greeted him as he ducked through the front door. No one even looked up when he entered.

Perfect.

Dare grabbed a mug of some unnamed dark beer from the bar and found a table in a shadowed corner. One drink to give him a minute to process what had just happened before he needed to be back on the ship. He didn't think he could face Finn yet. Dare becoming a Warden had been her idea, and she was bound to feel guilty for what had just transpired.

And he wanted to blame her, even though it wasn't her fault. He wanted to blame Verity for not warning him. And he wanted to blame Zahra for kicking him out, but she did what she had to do. He wanted *someone* to blame, but the only one left was himself.

He'd have to do.

Dare finished the beer in a few quick gulps and ordered another. He had time for one more.

He finished the second nearly as quickly and was working on a third when a man approached his table and slid into the chair across from him.

"Lord Wilhaven?" the man inquired.

Dare snorted into his mug. "Definitely not."

"Perhaps *Warden* Wilhaven would be more to your preference?"

Now what? He'd been in Valda for four godsdamned hours. Dare set his drink on the table and looked the man up and down, taking in the finely tailored clothes, far too fine for an establishment such as this. "And you are?"

"You can call me Willem. I represent Head Councillor Myra Gartend."

Dare tensed. The Valdane Council. He wasn't surprised they'd tracked him down, but he was surprised they'd done it so *quickly*. And apparently word had reached them of his shift in allegiance. That didn't bode well.

"What service can I be to the Council?" he asked, taking care to keep his voice steady. He took a long swig of his drink.

"We understand that you are part of an envoy on its way to Whitehollow."

Dare stayed silent. No point in making this man's job easier by confirming anything.

"We also understand that a committee will be meeting there to discuss the tragic attack on the great city of Taernfane," Willem continued, undeterred. "And further, that you are the only individual with knowledge of certain circumstances surrounding that event."

Dare scoffed. "Circumstances? You mean Valda's involvement."

Willem didn't even bat an eye. "Valda considers King Dominic Drahkon a friend and ally. The Council would never condone the events of last autumn."

"Really?" Dare leaned back in his chair. "You expect me to believe that the Council's spymaster attacked a foreign city of her own desires, without the Council's knowledge or involvement?"

The man smiled, a cold, flat grin. "Yes. Though our preference would be for you to report that she wasn't there at all."

Dare snorted a laugh. "She killed a dozen of the king's guard, at least. There were plenty of witnesses."

"How many witnesses, exactly?" The man's smile didn't change. "How many people actually *saw* her? There was you, your fellow Crimson Brother, the former Secretary to Duke Wilhaven, and your two mercenary friends, correct?"

Dare's hand clenched into a fist beneath the table.

"Five witnesses. Though the mercenaries declined to make the journey, did they not? Of the three remaining, how many know her occupation? Of her ties to Valda?"

"All three of us," he said slowly. Perhaps with a bit of luck, Willem wouldn't realize—

"Ah, but *you* know, of course, given the nature of your employment by the Council. But your associates? They only know because *you* told them. Isn't that right?"

Where is he going with this? Dare swallowed, reaching out for the expansive presence that had become more and more familiar lately. *Tykaras? Are you there?*

Nothing but silence answered.

"You, Warden, are the only one who has firsthand knowledge of the identity of Valda's spymaster. Councillor Gartend would like to keep that knowledge contained."

Dare had the sinking feeling that perhaps he should have stayed on the ship. *Tykaras?* he tried again. He kept his face carefully neutral in the mental silence. "What are you proposing?" he asked aloud.

"Councillor Gartend is prepared to work with you on one final contract, Warden." He slid an envelope across the table. "In exchange for the coin listed here, you are to officially report that you knew Tanithe Ash only through independent mercenary contracts, not through any connection to the Council, direct or implied. You are also to officially report that Tanithe Ash was *not* responsible for the attack against the city of Taernfane."

Dare glanced at the envelope where it lay on the table between them. "Regardless of her connection to the Council, I'm not the only one who saw that it was *Tanithe*, remember? You said it yourself."

Willem's smile didn't waver. "The archer, Fionna Garrison, saw her from, what? A hundred and fifty feet across a courtyard, through the trees and shadows?"

Dare's jaw tightened.

"And Secretary Gregor Thalesen? I'm sorry, *former* Secretary Gregor Thalesen claims he saw Tanithe Ash in the palace. But there are no witnesses to corroborate his story. There was chaos, demons attacking and the like. Death and destruction, Warden. Not everyone is made to handle witnessing such horrors. How do we know what he really saw? I wouldn't be surprised if they weren't even planning on having the two of them testify."

"Let me make sure I understand," Dare said, leaning forward, elbows resting on the table on either side of the envelope. "The Council wants to pay me to report that Tanithe has no connection to the Council *and* that she was never in Taernfane, despite the fact that at least two other people saw her there? That's absurd. What good does it do the Council if it's two-to-one that she was there?"

"Aside from the fact that the other two witnesses are unreliable, you're a Warden. Your word will carry more weight than both of theirs combined."

You're a Warden. The words hung in the air, settling over him like a cloud of dust, suffocating him. That was all he was now. No longer a Brother, no longer a free man able to pick and choose the jobs he wanted. No. He was a *Warden* now. And a piss-poor one at that.

"And if I refuse?"

Willem clasped his hands on the table, his calm, placid expression not faltering in the slightest. "It is well within your rights to do so. You are free to accept or decline Councillor Gartend's offer. Though, I've heard Whitehollow's become nearly as dangerous a city as Valda. The crime rate's really gone to hells, I hear. Lots of muggings. Quite a plague on the tourists, even those more experienced in the ways of life in a large city. But that's neither here nor there, I suppose."

"Yeah," Dare huffed. "I suppose not." The Council's message was loud and clear. Finn, Gregor, and Dare were loose ends—ones the Council weren't about to leave hanging.

Dare took up the envelope and tore it open. Everything about this proposal was ridiculous, though he supposed he'd better know how much they were willing to pay him to keep this quiet.

His brows rose as he read the amount listed. It was a truly obscene amount of gold. "This can't be right," he said. His eyes flicked up to the man across from him.

"I assure you, it's accurate."

Dare's mind raced with the possibilities of what he could do with that much coin. It could not only help Matron Nora keep the children she cared for clothed and fed in perpetuity, but he could bankroll at least one other orphanage with it. Maybe more than one.

"All you have to do is swear to me now a legally binding oath on your honor as a Warden, that you will never speak of our conversation or this deal to anyone, that you will tell anyone who asks that Tanithe Ash has no connection to the Valdane Council, and that she was never in Taernfane." He reached his hand across the table to Dare. "Do we have a deal, Warden Wilhaven?"

Dare stared at the numbers on the paper. It was more money than he'd ever seen, even when he was still living in Brookshire as *Lord Darcy Wilhaven*. And all they needed was an oath. A *legally binding* oath, but since when had Dare had a problem with breaking the law? Plus, any efforts by Valda to point out the legality would result in them admitting to bribery.

It would be so easy! He could swear it now to this agent of the Valdane Council, then tell Verity everything ahead of the hearing. Sure, she might not be too happy about the oath thing, but when she saw the money it brought in, when she saw the good the coin could do and the justice that breaking the oath would bring against Tanithe and the Valdane Council . . .

She'd get over it. Eventually.

"Alright." Dare clasped Willem's hand. "I swear it."

"I'm afraid I need you to speak the words."

Dare smiled. "Of course. In exchange for the gold listed here"—he tapped the paper—"I swear on my honor as a Warden of the Flame that I will only ever tell anyone that Tanithe Ash does not work for the Valdane Council and that she was never in Taernfane. And I swear that I will never tell anyone about this conversation or this deal."

Willem released Dare's hand, his smile broadening. "Thank you, Warden." He handed Dare another envelope. "This is the official documentation for an account at the Bank of Valda, in your name, with the agreed upon amount. These documents will allow you to withdraw funds from any bank on the continent, or to transfer funds to any account that you wish." He rose and turned toward the door. "A pleasure doing business with you."

Dare stared at the paperwork in his hand, a faint warmth blooming in his chest. Verity would be upset at first, but she'd understand. Once he explained everything, she'd understand. Maybe something good would come out of this shit day after all.

CHAPTER 21

GREGOR LEANED AGAINST THE central mast of the ship, keeping out of the way as sailors hurried about the deck preparing to set sail. Verity paced along the starboard side while Finn stood on the rail, one hand on the rigging, watching as the last of the passengers climbed the gangplank.

"Where is he?" Verity muttered. "He said he was coming straight back."

When Finn and Verity had returned an hour ago, Gregor had asked if they'd found Dare. The expressions on their faces as they looked at each other had sent a wave of dread rippling down his spine. They had, and he should have been back by now.

And then Finn had told them both what had happened with the Crimson Brothers.

One of their Drahkonian guards, a man named Rhori with copper hair and pale, freckled skin, spent the last hour searching the immediate area near the docks, but with no luck. Gregor had tried to go with him, but Rhori had politely pointed out that Gregor had no useful knowledge of the city. And besides, he'd added, if trouble *had* somehow found Dare, Rhori would need to split his attention protecting both him and Gregor.

So instead Gregor had stayed behind and tried hard not to think of every possible horrible thing that could have happened to Dare in the meantime.

He'd failed miserably.

"I see him!" Finn called from her perch on the railing. "He's coming!"

Gregor straightened, though he didn't stray from the mast, as much as he wanted to dash to the rail and see for himself.

Verity shouted down the gangplank a few moments later. "Where the hells have you been?"

Dare crested the top of the plank, hands stuffed firmly in his pockets. He mumbled something to Verity as the sailors rushed in behind him and loaded the plank back onto the ship.

Gregor couldn't decide whether he was relieved or furious.

Verity's shoulders fell as she stepped closer to Dare, her voice lowering, though Gregor knew what she must be telling him.

Finn told us what happened. Are you alright?

As Gregor expected, Dare waved her off. "It's fine," Dare said. "Sorry I'm late. I got held up."

"Held up?" Verity demanded. "You said you were coming straight back. That was two hours ago!"

"It's a long story, my lady Warden," he said. He hadn't yet looked at Finn. Or Gregor. "I don't really want to get into it right now."

Dare brushed past Verity, but stopped dead as he finally spotted Gregor by the mast.

That's when Gregor noticed it—the stiffness in Dare's back, the way he walked almost too straight, like he was trying to prove he could.

"You're drunk," Gregor said softly, though a current of frustration swirled within him.

Dare stepped closer, rubbing a hand along the back of his neck. "I'm not *drunk.*" The added emphasis told Gregor what he needed to know.

"I asked you not to do anything stupid."

"I didn't," Dare protested. "I just—"

Gregor held up a hand to stop him. "Let me make sure I understand. You left the ship without telling anyone"—he closed the rest of the distance to Dare—"in *Valda* of all places. And instead of coming back right away like you told Verity you would, you went drinking for a couple hours. Is that right?"

Dare winced, his green and gold eyes darting to his feet as his face flushed red. "Well, when you say it like that . . ."

"How about if I add in that you left me here to worry about you? All day. Did you think I wouldn't notice you'd left?"

"I honestly didn't plan on being gone so long."

"That's not the point. You *left*, Dare." Gregor slid his glasses off and pinched the bridge of his nose. How could he make him understand? "I know you're used to being on your own, but you're not alone anymore. You have friends who care about you. Who worry about you when you disappear into the most dangerous city on the continent without a word."

"It's not the—"

"It is," Gregor interrupted, pushing his glasses back on. "Right now, for you—for *us*—with Tanithe out there, and who knows what the Council is planning with all of this. It *is* dangerous. I can't—" He stopped, hearing the tremble that had crept into his voice. "I don't want to think about what would happen," he continued slowly, "if Tanithe found you."

When Dare's eyes flicked down, Gregor followed them and realized his thumb was tracing one of the scars around his wrist. He let his hands fall to his sides.

Dare fiddled with something in his pocket before seeming to come to some sort of decision. He took Gregor's hands in his own. "You're right," he said. "I'm sorry." His thumbs rubbed softly against the backs of Gregor's hands.

The gesture tempered some of his irritation, leaving in its wake a kind of tired exasperation. "If I can't get you to *not* do anything stupid, can I at least get you to promise you'll tell me next time? *Before* you do it," he added before Dare could try to sidestep through that particular loophole.

Dare smirked, as though Gregor had just thwarted his plan. "I'll do my best," he said. Gregor narrowed his eyes at him, but Dare only tossed up his hands in mock innocence. "You're assuming I'll recognize it as stupid before I do it," he said. "That's giving me a lot of credit."

"You're a smart man," Gregor said, and he was proud of himself for holding on to his frustration in the face of Darcy's aloof scoundrel act. "I trust you can figure it out."

CHAPTER 22

LUCIEN'S SHOULDERS DIPPED. "FOR the record," he said, "this is a very bad idea." Jae hummed cheerfully behind him.

As soon as he was beyond the bounds of the Red Forest, his full control over the beast had returned, the locks and chains as strong as ever. He led the way through the southern woods, the worn paths still familiar. How Jae had managed to convince him to do this was beyond him. It was a terrible idea. It had been twenty years. Nearly twenty-one!

He'd made the right decision all those years ago. He knew he did. It had taken him time to learn the way of his beast, to learn to control it.

The visions of what he could have done to them if he'd gone back still haunted his dreams. His beast made sure of it.

She'd probably moved away long ago, Lucien reasoned. He would find the place owned by another family or, at worst, overgrown and in disrepair. He could handle that, he decided. He could handle another family hanging their clothes on the line or tending the garden. He could handle weeds and ivy growing up and over the sides of the cottage, its windows black and lifeless. He could handle that. He wasn't sure if he could handle—

The woods gave way to a wide clearing. The little cottage stood just up ahead, with smoke drifting from the stone chimney and its windows open despite the chill. The small garden he remembered had expanded. It rolled away from the house to the west toward the line of trees on the other side, which was farther away now than it used to be. Two secondary buildings stood just north of the cottage. One he knew well—he'd built it and the kiln behind it for Ethriel the year before he was changed. The other looked newer but was built in the same style.

Lucien took three steps on the gravel path and stopped. Even from this distance the smell of fresh bread wafted through the open window. There were other scents too, mixing and mingling through the clearing.

He'd often wondered if he would know her scent, were he to come across it now, as a shifter. Something smelled familiar. He couldn't quite place it, though it raised the hairs on the back of his neck.

"What are you doing?" Jae chided as she entered the clearing. "You can't give up now." She gave a playful shove against the small of his back. It wasn't much, but it was enough to get his feet moving again. "I'll wait back here," she said, her voice softer than he'd ever heard it before. "I'll give you some time."

Lucien took a few more steps up the path, toward the painfully familiar cottage. He could picture Ethriel standing in the doorway like it was yesterday, their little girl in her arms.

His vision of her was as clear as day, even as the cottage door swung open and Ethriel emerged. Her hair was the same orange-red of flames, though it was streaked through with silver, and her face bore the signs of the years he'd been away, unlike his. She didn't look up as she stepped into the afternoon sun, her attention on the pitcher she held in her slender hands. She was heading to the pump on the side of the cottage for water, no doubt.

It was her. Truly her.

Ethriel.

His wife.

The gravel crunched with his next step, and her eyes lifted and fell on him.

She froze. Her mouth worked, forming a question, but no sound came out at first. Lucien took a tentative step closer, his hands out and open at his sides, doing his best to appear nonthreatening.

She tried again to speak. "H-how?" Her voice was airy and light, as it had always been. "You're . . . you're dead."

His own throat tightened. "I'm not," was all he could manage.

When he spoke, she gasped—had she thought him a ghost?—and the empty pitcher fell from nerveless fingers. It shattered at her feet, scattering shards of fired clay across the stone steps.

Ethriel staggered against the door frame, one hand rising to her lips. He closed the distance, but he stopped himself at the bottom of the steps. He wanted to run to her—gods, he wanted to run to her and gather her up in his arms. But he didn't want to scare her. He never wanted her to be afraid of him. And so he held himself firmly in place, only a few feet away from her. Such an impossibly short distance after such an impossibly long time.

He watched. And he waited.

Ethriel inched forward. One hand held onto the door frame. The other stretched toward him. Her fingers were trembling. Her long, elegant fingers, rough from years and years of work, reached for him.

"You look the same. How is that possible?" Her eyes, like two bright sapphires, glittered as the tips of her fingers brushed along the edge of his beard. "Are you *my* Lucien?" she breathed. "My Luc?"

Lucien's knees nearly gave out. He closed his eyes as her fingers found the scar down the side of his face. *Luc*. She was the only one who had ever called him that. Only her. Only ever her.

"Yes," he said, his voice rough like the rocks beneath his boots. "It's me, Eth."

A choked sob erupted from Ethriel. She left the support of the door and fell against him. Lucien caught her, pressed his cheek into her hair, and breathed her in. Honeysuckle, woodsmoke, and wet earth filled his nose. She felt boneless in his arms, and he sank to the ground with her, kneeling amid the shards of broken pitcher and the gravel of the path.

Ethriel sobbed as he held her. She clutched his shirt with one hand, pulling him closer, but her other was clenched tight. She pressed her fist to his chest. She withdrew it and pressed it against him again. And again, harder this time. And harder, until she was pounding her fist against him.

"Where were you?" she whispered. Her whole body was shaking as she struck him again and again. "Where were you?" Even as she beat her fist against his chest, her other hand still held onto his shirt, keeping him close. She lifted her face to him, streaked with tears.

Lucien thought his heart might shred itself into a thousand pieces. He'd never felt so helpless as when he looked into her eyes. "Ethriel, I—"

"Where were you?" she cried. "They told me you were dead. *Dead*, Lucien." She struck him again. "Twenty years. Where have you been?"

He drew a long, deep breath. "That's a . . . long story."

Her beautiful blue eyes narrowed at him. "Then you had better get started." Her shoulders still shook and the tears still fell, but he could see the anger beneath the pain now. "Tell me."

Lucien swallowed hard. How could he tell her? How could he explain that he should have died, but he became a monster instead? That he'd stayed away to keep her safe, so he wouldn't hurt her?

She pounded her fist against his chest again. "Dammit, Lucien!" she screamed. "Where the *fuck* have you been?!"

"Ethriel? Is everything alright?"

Lucien's body tensed at the unfamiliar voice. He'd always assumed she must have remarried, must have found someone else to share her life with who wouldn't be forced to leave, but—

A man appeared from around one of the smaller buildings. Lucien took in the stranger all at once: shaggy black hair, brown shirt with the sleeves rolled up to the elbows, tan pants and sturdy boots, an axe over his shoulder.

The man's eyes swept over the scene in front of the cottage as he moved closer. "Hey, get away from her!" he shouted.

It took Lucien a moment to grasp what he was seeing. It didn't make any sense, and so he assumed the tears burning his eyes were playing tricks with his vision. But then the man's scent hit him, and he knew. He *knew*.

A growl tore from Lucien's throat as he stood, turning as Corvin Crosse sprinted toward him, shifting his grip on the axe he carried. "Step away from her," Corvin said, his deep voice a firm command. He slowed as he reached the path, brandishing the axe.

Lucien would only have one shot at this. He was certain the only reason Crosse hadn't blasted him as soon as he'd come around the corner was because he didn't recognize him. He'd only ever seen Lucien in his monstrous form.

Lucien closed the remaining distance with feral swiftness. One hand caught the axe by the handle before Crosse could complete the swing, and the other gripped him around the throat. His nails, always short and bitten to the quick, lengthened into sharpened claws.

Shock flashed over Crosse's face, his mouth opening in a silent yell as Lucien began to squeeze. Crosse dropped the axe as his fingers moved to rake at the hand around his throat. He had several inches on Lucien, but that hardly mattered. It would only take a moment. With the strength Lucien possessed, he could snap Crosse's neck before the bastard had a chance to call on any of his power.

"Lucien, stop!" Ethriel was beside him, her hands on his arm, pulling at him. "Let him go!"

Lucien stopped tightening his grip, but he didn't loosen it. Nothing but strangled gasps were coming out of Crosse. "He's dangerous," he snarled.

"He's not!" Ethriel cried, still pulling on Lucien's arm. She looked at him, and even with her eyes red from crying and lined in the corners from the years that had passed, he saw in them the stubborn defiance that only Ethriel could possess.

He wanted to listen to her. After the pain he'd caused, he wanted to give her everything she would ask of him. But *this*? If he did as she said, they would both be killed. "Ethriel, he's—"

"Let him go, Luc. Please."

Lucien hesitated only a moment longer before he dropped Crosse. The taller man collapsed to his hands and knees, coughing and choking.

Ethriel knelt beside Crosse, and Lucien's jaw tightened, fire rising in his throat when she set a hand on his back as the man recalled how to breathe. Lucien saw movement out of the corner of his eye. Jae was running up the path toward the cottage. He held up his hand, and she stopped, one hand resting on the hilt of the sword slung on her hip.

Crosse lifted his head, rubbing at his scarred throat. He spotted Jae at the same time that she recognized him. Everyone moved in the same moment—Jae drawing her sword, Lucien stepping toward her, hand still raised to hold, Crosse standing and grabbing Ethriel by the wrist. She rose with him. Lucien growled when he touched her.

Crosse's steel gray eyes darted from Jae to Lucien, the realization of who he must be—of *what* he must be—dawning. A memory of a courtyard in Taernfane, and a battle with a Warden of the Flame and a massive furred monster.

No doubt putting the pieces into place, Crosse tugged Ethriel behind him and stepped forward. "You!" he croaked. "What are you doing here? What do you want?"

"Vire's hells!" Ethriel shouted. She stepped out from behind him, never one to cower. Lucien felt a strange swelling of pride, even as her glare encompassed the three of them. "Everyone just *stop*!"

Everyone stopped.

Ethriel looked at Crosse, pointing at Lucien. "That's Lucien," she said. "He's my husband." She turned to Lucien and pointed back at Crosse. "That's Corvin; he's my farmhand."

"He's your *what*?" Lucien and Corvin blurted out together.

Ethriel ignored them, looking across the yard at Jae. "And who in the hells are you?"

Jae sheathed her sword. "My name is Jae. I'm a friend of Lucien's."

Ethriel considered her, then looked to Crosse and finally back to Lucien. "Fine," she said sharply. She wiped at her eyes with the back of her hand. "The three of you are coming inside. There will be no strangling." She turned to Corvin. "Or axes." A quick glance at Jae. "Or swords. We are going to sit at the table, and you are going to explain this to me." Her gaze fell back to Lucien. "*All* of it." Without waiting for a response, she stepped over the pieces of the shattered pitcher and went inside.

Jae brushed past Lucien's shoulder on her way to the cottage. "I like her," she whispered. She strode up the steps and followed Ethriel inside.

Lucien stared at Crosse, who rubbed at his throat again, still breathing hard. "If you hurt her," Lucien said through clenched teeth. Fangs. His teeth had sharpened to fangs.

"I haven't," Crosse said quickly. He held his hands out at his sides, palms up. "And I won't. Not ever. You have my word."

Lucien glowered. "That means nothing coming from you."

"Be that as it may . . ." He nodded toward the door. "If we don't follow her, I think you know there's going to be hell to pay."

As he stepped back to allow Crosse to pass, Lucien snarled, making sure to bare all his teeth. "Right behind you."

CHAPTER 23

JAE FOLLOWED ETHRIEL INTO the small cottage. She had to admit, Corvin Crosse working as a farmhand was the last thing she expected to find in a wooded clearing in Southreach. The fact that he was working for Lucien's wife made the whole situation that much more surreal.

Ethriel had left the front door open, so Jae kept an eye on the two men outside. The last time they'd crossed paths with Corvin, the Westholden captain had tried to kill them. Although it was clear that Ethriel wasn't worried about him, Jae wasn't about to drop her guard, even if she couldn't deny a fierce curiosity about how the Chosen of Ainam had ended up *here*.

Crosse's presence at the farmstead wasn't the only surprise, however. Jae had always thought she'd have so many questions for Lucien's wife. *How did you two meet? What was he like as a father? Was he always such a grump?*

But seeing this woman for the first time, her poise in handling these wild circumstances, and seeing how Lucien looked at her . . . Jae found she had no more questions.

Before the men joined them, Ethriel cleared the table, moving some knives and a clay bowl filled with cut vegetables out of the way.

Probably not a bad idea, Jae mused, schooling her features.

She stepped closer to the door, clasping her hands behind her back and hoping to stay out of Ethriel's way in the small cottage. "I feel like I should apologize for intruding," she said tentatively. "But that feels remarkably underwhelming, considering."

Ethriel snorted a laugh. "You have no reason to apologize," she said. "But I should say thank you."

"Thank you?"

Ethriel smiled softly. "Thank you for bringing my husband back to me."

"He brought himself back, ma'am," Jae said as she saw Lucien stalking Corvin toward the open door. "But that's his story to tell."

"Please, call me Ethriel."

Corvin entered the cottage first, Lucien only a pace behind. Ethriel stood at the head of the broad, scarred table and pointed at the other chairs surrounding it. "Corvin. Jae. Lucien. Sit."

They all did as they were told. Ethriel took her own chair last. "Now," she said firmly, sounding for all the world like an exasperated schoolteacher. "Who would like to start?"

To Jae's surprise, Corvin Crosse cleared his throat. "I'd like to speak first, if I may." His deep voice was startlingly pleasant, and not at all the maniacal, twisted shouting of the battle in Drahkonia where he'd nearly killed her.

He'd nearly killed them all, really.

Yet Ethriel looked at him with the same compassion as she had Jae only a few moments ago. "Alright," she said, nodding once.

Corvin brushed his hair out of his face. It had been close-cropped in Taernfane, though now that it was longer, his midnight black hair had a waviness to it. He focused on Ethriel as he said, "I should apologize for not being forthright with you when you first offered me work and a place at your table. I thought the less you knew about me, the better. My surname is Crosse. I was a captain in the Westholden army."

So he'd lied to her. Or at least withheld the truth. That must have been why she felt so comfortable around—

"I already know all that," Ethriel said flatly.

Corvin's jaw went slack. "You know?"

"I'm not an idiot," she explained. "I go to town every couple of weeks for supplies. Rumors have been flying around for months about the Westholden captain, Corvin Crosse, who deserted after his involvement with the attacks in Drahkonia last autumn." She leaned a little closer to Corvin and whispered,

"*Corvin* is not so common a name around here, I'm afraid. Given that the rumors were accompanied by wanted posters with your likeness on them, it wasn't difficult to put together."

Jae grinned, though both men gaped.

"You deserted?" Lucien asked skeptically.

Corvin leaned his elbows on the table. "I didn't. I was . . . forcibly discharged. But I hadn't realized there were wanted posters."

"Unfortunately," Ethriel said, "it seems Westhold put quite a bounty on your head after whatever actually happened."

The table was silent for a beat before Corvin asked, "If you knew, why didn't you turn me in?"

Ethriel scoffed. "I already told you, I'm not an idiot. I know how rumors work." Her face softened. "When you came here, you needed help. You've never given me a reason to think that you were anything other than a soul in need. You were clearly as ready to leave that life behind as it was ready to be rid of you. I'm not about to judge a person for the decisions of their past. It's what they do in the present that matters." Her eyes never left Corvin, but even Jae could tell that her words were meant as much for Lucien as they were for him.

No one spoke, until Corvin finally said, "I . . . don't know what to say."

Ethriel gave him a warm smile. "Why don't you continue with the story you wanted to tell?"

Remarkably, Corvin's cheeks flushed a scarlet red. "Of course. Two years ago, I was tasked with finding a weapon to aid Westhold in their expansion."

"Expansion," Lucien snorted. "You mean war."

Ethriel shot him a glare. "You'll get your turn to speak," she said sharply.

He crossed his arms over his broad chest and leaned back in his chair, but kept silent. Jae stared at Ethriel, amazed that she could cow Lucien with a look and so few words. *Lucien,* who was more stubborn than any man she'd ever met, quieted to little more than a frustrated huff by this willowy, red-haired woman.

Corvin clasped his hands on the table. "The weapon was thought to have been forged by the gods. Most thought it was a fool's errand, but I believed the legends to be true.

"Not long into my search, I heard a voice. The Lord Ainam spoke to me. He told me that the weapon was real and that it still existed. If I found it, it would solidify the Glory of Ainam across the continent. He said He would grant me power. That I would serve as His right hand."

Corvin paused, watching Ethriel carefully, no doubt giving her a chance to call bullshit on his story, but she simply waited for him to continue.

"After more than a year of searching," Corvin went on, "I found it. But one of my men touched it before I could get to it, and the weapon awakened, merging itself with his body to be powered by his soul."

A chill ran through Jae as she was struck by the realization of what he was describing. Solace. He'd been just a man once, a soldier. One of Crosse's soldiers.

"It was . . . an unfortunate event," Corvin said, his voice flat. "For months, I was in charge of maintaining security around the weapon, of ensuring it was contained while we conducted more research on how to control it."

"You tracked down an all-powerful weapon without fully knowing how to control it?" Jae asked. She shook her head as she looked at Ethriel. "Typical men."

"My superiors were investigating how to control it while I hunted for the weapon," Corvin said, his voice tight. "But since no one expected that I would find it so quickly, they weren't as far along as—"

"They thought it didn't exist, so no one did anything until you found it and sent them scrambling."

Ethriel raised her hand just slightly to bid Jae stop, so she fell silent.

"We did what we could," Corvin continued, "but the weapon was taken from a Westholden military base. My soldiers pursued. To keep the tale brief, I ultimately tried to reclaim the weapon in the city of Taernfane." His eyes met Lucien's for a moment before drifting to Jae.

She stiffened beneath his gaze. She would not shrink back from him.

"I heard about Taernfane," Ethriel said gently. "Though I don't know how true those stories are. It all sounded fairly unbelievable."

"Stories will always expand to fill the space they're given," Corvin said, still looking at Jae. He swallowed, his throat bobbing, before finally returning his focus to Ethriel. "But I would hazard a guess that they're more true than they sound. By then I had learned how to control the weapon, so I . . . I unleashed it to force my opponent's hand. The Warden and"—he gestured to Lucien and Jae—"her friends. I needed them to see that it was dangerous. I needed them to understand."

Jae shifted in her chair, the rest of the battle playing out in her mind. The way Solace's face had gone slack when he'd turned his elemental power on her. How she'd only managed to avoid his first attack because of the warning Lucien had barked from across the courtyard.

The way Lucien lay unconscious in the grass after saving Jae from a fall that certainly would have killed her. She'd thought Lucien was dead or, at least, that he might be too hurt for his rapid healing to save him.

It had been Corvin's fault. That Lucien had been hurt and that Solace had suffered and died—everything was because of him.

Jae had worked hard to move past the events of last autumn. Meaning she'd tried hard not to think about it. If she thought about it for too long, it threatened to pull her under. But she couldn't let herself drown, so she pushed the thoughts away almost as quickly as they surfaced.

"But the Warden didn't relent," Corvin continued. "She defeated me in battle and . . . well, when I awoke, she and her friends were unconscious, and the weapon was gone. I knew what had happened. The weapon had been destroyed, releasing the power that held the elemental gods in slumber. So I fled the city.

"I wanted to return home, but I had failed. In every conceivable way, for every duty that had been given to me. As punishment for my failures, my superiors tried to have me killed."

"You mean the wanted posters?" Jae asked, swallowing down her hatred of the man sitting so near her. She needed to remain focused, on alert. She couldn't let her emotions overpower her reason. That was how mistakes were made. That was how people got hurt.

Corvin shook his head. "Before that. The Westholden military doesn't fail. Not publicly, anyway. They had to make sure my very public failure couldn't reflect upon them. But that was also when Ainam . . . When Ainam revoked His blessing." He drew a shuddering breath.

And Jae held hers. Could it be that Corvin Crosse was no longer the Chosen of Ainam? Was his power truly gone?

"How did you come to be here?" Lucien asked. His tone wasn't exactly *compassionate*, but it lacked malice.

"After Taernfane," Corvin said, "I was hurt. I stumbled upon Ethriel and her farm as I attempted to make my way to Southport so I could get home. She patched me up and sent me on my way, no questions asked. I was grateful, both for her help and her discretion. When I reached Southport, I made contact with my commanding officer back in Westhold. They instructed me to return, but I knew something was wrong. They didn't ask for a debrief of the events, which meant they'd already heard what had transpired.

"As I spent the next few days deciding whether to face my fate back home or try to find a way to redeem myself in the general's eyes, as well as Ainam's, I was attacked by Westholden assassins. I begged Ainam to grant me my power back so I could defend myself and continue to serve Him, but my pleas went unanswered. Alone, without power, and already wounded from Taernfane, I was no match for them. I barely escaped with my life.

"I didn't know where I was going—I was half-dead and delirious—but somehow I found my way back here. To Ethriel and . . ." He trailed off, eyes shifting to the ceiling. "She saved my life. And seeing as I had nowhere else to go, she offered me a place here. It seems too meager a payment for what she did for me, but I help as I can. I hope one day to be able to repay the debt I owe her. And maybe once more be worthy of Ainam's grace."

Lucien studied Corvin, his face unreadable. Jae glanced between him and Ethriel, who sat with her slender hands clasped on the table.

"Thank you, Corvin," Ethriel said. Her voice was like the flutter of wind chimes. She turned her attention to Lucien. How was she so calm through all this?

He straightened under her gaze. "For my part," he began, "I should start a good deal farther back."

Having only just met Ethriel, Jae could already tell she and Lucien were opposites down to their cores. Ethriel, with her tall, willowy build, her voice like soft music, and her seemingly endless patience; and Lucien, all solid strength and ferocity, with his deep, gravel voice. Ethriel's obvious compassion coupled with

Lucien's cynicism. Her gentleness where he was rough. And yet they so clearly loved each other despite their differences.

Or perhaps because of them?

Her thoughts flicked briefly to Dare and her life alongside him ages ago. Back when he was Darcy. After he'd left her, she'd thought that they'd been too different to last. But now, watching Ethriel and Lucien, and catching glimpses of the life they once had together, she wondered if perhaps the trouble had been that she and Dare were far too similar.

Lucien opened his mouth to speak, but another voice interrupted the gathering.

"What the hells happened out here?" a woman called from just outside the door, broken pottery crunching under foot. "Ma, are you alright?"

The door swung open, and a young woman entered with a pack slung over one shoulder. Her dark hair fell in waves around her face, crimped as though she had just pulled it down from a tight braid. It highlighted her bright blue eyes and the smattering of freckles across her fair skin. Her face was a younger version of Ethriel's, but as Jae took in her broad shoulders and the wide curve of her hips, there was no doubt as to whose daughter this was.

The woman stopped short in the doorway, startled. She dropped her pack to the floor as Lucien stood and turned.

"The fuck are you doing here?" she demanded.

Lucien didn't flinch. Had he expected such a harsh greeting from his own daughter?

"Faith," Ethriel chided. "This is—"

"I know who you are," Faith said, never taking her eyes from Lucien. It seemed the resemblance was not lost on her either. She crossed her arms over her chest. "So I'll ask you again: what the fuck are you doing here?"

"*Faith*," Ethriel said again, her voice going sharp.

But the young woman didn't move, nor did Lucien back down from her glare. They faced each other, two immovable objects, neither willing to bend.

Ethriel stood. She slammed her open palm down on the table, causing Lucien and Faith both to snap their attention to her. "Stop it."

Faith thrust a finger toward Lucien. "He owes us an explanation," she said to her mother.

"He does," Ethriel agreed. "And we will listen. We owe him that much."

Faith stared at her, fists clenching at her sides, like they were the only two in the room. Like there wasn't an audience to her pain. "We don't owe him shit!"

"If you want an explanation," Ethriel said coolly, "then we owe him a place to provide one."

Faith's eyes didn't waver, though her shoulders slumped just slightly.

Ethriel gestured with a graceful arc of her hand toward the door. "Corvin, Jae, would you please give me a few minutes with my family?"

Jae stood quickly and joined Corvin, who was already making his way around the table. She cast a quick glance at Lucien, who met her eyes and nodded.

Jae followed Corvin into the front yard. She could keep an eye on him, at least. Even if she couldn't be inside with Lucien, she could have his back from out here by making sure Corvin Crosse didn't cause any problems.

Corvin strode a few feet down the path before turning toward the field to his right. A low half wall made of crumbling stone marked the division between two plots of Ethriel's garden, and he perched on one end, lifting his foot to rest on the edge of the wall where the stones stepped down into nothing.

Jae followed, though she stopped before approaching the wall. She watched him, one hand on her hip, the other resting on the hilt of her sword. The weight of her second sword strapped to her back was reassuring as she stared down the man who had tried to kill her and her friends a few months ago.

Maybe if she tried to focus her powers, she could get a read on him. Jae inhaled deeply, the way Verity had shown her, and imagined herself tossing her awareness out like a stone into a lake, the way Lanara had shown her. The ripples that returned to her, Lanara had explained early on, were the emotions of others around her.

In Taernfane, she'd found that it only worked on strong emotions. She was still learning her way around her powers, like how some emotions seemed as though they could pierce her awareness even without her trying to sense them. She wasn't sure why it happened sometimes but not others, but it seemed to be happening more lately. She'd made a mental note to ask Lanara about it when next the goddess spoke to her.

For now, Jae cast her awareness out, but nothing came back. Whatever Corvin Crosse was feeling, she couldn't sense it.

After a moment, Corvin cleared his throat. "I don't believe we've formally met," he said. Even sitting out here in the garden, his back was rigid. Still the soldier. He stood again, extending his hand to her. "I'm Corvin."

Jae didn't move. Was he serious? "I know who you are."

His lips pursed together. "But you have me at a disadvantage."

"You've heard my name," Jae said curtly, crossing her arms over her chest. Why he thought she would ever shake his hand was beyond her.

He must have figured it out because he finally dropped his hand and returned to his seat on the edge of the low wall. "Jae, right?"

She simply stared at him. She wasn't here to be polite or make friends. She was here to make sure their enemy couldn't stab Lucien in the back while his focus was elsewhere.

Corvin blew out a long sigh. "Right." His gaze drifted out across the farmstead. "May I ask you a question?"

She shrugged. "Sure." She made no promise of answering him.

He seemed to steel himself. "Is it true? Did your friends really awaken the old gods?"

It was Jae's turn to steady herself. "It's true."

"You're certain?"

Within her, the little droplet of Lanara's power sat nestled against her heart like a dewdrop on a leaf. "I'm certain."

Corvin shook his head, eyes widening slightly. "Incredible." Though to what extent he saw it as a blessing or a bad omen, Jae couldn't tell.

"And is your story true?" she asked, her curiosity getting the better of her. "Did you really lose your power?"

He leaned back, resting his hands against the edge of the wall. "It's true." He tilted his face to the sky and closed his eyes. "Ainam withdrew His blessing."

Jae still wasn't sure if she fully believed him. Her hand tightened on the hilt of her sword, ready to move at any sign of aggression.

"So you're no longer his Chosen?" she asked carefully.

"Not until I can redeem myself."

"You still want that?"

"Why wouldn't I?"

Jae gestured toward the expanse of the clearing around them. "To start with, he abandoned you. You said he left you to die."

"He left to *test* me," Corvin said. "To prove myself worthy of His grace. When I answered His call, I dedicated my life to serving Him." Corvin met Jae's eyes, an intensity within his steel gray gaze. "That doesn't change just because He wants me to atone for my mistakes."

"Mistakes?" Jae scoffed. This man had hunted her friends across the continent, tried to kill them and her, and was the reason Solace was dead. And how many other innocent people had he killed along the way? Yet somehow Jae suspected those weren't the *mistakes* he was referring to. That had all been part of his job. His mission from his god. Those were his conscious choices.

And given half a chance, he would make them all again.

Jae shook her head and waved her hand, dismissing both Crosse and his *mistakes*, before turning and heading back toward the cottage.

She could keep an eye on him from a distance just as easily.

CHAPTER 24

LUCIEN FACED HIS DAUGHTER. She'd been an infant last he saw her, and yet he knew without doubt or hesitation that it was her. He would know her blindfolded. She smelled of damp earth and pine trees. She smelled of *home*, if such a thing could have a scent.

She stared daggers at him with bright blue eyes. Ethriel's eyes.

"Sit down," Ethriel said, returning to her seat at the head of the table. "Both of you."

Lucien sat as ordered, while Faith took the seat previously occupied by Corvin. She leaned back in the chair, arms crossed over her chest. There was no warmth coming from her. Or fear. Only a near-feral anger.

Yes, he would know her anywhere.

Ethriel turned her attention to him. "I think you'd best explain what happened to you. And why you're here now looking like you haven't aged a day in the last twenty years."

He drew in a long breath, gathering his thoughts. And his nerve. He'd never told his story in its entirety. Even Jae only knew bits and pieces that she'd pried out of him over the years they'd traveled together.

"They told you I was killed. In an ambush at the edge of the Red Forest, right?"

She nodded. Her eyes glistened, but her face remained neutral.

"It wasn't an ambush. Not exactly. But my entire company was killed." He could still smell the blood clogging his senses, and he fisted his hands beneath the table. "I should have died."

"Who attacked you?" Ethriel asked. Her hands were clasped, knuckles white. "I could never get a straight answer out of anyone."

Lucien swallowed hard. "Shifters."

"Shifters?" Faith's voice was incredulous.

"Some of the other soldiers had wandered inside the forest's borders. I don't know what they were thinking—whether they heard something or if they were just being reckless. But the shifters came. They slaughtered everyone."

"Bullshit," Faith muttered.

Ethriel ignored her. "How did you survive the attack?"

Faith rolled her eyes. "How do you think? He probably ran away."

Lucien pulled open the collar of his shirt, exposing the deep indented scars of a bite beginning at the tendons at the base of his neck and dragging across his chest and shoulder. It was far too large for either human or animal.

Ethriel's eyes widened as she almost certainly realized where his story was headed. Even Faith's throat worked as she swallowed, staring at him.

"One of the beasts caught me in its jaws. It could have ripped my throat out, and I would have been dead like the rest of them. But I don't know what happened. I think another soldier stabbed it. Its blood poured over me before it could finish what it started." The pain, the guilt for *not* dying when he should have, tightened his chest. "I should have died there. But instead, I . . . changed."

"You . . . You're . . ." Ethriel struggled to find the words, so he supplied them for her.

"I'm a shifter."

Faith pushed up from the table and paced the kitchen. "That's bullshit," she said, much louder this time. She almost managed to hide the quaver in her voice, but Lucien could scent the fear coming from her now. It was subtle, but it was there. His heart ached.

"I wish it were," Lucien said honestly. "The next time I woke, I was healed, but I felt . . . *wrong*. Somehow." He'd never been able to put words to how it actually felt. But he would try. For her. For them, he would try. "It was as if I was suddenly sharing my skin with a monster that wanted only violence and blood, and it burned with rage if it couldn't have it. Only I couldn't tell where I ended and the monster began."

His breath caught, but he forced the words out. "It took me a year, I think, to even remember my name. To remember that I was a person and not just this monster. It was another seven years before I trusted myself around humans—before I trusted that I wouldn't lose control."

Beneath the table he flexed his hands. The scent of blood hit him, and he glanced down. His fingernails had lengthened into claws, piercing the soft flesh of his palms. As he watched, the tiny wounds slowly drew closed, leaving only little crimson smears. He willed his claws to retract. They shrank and retreated until only the bitten stubs of his nails remained.

"I needed to make sure both of you were safe," he went on, still staring at the blood on his palms. "I could never forgive myself if I hurt you. Either of you. So I stayed away."

Ethriel sat as still as death, but Faith continued pacing. "What about the other twelve years?" Faith asked. "You said it was a year to remember your own name and seven more to be around people. That's eight years. You were gone for twenty." She squared her shoulders as she faced him. "So what about the other twelve?"

Ethriel gave Faith a distinctly motherly look. Despite everything, Lucien's chest warmed at the sight of it. He'd always known Ethriel would make an incredible mother.

"I needed to be certain you were safe," he said again. "From me. From"—he gestured to himself—"this thing I'd become. I didn't want . . . I never wanted to hurt either of you. Not ever. And I . . ." Damn it all, the words still snagged in his throat. The words he'd thought a hundred thousand times, but had only ever spoken aloud once to Jae as they rode toward Taernfane.

"You didn't want us to see you like that," Ethriel supplied.

Lucien nodded. How did she do that? How did she always know his heart better than he knew it himself? Though he supposed that made a sort of sense. It had always belonged to her, after all.

Faith scoffed. "I can't believe you're buying any of this," she complained to Ethriel.

"It's the truth," Lucien said.

She faced Lucien. "Then prove it."

"You don't want that," he said, his voice dropping to an icy timbre.

"Then why now?" Faith went on. "Huh? Why are you here *now*? What's changed? You're still a monster, right?"

Lucien flinched. Her words were true, but hearing his daughter speak them aloud sent a bolt through his heart. "Yes," he said, jaw tight. "I am."

"Then what's changed?"

So much had changed and yet also, somehow, nothing had. Or at least, nothing that would matter to her. He sat in silence, trying to find the words to explain a thing he wasn't sure he fully understood himself.

The silence filled the cabin, nearly suffocating in its oppressiveness.

Faith was the one to break it. "Fuck this," she snapped. She stalked toward her room.

She was through the door, slamming it shut behind her without another word.

Lucien stared at the table, his hands still under it, out of sight. On this side, the grain of the wood swirled into a knot and continued on down the length of the planks. Just to the right of the knot was a divot gouged into the table. Lucien remembered that notch. He'd hit the knot with his plane, sending it skidding to the side at a bad angle and leaving a scrape deep into the grain. He'd been furious at the time, ready to throw the whole thing away. But Ethriel had talked him down.

Character, she'd said. It would give the table *character*. He'd grumbled something in his frustration, still ready to scrap it all and chop it up for kindling. But then she'd said, *Every time I see that notch, I'll think of you and how you made this for our family with your own hands.* And so instead of smashing it like he'd wanted, Lucien had put it down for the rest of the day, returning to it the next morning, ready to view it with fresh eyes.

Ethriel sat motionless, letting the silence settle around them both. She never minded the quiet, although she could fill it just as well as anyone else when she had a mind to. But she let this one linger, her piercing gaze fixed on Lucien.

Had he done the right thing coming back? Should he have stayed away and let them go on thinking he had died in those woods?

After a long while, Ethriel inhaled deeply, breaking the silence with only the sound of her breath. "I don't know what to say." Her eyes flicked down to her hands. "I'm sorry."

Lucien nearly fell out of the chair. "Eth . . ." It was a whisper on his lips.

"I'm sorry this happened to you." Her tear-rimmed eyes met his. "I'm sorry you were alone for so many years. I wish . . ." A tear slipped down her cheek, and she blinked quickly, ushering the rest away. "I wish I could have been there to help you. But I . . . I think I understand."

Her voice cracked and so did Lucien's heart.

"I would do anything to protect Faith," she continued, glancing toward where their daughter had stormed off. "And if I thought staying away from her was the only way to keep her safe, then I would do it. Even though it would kill me, I would do it. And I know it must have killed you too. But I'm glad you're here." She seemed to consider her own words for a moment before she gestured to the room. "I don't mean just here, though I'm glad for that too, but I mean . . . *Here*." She drew a shuddering breath. "I'm glad you're still here, Luc."

After he'd been turned, Lucien had wanted so badly to be done with it all. He had thrown himself away, cut himself down and burned himself up. But . . . maybe all he'd needed were fresh eyes.

CHAPTER 25

LUCIEN STOOD IN THEIR small kitchen—*Ethriel's* small kitchen. He could hardly think it was his anymore. He collected the clay plates from dinner, moving them to the wash basin that stood on a small table near the hearth.

Ethriel had been in the process of preparing dinner when Lucien and Jae arrived, and she had insisted on feeding them rather than having them fend for themselves with their own trail food.

Lucien couldn't say he minded. Ethriel's cooking had always been simple but delicious, and it seemed that hadn't changed.

The meal had been tense, but civil. Corvin and Jae had come back inside at Ethriel's invitation. Faith had come out of her room long enough to grab a roll and a hunk of cheese before storming off again, this time through the front door, muttering something to Ethriel about needing to go check the snares in the woods. Lucien doubted that was true.

"Corvin, could you bring in some water from the pump?" Ethriel asked as she wiped down the table and straightened the chairs.

"Of course," he said, hurrying to the door. He was back a few minutes later with two pails of water, which he deposited into the pot that hung over the hearth.

"Thank you." Ethriel surveyed the cottage, as though taking a mental tally. "I think we'll need some more firewood before long," she said, half to herself.

Corvin didn't hesitate before turning toward the door again. "I'll get some before it gets dark."

Lucien couldn't scent anything unusual on Crosse. And there was no fear or anything strange coming from Ethriel either. Whatever Crosse was up to, Ethriel certainly wasn't afraid of him. Lucien shot a quick glance at Jae, who seemed to intuit his question.

"I'll help you," she said to Corvin, following him outside. Lucien appreciated her keeping an eye on him so he could focus his attention on—

"Your turn to wash tonight," Ethriel said as she checked the temperature of the water.

Lucien's brow furrowed as he watched her.

"The dishes," she said with a quiet laugh. "I've had it for twenty years. I think it's fair to say it's your turn."

Lucien could hardly stop his grin as he took the pot from the hearth and moved the warm water to the wash basin.

Ethriel busied herself with tidying up the rest of the kitchen, occasionally bringing some forgotten utensil over and dropping it into the water. She hummed as she moved about the cottage, as she always had, the pleasant melody filling the small space. Ethriel's soft humming had been a constant presence in his life. One he hadn't truly noticed until it was gone.

When she walked past him the second time, her hand brushed the center of his back, between his shoulder blades. It was such a light touch, the gentle, casual caress she had done a thousand times in their life before.

Lucien's hands froze in the water, a plate held tight in his grip. He turned just enough to look at Ethriel over his shoulder, but she was already past him, still cleaning and straightening up. He doubted she even noticed what she'd done, that slight touch having been such a habit of hers. It had always been her quiet way of letting him know she was there.

Lucien returned his focus to the dishes in the basin, listening to Ethriel humming as she worked. A short while later, a knock sounded on the door. Ethriel opened it, allowing Corvin and Jae back inside to drop armfuls of firewood off near the hearth.

"Is there anything else you need, Ethriel?" Corvin asked. Lucien eyed him but managed to keep the growl from escaping his throat. The sun had set while they worked, darkness settling over the cottage and the farm.

"No, thank you," she said.

Corvin dipped his head. "Then I think I'll turn in for the night. Good night."

"Good night, Corvin," Ethriel said.

He paused by the door. "At the risk of sounding trite," he said, gray eyes darting between Lucien and Jae, "it was nice to actually meet the both of you." He ducked outside before either of them could respond.

Jae watched him leave, her mouth twisted up in concentration. Lucien would have to ask her what she sensed on him later.

"Where does he sleep?" Jae asked.

"One of the out buildings," Ethriel replied, still tidying. "Luc built the first one, but I had the second one made as a bunk for any farmhands helping out around here. We've had our fair share over the years."

Lucien couldn't deny his relief at the realization that Corvin didn't share a bed with Ethriel. Or Faith, now that he was thinking about it.

"I'll start setting up camp," Jae said, pulling Lucien out of this new, unpleasant line of thinking.

Lucien nodded, but Ethriel shot a look at them both. "Don't be ridiculous. You'll sleep here."

Finishing the last of the dishes, Lucien wiped his hands on the thighs of his pants. He started to argue, but Ethriel threw a towel at him from a shelf behind her. He caught it and dried his hands in silence.

Jae gave a short bow toward Ethriel. "We don't want to be a bother."

"It's no bother, and the nights are still cold. Our cottage might be cozy, but we have room enough."

Jae smiled. "Thank you, though I refuse to put anyone out of their bed. I'll be fine on the floor. Trust me, I've slept on far worse."

Ethriel nodded. "Fair enough. I won't pressure you any more than I already have. Let me just get you some blankets." With that seemingly settled, Ethriel disappeared into her room at the back of the cottage.

Lucien watched her leave, leaning back against the table, hands gripping the edge.

"How are you holding up?" Jae asked, her voice quiet.

Lucien grumbled, low and deep in his throat. "Can't you tell?"

"Don't be an ass."

A creak of wood from the table told him he needed to loosen his grip. "How do you think, Jae?"

"Not very well," she said bluntly. "Do we need to go?"

"I'm fine." At her look that silently called his bullshit, he growled, "I'll *be* fine."

She was making sure he was still in control. Being back here, seeing Ethriel and Faith, finding Corvin here—as a farmhand of all things . . . it was a lot. And Lucien was, admittedly, having trouble coping. As much as he hated it, he appreciated Jae keeping an eye on *him* too.

He had expected Faith's anger, and it was justified, though the hatred in her eyes when she looked at him was like being stabbed in the chest. But he had expected anger from Ethriel too. And while it was there to some degree, he'd also found something he hadn't expected. Compassion. Understanding. He wasn't sure he deserved it.

Lucien looked deep within himself, to where he kept the beast chained. It snarled at him, but the chains entwined with ivy were solid, the moss-covered locks secured.

He drew a long, steadying breath. "I'm fine," he said again, much more calmly.

Jae nodded, satisfied, as Ethriel emerged from her room with a pile of blankets. Jae took them from her graciously with a quiet "Thank you."

Lucien glanced toward the window, into the gathered dark. "Faith." There were dangers in the woods, even here. "It's late."

"She's alright," Ethriel said, smiling sadly. "She takes after you more than a little."

"She can take care of herself?" Jae asked, starting to lay out the blankets near the hearth.

"That," Ethriel said, not taking her eyes from Lucien. "And she's stubborn as all hells."

Jae snorted a laugh, and even Lucien angled his mouth in a small smile.

"She'll be back when she's ready," Ethriel added. She looked at Lucien for a long moment, hesitating as though there was something more she wanted to say. But after a breath, she bowed her head, fire-red curls falling over her shoulders. "Good night," she said softly. She turned to her room, took one look back at

Lucien as she stepped across the threshold, and then closed the door all but an inch.

Lucien stood in the center of the cottage, wrapped in the scents of Ethriel and home, committing them all to memory. In that moment, he wanted nothing more than to breathe deep for the rest of his life.

"What are you waiting for?" Jae whispered.

"What do you mean?"

Jae crossed her arms. "Lucien, you haven't seen your wife in twenty years, and you're telling me that you're going to sleep out here on the floor?"

"No," Lucien said, though it came out more of a growl than he intended, which only served to solidify his decision. He crossed to the front door of the cottage. "I'm going to sleep outside."

He stepped into the dark before Jae could voice her objection.

Chapter 26

LUCIEN STALKED THE PERIMETER of the plot of land he and Ethriel had carved for themselves more than twenty years ago. He'd meant for this to be the place where he lived out his days with her. He'd meant to be buried beneath the massive oak tree on the eastern edge of the clearing. He'd meant to see his daughter grow, and learn and love, to be married—or not, as she chose—and to stay or venture out into the world as she wished.

He'd meant for so many things to happen. And, conversely, there were many more things he wished hadn't happened.

On his second pass along the western edge, a soft rustle of movement in the woods pricked his ears, and soon the scent he already recognized—pine and wet earth, a hint of petrichor—reached him. The motion in the trees stopped as Lucien paused, angling his head.

"You can come out, Faith," he said, beckoning with one hand toward the shadows. "I know you're there."

Faith emerged, a scowl darkening her face. "What are you doing?" she asked, brushing past him and heading across the garden toward the cottage. "Were you following me?"

He fell into step beside her. "I couldn't sleep," he said. "I sometimes find it helpful to walk for a while."

She eyed him sidelong. "In circles?"

"Which is it?" Lucien asked. "Was I following you, or were you watching me walk in circles?"

A scoff was the only answer she gave him.

"Patrol," he continued. "It helps focus my mind. Calm my nerves."

"Oh, are your nerves in need of calming?"

Mother Taerna, she did not want to make this easy. And Lucien couldn't blame her in the slightest. But he also couldn't walk away from her. Not now that he was here.

"Faith, look, I—"

"Lucien." She turned to face him as they reached the crumbling stone wall that marked the midpoint of the fields. "Just stop. I don't care, alright? You may have my mother convinced that you never stopped loving us, that you never stopped thinking about us, but not me. You can stop trying so fucking hard. I haven't needed you for twenty years, and that's not going to change just because you decided to finally show up."

The hair on the back of Lucien's neck stood on end as the beast within him tugged at the chains, testing one of the locks. He rolled his shoulders, tamping it back down. "Faith," he said again. "I know this is hard—"

"You *know*?" she snapped. Faith stepped closer, squaring her shoulders as she confronted him, chin up, fists clenched. Only Jae ever went toe-to-toe with him like that. "What exactly do you think you know, Lucien?" She spat his name at him. "You think you know what it was like thinking for my whole life that my father was dead only to walk into my house one day and find him having a fucking chat with my mother? You think you know what *that* was like? Finding out that he wasn't missing from my life because he was dead but because he chose to be?"

Tension knotted Lucien's shoulders, the beast tugging harder on the chains as his anger simmered beneath the surface. "I didn't choose what happened," he said, teeth clenched.

Faith rolled her eyes. "Please. Even if you didn't choose to be turned into a monster, you certainly chose not to come back for twenty fucking years."

Monster. The word echoed through Lucien's mind. The beast roared with its always-burning rage. *Free*, it said. *Out.*

No. Lucien clenched his fists at his sides. "I didn't want to hurt you," he said, his voice dangerously close to a growl.

His daughter wasn't the least concerned as she stepped closer. "Well then you failed spectacularly."

"Everything I did," he ground out. "Everything was to keep you *safe*, Faith." His fists tightened, a sharp pain slashing at his palms.

Free.

"Bullshit!" Faith shouted back.

The beast tore at its chains. *Out*, it roared. *NOW.*

"Everything was to protect you and Ethriel. The both of you." Lucien's voice rose to match hers. "Everything I did was for you!"

"No, everything you did was for *you*!" She stepped into him, shoving him in the chest. "You were scared. You were scared, and you ran. Don't fucking kid yourself, Lucien. That wasn't for us. That was for *you*."

She took off past him, sprinting toward the house. She was fast for her build, and she was at the cottage door nearly before Lucien had collected his thoughts enough to turn around.

Rage skimmed along the surface of his body, raising his hackles. He ran his tongue along his sharpened canine teeth, which had elongated to fangs while Faith shouted at him. He willed them to shorten back to their normal length as he slowly opened his hands, looking down at the bloodied mess he'd made of his palms. His claws retracted as he breathed deep, and the wounds closed, the skin pulling together.

Slowly, focusing his mind on his steps, the sound of his boots in the garden, the rustling of the wind in the trees, Lucien walked back to the cottage. He stopped at the water pump along the side of the house and washed the blood from his hands. The slices he'd made in his flesh with his claws were fully healed. Like nothing had ever happened. That's how Lucien's existence was now. Every wound he received covered over, healed, only the deepest of them leaving a mark.

Lucien looked toward the cottage door, then toward the forest at the edge of the clearing. The beast was still clawing at its chains, though its baying had subsided to its usual dull roar. But it seemed to follow the movement of Lucien's eyes, seeing what he was seeing. It always did.

Run? it growled.

Lucien sneered. *Run.*

He sprinted down the path, and when the shadows of the forest surrounded him, he unlocked the chains and let the beast come out to play. Between one step and the next he shifted, lumbering forward on all fours as his bones snapped and joints popped into another shape, the shape of the beast that had ridden alongside him all these years. The wind whipped through his fur as he ran headlong into the darkness. But the beast could sense everything better than Lucien could in his human form, and the beauty of the forest at night opened to him.

He ran for hours, until the rage began to subside and the beast seemed . . . content . . . with this excursion. He circled back until the cottage came into view through the trees and shadows. Ethriel sat on the front step. Her hair cascaded over her shoulders in beautiful ringlets of fire, and she had a knitted shawl pulled tightly around herself.

Lucien shifted back into his human form before he stepped into the clearing. She tracked his movement as he approached, though she didn't move to stand, nor did she say anything.

When he reached the path directly before the steps, Ethriel slid to the side, giving him space to either sit or pass by her and into the cottage.

Lucien sat. The night was cold, but it didn't bother him. His skin still felt too hot from his anger and the run. It would take him a while yet to cool off.

Ethriel whispered, "Are you alright?"

"Not really," he said quietly. "But I'm not going to lose control, if that's what you're—"

"It's not," she said. She stared out at the darkness of the forest. "I trust you."

Something settled in Lucien's chest. Some pain he'd been carrying eased slightly. Overhead, the gibbous moon shone brightly, illuminating the clearing.

"I talked to Faith," Ethriel continued. "As much as she felt like talking anyway. I think she's just going to need some time. We all are." She set her hand on Lucien's arm, and it sent a shock of cold through him.

Her fingers were frozen. Instinct took over, and he scooted a little closer to her, wrapping his arm around her shoulders and pulling her into the warmth of his body. She stiffened at first, just enough that he paused, loosening his grip should she want to pull away. But she settled into him, leaning her head against his chest and tucking herself close. The skin of her arms was chilled even through her shawl.

"How long have you been sitting out here?"

"A little while," she said.

"Were you waiting for me?"

Ethriel nodded into his chest. "Part of me worried you wouldn't come back."

Lucien squeezed her shoulder and set his cheek against the top of her head. He'd certainly given her cause enough to worry about that. "I'm sorry." He closed his eyes, shutting out the rest of the world, if only for a little while. He ran his fingers over the knitted wool of her shawl. "I remember when you made this," he said after a time. "You were pregnant with Faith." The memory tugged at the corner of his mouth. "You were so worried you wouldn't finish it before she was born."

"You kept saying I had plenty of time," Ethriel said.

"You did have plenty of ti—"

"I did *not* have plenty of time, Lucien Zamorra." Her voice was stern, but there was a playfulness in it that he'd missed, along with his human name from so long ago.

He leaned into the twenty-year-old debate. "You finished it with six whole days to spare," Lucien said, trying to keep the smile out of his voice.

"That's only because she arrived a full eight days later than we expected and you know it."

Lucien chuckled into her hair as she snuggled deeper against his shoulder. They were silent for a while, and when Ethriel finally spoke again, her voice was sorrowful. "When do you need to leave?"

Lucien rubbed her arm through her shawl. He wished he could tell her that he was here to stay. But Taerna's visions still pulled him toward the Red Forest where he'd need to meet with Micah. He also wished he could at least tell her when he would come back. "A few days," he said. "I have business in the Red Forest. It's why Jae and I are in Southreach."

Ethriel sat up, though she left her hand on Lucien's leg. She searched his eyes. "The Red Forest?" The crease on her forehead appeared, the one she always got when she was worried. "The shifters?"

He nodded. "There's a bit more to my story that I didn't get to earlier."

She held his gaze, her blue eyes bright in the moonlight. "Tell me."

Lucien sighed and looked away. He wasn't even sure how to begin this part. He hadn't yet needed to explain it to anyone—everyone else he cared about was there when it happened. "You remember what Corvin said? About being blessed by Ainam?"

Ethriel nodded. "Yes. Hard to forget something like that."

"And also when he said that my friends awoke the elemental gods?"

Her brows furrowed. "Of course I do."

Lucien took a deep breath. "Only the six of us who were there, the head of the Wardens of the Flame, and the King of Drahkonia himself know what I'm about to tell you."

Ethriel's slender hand slid up to his cheek, caressing his beard, her fingers tracing a small length of the scar that followed the curve of his jaw. "Luc, you can tell me anything."

"When the gods awoke, they Chose four of us to be their champions, as Corvin was a Chosen of Ainam. Taerna Chose me."

Ethriel's hand paused against his cheek, but she didn't pull away.

He leaned into her touch. "I'm still figuring out what that means, but I have a responsibility. To Taerna. And there's something she wants me to do in the Red Forest."

Ethriel took a deep breath, then her fingers began their slow tracing again. "She speaks to you?" she asked. She didn't sound frightened, which Lucien had been worried about. But there was something there. Curiosity? Concern?

"Sometimes," he said. "It happened more when we were in Taernfane." At the tilt of Ethriel's head, he added, "Her power is strongest there. But she sometimes sends me dreams. Visions. And right now, there's a task I need to complete. And I . . . I don't know how long it will take me, Eth."

She focused on his face, like she was memorizing every curve and angle of his cheek, his chin, his jaw. "I understand." Her voice held the slightest tremble. Ethriel blinked, and a tear slipped from beneath her lashes, glinting in the moonlight as it slid down her pale, freckled cheek. "Will you come back?"

Lucien turned, all of his calm nearly leaving him in that instant as he cupped her face in his hands and pressed his forehead to hers. "As long as I have breath in my lungs and legs to carry me, or friends to drag me back, I *will* come back to you. I'm yours, Eth."

"My Luc," she whispered.

"Your Luc," he repeated. "I may have to go, but I won't *leave*. Not again. I promise you."

Ethriel threw her arms around his neck and kissed him. The strength of it, the urgency, surprised him, and he inhaled sharply. Her scent filled his nose—wet clay, woodsmoke, and honeysuckle. He pulled her into him, returning the kiss with as much need as she had. A quiet sob escaped her throat as she kissed him, as they relearned the touch and taste of each other.

Lucien's pulse quickened, and his breath hitched as she entwined her fingers in his hair. His thoughts wandered. Maybe he could let himself relax. The burdens he carried, maybe . . . maybe he could lay them down. Allow himself to let go, just for a moment—

The beast ripped at its chains. *Out!*

Lucien gasped and grabbed Ethriel's shoulders. He pushed her back, holding her at arm's length. Her hands slid from his hair and fell into her lap, and Lucien bowed his head, focusing on her hands.

"I'm sorry," he said between ragged breaths.

Her hands gripped each other, wringing her fingers like she wasn't sure what else to do with them.

He swallowed hard. "I . . . I'm not sure how to explain . . . I . . ."

"It's alright." Her voice was tight but steady. "I shouldn't have done that."

"No," he said firmly. He lifted his head. "No, Eth, I . . ." The slightest curve to his lip, a breath of a grin. "I'm grateful you did, I just . . . I can't."

"I think I understand," she said slowly. She gripped the edges of her knit shawl and pulled it more tightly around herself.

Lucien blew out a long breath. "You should go inside before you freeze."

She smiled, though it didn't reach her eyes. She drew her legs under her and rose to her knees. "Good night, Luc," she said, and she leaned forward and kissed his forehead.

"Good night, Eth."

Ethriel stood and slipped into the cottage, closing the door again behind her.

The beast growled in its cage, and Lucien growled back. He dragged his hands through his hair, still feeling the tug of her fingers. He sat on the stone stoop until even he was beginning to feel the cold seeping into his bones.

Inside, the hearth sent warmth and a soft glow through the cottage. Lucien crossed toward where Jae was stretched out in front of it, her arm beneath her head like a pillow. At her head, another set of blankets were laid out for Lucien.

Jae's eyes were closed, but as Lucien padded closer and lowered himself onto the blankets, she asked, "Are you alright?"

Lucien tugged off his boots. "No."

Jae opened her eyes at that, rolling onto her stomach so she could look at him. "Do you want to talk about it?"

"No."

Jae glanced from the closed door that marked Faith's room, to the other closed door that was Ethriel's. "Alright," she said, rolling back over.

Lucien removed his belt and set it beside his boots. "That's it?" he asked. "You're not going to pry?"

Jae tilted her head so she could see him, albeit upside down. "Lucien, I can't even pretend to understand what you're going through and how much will this is taking right now. But I know you know I'm here if you want to talk about it." She was silent for a moment, watching him, and then she rolled onto her stomach again and propped herself up on her elbows. "The amount of courage it took for you to come here . . . I know I pushed you to come, but I didn't realize—I don't think I could understand without seeing it for myself—what it took for you to do it."

Lucien watched the embers glowing in the hearth. "I don't feel very courageous right now," he said bitterly.

"I expect not," Jae said. "But I'm damn impressed. For what that's worth."

The corner of Lucien's mouth drew up despite himself. "It's worth an awful lot."

Chapter 27

The last small leg of the trip from Valda's bustling port to Whitehollow's slightly smaller one gave Dare a chance to sober up a little. He also took the opportunity to avoid the others as much as physically possible.

Verity led the way from the ship, and once they were safely off the docks and into the city proper, Chancellor Caelan summoned their attention.

"Well, we made it, and only a little worse for wear," he said, inhaling deeply. His attention landed on Gregor and Finn. "And you two are with me. Warden Corallan, I assume you'll be in touch about when next we should meet regarding the hearing preparations?"

Dare's mind snagged as Gregor and Finn both moved to Caelan as though this had all been previously arranged. What the hells? "Wait. What?" The others all turned to him, confusion plain on each of their faces. Did Verity really not have any concerns about Gregor and Finn being off on their own?

Verity's hands came to rest on her hips. "What do you mean, *what*? King Dominic asked Gregor to help with the logistics surrounding the hearing, and Finn's going with him so no one's left alone."

Thankfully Dare had sobered enough to bite back the scoff that threatened to escape. "What about me?"

Verity rolled her eyes. "You're coming with me to the Wardens' base."

When had all this been decided?

"Don't look so shocked," Verity went on. "It was all part of the briefing with King Dominic before we left Taernfane, remember?"

Dare thought back to their parting with the king, to his wandering thoughts that morning, and to the suspicion that he'd missed something important. It seemed he was right.

"Oh," he said, trying to regain some sense of balance. "Right."

Caelan cleared his throat softly. "They'll be guests of the Drahkonian embassy," he said, speaking to Dare. "Security there will be heightened ahead of the hearings. It's one of the safest places they can be."

Dare risked a quick glance at Gregor, who was frowning at him but seemed otherwise content to go where he was needed. "Of course," Dare said, nodding to Caelan.

"We'll see you soon," Finn called over her shoulder as they followed the chancellor. Gregor didn't look back.

When Dare turned to Verity, her stern eyes were fixed on him. For some reason his stomach sank.

"You and I need to check in with Commander Cairn," she said.

Dare swallowed hard. *And there it is.* "Can't we do that tomorrow?" The sun was beginning to set and he'd had a very long day. "We just docked."

Verity crossed her arms over her chest.

"Alright, alright, fine," he said, throwing his hands up in defeat. "Lead the way."

The Wardens' compound was largely how Dare remembered it. Lots of low, gray buildings and only a handful of people visible in the open training yards. As they crossed the courtyard, Verity stopped at the burning brazier in the center, the symbol for Pyrannis, patron of the Wardens, tucked behind its low wall.

She brought her hand to her lips, kissing her steel fingertips, and touched it to the top of the stone. Dare considered briefly whether to say something, to ask her what she was thinking about, but she simply stared at the flames. Dare had the overwhelming sense that he was intruding on something very personal.

After a moment, Verity inhaled a slow, deep breath, and turned to Dare. She blinked as though surprised to see him there. "Sorry," she said. She gestured in the direction they'd been heading. "We should go."

"As you wish, my lady Warden." Dare bit the inside of his cheek as he considered whether to ask his other question. He pushed forward despite his hesitation. "Are you good?"

"Yes," she said immediately. But then she stopped, her shoulders sagging. "I don't know." She leaned back against the low wall and looked out across the base. "It feels strange."

"Being back?" Dare asked, moving to stand beside her.

Verity shook her head in silence. When she spoke again, her voice was soft, like she was trying to keep it from cracking. "Being back without him."

Before Dare could think of something useful to say, Verity sucked in a breath. "But what about you?" she asked. "After what happened earlier today—with the Brothers? How are you holding up?"

This wasn't exactly something Dare wanted to talk about right now, especially with Verity—not after she hadn't even warned him this could happen—but he didn't want to drag her through her own painful memories either. If she needed to talk about something other than Drystan, he supposed he could oblige her.

He wanted to tell her he was fine, but he'd never lied to her, and this didn't seem like the time to start. "Not great," he said. "It caught me off guard. I'm, uh . . ." He swallowed thickly as he stuffed his hands in his pockets and tucked his elbows in tight to his sides. "I'm still reeling a bit."

Dare hated being so exposed. Gregor was the only person he'd ever been so open with—so honestly *himself*. And while he trusted Verity not to throw it back at him or to brush him off, it still made his stomach clench up.

"I'm sorry," she said. "I can't help but feel responsible."

"It's not your fault, Verity."

She was silent for so long, Dare thought that might be all she wanted to say, but then she turned to face him. "I didn't realize the Brothers required an oath of loyalty."

"It wasn't a—"

"It's not a formal oath, I know," Verity continued. "Finn explained it to me. But being commissioned with the Brothers came with an expectation of allegiance. I didn't realize. I'll be honest, Dare. I assumed the worst of the Crimson Brothers. After all this time, even knowing you, even knowing Finn, it didn't occur to me that a group of mercenaries would ever have an expectation of loyalty. And because of my bias, you were blindsided. And I'm ashamed that I didn't realize how important the Brothers were to you. I should have. I'm truly sorry, Dare."

Dare's breath left him in one long exhale. Gregor was right. He had friends now. Friends who cared about him. Friends who would miss him if he were gone. Verity cared, and despite her frustratingly noble streak, she meant well and only ever wanted to help him.

"Thank you," he said when he could find his voice again.

"Looks like I'm really stuck with you now," Verity said.

Dare huffed a small laugh. That's what he'd told her just after she'd freed him from his parents. His shoulders loosened along with the knot in his chest, and he pulled her into a side hug. "I wouldn't have it any other way, my lady Warden."

They walked in silence to a building at the far side of the compound. Inside, Dare recalled the large doors as soon as he saw them, as well as the bench on the opposite wall. He and Solace had sat there when they first came to Whitehollow, while Verity and Drystan reported to their commander. The four of them, travel-worn and weary.

And now it was just two.

Dare moved to the bench to wait for Verity to report to Cairn. No doubt Cairn would have questions and would probably need to decide what would be done with him. Would Cairn cut him loose? If so, what then?

Dare sat and leaned against the wall, stretching out his legs.

"What are you doing?" Verity asked. She beckoned for him to stand. "Come on."

Dare sat up straighter. "Don't you need to report to your commander?"

Verity's mouth quirked to the side. "He's your commander now too," she said dryly. She held out her hand for him.

Dare studied the smooth metal plates of her fingers, the perfect joints and nearly invisible seams where they overlapped. Cairn was his commander now. Not Zahra. Not even Verity. Cairn. Dare remembered the derision in High Commander Joseph Cairn's gaze when he had first met the leader of the Wardens of the Flame.

He took her hand, and she pulled him to his feet. "Verity, are you sure this is a good idea?"

She tugged him toward the doors.

Dare found himself leaning back, away from the office. "Our last conversation didn't end on the best terms." Dread settled in the pit of his stomach.

Verity hadn't let go of his hand yet. She raised her fist and knocked on the door. The metal rap echoed through the empty hall. "I know." She gave his hand a gentle squeeze before finally releasing it. "But you're a Warden now. It'll be different."

Dare hoped she was right.

"Enter," a powerful voice boomed from the other side of the door. Dare swallowed his unease as Verity pushed open the heavy doors and stepped inside. He followed.

He would follow her through the Black Gates themselves if he had to.

Cairn's office was largely what Dare had expected from a man like the commander. A massive table in the center with maps and parchments spread out across it was the only remotely messy area in the whole room, and clearly only because it got plenty of use. Everything else was neat and orderly—the bookshelves lining the walls, the desk on the far side of the room with its organized stacks of books and papers, quills in a line beside bottles of ink. High Commander Cairn sat at his desk, studying some documents, but he looked up as they entered.

Cairn's attention immediately fell on Verity, and he rose. He was wearing a gray shirt tucked into dark brown pants, and a brown leather belt with a loop for a sword. The sword, Dare noted, was leaning against the side of the desk, just within arm's reach of the commander.

Verity straightened and saluted, her closed fist over her heart. "Commander Cairn," she said formally.

Cairn crossed the room in three long strides and gathered Verity up into his massive arms.

That surprised Dare, who stood a few paces behind and suddenly felt very much like he was intruding again.

Verity returned the hug and stepped back as Cairn set his hands on her shoulders. "Welcome home, Warden Corallan," he said. "You have my condolences for the loss of Warden Serah. Drystan was . . ." The man sighed heavily. "He was an outstanding Warden and a better friend."

Dare couldn't see the expression on Verity's face, but she nodded. "He was," she said gently. "Thank you, Commander."

As though noticing him for the first time, Commander Cairn's attention landed on Dare. His face lost all its warmth, and his arms fell stiffly to his sides.

Verity moved back, gesturing to Dare. "Commander, this is—"

"I remember," Cairn said brusquely. "The mercenary."

Dare bit his tongue, but he shoved his hands in his pockets and let a casual slouch slide into his shoulders as he met Cairn's eyes with a level gaze.

Verity shot Dare a look that said *play nice*, which Dare thought was rather unfair, considering her commander was the one giving him a stare-down.

"Commander," Verity said, doing her best to interrupt the staring contest. "I trust you received the letters I sent. Dare's a Warden now."

Cairn crossed his arms. "That remains to be seen."

Inwardly, Dare bristled but didn't let it show on his face. He wouldn't give the commander the satisfaction.

Verity looked between the two of them. "I gave him the oath myself," she said, a lilt of confusion slipping in for just a moment before she pulled it back. "All respect, Commander, Dare *is* a Warden."

"I understand that you swore him into the order," Cairn said to Verity. "But that doesn't make him a true Warden." He looked back at Dare. "Where do your allegiances lie? There can be no question, no doubt, as to where your loyalty falls when the situation is dire. Will you uphold peace? Justice? Neutrality? Or will you take the easy road and follow the coin?"

"Sir—" Verity began, but Dare stopped her.

"I'm no longer commissioned with the Crimson Brothers," Dare said. It was the first time he'd said the words aloud and was grateful his voice remained steady. "You have no reason to doubt my loyalties."

"Ah," Cairn said, taking the measure of him. "They cut you loose, did they?"

Dare's back stiffened.

"Well, you'll need to prove yourself if you expect to have a place here. Trust when I say that I will watch your progress with great interest. If you so much as set a toe out of line, I will personally see to it that your brand is removed and you're extricated from the order."

As they regarded each other, Dare seethed.

Cairn's eyes narrowed on him. "Is that understood, *Warden*?"

Dare gave a sloppy salute, leaving one hand in his pocket. "Absolutely."

"*Commander*," Cairn prompted.

Dare's grin was dangerously close to becoming a sneer as he straightened, gave a proper salute as he'd seen Verity do it, and said, "Absolutely, *Commander*."

Apparently satisfied, Cairn turned toward his desk. "I assume you just arrived in the city?" he asked, addressing Verity this time.

"Yes, sir," she said.

"Go to your quarters and clean up. Rest for the night. We can meet in the morning for your debrief."

"But sir, I—" Verity silenced herself as Cairn's brows raised. "Yes, sir."

Cairn's tone softened, frustratingly so, as he said, "Verity, I know you want to provide your report and get back to work. And you will. But take some time. Rest for a moment. We'll speak tomorrow, first thing." Cairn looked between the two of them before he added, "We're short on available quarters, right now. Why don't you put him in Warden Serah's room for the time being, until I can find a proper place for him?"

Dare's aloof demeanor slipped. "I couldn't—" he began at the same time that Verity's mouth fell open with an urgent, "Sir, I—"

"Dismissed," Cairn barked, returning to his chair without another look.

Verity saluted again, catching Dare's eye as she passed him and headed toward the door.

Dare kept silent as Verity led him back across the courtyard to the long building that apparently served as the Wardens' barracks. She ushered him inside. There was a small room that looked something like a front office, with a kindly older man sitting behind a desk and lots of papers and parchments scattered around him in a far more cluttered manner than Cairn's office. Verity stepped inside, but with her, the older man, and the desk, there was little room for anything else.

Dare stood in the hallway, his mind rushing and reeling with conflicting thoughts. How dare Cairn assume the worst of him yet again, but also, what the fuck was he even doing here? Who was he trying to fool?

Verity returned quickly and gestured for Dare to follow up a set of stairs and down a long hall lined with doors. She unlocked one of them and took a decisive breath before she turned the latch and pushed the door open.

The room was small, though not as small as Dare had expected. There was a narrow bed against one wall with a heavy, moss-green blanket tucked neatly around three sides; a short dresser; a chest at the foot of the bed; and a small writing desk with a single, hard-backed chair. On top of the desk were a few papers at haphazard angles and a quill left beside a page that looked about half filled with a tidy script. On the dresser stood a line of books, all worn covers and creased spines. They were perfectly arranged in a neat and orderly row, except for one narrow gap, just wide enough for a single book.

Dare crossed to the dresser as Verity stepped to the side of the door. Dare's fingers ran along the line of books, brushing lightly across the leather of the volumes. He paused at one with a faded blue cover, remembering his conversation with Drystan in the Snapdragon so many months ago, when he'd returned it to him along with one other. It felt like another life entirely.

Another memory flashed through his mind, of his friend turning to dust and drifting through the Black Gates of Death. Dare's eyes burned.

"He always loved to read," Verity said, suddenly beside him. She looked at the line of books. "When I first came to the Wardens, I . . . couldn't do anything, really. I'd just lost my arms and had some other broken bones. All I could do was lay on this cot they had for me in a little tent. I just lay there, for days on end. And Drystan . . . he would come visit me, and he would read to me. He would find a book somewhere in that blasted Warden's camp, and he would come and sit beside my cot and read. Or if he couldn't find a book, he would tell me stories." She chuckled softly. "And they would always have these *terrible* endings.

"But I remember when he first started visiting, I used to wish he wouldn't. I just wanted him to leave me to my despair. I didn't talk to him—didn't talk to *anyone* for weeks. I had nothing left, and I thought my life was over. I wanted to die. I wondered, who is this boy who's taking pity on some poor, scrawny, helpless girl? But then, after a while, I realized it wasn't pity. I realized he needed it just as much as I did." Verity wiped a tear from her cheek as she finally turned to Dare. "Did he ever tell you his story?"

Dare shook his head. "No. He said he would someday, but . . ."

She nodded as she crossed slowly to the bed. She sat on the corner. "Have you ever heard of Phillip Kalon?"

Dare leaned back against the dresser, folding his arms over his chest. "Of course." With the circles he ran in while he was in Valda, it was hard not to know the name. The man was practically a legend. "He's one of the greatest thieves of all time. Runs a crew somewhere in Weryn, if I recall."

"He does. Or did, at least. Drystan was part of his crew."

After Dare picked his jaw up off the floor, he managed to form words again. "Drystan ran in Phillip Kalon's crew? Vire's fucking hells, how'd he get caught up in that?"

"Pretty easily, to be honest. Kalon was Drystan's father."

"You're shitting me."

Verity shook her head. "They had a job that went wrong, and Drystan got caught. The soldiers that caught him shattered his knee so he couldn't run away. They beat him, nearly killed him."

She took a breath, but her voice cracked as she continued, "He was about to be hanged, but Warden Sylus stepped in. She saw something in him . . . Thought he deserved a second chance. So she conscripted him right there and brought him to that camp. One of the Wardens at the time was a devout of Ainam and managed to work a miracle of healing magic on him. They were able to repair his knee, but it was incredibly painful, and he had to learn to walk again. That's when he would come see me. When he'd just been through hell, he would come to my tent and read to me."

Dare watched her. He had hardly dared to breathe while she spoke, lest she remember he was there. What could he say? *I'm sorry* seemed pathetic, but *I understand* felt like a damned lie.

"I know I didn't know him nearly as well as you, Verity," he said after a time, moving to sit beside her on the bed. He pressed his hands together between his knees. "But he always treated me kindly, even when we first met. He was probably the most genuinely kind person I ever had the good fortune to meet. And if *I'm* feeling the weight of his loss, I don't think I can imagine what you must be feeling."

She didn't look at him; she just stared across the room at the row of books with the gap that marked one missing volume. One absence. One loss.

"I don't need to sleep here," Dare said. "In this room. This is his, and I . . . I can sleep in town."

"It isn't safe."

"Then I'll go to the embassy with the others," he said. "I'm sure Caelan would—"

Verity turned to him then, her eyes rimmed with the silver of tears threatening to fall. That stopped him from saying anything more.

"Stay, please," she said. "My room is right there." She nodded to the wall behind the dresser. "It . . . It won't feel right to know that it's empty." Verity grabbed Dare's hand in hers and gripped it tightly. "Please. I would be honored if you would stay."

Dare's heart lurched in his chest, but he drew Verity's hand up to his lips and set a soft kiss upon her knuckles. "As you wish, my lady Warden."

THAT NIGHT, VERITY COULDN'T sleep. In some ways it was nice to be back in Whitehollow, back in her own room in the Wardens' barracks, but to be back here without Drystan felt wrong.

She tossed and turned for a few hours before getting up and lighting the small lamp on her desk. If she couldn't sleep, she could at least take care of some things. Verity sat down and jotted a few quick missives—one to Gregor and Finn, letting them know that she and Dare would meet up with them at the Drahkonian embassy tomorrow afternoon, one to Chancellor Caelan asking for a meeting to discuss the upcoming committee hearings, and one to Dare instructing him to meet her at the training circle closest to the brazier at the ninth chime. That should give her enough time to provide Cairn with her report and meet Dare there.

Although she had originally wanted Dare with her when she gave her report to Cairn, after the tension of yesterday's meeting, she thought giving them a reprieve from each other might be a good idea. She mumbled the incantation for the Sending spell three times, one for each note, and sent them along to their destinations.

When she finished with the notes, she took out a new sheet of paper and wrote another name as the salutation at the top of the page.

Drystan, the pen scrawled. Verity wrote as though she were writing to him, updating him on all the events of the last several months. She wrote about swearing Dare into the Wardens, and how she thought Drystan would be proud of him. She wrote about becoming the Chosen of Pyrannis, and how she knew he'd appreciate the irony. And she wrote about Finn and Gregor and Jae and Lucien.

I wish you'd had the chance to meet them. I think you'd love them all. Especially Finn. She's an archer, like you.

When she was done, she stared at the note, at the spots where the ink smeared and bubbled on the page where her tears had landed.

She signed it, *I miss you. V.*

Verity picked up the pages and, as the sky lightened through her narrow window, she summoned a spark of flame to her fingertips, setting the whole thing alight.

Verity entered the commander's office just before the eighth chime. High Commander Cairn was standing at the central table, already poring over some maps, though he glanced up as she entered. "Warden Corallan, excellent. I need to update you on what's been happening to the north."

The Wilds. She'd been away from this part of the continent for so long, and news from the Wilds was slower to make its way south to Drahkonia. "What's been happening?"

Cairn gestured her over to the table. "It's the shifters. They'd started mobilizing when you left, and then they began raiding towns along the fringes, but they've considerably upped the ante." He tapped a spot where several black markers had collected on the map. "Our latest reports have shown them gathering in even larger numbers here, due north of Valda. We intercepted some communications a week ago that suggests they're planning to move on the city."

"They're planning an attack?" Verity asked, staring at the map, forcing her eyes to stay focused on the Wilds and not drift south and east to the Crescent Mountains, or further south still, to Brookshire. Or to Southreach, where Lucien and Jae had stayed behind. She shook her head, bringing her thoughts back to the present. "On Valda? Sir, wouldn't that be suicide? The city guard is practically an army."

"That may be true, but these beasts are savage monsters. Any one of them can kill at least a dozen men if given half a chance."

Verity tensed, sliding her hands behind her back so the commander wouldn't see her tightening grip. If they were *mobilizing*, didn't that confer a measure of intelligence to their actions? She was ashamed she'd never made the connection before. Lucien was no monster, no savage beast. She had to believe that there were others like him, too. Others who had managed, somehow, to maintain their humanity.

"We've set up a camp just outside Lostward, and we have Wardens all along the borders of the Wilds, trying to help the impacted villages," Cairn continued. "But this rumor that they're planning to move against Valda is concerning to say the least. I've sent Warden Sylus to speak with the Council and get their assessment of the situation. Our missives are being given the runaround by their clerks, and I want answers regarding the severity of this threat."

He studied the map for another moment. "If these monsters were to make it into the city, the devastation they'd wreak would be catastrophic, considering what they've been doing along the border towns."

Something in his tone made Verity's ears prick. "What they've been doing?" she asked.

Cairn's brows rose. "You haven't heard? I thought that part was old news by now."

She shook her head. "Heard what, sir? I thought they were leading raids on the villages along the edge of the Wilds."

"Not just raids," Cairn said, his face darkening into a glower. "They're not just killing people. They're turning them."

Verity's stomach clenched into a knot. "Turning them? Sir, you're saying they're—"

"Making more shifters. Yes."

"Have they turned any Wardens?" Verity forced herself to ask. She wasn't sure she wanted to know the answer.

Scratching at his beard, Cairn straightened from the map. "Two. Wardens Elian and Sorrun, according to the most recent reports."

Verity's fists clenched at her sides. She knew them. Nathalie Elian and Mattias Sorrun. They were good Wardens. They'd been partners the way she and Drystan had been.

"Are there any plans to rescue them?" she asked.

"Rescue them?" Cairn's brows rose. "From what? Their own diseased blood?"

She stiffened. Her mind darted to Lucien. What must he have gone through to become the man she now counted among her family? "I . . . Sorry, I just mean . . . Has anyone tried to make contact with them?"

"They're gone, Verity." He rounded the table toward her, giving her his full attention. "I know they were our brothers," he said, his voice going gentle. "And their loss is felt throughout the ranks, much like Drystan's is. I'm sorry this is news I have to give you so soon." He studied her for a moment. "Are you sure you're feeling ready to return to your duties?"

She couldn't tell Cairn about Lucien, about her suspicion that others must be capable of the same. Perhaps once this business with the trial was over, Verity could ask Lucien for help. Maybe she could travel to the Wilds herself and see if she could find them. Maybe there was hope for them, or for others who'd been turned. But that was a problem for later, so she pushed the thought from her mind. Right now, she needed to focus on the task at hand.

She gave Cairn a sharp nod. "Sorry, sir. I'm fine. Truly."

One of his rare smiles flashed across his face for just a moment before he returned to the far side of the table. "As for the other reason you're here this morning," he said, his expression stern, "are you prepared to give your report, Warden Corallan?"

"Yes, sir."

"Excellent. I read the reports you sent from Taernfane and forwarded them to Lorekeeper Harrow, to keep her up-to-date. I'd like your full, unbiased account of the events that transpired after you left Whitehollow with Warden Serah, the mercenary, and the boy, Solace."

Verity spoke on the events as best she could, taking care to highlight Drystan's and Solace's bravery, as well as the many contributions from Finn and Dare.

She hesitated for a moment when she came to the events in Brookshire. She hadn't written much about that part of the journey in her reports home, focusing mostly on Drystan and Solace, and the awakening of the gods, including her being Chosen by Pyrannis. She hadn't written about any of the others, though.

Back in Taernfane, the four of them who'd been Chosen had all agreed to keep it a secret for now, telling only King Dominic the full story. Verity petitioned the group to let her tell Commander Cairn as well, and in the end, they'd agreed—but only that she could include notes about herself. They asked her to keep the other three out of the written messages for the time being.

Drystan's voice drifted into her mind. A memory of something he'd always tell her whenever she'd muck things up by telling too much of the truth. *You don't have to lie. Just don't tell them everything.*

As she gave the details to Cairn, she left out Jae and Lucien entirely, not because they hadn't been critical to the mission, but because she was worried she would have to explain too much about Lucien. Given everything that was happening in the Wilds and Cairn's reaction to the shifters, she couldn't bear the thought of divulging Lucien's secret and betraying his trust. She kept the other Chosen a secret for now. A Warden of the Flame being Chosen by Pyrannis after his awakening made sense, theologically speaking. There was no reason to assume any of the other gods had done the same.

Cairn had returned to his desk part way through, jotting a few notes on a scrap of paper as Verity spoke. He asked a few clarifying questions, especially about her conversation with Pyrannis in the courtyard. By the end of her tale, he scribbled something else down on the paper and underlined it.

"Thank you, Verity," he said. "Your perseverance in the face of such a challenging mission is commendable."

Verity saluted, grateful to be through with having to withhold information. Her skin was hot and clammy, and she wanted nothing more than some fresh air.

"I do, however," Cairn continued, "need to ask you for additional details on one particular area. I'd like to discuss the mercenary and why you saw fit to swear him in as a Warden of the Flame." Cairn circled the desk, crossing his arms over his chest as he leaned back against the edge. "You know how serious the Wardens' oath is. I don't need to lecture you on the importance—on the sanctity—of that vow."

Verity's back straightened, defensiveness tightening her muscles. "No, sir. Dare was being held captive, and we needed him to complete the mission, to get Solace to Taernfane. It was the only way we could get him out without—"

"Without interfering?" One thick eyebrow arched at the question. "Swearing him into the Wardens to get him out of jail seems awfully close to interfering as it stands."

"He wasn't in jail, sir," she said quickly. "He was being held unlawfully."

"By whom?"

"Sir, we needed him to complete the mission."

"Why did you need him? What skills did he bring to the mission that you were lacking?"

Verity swallowed. She'd justified her actions in Brookshire by saying that they'd needed him, but in truth . . . ? "He was a member of our team, and I wasn't going to leave him behind. Not when he was being held against his will."

Cairn nodded. "Held by whom?" he asked again.

"Duke and Duchess Wilhaven."

"His parents."

"Yes."

"You intentionally blocked Duke Wilhaven from being able to name his own son as his successor."

"Dare didn't *want* to be his father's successor," Verity said, her voice rising.

"That was not your decision to make." He matched her volume as his dark eyes narrowed.

"Shouldn't it have been Dare's?"

"That may be," Cairn conceded, "but that was for him to sort out with the duke and duchess."

"They weren't going to let him sort anything out," Verity said. Her jaw ticked as her temper flared. This was ridiculous. Cairn hadn't been in Brookshire. He hadn't seen what the duke and duchess were like. How they'd abused Dare. Neglected him. "They locked him in the dungeon they have in the basement of their manor. A dungeon! How rational do you think these people are that they could do that to their own son? He was *trapped* there. I couldn't just walk away!"

"It was not your concern, Warden Corallan," Cairn snapped. "Are you sure you weren't just looking to replace—"

Verity staggered back, even as he bit off the words before he finished the thought.

But Verity knew what he'd been about to suggest. Rage burned within her. How could he even think that? She took a deep breath as she straightened, pulling herself up to her full height, standing at attention.

"Commander Cairn," she said, her tone slow and measured, rigid. "Sir. Regardless of your personal feelings toward him or the timing of his oath, Dare has demonstrated all the virtues of a Warden of the Flame. He has been selfless, just, and he has protected those weaker than himself. The world is a better place, a safer place, because he walks in it. You know what this order—this *oath*—means to me. After all my years as a Warden under your command, do you honestly think that I would *ever* swear someone into the order who didn't deserve it? Someone who hadn't *earned* it?" Verity raised her chin. "And I would request that you show me the respect of not suggesting I swore Dare into the Wardens because I wanted to replace my best friend who'd just been killed. I think I've earned as much."

Cairn watched her carefully, though he kept his mouth clamped shut.

Through the window, the ninth chime echoed across the base. If she spent one more moment in this room, she was going to scream.

"Am I dismissed, sir?"

He nodded. Verity ignored the tightened, pained expression on his face, leaving without another word passing between the two of them.

She sped out of Cairn's office. She needed to get outside. Her blood was ready to boil in her veins.

Outside the building, Dare perched on one of the stone steps, rolling a coin over his knuckles.

"What are you doing here?" she barked, hardly slowing as she passed him.

Dare's footsteps crunched on the gravel path as he jogged to catch up to her. "Waiting for you."

"I told you to meet me in the training yard."

"Yeah," Dare said, coming up alongside her. "And when you weren't there, I came looking. One of the pages said he saw you go into Cairn's office. So I waited for you."

"It's barely the ninth chime."

"And you're always early."

Verity felt him watching her as they walked.

She was grateful Dare had decided to wait outside rather than in the hall by the commander's office. She didn't want to think about him overhearing that conversation.

Even the thought of what Cairn had implied caused her hands to clench into fists.

"Verity, did something—"

"It's nothing," she said, taking a deep breath to steady herself. It *was* nothing. Cairn didn't know what he was talking about. Not this time. "Let's just get to the training yard. We have a lot of work to do."

They walked in silence until the empty training circles came into view.

"What fresh hell do you have for me today, my lady Warden?" Dare asked, though Verity could hear the smile in his voice. "More punching drills? Running in circles?"

"Breathing," she said. It would be the first part in trying to teach him to meditate, and she had to admit she could use some of it herself at this point.

"I already know how to breathe," he groaned, and it nearly had her wheeling on him in frustration.

She managed to contain it, pinching the bridge of her nose instead. "This is the first step in controlling your abilities," she said, swallowing her irritation. "You've got to be able to focus and clear your mind in order to work with magic at all. If you can't meditate, you're not going to have any luck.

"Magic?" The humor in Dare's voice faded, replaced by a nervous trepidation. "We're starting today? Now?"

"I see no reason to delay," she said. "You have something else to do?"

Dare sighed. "Fair enough. But out here?"

She threw her arms out to the side. "There are distractions everywhere, and the yard is quieter now than it usually is. You've got to be able to concentrate no matter where you are, regardless of whatever else is going on around you."

Verity crossed toward the center of the thirty-foot ring. "You said you wanted me to teach you," she said, looking back at him where he stood at the edge of the circle, his shoulders hunched. She gestured to the space around her. "This is how I teach you." She nodded toward the chalk line that marked the edge of the circle. "You're either in or you're out, Dare. Make your choice."

CHAPTER 29

DARE STOOD AT THE edge of the circle, staring down at the scuffed line of white at his feet. In or out. Those were his choices. He was either going to trust Verity to teach him magic, or he wasn't. He was either going to be a Warden, or he wasn't. He couldn't stand on the line forever, waiting for someone else to push him one way or the other. He needed to take the step. Make the choice.

Verity looked stressed, with lines etched across her forehead and around her mouth. The conversation with Cairn was certainly to blame, and he could understand why.

Dare had been looking for Verity, and the page had pointed him toward Cairn's office. And Dare had entered the building and jogged down the hall until he'd come to the familiar bench. And he'd been about to sit down to wait when he heard the argument through the door.

"I wasn't going to leave him behind. Not when he was being held against his will."

Dare had wondered briefly, foolishly, if she was talking about Solace. But the rest of the argument dissuaded him of that thought. He'd listened as Verity defended her decision to swear Dare into the Wardens.

And then: *"Are you sure you weren't just looking to replace—"*

The words had been a punch in the gut through the closed door. Dare had almost left in that moment, but he couldn't deny that the question had been skirting around the edge of his own mind whenever he'd found himself with too much time to think. He'd pushed the thoughts away whenever they'd started to intrude, assuring himself he was being foolish to even consider such a thing . . .

But Cairn suspected it as well. And if the thought had occurred to him, who else had thought of it?

The silence that followed the question had Dare's palms sweating, but then Verity's answer had floated through the door, calm and even, if a bit sharp.

She'd defended him. Not just her decision, but *him*.

"The world is a better place, a safer place, because he walks in it."

Verity's words—the strength and certainty in them—had steadied something in Dare's chest. He'd turned it over in his mind as he'd hurried back to the steps at the front of the building. He'd barely gotten his coin out to roll over his knuckles by the time Verity stormed past.

Dare hadn't expected Verity to start his training so soon. But here he was, and regardless of whether she'd made him a Warden as a replacement for Drystan, Dare was sure as all hells standing in his shadow. Dare needed to try to do the right thing. Verity trusted him. More than that, she believed in him. Maybe he could earn the faith that she placed in him. Maybe he could live up to Drystan's memory somehow.

Dare stepped into the training ring and crossed to Verity. "Alright," he said. "Tell me what I need to do."

"Remind me again why I let you talk me into this," Dare grumbled. They sat in the center of the empty training ring, where they'd been for the last three hours. He was pretty sure his ass had fallen asleep.

Verity shushed him without opening her eyes. "Concentrate on your breathing," she said sternly. "And close your eyes."

Dare sighed. How she knew he was distracted and staring off at different parts of the compound was beyond him. He closed his eyes as instructed.

"Now focus on your breathing," she said again. "If you get distracted—"

"Acknowledge the feeling and move on," he recited back.

"Good, so you *are* listening."

Dare smirked. "You're distracting me, my lady Warden."

"So acknowledge it and move on," she said, and he could hear her own grin. "And stop smirking."

Dare laughed, but then pulled his focus back inward, relaxing into his breathing. He paid attention to the slow in and out of his breath as she'd been teaching him over the last few hours. How his chest expanded—no, that was wrong, he was supposed to be breathing lower, from his gut. He tried again, felt the expansion of his stomach as he breathed deep. Dare rolled his shoulders and shifted his legs, trying to get comfortable, but he found his focus returned more quickly to his breathing. Minutes passed.

"Keep focusing," she said, distracting him again. "Picture your breath as flowing in and out of your body."

"Verity, if you keep—" But a sudden jolt snapped his eyes open, and he yelped. Verity was looking at him, her hand still extended where she'd touched his forearm. "What the fucking shit, Verity?"

"You have to be able to remain focused, despite distractions." She paused for a moment before adding, "Magical or otherwise."

"Can you warn me next time?"

"If I warned you, that would defeat the purpose."

Dare sighed.

"Try again," she instructed. "Close your eyes."

With a groan of displeasure, Dare obeyed. Soon he felt something on his arm again. This time it was less of a sharp shock and more of a persistent tingle. An itch.

"Remember," Verity said calmly, "focus on your breathing. Picture your—"

"I know," Dare interrupted. "Picture my breath . . ." The itch on his arm was turning into a sting. He grimaced.

"Concentrate," she insisted. "Acknowledge the feeling and picture the discomfort flowing out of your body with your breath."

Dare breathed in deeply. The stinging grew sharper, but he tried to picture it as an insect sitting on his forearm, biting him. When he exhaled, he imagined his breath blowing at the little bug, shooing it away.

To his surprise, the discomfort lessened, albeit only slightly. He tried again. Again. Again. By the fifth cycle, the pain was barely more than a mild irritation on his forearm, easily ignored.

"Warden Corallan!"

Dare opened his eyes at the shout, and the annoying stinging turned into a thousand needles all stabbing into his skin. "Fuck." He yanked his arm away from Verity.

He expected to be chided for losing his focus, but to his surprise, she smiled at him. "That was good." She folded her legs beneath her and rose gracefully, turning toward the young Warden who had called her name. "Jonah," she said, a cheerful lilt in her tone. "What a surprise. How are you?"

"I'm well, Warden," the young man said. "Thank you." He cleared his throat, toeing the ground with the edge of his boot. "I'm sorry to interrupt, but I wanted to . . . that is . . . I was sorry to hear about Warden Serah."

"Thank you," Verity said, though her voice tightened. It was subtle, but it was there. Dare doubted the young Warden would even notice her discomfort.

Still rubbing at his arm, Dare rose and turned to the man. He was young—probably in his early twenties if he had to guess. His dark hair was cut short. Dare suspected from his tall, lithe build that the Warden would be fast and light on his feet.

As he stood, Verity gestured to him. "Jonah, this is Dare. He's a new recruit."

Dare arched a brow at this description but kept silent. He'd rib Verity for it later.

"Jonah Ashcroft," the young man said, extending his hand. "Nice to meet you, Warden . . . *Dare* . . . ?" Clearly he wasn't sure if *Dare* was his given name or his surname.

Beside him, Verity cleared her throat. "It's, um . . ."

But Dare simply smiled and took the young man's hand in his own. "Wilhaven," he said. "Dare Wilhaven."

Verity tried and failed to fully hide her surprise.

Jonah nodded, shaking his hand firmly. "Warden Wilhaven. A pleasure. Have you been with us long? I don't recall seeing you at training."

"They have you training the recruits now?" Verity asked.

Jonah ran a hand through his hair and grinned somewhat sheepishly. "Sword fighting," he said. "They called the master-at-arms out to the Wilds three weeks ago."

"Oh." Something flickered across Verity's face for a moment, but then her smile renewed itself. "Well, if he can't be here to train the littles, I can think of no one better."

Color flooded the man's cheeks. "Thank you, Warden. That means a lot coming from you." Jonah cleared his throat and gave them both a quick nod. "Again, sorry to intrude. I'll let you get back to your training." He turned with a wave and darted across the yard.

When Dare turned to Verity, she was watching him. "You're alright using your family name?" she asked, her brows drawing together.

He hated when she looked worried for him. He waved a dismissive hand. "At this point, I think the damage has been done. Besides, I'm no longer in hiding so much as I'm now a lord living in exile." He straightened, adjusting the collar of his shirt and puffing out his chest. "That persona should suit me rather well, don't you think?"

Verity gave a firm backhand to his stomach, knocking half the air out of his lungs with a loud puff. "I think you'd better stick to *irritatingly charming scoundrel.*"

Dare, deflated, perked up again. "You think I'm charming?" He winked as she rolled her eyes.

"Don't you think it might anger your parents, though?"

"Honestly, I don't hate the idea of annoying them from a distance. Seems like the least I could do."

Verity let out a quiet snort before gesturing to the ring. "Let's call it for now," she said. "We can pick it up again tomorrow."

That caught him off guard. He expected another hour of this, at least. "Really? Didn't you want me to try that again?"

Verity shook her head. "Not today," she said. "You did great."

He blinked. "Really?"

Verity chuckled at the shock in his voice. "Yes, really. Why is that hard to believe?"

Dare looked at the ground where they'd been sitting. "I don't know," he mumbled, rubbing at the back of his neck. "I thought I kind of fucked that last one up. That little sting got bad when I slipped up. I figured I just made it worse when I got distracted."

Verity stared at him, her mouth open. "Are you joking?" she asked. "I was slowly increasing the power on the spell while you were focusing," she said. "I couldn't drop it fast enough when Jonah interrupted, but you stayed calm and focused through . . . well, through nearly as much magic as when I cast that Banishment spell through you back in Westhold. Even after you got distracted, you stayed calm. I remember that much power laying you out flat last time."

It had. It had knocked him on his ass, and he hadn't been able to feel his fingers for minutes afterward.

Dare flexed his hand, everything moving as it should. "It's you who's joking now, right?" he asked. "It's not nice to toy with my emotions like that, my lady Warden."

Verity shook her head again, her reddish-brown braid swaying where it hung over her shoulder. "Dare, I swear to you."

That couldn't be possible. He remembered clearly how it had felt that first time Verity had cast magic through him. The jolt of it, the lingering tremor in his hands, the numbness. Had he really just sat through nearly that much magic again and hardly noticed? Were these tricks Verity was trying to teach him actually working?

"Dare?"

He shook his head, focusing on her face. "Sorry, I just . . ." He had never imagined . . .

She set her hand on his arm. "Are you alright?"

"I . . ."

He had never dared to imagine a world where magic didn't hurt him. And if it didn't hurt him, what if . . .

"I'm fine," he said quickly, cutting off his own thoughts before they could spiral. "I think it was just more than I realized. You're right, we should call it for today."

Verity's lips tightened but she nodded and let her hand fall. "Alright. Do you want to head back to the barracks? Get some rest before we meet up with the others later?"

Dare slid his hands into his pockets and stared across the yard, toward the city on the other side of the long, gray stone wall. "I'm, uh . . . I'm going to head into town." His mind kept circling back to the feeling in his arm, the slight annoyance that had actually been a strong channel of magic.

Once, he reminded himself. *You did it once. That doesn't mean—*

"Dare, wait." Verity pressed her lips into a thin line. "You shouldn't go alone."

"I'm not going far," he said, angling himself toward the city. "I just . . . I need a few minutes. I'll meet you at the embassy later, alright?"

He thought for a moment that she might argue, but she only nodded. When she waved him farewell, she smiled, pure and genuine. "Good work today, Warden." She turned toward the barracks. "I'll see you later."

Dare nearly sprinted into town. There was only one person who would understand.

CHAPTER 30

Dare had no idea if Gregor would be busy when he got to the embassy, and he realized, as he bounded up the steps two at a time, that he didn't even know where Gregor would be in the expansive building. An old manor house toward the center of the city, it had been converted for use as the Drahkonian embassy some years ago.

He hesitated just inside the building's front door, his mind a maelstrom. He briefly considered just yelling for Gregor until he found him, but a door at the end of the hall opened, and a man appeared carrying a small tray tucked under his arm.

"Can I help you?" the man asked.

"I'm looking for Gregor Thalesen. He's here as a guest of Chancellor Caelan."

"Certainly, my lord. May I give him a name?"

"Oh, right. Yes, I'm—"

"Dare?"

Looking up, Dare spotted Gregor at the railing of the second-floor hall that overlooked the foyer. Dare hurried up the stairs as Gregor gave the man a wave of reassurance.

"Jashua, this is Warden Dare Wilhaven."

"Oh, of course, sir," Jashua replied. "Warden, you're welcome here at any time. Chancellor Caelan was very clear that the embassy is open to any member of your group."

"Thanks," Dare called over his shoulder, already most of the way up the stairs.

Gregor was barefoot, standing in the hallway in his crisp white shirt, though it was untucked and the top two buttons were undone. His glasses sat perched on the end of his nose.

"What's going on?" he asked, leading Dare to the first door just past the balcony.

Dare followed him, pacing the room as Gregor closed the door. He couldn't sit still. Not right now, not with so many thoughts and feelings swirling through him.

Gregor crossed the few steps to Dare and caught him by the forearms, stopping him. "What's happened?"

Dare wasn't even sure where to begin. He just knew that he was going to lose his calm any second, and he needed to be somewhere he could allow that to happen. And only Gregor would understand.

There were too many thoughts running through his mind, all vying for use of his mouth. "I—Verity and I, she—We were training, and it didn't—*Fuck*."

Gregor firmly guided Dare to the bed and set his hands on Dare's shoulders, pushing him to sit. "Breathe," he said, kneeling in front of him. "Start again."

Dare did as he instructed, breathing in deeply. The familiar scent of vanilla and citrus helped steady his racing thoughts. "You know Verity had this idea that she could work with me to make my Perception of magic less . . . shitty, right?"

The corner of Gregor's mouth tipped upward, the dimple appearing beneath his right eye. "Yes, I'd heard something about that."

Dare took another breath. "It worked," he said. He hadn't spoken that thought aloud yet, and he nearly choked on the words as they came out, half laugh, half sob. "I mean, mostly, and it was just the one time, but it worked. Gregor, it *worked*."

Gregor's smile broadened. He stood, pulling Dare up with him and into a fierce hug, enveloping him in the strangely pleasant magic of his own. "Darcy, that's wonderful. How do you feel about it?"

Dare stepped back from the embrace and dragged his fingers through his hair. "I don't know," he admitted. "I don't know how to feel. It's—gods, Gregor my mind is in seventeen places at once." He paced the small room again. "It's exciting, because it means . . . there are *so* many things it could mean! But also . . ." His breathing quickened as everything started to jumble and spiral again. Dare shook out his hands as he paced. "Also, it means that if I can do this now, I could have done it *then* too. What if I could have learned this before? What would it have been like . . . if I . . . could've . . . ?"

Gregor caught him in his pacing again, reeling him back in. "You can't do that," he said, his voice as calm as ever, but stern. "There's no way to know whether you could've learned as a child what Verity's teaching you now. You might have been too young to understand, or to grasp it. And you would have needed someone to teach you." Gregor raised his brows as if to say, *And who exactly do you think would have done that?* He slid his hands down Dare's arms until they held his fingers in their grip, firm and steady. "I believe you're learning this exactly when you're meant to."

When he was *meant to*, as though it was fated to be. That made more sense than Gregor could know or than Dare could truly wrap his mind around, and he thought he got the whisper of another touch, as a gentle caress that was somehow expansive enough to encompass worlds slipped down his back, but it was gone as soon as he turned his focus toward it.

"What did Verity say?" Gregor asked.

"Not much," Dare admitted. "I think she was surprised though. She said it was . . . a lot of magic." The idea still felt so different to him. Could this be real? He was getting ahead of himself. "Anyway, it was just once," he added. "Who knows if I'll even be able to do it again. Plus, it snapped as soon as I got distracted." He forced a laugh, trying to convince himself that this whole thing wasn't as world-shattering as it seemed. "It won't do me much good if I can't be doing or thinking about anything else for it to work."

Gregor released Dare's hands to cup his face, rising onto his toes to plant a kiss on Dare's forehead. "I know you'll be able to do it again," he said. "And it will only become easier with practice."

He was right. Dare set his hands on Gregor's waist. "Gods, what would I do without you?"

"Well, you had more than a decade to find out," Gregor said softly. "What's the answer?"

Dare closed his eyes, feeling the gentle thrum of Gregor's magic, breathing in the scent of him. "Nothing that wouldn't have been made better by having you with me."

Gregor's lips pressed against his, and Dare's heart fluttered in his chest.

"I'm happy for you, Darcy."

Finally approaching calm, Dare looked at Gregor—really looked at him. The untucked shirt, the disheveled hair, the dark circles under his eyes. "Aetherann's gusty ass, you look like you just woke up."

Gregor's eyes narrowed at the blaspheme for only a moment before a sheepishness overtook his expression. "I did," he said.

"It's after midday," Dare exclaimed. "Who are you and what have you done with Gregor?"

Gregor swatted at his chest, but it was a halfhearted attempt at playfulness. "I've been having some trouble sleeping since we left Taernfane," he admitted.

Oh. Had Dare really been so caught up in his own bullshit that he hadn't noticed Gregor wasn't sleeping? They hadn't been able to share a room on the ship, and last night was their first in Whitehollow and Dare had stayed at the Wardens' base, but still. He should have noticed. Were Gregor's nightmares getting worse and keeping him awake, or was something else bothering him?

Before Dare could ask more about it, Gregor rubbed his face, pushing his glasses on top of his head. "I'm alright," he said, though he sighed deeply.

Ainam's bollocks, Gregor always was a terrible liar.

"I'm just tired," Gregor went on. When he lowered his hands and with his glasses still on his head, a dullness clouded his ice-blue eyes, though the smile on his lips was genuine, the dimple reappearing. "I'm happy for you," he said again.

"Why don't you get some more rest?" Dare suggested, taking a step toward the door. "We have a couple hours before we're meeting with Verity and Finn."

Gregor nodded solemnly, like he was conceding defeat, but as Dare reached the door to leave, Gregor's hesitant voice stopped him.

"Would you stay?"

All at once, their argument from the day before stormed Dare's memory, and his face warmed with embarrassment that he hadn't remembered Gregor was angry with him before bursting in here with his own shit.

"Would you want me to?" Dare asked. "Are you still pissed?"

Gregor gave a one-shouldered shrug. "I'm still annoyed that you seem to care so little for your own safety," he said. "But I can be angry and still miss you." His mouth quirked to the side. "I can be *pissed*, as you said, and still want to be with you." Studying Dare for a moment, Gregor seemed to come to some sort of decision. "Besides, I have something for you." He crossed to the small chest at the foot of the bed and opened it, crouching to rummage around inside.

Dare's curiosity nudged him away from the door and closer to Gregor, who closed the trunk with something held within his fist. He extended his other hand to Dare. "Give me your hand."

Dare did as instructed, holding his palm open.

Gregor's face turned a flustered shade of pink as he pressed something cold and metal into Dare's palm. "I wasn't sure what to do with this," he said, not taking his hand away. "I thought maybe I should throw it away, but something made me hold onto it. And now, with what you accomplished today—"

"I didn't accomplish anything," Dare interrupted.

"But you did." Gregor squeezed Dare's hand between both of his, and the metal object warmed at their touch. "You took the first step. You opened a door you never thought you'd open, and you walked through it. And I think I held onto this so that I could give it to you."

He released Dare's hand then, and Dare found himself staring down at a small, iron key. But a key to what?

"That," Gregor continued, reading the confusion on Dare's face, "is the key to the dungeon beneath Wilhaven Manor."

Dare swallowed thickly, his palms beginning to sweat.

"I had it on me the day Verity came to get you out, when your father sent me to bring you before him. I don't know why, but I kept it in my pocket instead of returning it to the ring of household keys. Then a few days later, Tanithe—" His voice cracked and he cleared his throat before starting again. "I want you to have it. I want you to remember. I want you to remember that you escaped, that you got out. What you accomplished today—the door you opened with Verity—leads you forward. This key is to remind you not to look back, because no one can chain you down again."

When Dare finally tore his stinging eyes away from the key, his vision blurred.

"I'm sorry," Gregor blurted out, gathering Dare up in his arms. His fingers brushed the tears from Dare's cheeks, leaving little airy tingles of magic in their wake. "I didn't mean to—"

But Dare threw his arms around Gregor's neck, the key clutched tightly in his hand. The tears fell hard enough that his shoulders shook, but Gregor just held him tighter. "Thank you," Dare choked out.

Dare remained in Gregor's arms until the tears stopped and his breathing steadied. "Alright, alright," he said, pushing himself back and wiping his eyes with the heel of his hand. "I've kept you from sleeping for long enough." He pocketed the key and waved Gregor toward the bed. "Rest. I'll wake you before we have to be anywhere."

Gregor looked as though he might say something else, but he slumped into the bed in silence, setting his glasses on the small table and pulling the blanket over his shoulder. It wasn't long before his breathing slowed.

Dare slipped off his boots and climbed into the bed beside him, tucking his hands behind his head. After a while, he let his mind wander through memories of the time he'd spent with Gregor growing up in Wilhaven Manor. He hadn't known the word for it then, or even how to describe how it felt. But when he was in that cell beneath the manor, wondering whether Verity and Solace would leave Brookshire without him . . . Seeing Gregor again was like being reunited with a piece of himself he hadn't realized was missing.

Everything changed for Dare in that dungeon, but Gregor . . . he'd been the one constant through everything.

Beside him, Gregor stirred in his sleep.

Your mind wanders, Child.

Dare tensed as the voice of Tykaras drifted into his thoughts. *I was just meditating for hours,* he replied. *I figured I was overdue.*

Your memories, Tykaras continued, *seem like happy ones.*

Dare rolled his eyes. *Are you snooping?* he asked, his tone sharp. *Or was I shouting out my thoughts again?*

You seem bothered.

Yes, well, I am bothered.

There was a brief pause before Tykaras said, *That feels pointed.*

You disappear for months, leaving me to think that I've lost my mind. Then you just pop in whenever you feel like listening into my thoughts. Dare sighed and tried not to fidget. *It's bothersome.*

I do have other demands on my attention, Child.

So you keep saying.

Gregor rolled over, draping an arm over Dare's stomach, his head nestling into the crook of Dare's shoulder.

A twinge of shame flashed through him. Although he was still wrapping his mind around it, Dare needed to remember that this was a literal *god* he was dealing with. He was letting his frustrations get the better of him when he should be enjoying this quiet, peaceful time with Gregor.

You're right, Dare said. He set his arm around Gregor's shoulders, pulling him in closer. "Forgive me," he whispered, though whether it was to Tykaras or Gregor, he wasn't certain.

Gregor stirred again, eyes fluttering open. "Did you say something?"

Dare squeezed Gregor's shoulder. "Just talking to myself." In a manner, that was true.

There is nothing to forgive, Child.

Gregor pushed himself up onto his elbows, confusion flitting across his face. Then he shook his head as though clearing the last threads of a dream from it.

Dare wished he could do something more to help him. He was pale and drawn, a sorrowful version of the Gregor he knew. Dare couldn't even remember the last time he'd seen Gregor sketch anything.

Gregor angled his head toward Dare. Apprehension tightened the lines of his face as he said, "There was something I wanted to talk to you about."

Dare rolled onto his side, propping his head up on his hand. "Anything," he said.

At the same time, Tykaras said, *I will leave you in peace for now.*

Dare did his best to split his attention between the man lying beside him and the god in his head.

But remember, Tykaras continued, *that I am not beholden to you. Do you understand?*

Whatever Gregor had been about to say seemed to fade away as his pale blue eyes focused on Dare's face. A muscle ticked in his jaw. "Is something wrong?"

Yes. "No," Dare replied, one in his mind to Tykaras and the other aloud to Gregor.

We'll speak again later. There was a gentle farewell, like a hand gliding down his back, and then Tykaras was gone.

Gregor tensed. His brows furrowed. "Dare, is there anything you want to tell me?"

He gave his best smile. "Of course not," he said. And it was the truth—he didn't *want* to tell Gregor anything. Not yet. "But you said there was something you wanted to tell me?"

Gregor sat up, turning away from Dare, though in the afternoon sun that slanted through the window, his face had gone white, like he'd seen a ghost.

"I . . . think you should go," Gregor said.

"What?" Dare sat up. He couldn't have heard him right. Everything was fine—*good*, even. But now— "What's wrong?" He reached for Gregor's arm, but Gregor stood and moved toward the window, one hand rubbing at his temple.

"I'd like to be alone," he said, turning his back to Dare completely. "Please."

Dare stood. "Wait. You wanted to talk?" He wanted nothing more than to pull Gregor into his arms, as Gregor had done for him no more than an hour ago, but at his first step closer, Gregor flinched, drawing his arms in tighter. The motion froze Dare in place. "Gregor—"

"Forget I said anything," he said. "Please, Darcy . . . I need . . ." He sighed, bowing his head toward the window. "Please just go."

Dare's chest tightened, but he nodded, even though Gregor's back was still to him. He tugged his boots on and hurried into the hall, closing the door behind him.

He heard the click of the lock before he was more than a few steps away.

CHAPTER 31

DARE HURRIED OUT OF the Drahkonian embassy and into the streets of Whitehollow. What had he done to upset Gregor this time?

There was at least an hour before Dare had to be back at the embassy for the meetings Verity had arranged. He already hadn't been looking forward to them, and now this.

They'd only just arrived in Whitehollow yesterday, dammit. Why was everything already so complicated?

Dare wandered the city, letting himself get lost in the flow of the crowds. He'd hardly had a chance to explore Whitehollow the last time he was here. Now seemed as good a time as any. Except, he remembered belatedly, for Verity's warning about not being in the city alone. Tanithe's whereabouts were still unknown, and with Whitehollow being so near to Valda, wandering the streets on his own wasn't a wise idea.

Still, Whitehollow was much smaller and safer than Valda, and Dare had been handling himself on those streets since he was eighteen. Whitehollow was tame by comparison. And certainly as long as he kept his wits about him, he'd be able to spot Tanithe before she spotted him.

The next corner he rounded put him at the edge of the market district, with several stalls and carts sprouting up between the permanent storefronts. One vendor called out to him, beckoning Dare over to her small handcart laden with trinkets, jewelry, and precious stones of all shapes and colors.

Aiming to pass her by, Dare dipped his head, ignoring her. But the woman waved her arm like she knew him, the flowing sleeve of her green dress sliding down around her elbow. "Shadows follow you, my friend."

Dare's attention snapped up. "What did you say?"

The woman gave an awkward laugh, her eyes darting to the side in confusion. "Um, I said *a fine day to you, my friend.*"

He shook his head. Damn, this shit with Tanithe was really getting to him. "Sorry," he mumbled, approaching her cart. The least he could do after acting so weird was look at her wares. "It's been a long day."

The woman smiled, her round face lighting up. She was petite with pale blond hair that was braided into a crown around her head, woven through with small pink and white blossoms. "I hear you there," she said.

Dare forced a friendly smile. "I like your flowers," he said with an upward nod.

"Thank you." She touched the delicate petals. "Honeysuckle and raspberry blossoms. They've always been some of my favorites."

Something tugged at the back of Dare's mind, something familiar, but whatever it was sat at the edge of his recollection. Pushing the feeling away, he browsed the assortment of trinkets. Perhaps there was something he could find for Gregor, to apologize for upsetting him, even if he wasn't quite sure what he was apologizing for. But Gregor had never been one for anything ostentatious.

"Do you have anything for someone who doesn't wear much jewelry?" he asked, rubbing a hand across the back of his neck.

The woman nodded sagely. "Oh, of course." She rummaged behind the cart for a moment before pulling out a small box. It opened on a hinge, and inside was a flat piece of wood carved in the shape of a bird. "It's a cloak pin," she said as Dare leaned forward to examine it. It had a beautiful light gold hue and was polished to a high shine.

"That's stunning," Dare said.

"It's ash wood. Some say it represents healing and life." She offered the little box to Dare, and as she reached across her cart, the sleeve of her dress slid up just enough to reveal a black leather bracelet. Etched into the wide band was an eight-pointed star.

Dare's hand paused as he reached for the box. He'd seen that bracelet before, but where?

Taernfane—the woman selling flowers had had the same bracelet. *The flowers . . .* She'd sold him flowers in Taernfane.

His eyes darted to the flowers woven into the jewelry vendor's hair. "Honeysuckle and raspberry blossoms," he murmured.

"What's that, my friend?" the woman asked. She still held the box out to him with the small wooden bird.

"Nothing." He took a step back though, stuffing his hands in his pockets. "I'll pass. Thanks anyway."

"Have a pleasant day, Warden," the woman said. She grinned as he hurried away.

Shadows follow you, the woman had said when she first saw him. At least, that's what he thought he'd heard. That crazy old man in Southport had said the same thing the night before they left. *Shadows follow you. Shadows and ash.*

Tanithe Ash. Shit. Dare wanted to kick himself for not making the connection sooner. She was fucking with him. Had she been in Taernfane after all? Was she in Whitehollow now? At the far edge of the market, Dare cast one last look back, finding the vendor easily through the crowds.

She was still watching him.

As their eyes met, the woman raised her hand, fluttering her fingers in a gentle farewell.

Dare turned and sped out of the market square.

By the time he got back to the embassy, it was nearly half an hour past when he was supposed to meet with Verity and the others. Despite the increased security at the embassy, Dare had taken a circuitous route back, making sure he wasn't followed. When he was escorted to the meeting room, Chancellor Caelan was there as well, and was currently explaining the structure of the hearings that were to take place.

Verity gave Dare a look that very clearly said *Where were you?*

Dare mouthed a silent *sorry* and joined the others at the elliptical table, taking the open seat between Finn and Gregor. Gregor sat with his back straight, hands in his lap, though one hand traced the scar around his wrist.

It was bad enough that Dare was seeing Tanithe around every corner, but Gregor had to deal with the physical reminder of her—of what she'd done to him—every day. The thought of it turned Dare's stomach. He owed Tanithe for hurting Gregor, for making him afraid. He would make sure she got what she deserved.

"Does that sound alright with you, Warden Wilhaven?"

Everyone was watching him.

Dare cleared his throat. "Sorry, what?"

Across the table, Verity rolled her eyes.

"I was saying," Caelan said smoothly, "that Miss Garrison and Mister Thalesen will give their testimony first, followed by you. Drahkonia and Valda have agreed to abide by the decision of the inquest committee. We want to make sure we put our best foot forward, and your testimony, Warden Wilhaven, is critical."

"Do we all have to testify?" Finn asked. "I mean, if Dare knows Tanithe was responsible and that she works for the Valdane Council, *and* his word as a Warden will be weighed so strongly, what could Gregor and I contribute?"

"The more people who can say she was there removes doubt," Gregor said softly, his voice flat. "One person, even a Warden, could be mistaken. But three people all saying the same thing will carry more weight."

Caelan nodded. "Exactly that. The less doubt we leave in the committee's minds, the better."

"That makes sense," Dare said. "Sure, that won't be a problem. When's all this supposed to take place, anyway?" He needed to make sure he told Verity about the oath he'd sworn sometime before the meetings. Even though he knew she'd be pissed for a while, the worst thing he could do would be to keep it from her. If she found out on her own that he'd lied under a Warden's oath, he'd never hear the end of it. At least this way, he could control the narrative and make sure she understood all the good that would come out of it. But it was definitely not the time for that conversation.

"Two weeks, if all goes smoothly, which honestly I don't expect. Not with Valda involved." Caelan turned his attention to Verity. "Has Commander Cairn discussed which Wardens he's selected for the hearing committee?"

"Not yet," Verity said.

The committee, it had been decided, would consist of three Wardens of the Flame, as well as Chancellor Caelan and a representative from Valda.

"Do you know who'll be speaking for Valda?" Dare asked.

Caelan referred to some notes stacked in front of him. "Nathanial Jorn."

Crossing his arms, Dare snorted. He'd met Magistrate Jorn only once while he was working for the Council.

"You know him?" Finn asked.

"Not well," Dare said. "But it figures they would pick him. Jorn is the one the Council calls in whenever they need an honest face. He's kept in the dark about all the Council's backhanded dealings. He's a dupe."

"Of course," Caelan said, pushing himself to his feet. He paced a small circle near his chair. "They don't need to ask someone to lie or keep a secret if they send someone who has no knowledge of the events."

Finn glanced quickly at Gregor before focusing on Caelan. "Is Tanithe Ash going to be there?" she asked.

Caelan sighed deeply. "Unfortunately, Drahkonia's agents have been unable to locate her since the attack."

Beside Dare, Gregor stiffened just slightly. Dare wanted to let them all know what had happened to him in the market, but he didn't want to upset Gregor any more than he already had. If he was staying at the embassy, he'd be safe, wouldn't he?

But he deserved to know.

"I think Tanithe might be in Whitehollow," Dare said. "Or, at least, her agents are. I think she's been following me since Taernfane." He described his encounters with the flower seller and the jewelry vendor, noting the bracelets they each wore with the eight-pointed star. He also described the old beggar in Southport and what he'd said about shadows and ash.

Caelan listened, though he looked to Verity at the end of the tale. The Warden was watching Dare, skepticism painted on her face, though she was trying to hide it. Pyrannis's flaming bollocks, hers was not a face made for subtlety.

"Dare, I appreciate your attentiveness while in the city, but . . . A bracelet and something about shadows—which you admit you might've misheard . . ." She bit her lip before saying, "That's not a lot to go on."

"It's not," he admitted. "And you thought the pirates were a coincidence. What about now?"

Finn leaned back in her chair. "He's got a point. One or two of these things might be a coincidence, but when you add them all up, something doesn't feel right."

"Say it is her," the chancellor said. "What's her goal? Attempted kidnapping aside, of course. But merchants in two different cities, and a beggar selling fortunes in a third—that's a fair amount of coordinated effort. For what?"

"To get to us," Gregor said. He was staring down at the table, and his thumb had resumed tracing the scar on his wrist. "To get into our heads."

Dare's chest ached, but— "Gregor's right," he said. "She's always loved fucking with me. She wants us off-balance, second-guessing everything we see or hear, wondering if it's her."

Caelan widened his circle around the table, though he paused beside Gregor and set a hand gently on his shoulder. "But to what end?" Caelan asked, looking at Dare. "Is she only interested in chaos for chaos's sake, or does she have a larger plan?" He squeezed Gregor's shoulder before leaning against the edge of the table, dropping his hands to his sides. "What's her angle?"

"She doesn't need an *angle,* Chancellor. You don't know her like I do." Dare ran his fingers through his hair. "This is one of Tanithe's mind games. I'm sure of it."

Caelan nodded. "That's fair. I'll request security at the embassy be heightened further," he said. "And although I'm in no position to require anything of any of you, may I recommend that no one ventures into the city alone?"

"Agreed," Verity said, and the look she sent Dare's way was entirely too pointed. "Pairs only, or with one of the Drahkonian guards or a Warden escort."

Despite the tension in the room, or perhaps because of it, Dare couldn't help himself. "I wasn't aware *that* was one of the Wardens' services now. Looks like I joined up at the right time."

Finn tried—and failed—to stifle a laugh, while Caelan chuckled. "Lucky you," he said with an amused grin.

Verity's expression, on the other hand, was less than amused. "I'm serious, Dare. No more wandering off on your own. If you're right and everything really does point to Tanithe being in Whitehollow, you're the one she's going to come after."

Dare sucked in a breath between his teeth.

"Drahkonia's case against Tanithe Ash and Valda relies on your testimony," she continued. "You're the one in her sights."

"Lovely," Dare said, slouching into his chair. "Thank you for the reminder."

Not like he could forget.

Chapter 32

The full moon shone bright overhead as Jae walked a lap around the western field. Lucien had been on edge all day, and she could guess why. Their week was almost up. They needed to journey back to the Red Forest, and the whole mess was about to drag Lucien away again. And it was only because of Jae's pushing that he was here in the first place . . . that he would have to leave his wife and daughter again, not knowing whether he'd be coming back.

Although Jae felt terrible that she'd practically forced him to come here, she ultimately wasn't sorry about it. Over the last few days, Lucien and Ethriel had seemed to fall into some old rhythm—though there was a tension there, like a pull between them they were both trying to resist. Faith was still angry, though at least she'd moved on to quietly sulking rather than actively baiting Lucien. Maybe Faith would stop acting like a child and give Lucien a chance, but it didn't seem likely to happen before they left for the Red Forest, and it was hardly Jae's place to say anything. Not that that would typically stop her, but this was Lucien's family. She owed it to him to bite her tongue.

And then there was Corvin Crosse. Jae still hadn't managed to wrap her head around him or his presence. If she and Lucien were leaving, that would leave Ethriel and Faith alone with Corvin. To be fair, it seemed clear that he'd been telling the truth about losing his connection to Ainam, and that he genuinely cared about helping Ethriel and Faith. But otherwise, he was a mystery. Even though Ethriel and Faith trusted him, that didn't mean Lucien and Jae did. They'd seen what he could do, after all.

A gentle breeze stirred the grass, causing it to sway and flutter. As her thoughts wandered much like her path through the fields, the moonlight brightened overhead. Jae tilted her face to the sky. She'd expected this. It had happened at the same time every month since she'd first heard the goddess's voice.

Good evening, said Lanara, goddess of water. *You have traveled far since last we spoke.*

Jae smiled. Talking to Lanara was always like talking to an old friend. *I have,* Jae answered. *And farther yet to go.* Jae recounted the events of the last month. She was never sure how much the goddess was aware of what was happening when her direct attention wasn't on Jae, and Lanara seemed to enjoy hearing things from Jae's perspective, with her colorful language and all.

I am certain my sister is grateful to have you helping her Chosen on his course, Lanara said when Jae finished her story.

Do you talk to each other much? Jae asked.

Lanara laughed, and the sound was like a stream rushing over river stones. *You are curious whether I know what Taerna wants her Chosen to do.*

I don't understand why Taerna's being so secretive, Jae admitted. *If she wants Lucien's help, why doesn't she just tell him what she needs him to do?*

The goddess was silent for a time. *There is a pond and there is a tidal wave,* she said. *How does the tidal wave fit within the pond without washing it away completely? Does the pond widen, deepen? Or does the wave distill down to what will fit in the pond? And in either case, how? I do not know the answer and, I suspect, neither does Taerna.*

Jae considered Lanara's words.

I do not know the workings of my siblings, Lanara went on. *We do speak sometimes, but we are as different from each other as . . .* The goddess hesitated, as though searching for an appropriate comparison.

As fire and water? Jae supplied.

Another bubbling laugh. *Yes, precisely.*

Jae continued her walk through the garden and field, pondering whether to ask the other question she had. Lanara was a goddess, after all. She likely had much more important things to attend to than Jae and her foolish questions.

You are my Chosen, Lanara said, sensing her thoughts. *You are special to me. Ask your question. I will answer if I can.*

Jae's heart warmed. *I've been practicing the powers you've gifted me,* she said slowly, thinking through precisely what she wanted to ask. *But I've noticed that I can sometimes feel the emotions of others even when I don't mean to. Why does that happen?*

Lanara hummed, the whisper of distant waves against the shore. *You remember what I told you about the ripples on a lake when you cast a stone?*

Yes. I cast my awareness out like a stone and can feel the ripples of others' emotions.

I did not explain fully. Your awareness is not truly the stone. Their emotions are the stone, and you are always standing on the edge of the lake. Some emotions are small; the ripples they make on the surface are small and only perceived when you look for them. But others, if they are strong enough, may reach you where you stand at the bank.

That explained some things, but not everything. *When I'm near Lucien,* Jae said, *it's like I can feel what he feels all the time. It's . . .* She knew the word she wanted, but it pained her heart to even think that about him.

Exhausting? Lanara asked.

Sighing, Jae bowed her head. *Yes.* Gods, being around Lucien had been so exhausting since this power awakened inside her.

You are more sensitive to the emotions of those whom you care about. It is as though your feet stand in the shallows of their ponds rather than on the shore. And in the case of your friend, whether it is the shifter in him or it is simply his nature, his waves swell higher than most. If you imagine a levee in your mind, you can block out all but the strongest of waves.

Jae closed her eyes, picturing a levee circling her.

Like this, Lanara said. In her mind's eye, the levee grew taller, more solid.

Jae practiced erecting the levee herself until Lanara's flowing voice approved.

Well done. That should help limit the flood of emotions from others when you do not wish to sense them. I have to attend to duties elsewhere, but we will speak again soon.

The compressing weight of Lanara's attention lifted, and Jae felt as though she were floating back to the surface of her own awareness after being deep underwater.

Jae spent a while yet outside, enjoying the light cast by the full moon. She made one last circle of the near field and was starting toward the cottage when a wave of emotion crashed over the levee she'd left up around her mind.

She gasped as her heart raced with a sudden, nearly overwhelming fear. Her eyes burned.

Where was it coming from? Jae spun once, scanning the expanse of the field for signs of anyone. Alone in the empty field, the next rush of panic nearly brought her to her knees, her vision blurring with tears as a deep sorrow joined the fear in her chest. She'd never felt anything this strong before, not even from—

Lucien.

He'd left hours ago for one of his evening runs. Had something happened to him? Was he hurt somewhere?

Jae took off across the field. It was coming from somewhere to the west. She swallowed the fear, reminding herself that it wasn't *hers* to begin with, and ran.

She still couldn't see anyone else outside, but there had to be someone here. Even with Lucien, the range on her power had limits. Her heart was pounding so hard she thought it might burst from her chest. Jae rounded the corner of the low wall that marked the far edge of the field and caught something out of the corner of her eye. A figure in the darkness, kneeling, his back to the wall and the farm.

Corvin Crosse. His eyes were closed, but the fear and sorrow assailing her were rolling from him in waves.

"Crosse?"

He didn't move.

Jae took a hesitant step closer. "Crosse," she said again, a little louder this time. "What's wrong?"

He didn't respond, but another pulse of fear rippled from him. His jaw was clenched tight, and the muscles of his shoulders and arms were rigid. Was he even breathing?

Her eyes watered. The levee she'd built with Lanara was decimated, and without time to focus on fortifying it, Jae was about ready to curl into a ball right there in the grass.

Instead, she crouched in front of him, gripping his shoulders tightly. She didn't know what else to do. The fear clawed at her throat. No one deserved to feel like this. Not even Corvin Crosse. Jae shook him hard. *"Corvin!"* she shouted. "Wake up!"

Corvin's steel gray eyes snapped open, and he gasped like he'd been drowning. He fell backward, collapsing against the stone wall as his focus settled on Jae.

Just like that, the panic lessened, though the sorrow intensified.

Jae tried to push the feelings away, willing her tears not to fall. "Are you alright?"

Corvin nodded, one hand moving to his throat where his fingers rubbed at the scar around his neck. His hand was shaking. His whole body was shaking.

"What the fuck happened?"

He leaned his head back against the wall and closed his eyes again. He drew a slow, steadying breath. "I, uh . . ." His voice trembled. Another breath. "I just need a minute," he said, steady this time. "Please."

Jae sat back on her heels, watching him carefully. The fear receded fully and was replaced with something else, or maybe many somethings. She couldn't tease them out, but whatever emotions they were, they knotted her guts, making her feel sick to her stomach.

The knot of feelings slowly ebbed as he steadied himself.

After a few minutes, Corvin opened his eyes. They widened at Jae's presence. "You stayed," he murmured. Before Jae could say anything, he shook his head. "You told me," he said slowly, "the day you came here, that you were certain you and your friends had awakened the old gods in Taernfane." He watched her for a long moment, searching her face through the moonlit darkness. "You were blessed by them that day, weren't you? That's why you were so sure."

Jae's finger twitched toward the knife she kept in her boot, but she didn't reach for it. Not yet. Not unless he made a move. "What makes you say that?" she asked.

Corvin rubbed his face, breathing in a deep sigh. "Ainam told me."

"I thought Ainam hadn't spoken to you since the courtyard," she said carefully.

"He hadn't." Corvin lowered his hands. "Until tonight."

Lanara's tears . . .

"Is it true?"

"What does it change if it is?"

"Nothing," he said. "I just need to know."

"You need to know if I was blessed by a god?"

Corvin leaned his head against the wall again, as though he was too exhausted to hold it up. "I need to know if Ainam was lying."

Jae's whole body tensed. What did it mean that Corvin thought Ainam might be lying to him? And what would it mean that he wasn't? "It's true," she said, watching him for any movement. If he reached for her, she'd be on her feet with her blade through his throat.

But only another strong ripple of emotion reached her. This one was all too familiar. It was how she'd felt last fall, after Solace died. How they'd all felt. It was the first emotion she'd experienced from the others, the first she was able to name. She knew it well.

Grief.

"And Lucien?" Corvin asked. "Him too?"

"That's for him to say," she replied.

Corvin nodded as though she had given in and spilled all of Lucien's secrets. "Of course he would be. And some of the others too, I would guess. Four gods and four blessings . . ." He sat in silence, staring up at the band of stars overhead.

"What did he say to you?" Jae asked. She still sat poised on the balls of her feet, her muscles coiled and ready to spring.

"He said that when the weapon awoke the old gods, you and Lucien received their blessings."

Jae hesitated a moment before she asked, "Were you trying to get your power back?"

Corvin dropped his gaze to meet hers, the gray of his eyes almost silver in the moonlight. "Would you blame me if I were?"

"After everything that's happened?" she asked. "Yeah, I would."

A soft, sad kind of laugh escaped him.

She couldn't stop her curiosity. "Did it work?"

Another wave of grief crashed into her. "No."

"Did Ainam say why?"

"There were conditions that I was unwilling to accept."

"What kind of conditions?"

"It's late," Corvin said. Bracing his arm against the wall, he levered himself to his feet. "I should get some sleep."

Jae stood with him, her lips twisting at his blatant evasion. "I guess Ethriel keeps you pretty busy around here, huh?"

"There's a lot of work that needs to be done," he agreed. He set a hand on the top of the wall to steady himself, then headed across the field toward the cottage.

Jae jogged up alongside him, and they walked through the dark in silence.

"Will you try again?" Jae asked when they reached the smaller building where Corvin kept a room. "With Ainam?"

He stopped at the door, one hand tightening on the latch. "That is not a question for which I have an answer."

"I'm sure you don't give a shit what I think," she said, crossing her arms, "but Ainam seems like an asshole. Especially if what I saw out there"—she gestured toward the western edge of the farm—"is any indication."

Corvin pushed the door open, every muscle tense. "You don't know anything about it. Good night." And he shut the door firmly behind him.

Corvin had fully reined in his emotions during the walk back from the crumbling wall, but what had happened to him out there in the dark? What conditions had Ainam set for Corvin to regain his status as Chosen?

And what was so abhorrent that Corvin Crosse, the man who had hunted Solace across the continent, who had tried to kill nearly all her friends, and had shot her out of the sky, was sick to his stomach over it? What line was the man who'd killed Solace—for it was Corvin's actions, if not his actual blade, that had murdered him—unwilling to cross?

She needed to tell Ethriel about this. Even though he hadn't succeeded in regaining his powers, even Crosse had said there was no guarantee he wouldn't try again. And if she and Lucien were going to be leaving him behind with Ethriel and Faith, she needed to make damn sure Ethriel knew as much as possible.

Jae jogged the short distance to the cottage and stepped inside. It was empty. Faith had gone to visit friends who lived a few miles away and wouldn't be back until the morning, and Lucien was still out, but she'd expected to find Ethriel inside. She turned and crossed to the second outbuilding that stood nearby. A soft glow came from under the door. She knocked.

"Yes?" Ethriel's voice called from inside.

"It's Jae. Can I come in?"

"Of course. Please do."

Jae hadn't been inside this building yet and wasn't sure what she'd been expecting. Ethriel sat in the far corner of the space, a pottery wheel in front of her. One foot pushed rhythmically on a pedal beneath the table while her hands, wet and covered in clay, worked around something that looked like a vase or pitcher. The walls were lined with a hodgepodge of shelves in different styles, which contained everything from tools to stoppered jars to unfired bowls, plates, and cups.

"Sorry to interrupt," Jae said as she took in the space and everything in it. "I had no idea this was here."

Ethriel smiled at Jae, though she kept working on the clay between her hands. "Luc built it for me," she said. "He wanted to make sure I had space for all my *dirt*, as he lovingly calls it." The pottery wheel slowed to a stop, and Ethriel pulled one side of the clay out at the top, forming a pour spout. "I like to come out here at night when it's quiet. And also I need a new pitcher."

Wiping her hands on her apron, though it did very little to clean the wet clay from her fingers, Ethriel paused in her work and rose. "What can I do for you, Jae?"

"I was hoping to talk to you," she said slowly. She wiped her own palms on her pants, unsure why she was suddenly nervous. "About Corvin."

"This sounds like we could use some tea," Ethriel said. "What do you think?"

Jae couldn't help but smile. "That sounds lovely. Thanks."

Ethriel led Jae back to the cottage, where she washed her hands properly and set about making them some tea. While the leaves were steeping, Ethriel sat beside Jae at the kitchen table. "What did you want to talk about?"

Jae relayed her conversation with Corvin, including everything she knew about what sorts of powers Ainam had granted him in the past. "I'm sorry," she said when she reached the end. "But I thought you should know."

Ethriel nodded, eyes unfocused as she sat deep in thought. "What did Luc say?" she asked.

"I wanted to talk to you first."

Ethriel arched a brow. "Why?"

Jae shrugged. "Because it's your decision if you want to do anything about it."

A smile pinched the corners of her eyes. "I knew I liked you." She took a sip of her tea. "Thank you for telling me about what happened. And thank you for respecting me enough to let it be my decision, but I won't be sending him away."

"What? Why?" Jae blurted out. "He's dangerous." Her hands tightened around her teacup, but she forced them to relax. "He's hurt people. How could you want to keep him around after everything he's done?"

"If you were in my place, you would tell him to leave?"

"I would," Jae said without hesitation.

Ethriel hummed into her tea as she sipped it. "You've traveled with my husband a long time." She set down her cup. "When did you find out he was a shifter?"

Jae sipped her own tea, thinking back. "We'd been traveling together for a few months."

"Were you scared?"

"Of course."

"And what would you have done," Ethriel continued, "if someone had come to you a few days later and told you he was a shifter and that he was dangerous?"

Jae had been terrified the first time she saw Lucien in his bestial form. But he'd only ever helped her, been kind to her, protected her when she'd needed it before she learned to protect herself.

And he'd taught her that too.

Oh.

Ethriel smiled as the realization must have dawned on Jae's face. "I'd guess you would've told them they could go to hell," she said warmly.

Jae nodded, embarrassment heating her cheeks.

"I'm not saying that whatever you and Luc have is the same as Corvin and I. In fact, I suspect it's vastly different. But what I am saying is that you made the decision to judge Luc based on his actions—the ones he'd taken since you'd known him—and not the ones he'd done before you met him. Right?"

Jae nodded again.

"I'm choosing to do the same," Ethriel said. "With both of them."

CHAPTER 33

THEY'D BEEN IN WHITEHOLLOW for a week, and Verity was doing her best to focus on her duties. She was getting reacquainted with her role at the Wardens' base, helping where she could. She spent some time practicing her abilities as a Chosen of Pyrannis, though with Gregor busy at the embassy, she was hesitant to push herself too far without his calming presence. She also spent time with Dare nearly every day, training him on his Perceptive talents as well as hand-to-hand skills. It was keeping her busy, though Finn had managed to drag her into the city a couple times.

You said we should only go out in pairs, Finn had said, her eyes alight with mischief. *And if I have to have one more boring, formal dinner at the embassy, I'm going to scream.*

Verity couldn't help her amusement and acquiesced to accompanying Finn for an evening out. It had been so much fun, they'd gone again just last night. Though during that outing, Finn had mentioned she hadn't seen Gregor in a few days, despite her room at the embassy being right across from his. Since it was a rare morning for Verity where she had nothing to do, she decided to head into the city proper and check on her friend.

Verity knew she should follow her own instructions and not leave the Wardens' base alone, but it would take too long for one of the Drahkonian guards to come over from the embassy to escort her, and she doubted Dare was even awake yet. As she headed to the gates, she spotted Jonah Ashcroft running sword drills alone in one of the nearby training rings. She paused to watch him, smiling as she remembered their sparring match from months ago. It looked like he'd been practicing since then. His movements were more fluid and confident.

Jonah noticed her and lowered his sword. "Warden Corallan." His face was flushed red from exertion, and he wiped sweat off his brow with his sleeve.

"Please, call me Verity," she said.

He ran a hand through his dark hair, that boyish grin making him look so much younger. "You're not looking for another sparring match, are you?"

"No, no," she chuckled. "I was actually hoping to ask you for a favor." Verity briefly explained the situation. "If you're not busy, would you mind walking with me to the Drahkonian embassy?"

Jonah set his fist over his heart in a quick, almost casual salute. "Sure thing, Verity. Give me a minute." He dashed off to the barracks to clean up, returning soon after in black pants and a faded red shirt, his sword slung on his hip. "Lead on."

They walked in companionable silence mostly, though Jonah was happy to chat whenever Verity started a conversation. He didn't even seem to mind when Verity asked to make a detour to a small café. Once they arrived at the embassy, Jonah parked himself on a bench out front.

"You don't have to wait for me," Verity said as she started up the front steps, parcel from the café in hand.

He shrugged, draping his arm across the back of the bench. "I don't mind. You're going to need someone to walk you back, right?"

"Well, yes," she admitted.

"Then I'll be here."

"Alright, I won't be long."

Inside the embassy, Finn was leaning on the railing at the top of the stairs, overlooking the foyer. "Who's your walking buddy?" she asked as soon as the door had closed behind Verity.

Verity climbed the stairs, joining her on the upper landing. "Another Warden. His name's Jonah."

"Jo-nah," Finn said with a little singsong lilt. "He likes you."

Verity rolled her eyes. "He's just being nice. How long were you watching us outside?"

"Since you walked up." Finn prodded her in the side. "He's waiting out there to escort you back to the base, isn't he? How fast did he agree to walk you here?"

"You're being ridiculous."

"He likes you," Finn replied playfully. But then her eyes lingered on Verity, a breath passing between the two of them before she said very softly, "But I get it. What's not to like?"

Verity's stomach tightened, her face heating under Finn's assessment. She turned quickly and nodded down the hall. "Is Gregor here?"

"I assume so," Finn said, her expression turning serious. "I still haven't seen him, and he hasn't answered when I knocked."

That was concerning. Verity moved to Gregor's door and knocked.

"Gregor?" she called as Finn went into her own room. "It's Verity."

Gregor opened the door a few moments later, a book in his hand with his thumb holding his place as it hung by his side. She hadn't seen him for a while herself, and the circles under his eyes had darkened considerably, like he hadn't slept in all that time. He looked terrible.

Gregor's lip twitched. "Morning, Verity." He leaned against the door frame.

"Good morning. I wanted to check in and see how you were doing. And I brought you something." When he didn't move, she added, "May I come in?"

Gregor stepped to the side without a word, and Verity slipped past him into the small room. It wasn't messy by any measure, but it did look more *lived in* than other spaces she'd seen Gregor occupy.

"Have you gotten out into the city much?" she asked, though she recognized it as a foolish question as soon as she asked it.

"Finn dragged me out shortly after we arrived." Gregor tossed the book onto the small table. "But at the first crowded place we came to, I was so worried that either Tanithe was going to find us or my *gift* was going to start up that I panicked and we had to come back."

"Oh." She clasped her hands behind her back, unsure what else she should say. "I'm sorry I've been busy the last few days. I—"

"Verity, I'm not really in the mood for small talk today," Gregor interrupted, rubbing his temple and closing his eyes for a moment. "Can you please just tell me why you came by?"

"Oh, of course. Sorry." She set the small parcel on the table.

Gregor sighed deeply. "No, I'm sorry. That was rude of me. Please, sit. Stay." He gestured to the table. Verity took the chair nearest her while he sat on the other side. "I've hardly slept since we left Taernfane. I admit it has me a bit on edge."

Verity leaned forward, giving him her full attention. "That sounds terrible. Do you have any ideas as to what's causing it?"

Gregor tore his glasses off and tossed them onto the table. "Yes," he snapped, "I think I have some idea." He breathed another heavy sigh, inhaling deeply as he rubbed his hands over his face. "I'm sorry," he mumbled into his hands. "I really am poor company today." When he looked at her again, he smiled, though it was strained. He nodded toward the bundle Verity had set on the table as he slid his glasses back on. "What did you bring?"

Verity slid the small parcel across the table, a silent invitation for him to take it. "Nothing much. Just a cinnamon muffin from a café down the street. I thought you might like it."

"Thank you," he said sincerely. "I appreciate it. Though I can't imagine you came all the way here just to bring me this."

"No," Verity admitted. "I wanted to check on you. I've been worried about you. We all have."

"I know," he said. "I'm sorry. It's this . . ." He gestured vaguely to his head. "And this city isn't helping anything. At the palace in Taernfane, I could at least find a quiet place to think, but here"—he waved a frustrated hand in the general direction of the room's one window—"it feels like I'm under attack. And I don't know if this is Aetherann's idea of a lesson or if it's just getting worse. But I can't sleep. Every time I close my eyes, I swear I can hear the thoughts of half the damn city."

"And he still hasn't spoken to you?"

Gregor shook his head. "Silence," he said. "Infuriating silence."

A warmth kindled to life within Verity, and the spark she'd come to know as Pyrannis bounced inside her. *Aetherann has always been fond of his mysteries.*

Gregor's head snapped up, his eyes locking on Verity. His mouth opened, but no sound came out.

Verity watched him carefully as she felt the crackling laughter of Pyrannis through that little spark. The words had definitely been inside her mind, as the god of fire always spoke to her. But . . . "You heard him?"

Gregor nodded slowly, eyes wide. "Was that . . . ?"

That is intriguing, Pyrannis continued. *Never have I had a Chosen so near to one of my brother's. Curious.* The spark flared a bit brighter, casting a glowing warmth all through Verity as Pyrannis turned more of his attention toward her. *Hello, little windspeaker.*

Gregor jumped out of the chair and practically fell against the wall in his haste to put space between him and Verity.

She stood with him, reaching for him in case he needed a steadying hand.

He blinked a few times, his composure seeming to trickle back to him in pieces. "I didn't know I could hear . . . I didn't know it worked like that," he managed. His gaze grew distant, as though losing himself in some thought or memory.

"Gregor?"

He startled. "Sorry," he mumbled, rubbing his face again. "I feel like a complete fool. I should have been able to figure this out by now."

Verity considered what she could say to Gregor to help this hurt, this weight that had been pressing on him for months, but Pyrannis spoke again.

Little windspeaker, my brother houses the domains of knowledge and mysteries. He is wisdom made manifest. He does not *suffer fools. He Chose you. He would not give you a challenge beyond your means.*

"Do you really believe that?" Gregor asked softly.

I know this for a truth.

Gregor's eyes glistened with tears, though he blinked them back hurriedly. "Thank you," he said, his voice hardly more than a whisper.

"Get some rest, Gregor," Verity said. She might not be able to help him with this particular struggle, but she had another idea of something that might make his time in Whitehollow a little more bearable. "Is it alright if I come back tomorrow?"

He nodded, and Verity bid him farewell.

Out in the hall, Pyrannis's voice echoed in her mind. *Did I help cauterize your friend's emotional wound?*

She grinned as she stepped out into the sun where Jonah was waiting for her. *I think maybe you did.* A question itched at the back of her mind. *Pyrannis?*

Yes, Verity Corallan?

You said you'd never had a Chosen be so close to one of Aetherann's Chosen before, right? Beside her, Jonah walked in silence, his attention fixed on their surroundings.

That is correct.

Why is that?

To Choose a mortal is not something that I, nor any of my siblings, do lightly, Pyrannis answered flatly. *It is a rare thing, to find a mortal so worthy of our power. And it is even more rare for us to find more than one at the same time.*

Verity's mind reeled. *You mean, for all of history, only one of the Four has had a Chosen at any given time?*

So far as I am aware, Pyrannis answered. *Though I do not profess to know all the comings and goings of my siblings.*

Then what does it mean that all four of you have a Chosen at the same time now?

Pyrannis's crackle of laughter snapped through her mind. *I do not know, but I am curious to find out.*

CHAPTER 34

"THANK YOU FOR WALKING with me," Verity said to Jonah as they returned to the Wardens' base.

He smiled a lopsided grin. "It's nothing. I'm glad I could help out."

Splitting off from Jonah, Verity headed across the base to the one building that was set back the farthest away from everything. She knocked on the door.

It swung open a few moments later. "Warden Corallan," Lorekeeper Ardyn Harrow said, peering at her over her half-moon glasses. "What a pleasant surprise. Please, come in."

Entering the workshop, Verity's mind flooded with the memories of the last time she was there. Her muscles tensed as she passed the bookshelf where she'd waited with Drystan for Dare, who'd been late that day—dealing with the aftereffects of Tanithe's mind magic, she'd learned later.

The stool where Solace had sat for his interview with Harrow was in a different place, pulled up next to a workbench on the other side of the room. Even so, Verity couldn't help but picture Solace hunched over it, his shoulders rounded and his hands tucked in between his knees. He'd been so frightened and unsure back then.

"What brings you to my humble laboratory?" Harrow asked, pulling Verity out of her thoughts. Harrow motioned for her to have a seat in one of the more comfortable chairs that formed a small reading nook in the far corner.

"I, um . . . Lorekeeper, you read my report about what happened after we left Whitehollow, correct? Our mission to go to Aetherann's Reach?"

Harrow's expression fell, the gentle lines of her face deepening into a frown. "Yes, I read it. I was most saddened to hear of the loss of Warden Serah, as well as the young man you'd brought to me. It was regretful what happened to them both."

Verity's throat tightened as she nodded. "Yes," she said. All this time, and she had yet to find the right word to describe their loss. "It was . . . tragic," she settled on at last. But she pressed on; there was another question she needed to ask. "Did you read the *full* report?" Lorekeeper Harrow was a busy woman. It wouldn't have surprised Verity if she'd skimmed parts of it, or—

"I read it in its entirety," she said, reaching out to pat Verity's steel hand. "Chosen of the Lord Pyrannis. Following in Lyran Corovar's footsteps. I never thought I would see a Chosen in my lifetime."

Verity's face heated at the comparison to the founder of the Wardens of the Flame. "That's what I was hoping to talk with you about," she said. "I've met briefly with Commander Cairn, but I'm . . . not sure what I need to do."

"About what, exactly?"

Verity gestured to herself. "All this. I don't know what I should be doing."

"As a Warden?"

"As a *Chosen*."

Lorekeeper Harrow smiled. "You are Verity Corallan, Warden of the Flame and Chosen of Pyrannis. This *Chosen* business is just one small piece of who you are. It doesn't change the fact that you're Verity Corallan. It doesn't change the fact that you're a Warden of the Flame."

Setting her hands on her knees, Verity leaned forward. "But what am I supposed to *do*? What responsibilities do I have?"

Harrow suppressed a grin. "Perhaps this new journey you find yourself on isn't about responsibilities?" she posited.

Verity shifted uncomfortably. Dare would certainly be having a laugh at her expense right now, if he'd heard her question.

"Does Pyrannis speak to you?" Harrow asked, adjusting her glasses on the end of her sharp nose.

"Sometimes," Verity admitted.

Harrow leaned in, intrigued. "And what sorts of things does he say to you? Not the specifics," she added with a quick wave of her hand. "Generalities will suffice."

"He asks a lot of questions. He's curious about humans." She thought back to the first time the god spoke to her, in the middle of an elemental maelstrom in the central courtyard of Drahkonia's palace. "He asked me to be his hand in the world. To help protect the balance."

"Has he expressed any displeasure in how you've been conducting yourself since becoming his Chosen?"

"No . . ."

"Do you have the sense that he would tell you such a thing, were it to be the case?"

Verity considered whether Pyrannis would be straightforward with her if he was unhappy. "He's been direct about everything else," she said. "I don't have reason to believe this would be any different."

The lorekeeper leaned back in her chair and crossed her legs beneath her gray robe. "It sounds to me like you have your answer."

"You think he'll tell me if there's something he wants me to do?" *Like Lucien and his mission from Taerna.*

"I think that *you* think that," Harrow said, "but you're worried that you should be anticipating what's needed. But this is uncharted territory for many reasons, Verity. How can a mortal hope to anticipate the needs of a god?"

Now she thought of Gregor and the silence from Aetherann while he struggled with his gifts.

"Lorekeeper," she said, taking a breath to steady herself. "Do you have any—"

"Books you could borrow on the subject?" She smiled and gave Verity a knowing wink. "I believe I have one or two." Harrow busied herself about the workshop, checking shelves and stacks of books scattered around. "When followers of Ainam swept across the continent after the holy wars five hundred years ago, they destroyed many of the historic and religious texts pertaining to the Four, especially when it comes to Chosen of the gods." She returned with two large tomes.

Verity recognized one of them from the meeting with Solace.

"This one," Harrow said, handing Verity the familiar book, "focuses on the history of the Wardens, including many of the deeds of the order's founder, Lyran Corovar. As you know, he was a Chosen of Pyrannis himself, so you may find some helpful insights there." Harrow set the other book on top of it. "And this one is a collection of tales about the Chosen from various scholars and monks, though one of the monks claimed she was a Chosen of Aetherann herself. I don't know how much detail she goes into, but I recall her stories were interesting at least. They're all framed as legends, but perhaps it will provide some useful information for you."

Verity stared at the leather covers. It was a place to start. It was something she could hold in her hands and read and internalize. Maybe if she understood the lives of earlier Chosen, even if only a few stories about them, she'd have a better sense of what she needed to do. And maybe they could help Gregor too.

"Thank you, Lorekeeper," she said. She thumbed the pages of one of the books. "Do you know if more than one Chosen of the gods has ever existed at the same time?"

"Do you mean, more than one Chosen of Pyrannis, for example?"

"That," Verity said. "Or a Chosen of Pyrannis and a Chosen of one of the other gods."

Harrow steepled her fingers, bringing them to her lips as she considered the question. "As I recall, no. Though you could check the dates within the stories to verify that." The lorekeeper angled her head. "Are you thinking there may be others who were blessed as you were when the gods awakened?"

Verity swallowed hard. She didn't want to give the others away—that was their information to share as they chose, but she couldn't lie to Lorekeeper Harrow.

You don't have to lie. Just don't tell them everything.

"It's something I was curious about," Verity said truthfully.

Harrow nodded, brows rising. "It's a fair question. I should be interested to hear if there were any others as well. Speaking of your status, have you decided who you want to tell about your new power?"

The question caught Verity off guard. "How do you mean?"

"Are you planning on keeping this a secret," she began, "or tell the world? Or perhaps something in between?"

"I hadn't considered it." The four of them who'd become Chosen in the courtyard of Taernfane had agreed to keep their powers a secret for the time being, telling only Dare, Finn, and King Dominic—and they knew Verity would need to include the news about herself in her report to Commander Cairn—but they hadn't discussed how long they would keep that secret. The news of the gods reawakening would spread across the continent, and rumors would surely start along with it. How long could they hope to keep their power hidden from the masses? From army generals and monarchs?

From the Valdane Council? What would happen if they found out about the Chosen? What would happen if Westhold found out?

A shiver ran through Verity.

"Think about it, Warden," Harrow said. "Beyond your friends, the commander and myself, no one else in Whitehollow yet knows about your connection to Pyrannis. But nothing can remain a secret forever. It will be far better for you to choose how and when your story is told. The last thing you want is for that decision to be made for you."

Verity nodded solemnly. "It's a lot to consider."

"It is. Is there anything else I can help you with, Warden?"

"Actually, yes." Her eyes drifted across the shelves of tonics, poultices, and other alchemical dabblings. "Do you have anything to help with sleeping?"

"Too much or not enough?"

Verity couldn't help the quiet chuckle that slipped out. "Not enough. My friend has been having difficulty sleeping lately. I think . . . I think he's troubled by some horrible things that happened to him."

Harrow nodded, running a hand along her chin. "Yes, yes, I have just the thing." She crossed to a tall bookshelf and moved aside a few glass jars until she came to one filled with dried leaves of different colors. She took a small pouch and scooped some of the leaves into it. "Have your friend make a tea from this," she said, handing the pouch to Verity. She then scribbled something on a strip of parchment and handed that to her as well. "An hour before he goes to sleep. Only one cup and no more than once every other night. Too often will make it difficult for him to rouse and can cause him to sleep far more than he should. He can add cinnamon to it if he wishes; it helps with the aftertaste."

"Thank you," Verity said, depositing the tea in a pouch on her belt. "He, um . . ." Verity hesitated at how to describe Gregor's trouble without explaining too much. "He's been having a hard time since we arrived in the city. I think there are too many people for him. He could use a safe space—somewhere quiet—that he could retreat to when he needs it, and I was wondering . . ."

"You were wondering if he could come here?" Harrow finished for her.

Verity nodded. "In addition to the relative seclusion, I think he'd really like it here. And I think you'd like him."

Harrow surveyed her own workshop. "It is a bit off the beaten path, isn't it?" She smiled warmly at Verity. "I'd be happy to meet your friend and offer him a refuge here. Please bring him by anytime."

"Thank you, Lorekeeper." Verity stood, scooping up the books as she turned to leave. "I really appreciate your help."

Harrow smiled as she opened the door for Verity. "Take care, Warden Corallan. May Pyrannis's blessings burn brightly."

Verity crossed the courtyard from the lorekeeper's office, the books from Harrow tucked under her arm. She could skim through them tonight and then, when she visited Gregor tomorrow, she could bring him the tea, share anything she'd learned, and offer to introduce him to the lorekeeper.

Across the courtyard, one of the training rings was occupied. Two recruits sparred while others watched and Jonah circled the two in the center, likely arbitrating the match.

Verity paused at the brazier of Pyrannis. The fire danced and almost seemed to burn a little brighter as she watched.

"The flames react to your presence," Joseph Cairn said from behind her. The Warden commander joined Verity at the brazier, watching the fire flicker.

"Commander Cairn." Verity turned and saluted, which he dismissed with a wave.

"That hardly seems fitting now, considering."

Verity tensed as Cairn leaned against the wall. "Sir? You're still my commanding officer."

"I am." Cairn turned his back to the flames and gazed out across the training rings instead, crossing his arms. "I was hoping you could come by my office later. I want to speak with you more about your connection to Pyrannis."

A little rush of nerves fluttered through her. "Oh?" She'd wanted to have this conversation herself, but she wanted time to prepare and do some research first.

"Yes. I have a few questions for you, as well as some thoughts I'd like to discuss."

Verity watched the fire.

Cairn inhaled deeply and bowed his head. "I had hoped—"

The whine of an arrow pierced the air. Cairn jerked. Verity spun and the fire flared, roaring up. Arms falling limp to his sides, Cairn slumped back against the wall. He dropped to the ground before Verity could move, an arrow protruding from his chest.

Verity fell to her knees beside him. Cairn's eyes stared unseeing at the sky.

He was dead.

CHAPTER 35

Dead.

She was there, beside him. Yet she couldn't stop it. Couldn't help. Couldn't—

Shouts rose. Footsteps, shadows moving around her where she knelt over Cairn.

"What happened?" someone cried.

More shouting. "The commander!"

Verity stared blankly down at Cairn's body.

She'd been right there . . .

Somewhere at the edge of her perception, others crouched beside the commander. Strong hands gripped her arm, lifting her to her feet.

"Warden Corallan?"

Someone ushered her at a hurried pace to the covered entranceway of a nearby building.

She'd been standing right beside him. And now he was dead. She should have done something . . .

"Verity?"

Do something . . . She should *do* something.

"Verity!"

Verity shook her head, trying to clear the thoughts that were bogging her down. She blinked. Brown eyes stared back at her.

"Verity, are you alright?" Jonah asked. His hands tightened around her elbows.

"I . . . I was . . ." She turned toward Cairn's body. Several Wardens now crowded around where the commander lay at the base of the wall, two healers among them. Some of the recruits stood nearby, watching in stunned silence.

Jonah followed her gaze, then turned with her, gently steering her away from the growing crowd and just around the corner of the building. "Did you see what happened?" he asked, his voice softening.

Did she see? She saw Cairn hit the ground, an arrow in his heart.

But they were in the very center of the compound. That meant . . .

"Whoever did this," she managed, "was inside the base."

Jonah's eyes widened.

"Vire's fucking hells. Verity!" Dust flew as Dare skidded to a stop beside her. Words passed between Dare and Jonah, but Verity couldn't follow it. Not when Cairn's body lay in front of Pyrannis's brazier, not two dozen yards away. And she hadn't been able to do anything.

Verity was vaguely aware of being guided farther away. Where was Jonah taking her? No, she needed to go back—to help. She turned toward Cairn, toward the crowd of Wardens in the center of the courtyard, but the arms around her shoulders held her firm.

"I've got you, my lady Warden."

She stopped. "Dare?"

Dare pulled Verity into him, holding her so tightly that it cleared some of the fog from her mind.

She wrapped her arms around him. "I was standing right there," she whispered into his shoulder. Tears welled in her eyes and slid down her cheeks. "I couldn't do anything."

"I know," he said gently as he held her. "I know, it's alright."

"He was dead before he hit the ground." Verity pulled out of Dare's arms just a little, wiping at the tears that were falling freely now. "What good is this power I have if I couldn't even do anything?"

Dare pulled her in close again. "I know you're upset, so I'm not going to dignify that with a proper response, because you know damn well what good that power is. And you don't need me to tell you that just because you couldn't help Cairn, it doesn't mean you can't help others. That you *haven't* helped others."

She pulled away again, taking a step toward the courtyard. "I should do something," she said. "I should help."

"Verity, there are a dozen Wardens already helping," Dare said, grabbing her wrist before she could get very far. "They've got it under control." He gave her arm a gentle tug. "Let's walk."

Verity nodded and allowed Dare to lead her away from the commotion. When they rounded the corner to the barracks, Dare gestured to the door. "Do you want to go inside?" he asked. "I can walk you to your room."

She nodded for lack of anything else to say or do. She managed to fish the key out of her pocket when they reached her room, but Dare took it from her and unlocked the door, pushing it open for her.

"Is it alright if I stay?" he asked as she stepped past him.

"Why didn't I do something?" Verity asked, searching Dare's eyes for an answer.

"What do you think you should have done?"

Verity threw her arms up as the tears started falling anew. "I don't know. I should have done *something*. I should have reacted faster. Or if I'd been paying closer attention, maybe I could have stopped it. But I just froze. What kind of a Warden am I?"

"This wasn't a battle, Verity," Dare said gently. "Or a mission. You were in your *home*." A muscle tensed in his jaw. "You're allowed to let your guard down at home. That doesn't make you a bad Warden. You should have been safe here."

But no, this wasn't right. That arrow had come from somewhere in the base. There was a murderer somewhere within the compound walls. In her *home*.

"I should go," Verity said, turning back toward the door. "I need to find who did this. I need to—"

"You need to stop," Dare said, blocking the doorway with his body. "They're already looking for whoever's responsible. I heard them organizing a search when I found you." He held out his hands in front of him, palms open toward her like she was some kind of frightened animal he was trying to soothe. "Verity, you need to rest. There's nothing else you need to do right now. Everyone has it under control." He gestured to the narrow bed along the wall. "Just rest. Please."

Rest. Yes, she just needed to set down the books, and—

Verity looked down at her empty hands. "The books!" Where had she dropped them? When? She moved toward the door again.

"Verity!" Dare snapped. "Stop, please. I will take care of it, alright? I promise. But I need you to stop. *Please.*"

She stopped at last and blew out a long, slow breath, running her hands over her face. Then she sat on the edge of the bed.

"Thank you," Dare said. "I have your key, and I'm going to lock the door behind me. Then I'm going to find your books and bring them back here, alright?"

Verity nodded.

"Wait here for me, Verity. Don't open the door for anyone. I'll be right back." Dare hesitated by the door. "I promise," he said again before he disappeared into the hall.

Verity closed her eyes, trying to focus on her breath, trying to will her body to stop shaking.

Trying to stop picturing Commander Cairn's blank eyes staring up at nothing.

It took her much longer than usual, but eventually she was able to clear her mind, focusing solely on her breathing.

Verity startled out of her meditation when someone knocked at her door. She wasn't sure how much time had passed since Dare had brought her here. Or when he'd come back, but he jumped up from where he'd been sitting in her chair by the desk, the books from Harrow beside him.

Verity stood to open the door, but Dare held his hand out to stop her. "Who is it?" Dare asked. The sharpness of his voice surprised her.

"I need to speak with Warden Corallan," Lorekeeper Harrow said from the hall. "May I come in?"

Dare looked to Verity. He whispered, "Want me to tell her to fuck off?"

Verity exhaled a soft laugh and shook her head. "Please come in, Lorekeeper."

Dare unlocked the door and Harrow stepped into the small room, a few loose pages of parchment gripped tightly in one hand. "Warden Corallan, Warden Wilhaven," she said, nodding a greeting to them both. "I will keep this brief and to the point." She inhaled sharply, lifting her chin. "The late Commander

Cairn has named you his successor. Verity Corallan, you are to be the new High Commander of the Wardens of the Flame."

Verity blinked, Harrow's words reaching her through the fog.

High Commander of the Wardens of the Flame.

"Wait—*what?*" She shook her head, trying to even wrap her mind around how ridiculous that thought was. "How is that possible?"

Harrow offered her the parchments. "It seems Joseph documented your status as a Chosen of Pyrannis and drafted orders for you to succeed him as high commander in the event of his death or retirement."

"Well, that was timely," Dare muttered, sinking back into the chair.

"Unfortunately so," Harrow said flatly. "These orders were just found in his office, and I'm afraid the news has already spread."

Verity took the papers and flipped through them. Sure enough, they noted Verity's power as a Chosen of Pyrannis and expressed that, given her direct connection to the Wardens' patron deity, she should be given command of the Wardens stationed in Whitehollow.

"Had he spoken to you about this yet?" Harrow asked.

Verity shook her head. "No, I think . . . I think this might have been what he was starting to tell me when he was shot."

High Commander of the Wardens? No, that couldn't be right. She wasn't qualified. Could she be responsible for the lives of every Warden based in Whitehollow? While not every Warden would fall under her command, Whitehollow was the primary base, with the others being smaller outposts.

More than half the Wardens in the order would be under her command if—

"Wait a fucking minute." Dare dragged his fingers through his hair as he leaned forward. "Doesn't Verity get a say in any of this?"

"Of course," Harrow replied quickly, though she hadn't looked away from Verity. "It's your choice. Though know that Cairn trusted you with this responsibility, and these documents have already seen the light of day. There will be fallout to be dealt with if you refuse."

Dare jumped to his feet. "That's not fair! You can't force her to—"

"I'm not forcing her to do anything, Warden." Harrow finally turned to Dare. "I'm merely informing her of the consequences of her actions should she decline.

The choice is hers to make, but she should be aware of the probable outcomes, wouldn't you agree?"

Dare fell silent.

Verity drew in a lungful of air, but her breath shook. It was all too much. There were too many things happening all at once, and too much was going on inside her head. She needed a minute to sort things out, and she needed to be able to talk with Lorekeeper Harrow without Dare trying to defend her.

"Dare, could you give us a few minutes please?" Verity asked.

His eyes darted between her and Harrow.

Verity pulled out the pouch of tea leaves and instructions Harrow had given her earlier and handed them to Dare. "Could you take this to Gregor?"

Dare nodded, his face grave. "As you wish, my lady Warden." He took the tea, then gave half a bow to Harrow before he left, closing the door behind him.

"Before you make your decision," Harrow said once Dare was out of the room, "there is one more thing you should know. They found the man responsible for Cairn's murder."

Verity startled. "They found him?"

"Yes." Harrow took a steadying breath. "Warden Pendal."

"A Warden killed the commander?"

"It seems so, though he says he was hired to do it."

Verity sat back down on the edge of the bed, her knees threatening to stop holding her up. Warden Edwin Pendal. She didn't know him well, but . . . "He confessed?"

The lorekeeper nodded. "Apparently he swore an oath to kill Commander Cairn in exchange for a truly absurd sum of coin. He says he had no intention of following through—the amount he was paid up front for the attempt was more than he'd seen in his life. He planned to only wound the commander so that he would recover. But he couldn't."

Verity stilled, watching Harrow. "What do you mean he *couldn't*?"

"He said his brand burned like fire every time he tried to do anything to break his oath. He swears that he was bound to murder Cairn and had no choice but to follow through."

Her mind reeled. It was all too much. "I don't understand," she said. "His Warden's brand stopped him from breaking his oath?"

Harrow nodded. "It certainly seems that way."

"Who hired him?"

"He hasn't yet said. Further questioning—and further testing—is in order here. But this is a task I would entrust only to the High Commander of the Wardens."

Commander of the Wardens. It was a responsibility she had dreamt of in her early days as a Warden, until she had seen the toll it took to be responsible for so many lives. But Cairn trusted her with this. And Pyrannis had trusted her with his power.

But Cairn was dead. Verity had been standing right there. And she'd done nothing.

She'd done *nothing*.

And if she turned down this responsibility, that would be more of the same. More standing by. More doing nothing. She'd promised herself long ago she'd never *do nothing*—not when she had people to protect, a duty to uphold.

Who would take command if not her? Would their next high commander care about those under their leadership the way she would? Would they lead with compassion? Would it be someone she could trust?

"I apologize for needing to rush your decision, but I'm afraid time is not on our side with any of this," Harrow said. "So I need to know now, Verity. Will you serve as High Commander of the Wardens of the Flame?"

Forward was the only direction open to her. Backward was never an option. She had a responsibility. To Cairn. To Pyrannis.

To Drystan, and to the Wardens who had saved her life nearly a decade ago.

Verity set her hand over her chest, her palm over the symbol of the Wardens branded into her skin.

"I will."

Harrow's shoulders relaxed, as though a weight had been lifted. "I'm pleased to hear that," she said. She smiled softly. "I wish I could give you time to rest, but unfortunately there are a few matters that need to be tended to most urgently." She gestured toward the door.

"Of course." Verity grabbed her sword, slid its scabbard through the loop on her belt, and followed the lorekeeper outside.

Dare was waiting in the hall, leaning against his own door. He straightened as soon as Verity emerged. He took one look at her, and his face fell. "You don't have to do this," he all but whispered.

But if not her, then who else?

Verity straightened to her full height, her jaw set. "It's already done."

Dare's hand flew to his forehead. "For fuck's sake, Verity, at least take some time to think about this! What you're doing is—"

"My duty," Verity completed for him. "And I won't run from it."

Dare simply stared at her, his gaze hardening into a mask of ice. Only then did she realize—did she remember.

"Dare, I didn't mean—"

"It's fine," he said, heading down the hall. "I'll just get out of your way."

Verity stood still until Dare had disappeared around the corner. She hadn't meant to imply that Dare running from his family was the wrong choice. She'd helped him escape them, after all. But it wasn't the right decision for her. She needed to do this.

She wanted to go after him, but now was not the time. She had a responsibility to uphold. Verity angled herself toward Lorekeeper Harrow. "Lead the way."

Chapter 36

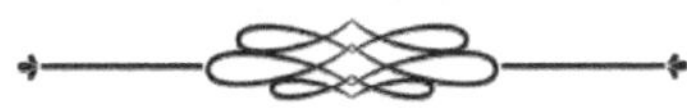

GREGOR SAT IN ONE of the embassy's meeting rooms with Chancellor Caelan, surrounded by disordered piles of documents, quills and ink, and coffee cups scattered everywhere. Although they'd started with neat and orderly stacks of parchments a few hours ago, by midday the table was a complete disaster.

The Valdane Council, in their efforts to *assist* with the committee hearing, had sent hundreds of documents—with no discernible organization, Gregor had noted with dismay—for Drahkonia's perusal ahead of the meeting. The chancellor had paled at the boxes that had arrived via courier and immediately asked Gregor for his assistance in sorting through the bewildering welter.

At first, Gregor had been happy to have something to occupy his mind—especially after the alarming event at the Wardens' base only two days prior—but after hours spent digging through pages and pages of irrelevant information, dates, figures, and lists, his frustration with Valda was mounting.

"They're doing this on purpose," Gregor said, pushing his glasses on top of his head. "They're purposefully trying to bog us down in the minutiae so we either miss something that's actually relevant or we just give up."

"Of course they are," Caelan said, dropping the parchment he'd been staring at onto the ever-growing stack of useless documents. "Which means there's something they don't want us to find. I've already found gaps in a few areas. I'll need to go back to them with a request for the missing information. It's all part of their game." He picked up a leather folio bound together with a length of cord, the pages within sticking out at odd angles. "Do you need a break?"

"No, no." Gregor repositioned his glasses as Caelan slid the folio to him across the table. "Let's keep going." He untied the cord and flipped open the leather cover while Caelan picked up another stack of papers. Gregor skimmed the first few pages, though he slowed as his eyes snagged on one of the headers.

It was a ledger for supplies and staff and troop movements for Valda. It was unlikely that Valda would have *attack Taernfane* as a line item, but if there were unusual expenditures around the dates of the attack, it could give them a direction.

"This could be something," Gregor said, flipping a few more pages. "But this one is from six years ago. Did they send more recent ones?"

Caelan gestured to the box the folio had come from. Inside Gregor found more of the same. He scooped up as many as he could carry and set about looking for the most recent files. They had folios representing seven of the last eight years—the one for two years prior was missing, but that shouldn't matter for this.

"Here," he murmured when he found the correct year. He thumbed through the pages. "Wait." Gregor flipped back and forth between a couple of sheets. "There are pages missing. The entire third quarter of the year!" Which, of course, was precisely when the attack had taken place. Gregor slammed the folio shut. "Dammit."

Caelan rose and poured another cup of coffee, which he handed to Gregor. "I'll add that to my list of missing files to request." He perched on the edge of the table. "But I think we're going to need to push the trial back by at least a week or two. I'll notify Commander Corallan."

Commander Corallan . . . When Dare had arrived at the embassy two days ago with news of Verity's unanticipated and, frankly, unprecedented promotion, none of them knew what to think. Verity was High Commander of the Wardens and news of her status as the Chosen of Pyrannis had spread. What would that mean for her? Would people welcome a Chosen of the old gods?

And what did it mean for the rest of them? For Lucien, Jae, and Gregor? Would people assume that the imbuing of one Chosen of the Four implied the existence of others? Would curious stares focus on the others who were there in the courtyard that day? Or would the simple connection of a Warden of the Flame becoming a Chosen of Pyrannis be sufficient for most to conclude that it was a one-off event?

So far, no one had asked any questions. At least, not around Gregor. But even still . . . What then? It was selfish to worry about himself when things had changed so drastically and so abruptly for Verity. He knew he should check in with her, but—

A knock sounded on the door and one of the embassy's pages entered.

"There's a Warden downstairs for you," the young woman said to Gregor. "Says the Warden commander asked him to escort you to the base for a meeting."

"What fortuitous timing," Caelan said, pushing off from the table. "Hold on a moment while I draft a missive to her about the delay."

Gregor hesitated. Between the idea that Tanithe could be lurking somewhere in Whitehollow and his *gift* from Aetherann that seemed like it could trigger at any moment, the thought of venturing into the city made his heart race.

"O-of course," he said after a moment, silently cursing himself for the nervous stammer. If one of his friends needed him, he would steady his nerves. He would push through and do what needed to be done.

Gregor followed the Warden through the streets of Whitehollow. It was crowded but blessedly silent. He breathed a little easier, though it was short-lived. As they rounded a corner, a breeze blew down the street. It wasn't particularly strong or out of place, as cities along the coast of Cloud Bay were often prone to the occasional gust of sea air. Yet it was remarkable for the scent it carried with it: honeysuckle, with something lighter, softer, hidden behind it, like a warm spring day.

Gregor halted his steps, head swiveling as he searched the crowd. *No, no*, he pleaded silently. *Please, no, not here.*

"What's wrong?" The Warden escorting him came up beside Gregor, his hand resting on the hilt of his sword.

Gregor barely registered the question. The scent suffocated him, his wrists aching at the memory of rope biting into his skin as Tanithe Ash dragged him through darkness and shadow. Her whispered words in his ear. Her threats. Her promises.

I will kill you, Gregor Thalesen.

His chest tightened even as the breeze blew onward, taking the floral scent along with it, passing as quickly as it arose.

"Sir?" the Warden asked. "Are you alright?"

Was his mind playing tricks on him, as it had before they'd left Taernfane, when Dare had brought him flowers? Or was the wind trying to warn him?

"I don't know," he said quietly, checking the crowded streets once more. "It might be nothing . . ."

The Warden's young face took on a hardened edge. He gripped his sword. "Or it might not be. What did you see?"

Gregor shook his head, his thumb tracing the scar around his wrist. "I didn't see anything," he admitted. "It was more of a feeling. Something familiar."

The Warden—Jonah, he'd said his name was—took Gregor by the arm and ushered him forward. "From what little the commander's told me, that's enough for me. Come on."

Although each shadow they passed had Gregor's heart thundering, Jonah guided them swiftly the rest of the way, and they reached the Wardens' base without running afoul of anyone or anything.

"Thank you," Gregor said. He'd expected his nerves to calm once he was through the gates, but . . .

. . . But the Wardens' late commander was killed within these walls, his mind helpfully reminded him. *In his own base. What if it was her doing?*

"Don't thank me yet," Jonah said, his eyes still alert as he gestured for Gregor to follow him, as though he'd had a similar thought. "You're not getting rid of me until I've deposited you with the commander."

The Warden guided him across the base until they came to a long, low building. Inside, Jonah brought him to a large set of doors. He knocked and pushed the door open in almost the same movement.

Verity looked up from the desk as they entered. "Thank you, Jonah," she said, but then her brow furrowed as she looked between them. "Is everything alright?"

Jonah saluted her. "We didn't have any trouble, though he thought he felt something on the road, about halfway here. I didn't see anyone suspicious."

"It was probably nothing," Gregor said, his face heating. "I think my mind was playing tricks on me." He wanted nothing more than to believe that was true.

Verity gave him a look that said *we're going to talk about this more* before returning Jonah's salute. "Thank you for taking the potential threat seriously. You're dismissed."

Jonah spun and left the room, closing the door behind him.

"I don't know whether I should congratulate you on your promotion," Gregor said, hoping for a swift change of subject, "or offer my condolences."

Verity huffed a laugh. "Both feel appropriate at this point."

"I'm sorry I haven't been by since it happened."

"It's been two days, Gregor. And we've both had more than a few things to occupy our time." She crossed her arms, shifting her weight to one leg. "Now tell me about this thing you felt on the way here."

Gregor inhaled deeply and explained what he sensed on the walk from the embassy, how the scent of spring flowers and honeysuckle had sent his pulse skittering.

Verity listened, and there was no judgment or pity in her eyes. "Scent is a strong trigger for memories," she said, setting her hand on Gregor's shoulder. The weight was comforting, and his shoulders relaxed away from his ears.

"You don't think it's foolish?"

"Of course not. Regardless of whether Tanithe is doing this to mess with us, it's not foolish to have a visceral reaction to something like that."

Gregor was almost afraid to ask his next question, but the words came out in nearly a whisper. "Do you think it's her?"

Verity's lips twisted as she considered her next words. "I don't know," she said. "It seems too subtle, too much of a coincidence, but Dare would point out that I said the same thing before, and this is yet another coincidence. And it would support his theory, given the connection to flowers." She leaned back against her desk, crossing her arms again. "I don't know what to think about all this, Gregor. I wish I had the answers for any of it. But what I do know is that we're going to take this seriously. I'm not letting her get near any of you if I have anything to say about it."

Some of the tension Gregor was carrying eased. "That means a lot, Verity. Thank you." He sank into one of the chairs angled toward the desk. "And how are you holding up with all this?"

"Honestly?" Verity tilted her head back, searching the ceiling for an answer. "Between learning my new responsibilities, planning Commander Cairn's funeral, and preparing for the inquest hearing, I'm completely overwhelmed."

Gregor could certainly imagine how much work that would entail, especially if Verity didn't have anyone in a support role to help her. "Well, I have some news that may help with one of those things." He took the note from Caelan out of his pocket and handed it to Verity. At Verity's raised brow, he continued, "Chancellor Caelan needs to push back the hearings by at least a week or two. The Valdane Council . . ." He paused, trying to think of a diplomatic way of describing the situation, but the hours of scanning tedious, useless documents had left his mind in a fog.

"You don't have to be polite with me," Verity said with a grin. "Speak your mind."

"They're making things far more difficult than they need to be."

Verity chucked softly. "That doesn't surprise me somehow. But moving the hearing back helps a lot. I can focus on Cairn's funeral and dealing with the person responsible."

A twinge of curiosity had Gregor sitting up a little straighter. "You know who did it?"

Verity nodded, though she turned her gaze to the floor. "Yes, but I'd rather not get into it right now. It's . . . complicated." As she straightened, Verity flicked the end of her braid over her shoulder. "I asked you to come here because I was hoping to show you something. It does involve meeting someone, if you're up for it?"

"I think so," he said, smoothing the fabric of his pants. "Is it formal, or—?"

"No, very informal. Relaxed, even. Nothing to worry about at all." She smiled, though Gregor couldn't help the thought that, these days, he was always worried.

Gregor followed Verity across the Wardens' base to a small stone building set apart from everything else by far enough that, had it not still been within the walls of the compound, he would have thought it wasn't a part of the base at all. Smoke curled from the chimney, and the frosted windows gave off a soft, comforting glow.

Verity's knuckles rapped against the wooden door, and before long, a woman answered. She seemed to be a bit older than Gregor, with warm golden skin and dark hair that twisted into a loose bun at the back of her neck. She peered at them over half-moon glasses. "Ah, High Commander, good to see you." She stepped out of the doorway, the silver chain around her robed waist clinking as she moved. "Please, come in."

"Is now a good time," Verity asked, not following the woman inside just yet. "I wanted to introduce you to my friend. The one I told you about."

Told her about? What precisely had Verity told her about him, Gregor wondered. He tucked his hands behind his back, waiting patiently.

"Ah, the young man who needs a quiet retreat." She smiled at Gregor like an old friend. "I've been looking forward to meeting you."

Gregor looked to Verity, who nodded and gestured him inside. He stepped across the threshold as the woman said, "My name is Ardyn Harrow. I'm the lorekeeper for the Wardens based in Whitehollow. Welcome to my laboratory."

Laboratory? Gregor had to force his mouth not to fall open like a gaping fool. This wasn't a laboratory. This was a *sanctuary*. Bookshelves lined nearly every wall, even the nooks with odd angles, and were filled with books, trinkets, herbs and other jarred specimens, and at least a dozen other things that Gregor wasn't even sure how to categorize. There were tables covered in alchemical apparatuses and reagents among what looked to be several half-finished projects.

It was amazing. It was wonderful. It held within it the type of magic that Gregor could see and touch. Not *real* magic—though he wouldn't be surprised if there were more than one or two enchanted items among the collected oddities—but the kind of magic he'd always felt when learning something new.

"Lorekeeper Harrow," Verity said, a smile in her voice. "This is Gregor Thalesen. He's a dear friend of mine currently staying at the Drahkonian embassy."

Gregor pulled his attention away from the wonders of the lorekeeper's laboratory, his face heating as he realized both Verity and the lorekeeper were grinning at him. "I'm sorry." He gave Lorekeeper Harrow a formal bow. "It's a pleasure to meet you."

Still grinning, Harrow leaned closer to Verity. "You were right, Commander. I'm going to like him."

CHAPTER 37

LUCIEN WAS RESTLESS. HE'D tried to put it off for as long as he could, but the closer Micah's one-week deadline came, the more agitated the beast grew. Almost as though it were eager to go back. Did it know something that Lucien didn't?

Taerna needed him to move. Although he didn't fully understand the task the goddess had for him, he hoped it would become clearer in time. He didn't want to leave Ethriel and Faith, but the longer Lucien tarried at the farmstead, the more anxious he got.

The last few nights, he'd barely slept. And last night . . . well . . . Lucien had needed to go for a hunt in the woods in order to calm the beast. He'd already been worried about losing control and hurting his family, and the longer he lingered here, the more pleasure the beast seemed to derive from setting his control on edge.

That was why, on the day he'd set with Jae to leave, Lucien was already sitting at the table, dressed and packed, when Ethriel woke just before dawn.

She didn't look surprised to see him at all.

"I made coffee," Lucien said quietly, hoping to avoid waking Jae, who still slept on a blanket near the hearth. Better to let her rest before the next leg of their journey.

"Oh, gods," Ethriel whispered back. "I didn't think you'd resort to poisoning me."

Lucien's eyes narrowed. "I'm capable of making coffee, Eth," he grumbled.

"Yes, but not *good* coffee, unless Jae was able to bestow that skill upon you." She winked, joining him at the table. "Taerna knows I never could."

Lucien's face heated. "As a matter of fact, she threatened to gut me if I didn't do it the way she showed me," he said, his voice lowering still farther.

Ethriel stifled a laugh. "I'll remember that trick for next time." Lucien poured her a mug of coffee, and she wrapped her fingers around it. "You're leaving today?" she asked once he sat down again.

Lucien blew out a sigh. "I'm worried about staying here too much longer." He flexed his fingers, his knuckles popping. "I have to finish whatever it is Taerna needs me to do."

Ethriel nodded, watching the steam swirling from the mug between her hands.

"I don't suppose," Lucien went on, "I can convince you to send Corvin away?"

She looked up at that. "You too?" she asked. "I suppose I shouldn't be surprised."

"I don't trust him, Eth." Once Jae had filled him in on what had happened in the western field the other night, Lucien trusted him even less than he had before. "But I do."

"We fought against him in Taernfane. He serves Westhold. He serves Ainam. I just want to look out for you. For Faith. I need to make sure you're safe."

"When Corvin told you his story," Ethriel said, "he omitted a few details of his arrival on my doorstep."

Lucien's brow furrowed, but Ethriel waved the look away with a swipe of his hand. "No, nothing sinister. He didn't say how bad off he was when he arrived. When he came through the first time, he was beaten, but nothing a little time wouldn't have fixed on its own. But the second time?" She inhaled, shaking her head slowly. "He was in bad shape, Lucien. Really bad. I was certain he was going to die. I thought, this stranger showed up on my doorstep and is about to drop dead in my kitchen. He had a concussion, and his arm had the worst break I've ever seen. He had broken ribs and more cuts and bruises than I could count. That's what Westhold did to him. That's what Ainam allowed to happen to him. That's what he got for his *service*."

Ethriel traced her fingers around the outer edge of the mug. "It took me weeks to convince him to give me his name, because he didn't want to put Faith or me in danger, in case someone was hunting him. He thought the less we knew about him, the better." She met Lucien's gaze, and her eyes were bright, determined. "I believe he's a good man. I've gone twenty years without having you around to look out for me, and I think I've gotten pretty good at taking care of myself and Faith."

Her words pierced through Lucien's heart, true as they were.

"Given everything you've been through, I understand why you don't trust him, Luc," she continued. "But trust *me*."

His shoulders dropped. Trust her. How could he not? He owed her that much, at least. Besides, Lucien had no right to pop back into her life—into Faith's life—and start making demands and decisions about who they should trust. She was right; they'd been doing just fine without him this whole time.

"I do trust you, Eth," he said, his voice dropping to a low rumble. "But if he hurts either of you, I'll break him in half."

Ethriel set her hand on his. "I would expect nothing less." Smiling, she brought the mug to her lips and took a small sip. Her eyes widened. "Lanara's tears," she breathed. "You did learn something."

Lucien chuckled softly. "I had a good teacher. Or, at least, a very insistent one."

Ethriel glanced toward the hearth where Jae still lay asleep. "I never asked," she said slowly, "and it's alright if you'd rather not say, but . . . You and Jae. Are you . . . ?" One eyebrow slowly arched in question.

Lucien nearly snorted his own coffee through his nose. "She's young enough to be my daughter, Eth."

Ethriel only angled her head as though that meant very little. "For many men that would hardly be a deterrent," she said gently. "Especially in cases where one doesn't exactly appear one's age." She took another sip of coffee, eying him over the rim of the mug.

"Gods, no. She's like a little sister." But considering Ethriel started them down this line of questioning . . . "So, are you and Corvin . . . ?"

Ethriel swatted his hand. "Lucien, he's young enough to be my son."

He shrugged, letting Ethriel infer what she wanted from the gesture.

She rolled her eyes. "You're insufferable." But the wistful smile on her face showed the truth.

"Eth, I . . ." He hesitated. He'd blurted out her name before his mind had caught up with what he wanted to say, and now he sat there like an idiot. What could he even say to her? So instead, he memorized the lines of her face, the bright, flame-red shade of her hair, the unruly curls. And her scent—wet earth, wood smoke, and honeysuckle. He committed that to memory too, although he doubted he'd ever be able to forget it.

"Let me pack you some things for the road," she said softly as she stood. Her hand drifted to Lucien's shoulder as she passed him, and she stooped just enough to place a gentle kiss on the top of his head. "I love you too," she murmured. Then she was behind him, gathering fruit, bread, and some cheese that had been left from their dinner the night before.

Lucien bowed his head as she worked. He didn't deserve this. He didn't deserve her.

Lucien double-checked and triple-checked his gear while Jae packed and Ethriel gathered things she insisted they take with them, including one of Lucien's old hunting knives and enough food to keep both of them fed the whole way to the Red Forest.

Soft footfalls squelched in the mud behind Lucien as he filled his water skin at the pump on the side of the cottage.

Faith leaned against the corner of the building, her arms crossed over her chest. "So you're leaving?" she demanded.

"I have something I need to do." Lucien kept his focus on the pump. He hooked the full skin on his belt, then splashed some water onto his hands and ran them through his hair.

Faith scoffed. "Of course."

"I know you don't believe me," he said, "but I'm coming back."

"Sure." She pushed off the wall and headed down the gravel path toward the forest. "I'll believe that when I see it."

"Look after your mother," Lucien called.

"I don't need to," Faith snapped over her shoulder. "She looks after herself just fine without you."

He swallowed a growl and splashed two handfuls of cold water onto his face. She was right, on both counts. But he hated the idea of leaving them alone with Corvin, despite Ethriel's assurance that she trusted him.

After all, she had trusted Lucien too, and he had broken her heart.

Lucien rounded the corner of the cottage and found Jae standing near the door, her pack slung over her shoulders and a knowing look of concern on her face. He brushed past her and stepped inside to grab his own things.

Ethriel sat at the kitchen table, finishing the coffee he'd made for her earlier. "Did Faith say goodbye before she left to check the snares?" she asked.

Lucien snorted. "In a way."

"She's like you in a lot of ways. She'll come around eventually. Once you come back, she'll have time to get to know you."

His hand stilled on his pack. *Once I come back . . .* He just needed to survive the meeting with Micah first.

"You promised," Ethriel said, her voice growing stern, though he sensed the tremor in it just below the surface. "Remember that. You promised me, Luc."

"I know." He hefted the heavy travel bag onto his back. "As long as I have breath in my lungs and legs to carry me," he said, repeating the words he'd spoken to her on the cottage steps a few nights earlier.

"Or friends to drag you back," she added. Her deep blue eyes glittered with tears she refused to let fall.

Lucien nodded. "I promise." He would come back to her. No matter what.

No power in the world would keep him from her again.

Outside, Jae stood in the middle of the gravel path, checking the draw on her blades, and Corvin was making his way toward them from the forest, pushing a wooden wheelbarrow piled with firewood.

Ethriel followed Lucien outside and moved to Jae. "Look after him," Ethriel said. "You brought him back to me once. I'd be grateful if you could do it again."

Jae nodded solemnly and extended her hand to Ethriel. "I'll do everything I can."

Ethriel ignored the hand and instead pulled Jae into a tight hug.

Lucien watched, amused, as Jae's eyes widened at first, then closed briefly as she returned the embrace. "I'm so glad I got to finally meet you." Stepping back, she added, "We'll be back soon. I'm not about to miss out on all the embarrassing stories you must have about Lucien. I need to hear them all."

Ethriel laughed then, and the sound nearly had Lucien changing his mind about leaving. "Oh, the stories I could tell!"

Corvin dropped the firewood off nearby and wiped his hands on his pants. "Thank you," he said to Lucien, his voice low, "for trusting me." He cleared his throat as he extended a hand. "Travel safely."

Lucien eyed the offered hand for a moment before taking it. "I'm not trusting you," he said. "I'm trusting *her*." He tightened his grip. Lucien knew his strength, and he knew he was crushing Corvin's hand, but he held that grip and let a bit of the beast glint in his eyes. "If you do anything to betray her trust in you, there will be nowhere you can run from me that I won't hunt you down." He bared his teeth, which had sharpened to fangs. "And when I find you, I will rip your throat out."

Corvin's jaw tensed as Lucien's hand held fast like a vise, but he didn't try to pull away. "I understand," he said tightly.

Lucien held him there a moment longer before releasing him. Corvin simply tucked his hands behind his back as Ethriel came to stand beside them.

"Stay safe," she said, rising onto her toes to kiss Lucien's cheek just above his beard. "Come back to me, Luc," she whispered before stepping back. "And in fewer than twenty years this time, please."

CHAPTER 38

THE FOREST OPENED TO Lucien's senses. As he led the way, with Jae following just behind, the beast clawed at its chains. It wanted to run. *Later*, he promised it. *We'll run later.* After that, it seemed to settle into a quiet sort of restlessness.

Lucien angled his head to glance over his shoulder at Jae. "You're quiet," he observed. They'd been walking for a couple hours already, and she hadn't said a single word, which was more than a little unusual.

Jae shrugged. "I'm giving you some time."

"For what?"

"You know what," she said. "To process all of that."

"I'm fine," he grumbled.

Behind him, Jae laughed. "Yeah, alright. Sure."

"I don't need you to coddle me, Jae."

"I'm not coddling," she said, jogging up to walk beside him. "You're a grumpy old man, and I'm giving you space to be grumpy."

A rumble of a growl sounded from deep within his chest before he could stop it.

"See," Jae said, waving a hand at him. "That's what I'm talking about. But, if you insist on wanting to talk, what's your read on Corvin?"

"I don't like him."

Jae laughed again. "Yeah, I figured that out. I meant do you trust him?"

"No, but Ethriel does. And I trust her." They walked a few more yards in silence before he asked, "What about you?"

Jae shook her head, her dark curls bouncing. "I have no fucking idea," she said. "If you'd asked me a week ago if I'd *ever* trust Corvin Crosse, I'd have told you not a chance in Vire's hells."

Lucien eyed her sidelong. "But?"

"But it seems like he genuinely wants to help Ethriel. Like he's trying to be a good person. And I think he was being truthful about losing Ainam's power. But then again, he's trying to get it back." She shook her head again. "I don't know what any of that means. I don't know if we can trust him."

Lucien tried to push the worry from his head. He couldn't think about that. He had to trust Ethriel. He had to focus on the path in front of his feet—and the task Taerna set out for him.

If only he knew what it was.

But once it was done, he could go home to Ethriel and Faith. *Home.* He hadn't let himself think about that concept for the last twenty years, but now it almost seemed within reach.

Almost.

The beast stirred in its chains. Could Lucien ever really hope to lead a normal life as long as this monster lived inside his skin, waiting for the moment he let his guard down so it could take control? Could he be a husband to Ethriel? A father to Faith? Or would his presence there only put them in danger, just as he'd always feared?

In his last vision from Taerna, Lucien had seen what the shifters had once been. Not monsters, but wolves, two halves that made a greater whole. What he wouldn't give for a chance at that kind of peace. It was nothing short of beautiful.

But . . . But what had caused the shifters to change from wolves to feral monsters? Why was this dream out of his grasp?

Or was it?

As the forest gave way to gently sloping hills, the tall grass almost seemed to lean into Lucien, caressing his legs, the ground humming in answer.

Lucien glanced at Jae, whose attention was on the path ahead. He kept walking, but turned his focus inward, to the little shard of crystal that sat nestled against his heart. *Taerna?*

It wasn't long before the heavy, comforting weight of the goddess's attention draped over him. *I am here, little wolf.* Some of the grass stretched up to brush against his palm. *You have questions for me.*

I do. Taerna had shown him a vision of shifters being created in a type of ceremony or ritual. He hadn't thought too hard on it—it was in the past and was no longer the way of things—but now, questions clawed at him. He inhaled deeply before putting the first into words. *Why were the shifters created?*

Between one step and the next the earth split open, and in that darkness between spaces, the same rolling hills across which he and Jae now walked resolved into being, though a massive battle raged. Lucien's awareness was high above, like a carrion bird circling the battlefield.

Hundreds of people charged across the open plains, screaming, yelling, shifting into giant wolves as they ran. They charged a horde of . . . *Demons*—the word was supplied for him. The shifters were horribly outnumbered. Two, maybe three hundred against a thousand or more. But they charged, and their bravery, their serenity, their faith was palpable. They charged. And they battled.

And they won.

They were my children, Taerna said, her voice rough and jagged in his mind. *My sacred warriors. Protectors. When we were under siege, they fought against Ainam's boundless order and Vire's unrelenting corruption. But with each victory in battle, more of my children met their end, until . . .*

The vision darkened briefly, and when it returned, Lucien looked down upon a small group in chains. Sorrow and pain and grief overwhelmed his senses. They huddled together as best they could, bound as they were. Soon, a hooded figure approached. Not a demon, but not human. Something in between.

One of the shifters took a single step forward. His long, dark hair was caked with blood, but he held his head high. The others looked to him and found their own resolve. Their backs straightened, and they faced their captor united.

The figure extended their arm and laid a hand upon each of the bound prisoners in turn. The sorrow and grief turned to overwhelming rage as the wolf inside each of them twisted, gnawing at their bindings, writhing and howling to be released. This—the rage—was all too familiar, and as it was forced upon the shifters, Lucien's heart broke. He witnessed their descent, their madness. The hooded figure staggered and fell to one knee. They waved a hand before collapsing unmoving in the grass, their power drained to nothing for this one act against the goddess Taerna.

The captives' bonds fell away, leaving them free, but—

They were cursed, Lucien said.

The shifters changed and tore into the wilderness, their wolves no longer beautiful creatures of power but horrible, howling abominations.

As they ran, one paused and looked back. And *up* to where Lucien watched the tragedy from above. It was bigger than the rest, and its fur was a stunning fade of black, brown, and silver. Glowing green eyes stared at him.

I've seen him before, Lucien said. It was the beast that had attacked him during his other visions. With the shifter's attention on him now, that throbbing pain behind his eye began again.

His name was Korin, Taerna said, and her voice carried with it an earth-shattering grief. *He was my last Chosen. Korin and his pack fought honorably, but they were overrun. They were caught by a Chosen of Vire, and cursed by the very corruption they fought against. And they were consumed by it. They were the last of my children.*

Why didn't you do something? Lucien demanded. Rage built in his chest as the shifter stared at him, pacing on the field below as though trying to figure out how to reach where Lucien hovered far above.

I was weakened. I tried, but Vire had grown in power, and I could not stop it. And once it was done, and my children were lost to my grace, I could not bring them back to me before we fell to slumber.

The monstrous shifter roared, and Lucien's vision flashed white as the pain stabbed behind his eyes. A growl tore from his throat, the shifter's presence pushing his own control to the breaking point, but Taerna held him close.

Do you see? Taerna asked, even as the world around Lucien faded to black. *I needed my roots in the world. My climbing vines.*

Lucien snarled, clutching his head in his hands. The rage diminished as his awareness returned to him. The ground was solid beneath his knees, the sun warm against his skin. He sucked in a lungful of air, panting as he worked to regain control of the beast that bellowed deep within him.

OUT!

"No!" Lucien shouted back. When he dropped his hands, the world was as he'd left it, though Jae was facing him, her swords drawn.

The scent of her fear danced around him, drawing the beast's attention.

"Jae," Lucien said through clenched teeth. "I need you to back up."

"Lucien? What was—"

He growled, baring his fangs. "Back. Up."

Jae moved away but didn't turn her back. Good. Lucien set his palms against the earth and took a few deep breaths. When his heartbeat finally steadied and he could think about something other than hunting prey, Lucien met Jae's concerned gaze.

"I know what Taerna needs me to do."

Chapter 39

In the week since the Warden commander's assassination, Dare had hardly seen Verity. Their training had become far more irregular when Verity was forced to serve as the new high commander. As much as Dare hated that this role was thrust at her, he had to admit that it suited her. Verity took to it much like a baby bird who was forced to leave the nest but realized quite suddenly that it already knew how to fly.

On top of Verity's new position and increased responsibility, Chancellor Caelan called meetings with Dare nearly every afternoon. Sometimes Gregor or Finn was present as well, and Caelan would review how the trial was to be conducted and what Dare's role was to be. The trial had also been pushed back because of some bureaucratic bullshit. Even Gregor had seemed annoyed by the delay.

But they were all so busy, Dare barely saw any of his friends outside of those boring meetings and the few trainings with Verity that, against all expectations, had become something he looked forward to. So when he woke to a note from Verity saying to meet him at one of the training rings at the ninth chime, Dare was excited at the prospect.

Their practices still focused mainly on breathing exercises and meditation, though Verity had made sure not to neglect his hand-to-hand training completely either. As much as he wanted to hate all of it, Dare was making progress. He had managed to meditate through Verity casting magic at him a few more times, and it was getting easier to tune out the prickling, needling sensations the more he practiced it. Even the martial training was going well. He knew Verity was still going easy on him—he wasn't naive—but after months of practicing with her, his muscles were slowly beginning to remember the movements. It reminded him of when he first learned to lift a coin purse, throw a dagger, or roll a coin. He was far from an expert, but the progress was encouraging.

Maybe Verity was right.

Dare got to the training ring just as the ninth chime rang across the base. Verity glanced up at his approach. "Arriving at training on time? Well, that's a first," she teased.

"Do I get a reward?" he asked, flashing her his most sincere smile.

"Yeah." Verity crossed her arms over her chest. "You get to *not* run laps for being late." Dare laughed as she gestured for him to take a seat near her. "We're going to start with meditation, and then transition into some drills, alright?"

"Whatever you say, Commander."

Verity's brows climbed, her lips twisting into a grin. "Hm, I could get used to that."

They practiced some of the mind-stilling techniques for a while, but soon Verity moved them to the second half of their training.

"I want to try something different today," she said, crossing to the rack of wooden training weapons on the far side of the yard. She grabbed one of the longswords.

"Sword training?" Dare asked. It wasn't something they worked on all the time, but it wasn't exactly new. Verity had been adamant that Dare know more about a sword than just which end to hold.

"Not exactly." When she turned, Dare spotted two wooden weapons in her other hand, about the size of his daggers.

Dare caught them as she tossed them over. He spun each one, idly checking the balance as he eyed the much longer sword she held. "Well, this hardly seems fair."

"Swords are great," Verity said, rejoining him in the center of the ring, "but you don't carry a sword. I can teach you sword forms until you're old and gray, but it's not going to do you any good if you don't have one on you when you need it." She nodded toward the wooden daggers. "But I know you always carry half a dozen of those on you. So let's work with what you have."

Dare's mouth went dry as he recalled fighting Caleb in a snow-covered mountain pass—a spear arcing toward his chest. "I can't help but feel like you have a distinct advantage here," he said. "You've got more reach."

Verity shrugged. "With this, sure. But that's not the point. I would have thought that you of all people would know it's not the length of the blade, but how you wield it."

Dare snickered. "My lady Warden!" he exclaimed. "You besmirch my honor."

To her credit, Verity only winked. "You must be a bad influence on me." She swung her sword up and held it at the ready. "Show me what you've learned so far."

They sparred a round, Dare dodging frantically, lunging and twisting to stay outside of Verity's range while she remained on the offensive. When she tagged him with the wooden blade for the third time, she held up a hand for him to pause.

Dare was already breathing hard, while Verity barely seemed to register the exertion.

"You did well staying away," she said. "But that's never going to win you the fight. All it's going to do is delay your defeat until your opponent tires you out." She waved Dare closer. "Look, here's the range of my weapon." She swung the wooden sword slowly in a downward slash, stopping when she hit his shoulder. "Now, step closer."

Dare stepped toward Verity until her forearm, and not the blade of her sword, was resting against his shoulder.

She nodded toward his daggers again, and Dare lifted one, setting the blade easily beneath Verity's chin in such close quarters. "Who's got the advantage now?"

Dare studied the point of the wooden dagger against Verity's pale skin. "It's not about staying outside your reach, is it? It's about getting *into* mine."

"Exactly!" Verity tapped her forearm against his shoulder again. "It's counterintuitive, but if you understand their weapon and how it moves, you can work around it. A sword is only dangerous from here"—she gestured along the length of the blade—"to here. Any closer than that and it's practically useless. Now, we're going to take some of the drills you already know and add the daggers to it. Like this."

They trained for another two hours, until the sun was high in the sky and Dare had sweat through his shirt. His stomach rumbled.

"Good work," Verity said as she collected the wooden weapons and returned them to the rack.

"I think I'm getting better," Dare said with a little swell of pride as he noted that a few strands of Verity's reddish-brown hair had escaped her braid and were stuck to her forehead. *That* was a first.

"Of course. It's called *practice*." Verity drew out the word as though Dare were hearing it for the first time.

He peered at her. "I think I've been a bit too much of a bad influence on you." He laughed with her, then surveyed the training yard. "Same time tomorrow?" he asked.

"I can't tomorrow," Verity said, and Dare tried to hide his disappointment. "I have meetings all morning, and I have to brief the Wardens who are going to serve during the trial. It's in a week."

A week? Only a week before Tanithe would get what was coming to her for the hell she unleashed on Taernfane. For the hell she put Finn and Gregor through. Once Dare was back in Valda, he'd set up a few things that would all feed back into the account the Valdane Council had set up in his name, which he'd then transfer to Matron Nora's orphanage and let the Valdane economy do the rest.

"What's going on?" Verity asked slowly, as though afraid of the answer. "You're up to something."

Dare snapped himself out of his wandering thoughts. "What?"

"You're grinning like a fool," Verity said, a hand coming to rest on her hip. "And I *know* you can't be excited for the hours and hours of meetings for the trial that await us next week. So, what are you up to?"

"It's nothing." He laid on the sincerity. "Just a couple things I need to take care of back in Valda when all this is done."

She watched him. "So it has nothing to do with the trial?"

A smirk tugged at Dare's lips. "I didn't say that."

Verity rolled her eyes. "You'd just better know what you're doing."

"Of course! When do I not?"

"Seriously?"

He set a hand on his heart. "After all we've been through, my lady Warden?"

"*Especially* after all we've been through."

"That stings, Verity."

She groaned as they started the walk across the compound toward the barracks. "Will you just tell me what you're planning?"

He chuckled softly. He'd meant to tell her about the deal earlier, but the events of the last week had gotten in the way. It would definitely be in his best interest if he controlled when and how the story came out, so now was as good a time as any.

Dare began to tell her the story of his clandestine meeting in that shady little tavern in Valda, of the promise of more gold than he'd seen in his life, and the details of a tiny, meaningless little oath that would conveniently be ignored when the time came to make his official report and testimony.

He began. But as he opened his mouth, no sound emerged. A heat burned on the right side of his chest. His hand flew to the source of the discomfort, but nothing felt out of the ordinary to the touch.

Dare swallowed and tried again. The words refused to form in his throat, though the burning in his chest increased. Panic swelled in the pit of his stomach.

As they passed by the central courtyard, Verity looked off toward the shrine to Pyrannis, burning as brightly as it ever did.

"Fine," she said, still not looking at him. "If you're going to play games, just promise me you're not going to make me look like an idiot. And that you won't get yourself into any trouble. I have enough on my plate as it is. I don't need to have any more messes to deal with, understood?"

Something was wrong. Dare cleared his throat, the sound arriving as expected.

He tried to rein in the expression on his face before she turned, but apparently he wasn't fast enough. Or she was getting better at reading him. He hoped it was the former.

"What is it? What's wrong?"

"Sorry," he said, rubbing his hand along the back of his neck. He gave her a sheepish grin. "Lost in thought. I'll, uh . . . I'll do my best to stay out of trouble."

She eyed him and sighed. "That doesn't comfort me as much as it should."

You and me both.

The rest of the walk to the barracks was quiet. Dare tried twice more to explain to Verity about the deal he struck at the tavern in Valda, and twice more he was met with silence and a burning in his chest that seemed to grow stronger the more he tried to force the words out.

"What the fuck," Dare muttered.

Verity shot him a look. "What?"

He dragged his fingers through his hair. "Just . . . thinking out loud."

She gave him an appraising look all the way down to his boots and back up again. "Are you sure you're alright?" she asked.

He forced a smile. "Why wouldn't I be?"

"Really? I can think of a dozen reasons off the top of my head."

"Come now," he said, shaking off the knot of panic that had settled in his chest. "You think so little of me?"

"The opposite, actually."

Dare's shoulders sagged, and his heart lurched. "I have a lot on my mind," he said. "I'll be fine." He hoped he was right.

When they reached the hall with their rooms, Verity paused at her door. "If you want to take some time to go over your testimony for the trial," she said, "you know where to find me."

"Right . . . The trial." *Fuck me right in the fucking—*

"Let me know if you need anything, Dare," Verity said, cutting off his thoughts. "If you need to talk"—she gave kind of a helpless shrug—"I'll be here."

Dare forced himself to focus. She was worried about him. She was looking out for him.

Again.

He'd be damned if he dragged her down with him. He'd figure this out. He had to. "I'll be fine," he said again. "Thank you, my lady Warden. Truly."

Back in his room—Drystan's old room—Dare flopped onto the bed, pressing his palms hard against his eyes. "What the fuck am I going to do?" he muttered.

His chest was still sore from all his attempts to talk about the deal. Dare pulled the collar of his shirt down to see if anything looked out of the ordinary, but all that was there were his scars. The knotted burn scar from Solace, and the raised scar of his Warden's brand.

Oh . . . oh, fuck . . .

Dare thought back to the oath he swore in Valda. To the language he'd used in swearing it. *I swear on my honor as a Warden of the Flame—*

The bottom fell out of Dare's stomach. *I will never tell anyone about this conversation—*

No, it wasn't possible.

Was it?

Tykaras?

Nothing happened. Not that Dare could command the god to appear, but some days it seemed far easier to call on them than others. And this was not a time when he was willing to wait around.

Dare focused his mind. *Tykaras*, he tried again. *I need to speak with you.*

A familiar rush of expansiveness filled his chest, signaling that he had the god's attention.

I . . . Now that he had their attention what could he say? "I . . . may have a problem," he said aloud.

There was a pregnant pause, as though Tykaras was thinking of saying something, but held it back. After a moment, Dare heard only a quiet, *Oh?*

"I made—" The words stalled out again, the pain in his chest returning. Dare slammed his fist into the bed. "Fuck!"

Tykaras's attention came into sharper focus. *What did you do, Child?*

I made an oath, Dare said in his mind, pleased to find the thoughts flowed as they should. Thank the fucking gods for that.

You swore an oath?

"Yes." Perhaps Dare was imagining it, but he thought he heard something of an exasperated sigh. It did not inspire confidence.

On your honor as a Warden of the Flame, I presume?

Yeah, that tone was definitely not a good one. ". . . Yes."

You may have a problem.

Silence filled Dare's mind. "Well, shit."

What was the wording of your oath, Child?

Dare dragged his hands through his hair. *I swore I wouldn't tell anyone that Tanithe Ash was responsible for the attack on Taernfane. And I swore I wouldn't tell anyone about the oath either.*

Now Tykaras really did sigh, a deep, expansive breath that could fill the stars. *I see.*

The silence that followed was so long, Dare pushed himself off the bed and began pacing the small room. "And?"

And what?

"I tried telling Verity about the—*dammit!*—about *it*, and I couldn't. I actually couldn't."

Well . . . Tykaras's tone sounded very much like they were speaking to a small child. *You did swear an oath. As a Warden.*

"That matters?"

Pyrannis takes these things very seriously.

"Are you fucking joking?"

Why would I joke? Your brand burned when you tried to speak of it, did it not?

Dare did another lap around the room. "How do I get out of it?" he asked. He couldn't keep the desperation from his voice.

You don't, Tykaras said with a finality that stopped Dare in his tracks.

"So I can't break it? That's it?"

Correct. Tykaras seemed to consider their next words carefully. *This is a situation where I believe you would say, you're fucked.*

Dare resumed his pacing. It couldn't be that final. There had to be a way out of it.

There isn't, Child. I am sorry. The presence of the god lifted from Dare's awareness, leaving him alone again.

On his next pass by the small chest of drawers, Dare sent a firm kick into it. The neat line of books across the top wobbled, and he caught them before they toppled off the side.

Paper! Dare scrambled over to the small desk and pulled a sheet of parchment and a quill from one of the drawers. He dipped the quill in a pot of ink and set the tip to the paper.

Tanithe Ash attacked Taernfane, he thought. His fingers tightened around the quill, but his hand wouldn't move and his chest burned. *I was bribed to say that Tanithe wasn't in Taernfane.* This time his fingers scratched words across the page, but when he looked at what he wrote, Dare wanted to scream.

In his leaning scrawl were the words, *Tanithe wasn't in Taernfane.*

"Fuck." Tykaras was right. He was fucked. Well and truly fucked. If he couldn't break the oath next week during the hearing . . . If he had to tell the committee that Tanithe wasn't in Taernfane . . .

Dare let his head fall against the top of the desk, his hands crumpling the paper, smearing the ink.

Verity was counting on him. Caelan and Dominic were counting on him. And the others—Lucien, Jae, Finn, Gregor—they'd all nearly been killed by Tanithe. They were never going to forgive him.

And he couldn't even tell them why.

Hours passed and dozens of pages of crumpled parchment littered the floor, covered in a hundred or more half-scribbled phrases. All failed attempts to write what Dare needed so desperately to be able to say.

He let his head drop against the desk again, but a tingle of magic danced in the air, sending a quick shiver through his body. When he looked up, a neatly folded piece of paper lay on the desk just beyond his ink-stained fingers.

He opened it, and his stomach churned as he recognized the handwriting.

I have a proposition for you. We're in a position to help each other. And before you tell me to go fuck myself, you'll want to hear me out.

An address was written with instructions to meet at dawn.

Come alone, the note said toward the bottom. *I'll make it worth your while. I swear.*

Dare balled up the note and tossed it onto the floor among all the other discarded pages.

"Fuck."

CHAPTER 40

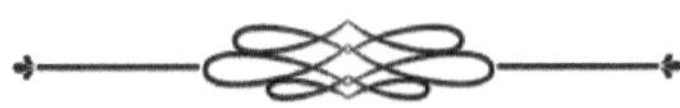

Dare had to admit, heading out alone to meet with Tanithe Ash was pretty high on the list of stupid shit he probably shouldn't do, but apparently he'd been on quite a roll ticking things off that list, so why not add one more?

The address on the note turned out to be a small café near the docks. The smell of warm, buttered pastries and strong coffee greeted him from half a block away, and nostalgia for his little apartment in Valda tugged at his heart. The place was crowded with a line a few feet out the door, but Dare spotted Tanithe sitting at one of the outdoor tables.

It took him a moment to recognize her. Instead of her usual black leathers with a dozen daggers strapped to her, she was wearing a fitted green top and a darker green . . . Was that a *skirt*? And instead of her bright red hair being tied out of the way, it was mostly loose, only pulled back in two small braids from her temples.

But that was definitely Tanithe. She gave him a predatory smile and beckoned him over with one slender, crooked finger.

Dare threaded through the crowd and took the seat opposite her. He braced himself for the overwhelming dizziness to wash over him, but it didn't. It crept in gently, almost beneath his awareness, turning his stomach like the beginnings of a hangover.

Before he could speak, a server came and asked if they wanted anything. Tanithe ordered two coffees and a plate of raspberry-filled puff pastries—Dare's favorite.

"Good morning, Dare, my dear," Tanithe said as the server left, her silky voice slithering across the table.

Dare kept both feet on the ground, ready to launch out of the chair if he needed to. "You look almost like a normal person," he mused.

"And you look almost like a functioning adult," she quipped back. Her hands gestured wide to encompass them both, as if to say, *And yet here we are.*

Dare crossed his arms. "What the fuck do you want, Tanithe?"

"Relax," she crooned. "Enjoy the morning. The coffee here is delightful, you know."

"You find yourself in Whitehollow often then?" he asked.

"From time to time." She angled her head to watch the patrons lined up for the café.

A quick glance revealed no weapons on her—at least none that he could see, though Dare had learned early on that not seeing them didn't mean she wasn't carrying them. As she uncrossed and recrossed her long legs, Dare realized she wasn't wearing a skirt but rather loose, flowing pants.

Tanithe's smile broadened with feline ferocity. "See anything you like?"

Dare had to suppress the urge to sneer. He knew that would only rile her up more. And a riled-up Tanithe was not high on his list of things to add to his day. "Not a thing," he said flatly.

The server returned with two coffees and the plate of pastries. Tanithe added some cream and sugar to hers and popped a raspberry pastry into her mouth while she waited for the coffee to cool.

Dare reached for neither, and she clicked her tongue at him. "Oh, come on, darling. After everything we've been through together?"

Dare forced a tight-lipped smile. He was well beyond feeling the need to indulge her in her little games. He noticed too, with no small amount of curiosity, that her presence still wasn't giving him the unnerving, dizzying vertigo that it had the last time. It simply roiled beneath the surface.

"Speaking of everything we've been through," Dare began. Why shouldn't he at least indulge his curiosity? She already knew all his secrets. Well, almost all of them. "Why is it that you don't feel quite as nauseating as the last time we met?" He grew bolder as her eyes narrowed. "Even Corvin Crosse's presence was more bothersome than this."

Tanithe looked as though she might gag. "Some people have no sense of subtlety whatsoever. Unlike that walking pile of shit, I prefer to keep my power close unless I need it." She let her eyes rake over Dare. "That is, unless you want me to let the chaos come out to play."

The ground rolled, and Dare had to grab onto the table to keep from falling out of his chair. And just as suddenly as it began, it stopped. No one else seemed to have noticed anything, but the residual vertigo still made Dare's vision wobble.

Tanithe laughed, delighted by her own little flare of power. He should have known better than to goad her.

He'd let her stall long enough. "I'll ask again, Tanithe. What the fuck do you want?"

"Charming as always," she said, derision oozing from her voice. She nudged the pastries a little closer to him. "Try one."

He knew this had been a bad idea. Dare dropped his hands, moving to stand.

"Stay, stay," she said, waving at him to remain seated. "Gods, you've gotten dull. That Warden is a bad influence on you. You used to be so much more fun." She brought her mug to her lips, her eyes rolling back almost sensually as she took a sip of coffee. "I've come to offer you a job," she said at last.

"A *job*? I find it hard to believe that the Council—"

Tanithe laughed. "The Council? Set your sights higher, darling."

He pinched the inner part of his arm with his thumb and forefinger to stop himself from drawing the dagger in his boot and lunging for her right there. He had a suspicion it wouldn't do anything except piss her off anyway. "You realize you have nothing left to blackmail me with, right? My secret's out. Damage done."

"Of course. I'm not an idiot."

Dare's blood heated. After what she'd done to him, to Gregor . . . "Tell me what in your twisted fucking mind makes you think I would ever willingly work with you?"

"Because *you're* not an idiot. At least, I'm hoping you're not. But perhaps I've been giving you too much credit all this time."

What he wouldn't give to be able to end her right here. To be done with the mind games and fuckery.

Tanithe watched him, pressing her lips together. "I don't like that I can't get into that fucked up head of yours anymore. I used to have so much fun checking up on you from time to time."

Gods above and below, how often had she—

"I presume," she continued, sizing him up, "that development has something to do with your new tag-along friend I met on the parapets?"

Dare's breath caught in his throat. She'd been there—of course! She was invading his mind with her magic, ripping him apart when Tykaras had intervened. *That* was the moment, when he'd said yes to Tykaras, and they'd shut Tanithe out. Apparently, the effect had been permanent. How had Tykaras accomplished that?

You could say it is a part of my purview, Tykaras answered, their attention focusing on Dare. Their voice sharpened to a razor's edge as they asked, *Why are you with the Chosen of Vire?*

She knows. About you.

She knows, Tykaras confirmed. *Which means Vire knows.*

There was no chance that was good, but . . . *How bad is that, exactly?*

Bad. I do not think Vire has a way to find out about the others just yet, so you would be the only other Chosen he knows about, aside from the Chosen of Ainam. I'm afraid that means—

I've got a target on my back, Dare finished. *Again. Just my luck.*

Tykaras's dry chuckle echoed in Dare's mind. *Indeed.*

Tanithe waved a hand. "It doesn't matter. Regardless, I want to bring you in on my little project. The ask is great, but so is the reward. For you and your *friend.*"

"Not interested."

Tanithe took a long, slow sip of her drink. "My dear, I haven't even told you the terms yet."

"Fuck the terms," Dare said, crossing his arms. He tried to conjure the stubborn defiance he witnessed so often with Verity. "Not. Interested."

"What if I sweeten the deal?" she asked, one delicate eyebrow arching. "What if I told you I could get you out of that silly little oath you swore back in Valda?"

Dare kept the old mask of cool indifference firmly in place, even as his palms began to sweat. "I don't know what you mean."

A slow smile played across her lips. "Don't you?" She took another luxurious sip of coffee. "I can absolve you of that oath, and you can go tell anyone you wish about all of that nasty business in Taernfane."

"Why would you do that? You'd be arrested and tried as a war criminal at best."

"Oh, darling," she said, her voice dropping low. "They'd have to find me first."

Dare leaned back in the chair, hands fiddling with the coffee mug, though he didn't move to drink it. "So what do you get out of it?"

Tanithe's gaze swept across the open seating area. "I don't want to go into specifics here," she said. "But all I would need is a small amount of your power."

Dare's brow knit. "My power?"

She waved a hand at him. "The power you wield from your friend," she said, "as well as your natural arcane magic." Her voice dropped to near a whisper. "After all Dare, you're a Perceptive."

That word alongside his name on her tongue made him shudder.

"And a Chosen," she continued just as quietly. "And by the god of luck, if what my patron tells me is true."

Dare shifted in his seat. He didn't like where this conversation was heading.

"Do you comprehend how rare of a combination that is? How powerful? My little pet project needs a bit more magic than what I can gather on my own, I'm embarrassed to say, but with your help?" Tanithe tilted her gaze to the sky, the sun highlighting the copper of her hair. "Oh, my dear, the things we could accomplish together."

Together. The thought turned Dare's stomach. Whatever Tanithe wanted his power for, she was only capable of evil, and any plan of hers would be dark and twisted. And regardless of whether or not she could actually free him from his oath, he'd figure out another way. There was no way he'd ever willingly work for Tanithe Ash again.

"Not a chance," he said coolly.

Under the table, Tanithe's foot brushed along the length of Dare's leg. "Oh, my little lordling. You know I always get what I want."

He slid his leg away from her. "Not always," he replied, matching her grin with his own as another thought came to him about that night in Taernfane. "By the way, how's your side?"

Tanithe went still. "Oh that," she said casually, though Dare saw a muscle twitch beneath her eye. "That was hardly a scratch, my darling. Hardly a scratch at all, made by little more than a rodent."

Oh, that struck a nerve.

Careful, Child, Tykaras warned.

"And if I get my hands on that rodent," Tanithe continued, her voice husky and low. "*When* I find him, I'm going to crush him beneath the heel of my boot until there is nothing left but bone dust and a dark splotch on the cobblestones."

Dare swallowed. His muscles tensed.

"And since you brought it up, I know he's here with you," she continued. "In Whitehollow. Should I pay him a visit?"

"Now that blackmail is out and persuasion didn't work, you're moving on to coercion?" Dare asked, boredom infusing each word even as fear clutched at his heart.

Tanithe leaned toward Dare. "You may have found a way to shut me out now, but don't forget, I've been in your mind more times than you know. I've seen the way you look at him. And I don't need to read your mind to know what it would do to you if I slit his throat. You're picturing it right now, aren't you? The look of horror on his face. The cold helplessness turning your stomach inside out. The light fading in his eyes as he—"

"Shut the fuck up," Dare snapped. Several patrons at nearby tables shot glances their way.

Tanithe simply smiled. "So what will it be, my precious little lordling?" She held one hand up as though weighing something in her palm. "Help me, you and your patron benefit from my plans, be rid of this oath, and your lover remains safe and sound? Or . . ." She held her other palm up. "Lose everything and everyone you care about. The choice is yours, darling."

No. He refused to accept those as his only two options. He'd find a way to talk to Verity. He'd warn Gregor. They'd figure something out. "Fuck you," Dare said, seething. "Are we done here?"

"Oh, my dear. You can go. But we're *far* from done. And in the meantime, I get the joy of knowing that you'll be watching around every corner, wondering if . . . wondering *when* . . . Wondering whether you'll be fast enough to stop my blade from sliding across his throat. Whether you'll be able to stop me from killing him."

She stood, all languid feline grace. And as she walked around him toward the main street, Tanithe leaned into him, far closer than Dare ever liked for her to be, and that little gut-twisting nausea doubled as she whispered in his ear, "Don't worry, Darcy. I'll make sure you're there to watch."

She sauntered away until she was swallowed by the crowd. Dare caught his breath, sinking back into his chair once she was out of sight. "Ainam's shining bollocks," he muttered under his breath. He didn't touch any of the food Tanithe ordered, but he dropped a couple of coins for the server before he left.

Before he could think too long about what had just happened, Dare took off at a run toward the Drahkonian embassy. He needed to warn Gregor.

He had enough forethought, at least, to take the long way around. Tanithe knew Gregor was in Whitehollow, sure, but that didn't mean she already knew exactly where he was. The last thing Dare wanted to do was lead Tanithe straight to him.

The guards stationed outside the embassy building waved him in immediately. "Good morning, Warden Wilhaven," one of them said.

Dare hardly slowed, dropping little more than a quick wave before he was inside and heading up the stairs. He knew he wouldn't be waking Gregor—he'd always woken with the sun.

At the upper landing, Dare skidded to a stop. Gregor *had* always woken with the sun, but Gregor hadn't been sleeping well since they'd left Taernfane. Verity had even had Dare bring Gregor a tea to help him sleep the day the Warden commander had been killed. The circles under his eyes were getting darker every day, and the way Gregor wrapped his arms around himself whenever they talked about Tanithe . . . Gregor was afraid. He was worried Tanithe was going to come after him again.

Could he really burst into Gregor's room with more bad news and no solutions? What purpose would that serve, besides frightening Gregor further?

Dare stared at the closed door to Gregor's room. Could Dare do that to him? And besides that, there was the fact that Gregor had asked Dare not to do anything stupid. Gregor was going to be furious at him.

He could tell Verity first, but she wasn't likely to find his excursion any more palatable than Gregor. And if he was being honest with himself, Dare was far more worried about Verity's anger than Gregor's.

Dare marched to the door on the opposite side of the hall and knocked.

Finn opened the door a moment later. "Dare? What's wrong?"

He glanced over his shoulder to where Gregor's door was still firmly shut. "I need to talk to you," he said. "Can we take a walk?"

"Let me get this straight . . ." Finn stared at Dare, clutching a coffee mug between her hands.

Dare sat across from her, taking a long drink of his own still-scalding coffee. He'd dragged her to a different café on a busy corner not far from the embassy and told her the story of his morning's encounter.

Finn shook her head like she still couldn't wrap her mind around it. "You got a message from"—she lowered her voice to a whisper—"Tanithe Ash saying to meet her this morning and to go alone, and you *did*?"

Dare swallowed. "Um . . . Yes?"

"What the hells is wrong with you?"

"I don't know, Finn. Tanithe's been in the wind for months since everything happened, but I've felt like she's been following us. Now we know she's actually here. In Whitehollow."

"Yeah, and that she wants to drag you into whatever insane scheme she has, or she's going to kill Gregor." Finn crossed her arms over her chest. "Great. Any idea what she wants you for?"

"I don't know," Dare said, the lie rolling easily off his tongue. Too easily. A pang of guilt twisted his stomach, but he pushed forward. This was not the time to try to explain about Tykaras. "Probably some job like she used to want me for in Valda."

"I hate to suggest keeping secrets," Finn said, frowning, "but I don't think you can tell Gregor. He barely comes out of his room as it is, and he hardly talks to anyone. If he knew for sure Tanithe was out there and was targeting him . . . Shit, I don't know what that would do to him."

Dare's shoulders slumped. "So what do I do?"

"Tell Verity?"

He winced. "She's going to be furious that I didn't tell her about the note before I met with Tanithe. I'll never hear the end of it."

"Security's already been doubled at the embassy," Finn said softly, as though thinking something through. "And it's only a week until the trial. If we keep an eye out . . . If we make sure Gregor stays safe . . ." She angled her head, considering.

"Then we might not need to bother either of them about it," Dare finished. And he'd need to stay away from Gregor, at least until Tanithe was captured. She'd said she wanted Dare to watch, and he didn't doubt for a moment that she meant it.

It might work, but gods did the thought of hiding this from both of them tie his insides into a knot.

Finn looked about as uncomfortable with the idea as he was, her lips down-turned like she'd tasted something bitter.

"Let me talk to Verity," she said after a moment. "I'll tell her I heard through a contact that Tanithe is in Whitehollow and might be targeting Gregor." Dare must have looked surprised because Finn added, "What? Do you think I've just been sitting around all day every day while the rest of you have been busy?"

"Fionna Garrison," Dare said, leaning back in his chair. "Have you been building a *spy network* in Whitehollow?"

"Impressed yet?"

Dare couldn't help the smile that slid across his face. "Always."

Finn scoffed quietly, rolling her eyes like she thought he was teasing her. "Look, I'll tell her about it, but I won't say I found out from you. Then Verity will know about it too, and we can make sure Gregor stays safe. What do you think?"

It was a good plan. And it would buy him some extra time to find a way to deal with his damn oath. Not to mention that he still needed to figure out how to tell the others about Tykaras.

One thing at a time, he reminded himself. And this—Gregor's safety—came first.

"I think," Dare said, finally circling back to Finn's question, "that I have no idea when you got smarter than me."

"Please." She returned his grin with a wry smile of her own. "I've always been smarter than you."

Chapter 41

Verity surveyed the map in the commander's office.

Her office.

She was still getting used to the idea of being High Commander of the Wardens, but somehow the role seemed to *fit*, settling around her shoulders like a mantle. It was like being a mage or, now, the Chosen of Pyrannis—it was a part of who she was.

Who she was meant to be.

She'd spent days going over the documents and notes Cairn had left behind, reviewing important topics with Lorekeeper Harrow, and interrogating Cairn's assassin. Although Warden Pendal hadn't been able to provide any useful information as to who hired him, Verity and Harrow had proved, without a doubt, that the Wardens' oaths were now magically binding. Not just for Wardens, but for anyone swearing a formal oath in their presence. She drafted a missive to the commanders of the other Warden posts, updating them on the situation.

It was bound to cause disruptions across the continent, though she hoped—perhaps, she was willing to admit, with a degree of naivety—that it would cause more good than harm.

With Cairn's funeral behind her now, and the hearing with Valda coming up in a few days, one problem had been needling at the back of her mind since Harrow had sworn her in as high commander. And she'd been putting it off for long enough.

Verity reviewed the most recent reports from the Wilds and adjusted a few of the carved wooden pieces on the map. The shifters were gathering at the southern edge of the Wilds, due north of Valda. At least one team of Wardens that she knew of had been changed, and their whereabouts were currently unknown. Several teams were stationed in Lostward, at the edge of the Wilds, and had been defending the small town, as well as its neighboring villages and camps, from the shifter raids.

But now that the shifters' focus had seemingly moved to a bigger target, could Verity redirect the Wardens in Lostward without risking the town's safety? And if so, should she redirect them to Valda, or move them west along the edge of the Wilds in a play to disrupt the shifters' plans?

And what were the shifters even doing? Why were their sights set on Valda, of all places? This wasn't just escalation. Valda was orders of magnitude larger than anything the shifters had raided before. So why Valda? Why now? Why not Whitehollow, which was due south from Lostward and far closer than Valda. What was their goal?

Verity thought of Lucien and his task from Taerna that had kept him in Southreach, where the Red Forest lay—the other territory that belonged to the shifters. She had a vague recollection of Duke Wilhaven commenting about shifters encroaching on Brookshire. Had he been referring to the shifters mobilizing in the Red Forest as well? Verity regretted not taking the time then to corroborate the duke's story; she'd been too focused on Dare and Solace at the time. She should check Cairn's notes again, in case any reports had come in from Southreach, southern Bremmaran, or even Weryn with news of shifter activity.

She hoped Lucien and Jae were staying safe.

After hours spent reviewing the most recent reports, drafting requests for status updates, and inquiring whether anyone at Lostward had seen the missing Wardens once they'd been turned by the shifters, Verity was restless. But there was still one problem that needed her attention.

Tanithe Ash.

Finn had reported that the Chosen of Vire was likely to be in Whitehollow and, even more distressing, that she was targeting Gregor, looking to exact revenge for the wound he'd given her in the palace last autumn.

Finn recommended not bringing the details to Gregor's attention, so as not to cause him further stress. Although Verity didn't like the idea of keeping this from him—and she had some concerns about what might happen if Gregor accidentally gleaned the information from their thoughts—she worried how he might react if he knew that his fears were not only well-founded but completely true. He was having a hard enough time right now, and Verity and Finn could work together to keep him safe.

It would be best not to worry Dare about it either. They could let him focus on his testimony for the hearing. Verity wrote a note to Caelan, asking him to increase the embassy's security again, as a precaution. It disappeared in the silver smoke of her Sending spell.

Verity was exhausted. Mentally, at least. Her body needed to move.

She considered trying to track down Dare for an impromptu training session, but he'd declined her most recent attempts at meeting up with him. In fact, now that she was thinking about it, Dare had turned down or skipped every training she'd tried to have with him since their sparring match earlier in the week. He'd been making such good progress—he'd even been on time for the last one—and then he'd just stopped coming. What had changed?

The mystery of Dare's strange behavior aside, there was one other person Verity was excited to train with again. It had been too long, as far as she was concerned. She scratched out a quick note to Gregor, asking if he'd like to join her at the base tomorrow morning, if he was up for getting out. It wasn't long after her own message had disappeared via the Sending spell that another appeared on her desk, written neatly on the Drahkonian embassy's enchanted letterhead.

I'd be delighted.

- Gregor

Of course, that still left the question of how to burn off her excess energy this evening. She left her office, locking the door behind her.

Maybe Jonah would be interested in a rematch.

Early the next morning, Verity met Gregor at the compound's front gate, the Wardens on guard there waving him through. Their two Drahkonian guards,

Rhori and Talia, were with him. Verity recognized them immediately, even though they weren't wearing their formal uniforms.

"It's nice to see you out and about, Talia," Verity said. Talia had been injured during the pirate attack on their way to Whitehollow.

"Thanks, Commander." She smiled, her eyes bright against her light brown skin. She brushed a lock of dark hair behind her ear. "They cleared me for duty a couple weeks ago, but this one"—she jabbed a thumb toward Rhori—"keeps stealing all the transport details."

"I'm not *stealing* them," Rhori said, his hazel eyes sparkling. "I just call them faster than you."

Talia rolled her eyes even as she smothered a smile. Verity and Gregor bid them farewell as the two guards turned back toward the embassy.

Rain fell steadily and had been since yesterday, leaving the roads muddy and slick. A chill hung in the air that reminded Verity she was back north and no longer in the southern, more temperate climate of Taernfane.

Gregor tugged his cloak more tightly around himself, water dripping from the hood. "Why do we always end up doing this in the rain?" he mused lightly.

Verity chuckled. "At least we'll be inside this time."

On the Wardens' base there was an indoor training ring that Verity and the others who were adept at magic often used when practicing some of their more powerful spells. The room and door were reinforced with steel and could withstand a fair amount of punishment from a group of Warden mages. It also happened to be the best place Verity could think of to continue practicing with Pyrannis's fire.

Her fire.

There would be no prying eyes, no one to stare in awe as the new High Commander of the Wardens created fire from nothing, and no passers-by to get too close if things should go wrong.

Before they reached the building that housed the training room, a familiar figure stalked across the yard, heading toward the gates at a hurried clip.

"Dare!" Verity called.

Dare's steps faltered as he spotted Verity and Gregor. "Oh . . . good morning, my lady Warden," he said, though it lacked much warmth. He favored Gregor with a smile that was halfhearted at best.

"Why don't you join us for training?" Verity suggested.

"I can't today." Dare moved to skirt around them. "I have a few things in the city that I need to take care of."

"Come for a little while," Verity said, holding out her hand. "Whatever you need to do in town will still be there in an hour."

Dare gave an apologetic half bow. "I really can't." He threw a wave up over his shoulder as he jogged off. "Another time!" he called.

"You're not going alone, are you?" she shouted after him, but he was already around the corner of the next building and out of sight.

"He's hiding something," Gregor murmured.

Verity inclined her head toward Gregor. "Did you hear something?" she asked, lowering her voice.

He didn't answer, but turned and continued in the direction they'd been heading.

"Gregor?"

"His tells haven't changed since he was seven," he said finally.

"You can tell when he's lying?"

Gregor shook his head. "I thought I could," he mumbled, almost under his breath. "I can always tell when there's more to the story than what he's offering up."

They continued walking, their destination not far ahead. "Has he said anything to you about why he stopped training?" Verity asked. If there was something she'd done wrong, and that was why Dare was avoiding her, she wanted the opportunity to fix it.

"I didn't realize he'd stopped," Gregor said, dashing Verity's hopes of getting any answers. "How long?"

"Nearly a week." Verity pushed open the door, and they stepped inside. Their cloaks dripped rain onto the stone floor, leaving a small puddle as Verity hung hers on a hook near the door. Gregor followed suit.

"Did something happen? Last I heard, it was going well."

"It *was* going well," Verity lamented, the worry rising in her voice. "He was doing really well, Gregor. His combat training, the Perceptive skills we were working on, everything. He was interested. Eager, even. There was this determination in him I hadn't seen since . . ." Her heart ached as she thought of Solace, of what she and Dare had had to do. She swallowed hard. "I don't know what happened, but it just disappeared. It feels like he's avoiding me."

She led Gregor down a hallway to the large training room. A few benches lined the perimeter, and a rack of various pads and training equipment sat against one wall.

"And you said working with him on his Perceptive abilities was going just as well?"

Verity nodded as she rolled up the sleeves of her shirt. "He was doing great. He could meditate more easily without getting distracted, and he could hold his concentration for longer. I was about to start teaching him to actually channel magic."

Gregor slid his glasses off and cleaned the lenses with the hem of his shirt. "Did you tell him that?"

"No, I don't think so."

"Maybe he sensed the shift coming and it scared him," Gregor theorized. "It wouldn't be the first time Darcy sabotaged himself when things were going well."

"You know him better than anyone," Verity said. "Any ideas on how to pick up where we left off?"

Gregor considered the question while he finished cleaning his glasses. "He's very smart, but he's not always the most self-aware. You may need to force his hand on this one. If he's scared to take the leap, he'll need a nudge."

"A nudge?"

"Or a shove," Gregor added, a dimple appearing beneath his eye as his mouth turned up at the corner. But the small smile faded again as he added, "You've brought him further down this road than he's ever gone before. He's probably afraid. The only magic instruction he ever received was from Duchess Wilhaven."

Verity cringed at the thought of Dare's mother teaching anyone anything. The woman was a manipulative terror. "That must have been horrible."

"It was." Gregor's shoulders slouched as though the sorrow of those memories still weighed down on him, even after all these years. "I wasn't allowed to be at any of those lessons, but from what he told me . . . This isn't an easy task you've set for yourself, Verity. Be gentle with him."

"You said to shove him a moment ago." Her tone was teasing, but her mind was focused on this new problem.

"I know," Gregor said, the dimple returning. "Just shove him gently." He blew out a deep breath, all the air in the room seeming to stir, though if Gregor noticed, he didn't say anything. "Are you ready to get started?"

Verity nodded, rolling her shoulders from where they'd been creeping toward her ears.

Gregor moved to one of the benches. "I'll be right here."

Verity practiced for an hour, creating and manipulating flame. It was getting easier, but she'd be lying if she said her heart didn't race every time the fire danced across her fingertips or licked up her arm. Gregor sat on the bench against the wall, occasionally offering words of encouragement.

She appreciated his steadying presence, though a question took shape in the back of her mind. Why Gregor, specifically? Ever since that day in Taernfane when she'd panicked and he'd come to check on her, Verity had felt comfortable practicing with Gregor around, but *only* with him. She hadn't asked anyone else to accompany her and, in fact, the thought of having anyone there besides him set her nerves on edge.

A theory started to form as she pondered whether Gregor's friendship and calming influence were the only reasons she felt so comfortable practicing around him.

"Gregor," she said as the flame she'd been manipulating winked out. "I'd like to test something, but I need your help."

Gregor leaned forward in interest. "Of course," he said. "What can I do?"

She beckoned him off the bench. "I'd like to see if you can use your magic to snuff out my fire."

"You think that would work?"

"I don't know. Do you want to find out?"

Gregor smiled as he flexed his fingers and a small gust of wind swirled around Verity in answer. "I'll admit I haven't tried anything like that before," he said, joining her in the middle of the room. "I've only manipulated the air to increase or decrease its strength. I'm not even sure how I would remove air from a space. And even then, I don't know if it'll affect magical fire."

Verity summoned a flame to her hand, letting it flicker and dance across her palm. "I'm hypothesizing that it's not the fire that's magic, just the summoning of it."

Gregor chuckled, light and airy. "You make it sound like a science experiment."

Verity shrugged one shoulder, holding the flame out for him. "Isn't it, though?"

He studied the flame, falling silent. He flicked his hand and the flame roared brighter, startling Verity into extinguishing it herself.

"Sorry," they both said together, then laughed at themselves.

Verity created another flame in her palm. "Try again?"

Gregor focused and tried a different movement with his hand, but again the flame grew instead of shrank, though this time Verity held onto it.

"The air's fueling it," Gregor murmured, still focused on the fire. "Even if I try to move the air away from the flame, the room's full of air—more just rushes in and the pressure difference causes it to flare up." Something danced in his ice-blue eyes. "Unless . . ." He stepped around her, looking at the problem from a different angle.

Something sparked in Verity's chest too. The puzzle of it was exhilarating.

"Extend your arm." Gregor moved to stand in front of her again, though he left a bit more distance between them. "It's like when I create a small cyclone of wind over my hand," he said, talking through his thoughts aloud, "but in reverse. If I create the cyclone around the fire, I might be able to pull the air out from the center of it."

"Worth a try," Verity said encouragingly.

Gregor swirled his hand in a small circle, and the air stirred. It whipped past Verity, and the flame flickered but didn't flare up or die out. He drew his bottom lip between his teeth as he concentrated. The circle of wind grew tighter, more focused around the flame on Verity's palm. While one hand still made small swirling motions, the other reached forward. He clenched his fist and pulled it back.

The fire snuffed out.

Gregor's breath escaped him in a puff, half laugh and half surprise. "It worked."

Verity had expected it would. That was why she felt most comfortable training with him; if things ever got truly out of hand, he'd be able to extinguish the flames with his own magic.

She created another flame in her palm. "Try it again."

They practiced for another hour until Gregor was able to create his vortex and pull the air out of the center in almost the same movement.

When they were finished and gathering their cloaks from the entranceway, Gregor said softly, "Thank you, Verity. I'm not sure I would have thought to try that if you hadn't suggested it."

"Thank you for being willing to try," she countered. "And for being here while I practice. It really helps." She let the silence sit between them for a moment before she added, "How are you doing with . . . everything?"

All the good humor seemed to drain from him, his shoulders sagging as he gazed toward the city. "Not well," he said.

She wished she had something more to offer him. "What about the lorekeeper's workshop?"

"Lorekeeper Harrow is very kind," Gregor said, "and spending time in her workshop has been a welcome reprieve. But I can't very well live there." He sighed, gesturing toward his head. "No matter how I try to tune it out or block it out, nothing works."

"If you want to work on it more, I'd be happy to do what I can to help. Even if it's just being there, like you've been for me."

Gregor was wincing almost before she'd finished the sentence, so she added quickly, "Or, if you prefer, I have these books from Harrow. They're full of stories about past Chosen. I've been meaning to look through them, if you'd like to give me a hand."

His about-to-politely-decline wince turned into thinly veiled curiosity. "What kind of stories?"

❋

Back in her office, Verity and Gregor flipped through the books from Lorekeeper Harrow. Verity focused on the one detailing the history of the Wardens and the Chosen of Pyrannis who founded them, while Gregor flipped through the book of stories.

They'd been reading for an hour in companionable silence, the turning of pages the only sound between them, when Gregor breathed a quiet "Huh."

Verity lifted her head from where it was angled over the tome in her lap. "Find something? About Aetherann?"

"No," he said, leaning forward. "Well, yes, but not exactly." He set the book on the desk between them. "These are reports from a Chosen of Lanara, though they were written by a scholar interviewing the Chosen, then translated by a third party."

Gregor pointed to a diagram on one of the pages. "This details how the power transfer works between the god and their Chosen. The connection is like a leaky water pump."

Verity raised a brow, causing Gregor to let out a chuckle. "Look, I'm just telling you what it says." He turned the book around so Verity could see the illustration, and sure enough, there was a water pump drawn there, with a small trough catching drips falling from the spout.

"It describes the connection like a water pipe, feeding into a basin," he continued. "The basin represents the available divine power within the Chosen. It fills over time, and the Chosen can draw upon that power easily."

"So if the Chosen uses that power faster than it refills, then the basin runs dry," Verity said, following the analogy to its logical conclusion. "The Chosen would be unable to access their patron's divine power until it replenishes. Is that right?"

"Yes, but"—Gregor flipped the page to show Verity the next illustration, which had water gushing into the basin at a rapid pace—"according to this, the Chosen can pull more power into themselves, like using the pump to add more water to the basin."

"Is that it?" Verity asked. "It almost sounds too easy. To be able to replenish the divine power, or draw on more of it at any time."

"Seems that way." He turned the book back around so he could keep reading. As he turned to the next page, his face fell. "Oh."

He didn't elaborate.

She leaned toward him, trying to glimpse the page that had stunned him into silence. "What is it?"

He angled the book so she could see the illustration of the same water pipe, pump, and trough, but with cracks along the length of the pipe and water spraying violently in all directions.

"Drawing upon too much power through the divine channel," Gregor said, reading from the text below the illustration, "will cause the vessel to fracture from the potent magical energy flowing through them. Little is known about the specific effects this fracturing has on the vessel besides a potentially fatal expulsion of power in the most extreme cases."

"Pyrannis's flames," Verity muttered.

"Literally, I fear in this case," Gregor replied, gaze drifting back to Verity. His face had gone ashy, and he swallowed hard. "When we were on the ship . . ."

Verity's mind raced back a few weeks to their journey to Whitehollow. Gregor had used his power from Aetherann to help them escape the pirates. And he'd described a strange sensation of opening a window to more of that divine power until it had abruptly slammed itself shut.

"Do you think," he continued, "that's what I . . . ? Did I nearly . . . ?"

Verity had so many questions. She needed to do more research, read more of the books, maybe even ask Pyrannis directly for his insight. "I don't know," she said. She took the book from him and skimmed the next few pages. "I wish I did. But, if it is, then the window slamming shut must have been Aetherann trying to protect you from drawing too much power at once. He must have been looking out for you."

Gregor stared at the space where the book had been. "Maybe," he said, his voice small.

Outside, the noon chime echoed across the base. Gregor shook his head, as though the sound had woken him from some sort of dream. "I'm sorry, Verity," he said. "I need to go. I told Lorekeeper Harrow I'd stop by today and help her organize her reagents."

Verity rolled with the change of subject. "When I introduced you, I didn't mean for her to put you to work." But honestly, she was glad Harrow had taken such a liking to Gregor.

"It's fine," Gregor said. "It's quiet, and having something simple to do lets my mind work on other problems in the background, like what to do about . . ." He let the thought hang as he stood. "Oh, and I did mean to thank you for the tea. It's been very helpful."

She rose with him. "I'm glad to hear it. Let me walk you over there."

The rain had mostly eased, and Gregor was silent on the walk to Lorekeeper Harrow's workshop. Verity didn't press him on what he was thinking about, though when they arrived at Harrow's doorstep, Gregor gave her only a quick farewell before ducking inside.

Verity returned to her office, her mind hard at work on another problem. Gregor and Dare were both struggling, each in their own way, but each was trying to tackle it alone. Verity knew *that* struggle well. She also knew that it often didn't work. She might not know how to help Gregor yet, but she had some ideas now of what she could do for Dare.

Starting tomorrow, she'd give him the shove he needed.

CHAPTER 42

DARE AWOKE TO A note from Verity on his desk. She must have sent it via a Sending spell earlier that morning. It gave directions to a building on the base and a time to meet. Maybe he could pretend he didn't see it? The hearing was in two days, unless it was postponed again—he could only hope—and he was no closer to figuring out either what Tanithe wanted with him or what he was going to do about this fucking oath.

But then he read the rest of the note, including the only four words that would get Dare dressed and headed out the door on time.

I need your help.

Dare found the building Verity mentioned and pushed open the heavy doors to the room at the end of the hall. They were reinforced with steel. In fact, the whole room looked reinforced, and there were no windows at all. What the hells did the Wardens need a room like this for?

Verity was already there, clearing a few training targets out from the center of the circular room. She looked up as Dare entered, brushing her hands on her pants.

"Verity . . ." Dare said slowly, eying the space she'd made in the center. "What are we doing here?"

"Training," she replied a little too quickly. She smiled.

Every nerve in his body was on alert. "You said you needed my help."

"I do need your help," she said. "I need your help figuring out why you've been avoiding training all week."

Dare sighed. He absolutely had been avoiding her. In two days, he was going to let Verity down in the worst possible way. He was going to let them all down and betray Drystan's memory in the process by calling himself a Warden. He knew Verity only wanted to help him, but he didn't deserve any of it.

"I really don't have time today," Dare tried.

Verity set her hands on her hips. "What else do you need to do?" she asked innocently.

Well, fuck. "Alright, fine," he said, taking a few more steps into the room. "What are we training?"

Verity took a quick breath as she stepped toward him. "You said you'd be willing to try magic, and I thought—"

"You're joking," he laughed, turning toward the door. Nope, not today. He could manage to choke down hand-to-hand training if she insisted, or even more meditation exercises, but Pyrannis's flaming ass, he was not about to deal with—

There were a few muttered words behind him, and a small pulse of magic rippled through the room, stopping Dare in his tracks. He angled his head toward where Verity still stood in the center of the room behind him. "What did you just do?"

"I put a force wall in front of the door."

Dare spun to face her, his temper flaring. "You fucking *what*?"

"It's not a strong one," she continued. "But it's enough to keep you in here."

He clenched his fists to stop his hands from shaking. "You're fucking locking me up?"

"I'm not locking you up." She inched closer to him, as though she were approaching a cornered dog. "I'm going to give you your first magic lesson, and then I'm going to teach you how to cast a basic Banishment spell."

Dare bristled at her hubris. How could she do this to him? "You're serious?" he snapped. "How long do you plan to keep me in here?"

Verity took another step closer and gestured toward the door. "You can leave when you can leave."

"What the fuck, Verity?"

"I was talking to Gregor—"

"*Gregor's* in on this bullshit?" Dare paced small circles in the room. "So you two are teaming up to torture me?"

"Gregor and I both think you need a shove to take the next step. And I thought giving you a challenge would be the only way you'd give it a chance. The only way you'd try." He didn't say anything, so she pressed on. "You were so successful with the meditations we did, focusing on your abilities, but then you haven't wanted to touch it since. What's stopping you, Dare? What are you afraid of?"

Dare rolled his shoulders back, still pacing the circular room. Every time he passed the force wall, it sent the slightest tremor through his arm on that side. One hand drifted up and found the thin metal chain he'd started wearing a couple of weeks ago, his fingers gripping the cold iron key that hung from it. "I'm not afraid," he said sharply.

Verity gestured to the center of the room. "Then come here and try. Dare, I'm not her."

He stopped pacing and turned to her. His heart was beating so hard it was pounding in his ears.

"I'm not your mother. I'm not going to push you too far. I'm not going to hurt you."

He rubbed the key around his neck. "You're not?" He jabbed a finger toward the door. "Then what the hells is that?"

"Motivation," she said flatly. "It's a challenge, Dare. I *know* you can do this. And I know you can do it without causing yourself pain. Give me a chance."

The iron key warmed between his fingers as Gregor's words came back to him. *I want you to remember that you escaped, that you got out . . . No one can chain you down again.*

Dare cracked his knuckles but moved to the center of the room. "Fine." He shrugged out of his coat and tossed it on one of the benches along the wall. His jaw tensed even as he said, "I'm trusting you, Verity."

Verity moved toward the center of the room and took a seat on the bare stone floor. Dare sat in front of her, crossing his legs.

"What do you remember from your lessons as a child?" she asked.

Dare heaved a heavy sigh. "Honestly, not much. I remember the breathing, I think. And that there are different types of magic, but I'll be damned if I can remember what they all are." He tried to think back to the lessons, to what nuggets of knowledge might have been left behind through all the shit.

"That's alright," Verity said, holding up her hand. "Magic is technically only one thing, but it can affect any type of energy that exists. You just have to manipulate the magic in different ways to affect the different types of energy."

"So like your fucking force wall over there," Dare said, jerking his head toward the door.

Verity grinned. "Yes. That *fucking* force wall is, well, force. That type of energy can also be used to affect momentum. You can use it to throw something farther, for example."

That sounded vaguely familiar. "There's also heat, light, and sound, right?" He belatedly remembered Tanithe's shenanigans and added hastily, "And mind."

"Yes, and of course there's manipulating magic itself." She nodded toward the force wall. "Like for a Banishment or a Sight ritual."

Dare considered Verity's words. *Any type of energy that exists.* "Are there any others that can be influenced?"

"There's also magnetic fields," Verity said. "And time."

"Really? Time? I don't think I've ever heard of someone controlling time with magic."

"It's incredibly difficult to accomplish. The theorems themselves are extremely complicated," Verity said. "Plus it requires more power than most mages can channel at one time."

Dare had learned early on that Verity wasn't *most mages.* "Have you ever done it?"

"Once, when I was in school."

"What happened?" He leaned his elbows on his knees.

Verity's lips tightened as though she were trying to suppress a grin. Or a grimace. "I managed to accelerate the decay on an apple, but then I slept for two days and almost missed the final exam in my 'art of governance' class."

Dare's eyes widened. "Damn . . . I hope you at least got an A on that project."

Verity's face flushed red. "It was an extracurricular," she admitted. That was definitely a grimace she was trying to hide.

He couldn't help but laugh. "Of course it was."

Verity waved her hands as if clearing the air in front of her. "That's all beside the point! Is there anything else you remember about magic?"

A memory of one of his mother's lectures floated into his mind. "And anyone can cast any of it, right? Even without knowing any of the spells or gestures." It was truly mind-blowing when he stopped to think about it.

Verity stretched her legs out in front of her. "Technically yes, though it's much easier for Perceptives and natural Channels. Over time, mages discovered that certain words or phrases or rote movements made conjuring a specific effect easier. So while it's true that you don't need to know the proper words to cast a spell, it helps focus the raw magic into the effect you want. Otherwise, the mage uses their will to shape the magic into the desired effect. It's a lot harder than it sounds, which is why trained mages memorize as many spells and rotes as they can." She leaned back on her hands. "Also, everyone has at least one type of energy that comes more easily for them to manipulate. Most formally trained mages have two or three specialties that come naturally."

"What're yours?" he asked, his curiosity getting the better of him.

"My specialties are magic energy, force, light, and, um . . ." She held up one of her steel plated hands. "Heat."

"You said two or three specialties. That's four."

The corner of her mouth ticked up. "I know."

Dare rolled his eyes. "Overachiever."

Verity let out a chuckle.

Dare's thoughts wandered over the different types of magical energy. He'd never let himself consider what might come naturally to him—what types of magic he might be good at. The idea of it was intoxicating, he had to admit.

Dammit, he hated when Verity was right.

"Are you ready?" she asked.

Dare shrugged. "As ready as I'm going to be."

They worked for almost two hours. Verity reviewed the mind-stilling techniques she'd shown him for controlling his Perceptive abilities, and she corrected his technique for the breathing exercises he'd learned as a child. Once he seemed to have that down, she taught him the incantation in High Aethirian for a Banishment spell.

The words were the easiest part for him to remember, since he'd maintained his fluency in the ancient language. It was one of the lessons his parents had imparted to him that he actually appreciated. It came in handy more than one would expect.

"Alright," Verity said once he could do each part individually. "Now do all three at the same time. No, not at the force wall yet," she added when Dare's gaze drifted toward the door.

"Well, what am I supposed to cast it at then?" he asked.

"Nothing yet. Without a target, the magic will just dissipate, but that's fine for now. We need to see if you can successfully channel first. Then I'll give you something small to aim at." She gestured for him to begin. "Go ahead."

Dare scoffed, shaking out his hands and rolling his shoulders. "Sure. No problem."

It was, in fact, a problem. Apparently *three* was beyond the limit of complex mental tasks he could manage at one time. Between the meditation, incantation, and breathing techniques, if he managed two of them, he messed up the third. Eventually he got the breathing and incantation happening at the same time, and that first sudden draw of magic sent needles shooting through his veins, shattering his concentration.

"What happened?" Verity asked, her voice urgent. She leaned forward onto her knees, one arm extending toward Dare. "Are you alright?"

Dare set a hand on his chest, the knotted scar easily felt, even through his shirt. "I'm fine," he said, but his voice shook. He hadn't been expecting that to work, and he'd forgotten the mind-stilling techniques entirely. "I, uh . . ." He leaned his head back, staring at the ceiling.

Magic. He'd almost *cast magic*. He inhaled slowly, trying to steady his breathing. "Can we take a break?" he asked.

Verity jumped to her feet. "Of course." She held out her hand. Gratefully, he clasped it and let Verity haul him to standing.

She set her hand on his shoulder, squeezing firmly. He used the sensation to ground himself. This wasn't Brookshire, and he wasn't a child. He was in a training room in Whitehollow with Verity. She wouldn't let anything happen to him. He thumbed the key on the chain around his neck. He took another deep breath and was pleased to find the tremor was gone.

"You had it that time, didn't you?" Verity asked, watching him intently.

He nodded. "I forgot the mind-stilling," he muttered. Blowing his breath out, he bent over and set his hands on his knees. "I panicked."

"It's alright." She squeezed his shoulder again. "You can do this. When you're ready, we'll try again."

Dare nodded and straightened, setting his hand on top of hers where it still gripped his shoulder. "I'm ready."

They sat in the center of the floor again, and Verity talked him through the different pieces he would have to keep in mind, and in what order. Then she took a small mirrored circle from her pocket and set it on the floor between them. "I'm going to create a small ball of light right here." Her eyes flicked up to Dare. "If you cast a Banishment, even a small one, it'll disappear."

"Right, got it." He tried to sound confident, but the idea was honestly terrifying him. *It's nothing*, he tried to convince himself. *It's nothing.*

Verity passed her hand over the mirror, and a sphere of light appeared, hardly wider than a gold coin. It bobbed and flickered with whatever small amount of energy she was expending to keep it shining.

Dare closed his eyes again, setting his hands on his knees. He focused on his breathing as Verity instructed. He calmed his mind, breathing slowly, in through his nose, out through his mouth. When the gentle thrumming of the magic from the little ball of light and from the force wall behind him had faded to the edge of his awareness, Dare spoke the incantation in High Aethirian. The magic rolled through him, riding his breath in and out, but not lingering in him any longer than just a quiet prickle through his blood. It rippled over him and through him, and then it was gone.

Verity gasped.

Dare opened his eyes.

She was staring at the little mirror. There was no ball of light floating above its silvered surface. "You did it," she breathed. "Dare, you did it."

Dare's breath left him in some combination of a chuckle and a curse. "Taerna's stone tits . . ." He stared at the mirror. "Fuck me."

Verity looked up, watching Dare carefully. "How did it feel?"

He let his body relax, his back rounding slightly. "It felt . . . not terrible," he said, taking a moment to settle on the proper description. "It was weird, but . . . that was it." He lifted his gaze to Verity's again. "Holy shit."

Her smile lit up her face. "Holy shit."

"Can I try that again?"

"Of course." Verity waved her hand over the mirror, and the sphere of light reappeared.

Dare tried again, following the same steps he'd done before, and again the light went out as he felt the ripple of prickling magic wash over him. He leaned back, casting a glance at the door. "You think I can take that on yet?" he asked, and he could feel the tug of a smirk playing at his lips.

"After two hours," Verity said, "I would normally say not a chance. But I've never seen anyone cast their first Banishment that quickly, so let's see what you've got."

Dare grinned at the challenge. "What do I need to do differently?" he asked. "I'm assuming it'll be different than the light."

"You'll need to focus the Banishment in a direction," Verity said, gesturing at the door. "An undirected spell will have too much power dilution to be effective against the force wall. You'll need to channel it out in front of you specifically. Also it'll need to be a lot stronger, so you'll need to channel more magic at the outset."

Dare nodded, turning to face the door where he still sat. "Sure," he mumbled, trying to keep all the things he'd need to do in his mind at the same time. "Should I stand?"

"No, stay seated," Verity suggested, though she rose and moved closer to the door.

He focused his breathing, quieted his mind, and channeled the magic, pulling it into himself. The stabbing needles started and intensified, but he blew the pain away on the next exhale, though not as much of it left this time. The prickling grew stronger, but he imagined the energy moving down his arms, into his hands. Eyes still closed, Dare extended his palms toward the door and spoke the incantation.

The needles shot through him, stinging his palms. His whole body was tingling. It was more magic than he'd tried before; he could tell that as easily as he was breathing. But after it was done, he couldn't feel any magical energy blocking the door.

"It worked," he said, though his voice came out in a whisper.

Verity crossed to the door and opened it without issue. "Incredible," she said. "Dare, you really are a natural at this."

He smiled. That one had certainly hurt more than the others, but it hadn't knocked him on his ass. And it had worked.

It *worked*.

Dare pushed himself to his feet and swayed as soon as he straightened, all the blood rushing from his head like he'd stood up far too fast after a night of drinking. The next sensation he felt was Verity's strong arms catching him, one hand on his arm and the other around his waist.

"Easy," she said gently.

Dare's knees wouldn't hold his weight, and Verity lowered him back to the floor.

"Just sit a moment."

Dare blinked hard, trying to get his head to clear, but he felt like he could barely think straight. "What happened?" he asked. He leaned forward, his elbows on his knees. His stomach churned. "Did I do something wrong?"

"No," Verity said, running a hand in small circles across his back. "Just inefficiently."

Inefficiently? So this was what it felt like to use too much magic at once? It was different from how he'd felt after Verity had channeled through him all those months ago, but not entirely. The same weightiness to his limbs was present again.

"I think you channeled more magic than you needed." She continued rubbing his back. "It gets easier. With practice, you'll have more control over how much magic you channel. And you'll be able to do more before you start to feel drained. It's kind of like a muscle. It takes training and practice, just like anything else."

She was silent for a few breaths. When she spoke again, her voice was soft and almost apologetic. "You know I wouldn't really keep you in here. But you needed the push, and this was the only way I could see to give it to you."

A ghost of a smile flitted across his lips. "I know."

They sat in the training room for several minutes. Verity stood and retrieved a skin of water from one of the edges of the room. She brought it to Dare, who drank gratefully. The water was cold and helped reinvigorate him somewhat.

Verity crouched beside him again as he took another long drink. "Are you ready to stand? We can head back to the barracks and you can get some sleep."

He nodded. "Sure, that sounds perfect." And it did. The idea of sleep sounded delightful.

Verity stood and pulled Dare up with her. "Are you good?" she asked, still holding on to him. "Do you want to lean on me?"

Dare took a tentative step, making sure that his legs would hold him without his knees buckling. "No, I'm fine," he said.

Verity smiled as she jogged to the other side of the room to collect the rest of their belongings before joining him at the door.

Outside, the crisp air was a welcome distraction, rousing his drowsy mind. Verity handed Dare his coat, but he slung it over one shoulder, not bothering to put it on for the short walk to the barracks.

"Dare . . ." Verity trailed off, letting his name float in the air.

He glanced at her sidelong, raising one eyebrow. Her face was serious as she looked out across the compound. "Yes, my lady Warden?"

He was rewarded with the corner of her mouth curling up in a soft smile at the nickname. The one he'd given her to irritate the hells out of her when they first met in Valda. He recalled fondly how Drystan had snorted a laugh when he'd first heard Dare use it.

"That was really well done," Verity said after a long moment. "I'm amazed at what you were able to accomplish in only a couple hours."

Dare smiled. "Well, I had a good teacher."

"No, it's not that. You picked that up incredibly fast, especially considering the extra steps involved for you. And the power you had when I had channeled through you before . . . I really think you have a gift, Dare."

His chest tightened at the compliment, some strange combination of pride but also uncertainty. He shook his head quickly, trying to stop his mind from wandering down the path of too many *what-ifs*. "Thank you, Verity. I don't need to be a great archmage. Just teach me enough to be useful. That's all I need."

CHAPTER 43

VERITY WAS STUCK IN meeting after meeting dealing with the details and logistics of the hearing. It was the day before the trial, and the Drahkonian embassy was bustling. Valda had finally sent over the last of the missing documents, but they'd only arrived early yesterday. According to Chancellor Caelan, Gregor had recruited Finn and several pages, and they had locked themselves in one of the embassy's meeting rooms since the files arrived.

Good, Verity thought. *That'll keep him safe.*

Unless something turned up in their search that necessitated another delay, the trial would proceed as planned. "Any news on Tanithe Ash?" Verity asked.

Caelan shook his head. "Nothing solid, though whispers have started that she's in the city."

That was more than they had before, and it corroborated Finn's reports. Verity wasn't sure if that was good or very, very bad.

"For the first part of the hearing tomorrow," Caelan said, "we'll present our side of the story, plus any evidence Gregor's able to turn up from the last of the Valdane documents. Then we'll hear the testimony from Finn and Gregor, and conclude our side with Dare's account of what happened. The Valdane representative will have the opportunity to ask questions throughout, as will I, should any arise. The Wardens acting as the arbiters will, of course, be able to ask any questions they have as well. Finally, Valda will provide any response to the accusations, after which the committee will make their decision."

Verity nodded along. Everything tracked with her understanding and expectations. "I've reviewed the schedule with the Wardens as well. We shouldn't have any issues."

Caelan snorted and muttered, "That would be a first."

Before Verity could comment, the door to the meeting room swung open. Gregor rushed in, several pieces of parchment held tight in his hands.

"I think I found something."

By the time Verity made it back to her room, night had settled over the city. During her last meeting, Harrow had reminded her that Joseph Cairn's quarters—a small home with several rooms on one side of the base—were technically now hers as commander, but she wasn't ready to leave her room at the barracks just yet.

She sat at her desk and got to work on the pile of paperwork that had fallen behind with the chaos of the last few weeks. Even though it was late, there were still important matters that needed to be dealt with. Before long, she paused in her writing and wiggled her fingers on her left hand. There was a lag in the movement. It wasn't much, just a split second, but it was noticeable.

It had been too long since she'd done proper maintenance on the mechanical elements. If she waited much longer, something could come loose, or worse. She was exhausted, but it was best to take care of it before she put it off any more than she already had.

With only a thought of how good her bed would feel once she was done with this last chore, Verity gathered up her small pouch of tools from her desk drawer and left the room. She turned right, walked the few feet to the next door in the hall, and knocked.

She was adjusting the closure on the pouch as the door swung open.

"What can I do for you, my lady Warden?"

Her heart sank. As she looked up, Dare stood in the doorway, leaning against the frame.

Of course it was Dare. Who had she expected?

Verity knew who, in the back of her exhausted mind, she'd thought would open that door. She'd been working off muscle memory, not thinking about what she was doing, and had half-expected Drystan to be there.

The way he'd *always* been there.

Verity opened her mouth, closing it again without a word. She turned to head back to her own room but stopped herself. What was she doing? She needed help with this, and regardless of who she'd expected, there was still only one person she trusted enough to ask for help.

"Verity?" Concern slid into Dare's voice.

She turned to him again, straightening her shoulders, her fingers tightening around the pouch. "Can I come in?"

Dare stepped out of the doorway so she could pass.

"I need your help with something," she said as he closed the door. "If it's not too—"

"Anything," he said before she could finish.

She smiled. He could do this. *She* could do this.

Dare's gaze dipped to the pouch. "What's that?"

"These are my tools."

He stepped closer, his curiosity piqued. "Tools?"

Verity set the pouch on the small writing desk and opened it, unfolding the leather flap. Inside was a collection of unique metal tools. "My arms function from both magical and mechanical components," she said quickly. "I need to maintain the mechanical parts to keep everything working as it should."

Dare stared at the tools. "You mean your arms can be damaged?" he asked, surprised.

"The parts inside can wear down or come loose if I don't keep them properly maintained. The outer plates are stronger, but they're not invulnerable."

"Huh," Dare muttered. He leaned against the desk, looking at the strange collection of implements. "What do you need *me* to do?"

She drew a slow breath. Drystan had been there from the beginning. She'd never had to *ask* anyone before. "I need your help to make the repairs."

His eyes grew round.

"There are a few spots where it's difficult for me to reach myself," she continued.

"Me?" He shook his head. "Verity, wouldn't you rather have Finn take a look? Or Gregor? This seems like something he'd . . . I mean, I don't know the first thing about—"

"I can talk you through it," she said. "I just need a steady pair of hands . . . and someone I can trust."

"But this is important. Really fucking important." Dare watched her carefully, searching her eyes. "You trust *me* with this?"

Verity held his gaze. "I do."

Something flickered across his face, and he looked down at the tools laid out on the desk. He ran his fingers lightly across them. "Alright," he said after a moment. "What do you need me to do?"

Verity sat in the chair and rolled up her left sleeve. "We'll start on the part I can do myself," she said. She picked up one of the tools with a thin, flat end. She slid it under one of the seams between the metal plates of her forearm. When she angled the tool like a small prybar, the plate popped off.

"Lanara's tits," Dare muttered. "I don't know what I was expecting. What are those there? Beside the gears."

Verity couldn't help but smile at Dare's wide-eyed curiosity. "They're called wires," she said. "They harness the magic that carries energy from my body through my arms to make them function. They're kind of like a self-sustaining periapt with very limited utility. Here." She handed Dare one of the other tools that had a small notched head at the end.

His throat worked as he swallowed. "Is this going to hurt you?"

Verity's heart squeezed. "No," she reassured him. "My hands and arms can only feel pressure. I can't feel pain."

Dare breathed out a quiet sigh.

"Right here," she said, pointing to an area beneath some of the wires. "There's a small bolt there that comes loose from time to time."

Dare reached into Verity's forearm with the small tool. His fingers barely brushed one of the wires when he yanked his hand back with a sharp hiss of pain. "Shit!"

Verity pulled her arm away from him, tucking it in close. "Pyrannis's flames," she gasped. "I'm sorry! The magic, I—I didn't think!" Dare had touched her arms, held her hand, many times and had never reacted like that before. The steel plates must dampen or block the magic from his Perception. She'd never considered that.

He shook out his hand, his face flushing red. "It's alright," he said, flexing his fingers. "Sorry, I should have expected that." He stooped to pick up the tool that had clattered to the floor. He gestured for her to set her arm on the desk again.

"Are you sure?"

"Come on, Verity. It just caught me off guard is all."

When her arm was situated in front of him again, Dare tightened his grip on the small tool. He inhaled deeply. He was using the breathing technique she'd been teaching him.

"That's good," she said encouragingly.

He glanced up. "A few lessons on meditation hardly makes me an expert."

"But it's someplace to start. You can do this."

Dare focused on his breathing as he set the tool into Verity's forearm, finding the bolt she'd indicated.

"Now twist it to the right," Verity said. "Good. And another here." She pointed toward one of the small bundles of wires. "You'll need to lift the wires out of the way gently to access it."

Dare blew his breath out in a long exhale. "This whole meditation thing is easier when my eyes are closed," he said quietly.

He pushed the wires to the side. His jaw tensed.

"What does it feel like?" Verity asked quietly. "If it's hurting you—"

"It's no worse than grabbing the thread of magic on a Warding spell," he said, concentrating as he tightened the second bolt. "This one was much looser." Dare twisted the tool between his fingers one last time.

"I thought it might be," Verity said. "Good. That was perfect." When Dare pulled his hands back, Verity took the steel plate and snapped it back into place, covering the inner working components. "Now for the ones I can't reach." She caught his eyes. He seemed determined, but . . . "Do you want to stop?"

Dare shook out his hands. "No, I'm fine. What's next?"

Verity took the small prybar and handed it to Dare before twisting her arm so she could tap on the steel of her tricep with her fingers. "You saw how I took off that first plate. There's another here. There's a seam at the bottom of the plate, near my elbow."

Dare held the little prybar, staring at the panel she indicated. He didn't move.

"I promise you can't hurt me, Dare."

"What if I damage something?" he asked.

Verity smiled. "I can block a sword with this arm," she said. She nodded to the tool he held between his fingers. "I don't think you can break it with that little thing."

Dare's face turned a brighter shade of red than it had earlier. "Fair point, my lady Warden." He set the end of the prybar into the seam above her elbow and levered it open.

Dare followed Verity's directions, adjusting a few gears and tightening a couple more bolts. The last two took him a little longer to finish than the others.

"There, I think that did it," he said. His hands shook a little as he pressed them flat against the desk.

Verity flexed her fingers and rotated her wrist, testing the motion. Everything worked as it should.

"That's incredible," Dare said. With the panel still removed from her tricep, he was watching the gears spin as she moved.

"Thank you for your help," she said, securing the access panel back in place. "That feels much better. I really should have done this sooner."

"No offense intended, but why didn't you? It seems too important to let slide for very long, considering."

Verity stared at her hands. "I . . . It was something that . . ." She swallowed. "Um . . . Drystan used to help me with it."

"Oh," Dare said. He fell quiet as he glanced around the room. Drystan's room. He mouthed another, silent, *Oh*. He slid the tools back into the small pouch. "I'm sorry, Verity." There was a weight to his words, a heaviness, as though he was trying to fill them with everything he'd ever done that he felt needed an apology.

Verity didn't know what to say. The pain of Drystan's death was less raw now with time and distance, but it was there, like a wound scabbed over that was still sore when pressed.

"Thank you," she said at last. And then, because something in her heart told her he might need to hear it said, Verity added, "You're a good person, Dare."

A lungful of air escaped him in a harsh laugh.

"You are," she insisted, setting a hand over his. "I see it, even if you can't. And Drystan saw it too, long before I did."

Dare didn't look up. He handed the closed pouch of tools to Verity and crossed to the door. "That's kind of you to say so, my lady Warden," he mumbled. He still wasn't looking at her. "It's late. You should get some rest. It's a big day tomorrow."

When he finally lifted his face, that calm indifference—the mask he used to wear so often—slid into place. She hadn't seen it in a long time, and it made her heart ache that he was feeling something he didn't want her to see.

"Dare . . ."

"It's alright. But I do want you to know that I'm sorry. I'm sorry for"—a wince flitted across his mouth for an instant before disappearing behind the mask again—"the things I've done. I hope one day I'll deserve the faith you have in me."

"Dare, wait." She joined him at the door. "What are you talking about?"

"It's late," he said again, this time with a not-so-subtle nod to the hallway. An invitation for her to leave. "Good night, Verity."

She stepped past him into the hallway, her pouch of tools clutched in her hand. "Thank you for your help tonight," she said, ignoring the hundreds of questions swirling through her mind. "I couldn't have done this without you. Truly. Thank you."

Dare gave her a sad smile. "I'm glad I could be of use," he said, then closed the door.

In her own room, Verity tucked her tools back into her desk drawer. Something was clearly going on with Dare. Something that went beyond his trepidation around working with magic. Maybe she could ask Finn for help in figuring out what was bothering him; she seemed to have a good read on people's emotions. Reading people had never been one of Verity's strengths.

She mulled the thought over as she readied herself for bed. There wasn't anything she could do about it right now. But tomorrow, after the trial was over, Verity would try to talk to Dare. It was the least she could do.

CHAPTER 44

Lucien thought leaving Ethriel had been hard the first time.

But now that he'd come back, and she'd seen the monster he'd become . . . and she still *loved him*, despite it all . . . Maybe in time she might even forgive him for leaving her and Faith for so long.

If he came back this time.

As long as I have air in my lungs . . .

The massive trees with their blood-red leaves loomed as Lucien and Jae entered the forest, and it didn't take long at all before Maldren Thorn found them, though she was alone.

. . . and legs to carry me . . .

"I wasn't sure you'd be back," she said, giving them both an appraising look. "And I see you brought your pet human again."

Jae stiffened, but to her credit, she kept her mouth shut.

. . . or friends to drag me back . . .

A low warning growl reverberated in Lucien's throat, and Mal tossed up her hands, as though that would be enough to curb his rage.

"Micah had better be here this time," he said through clenched teeth.

Mal gave a slow nod. "He's here. And he's expecting you." She gave Lucien a long look. "But the human stays here."

"She stays with me." Lucien wasn't about to let her out of his sight. Not here. Not with them.

Maldren crossed her arms over her chest. "Humans aren't allowed in the Glade."

"That's fine," he said. "She can stay at the edge. But she's not staying here."

"Lucien, you know the rules—"

"She's *not* staying here, Mal!"

She took a step forward to meet Lucien head-on. He glared back at her, letting the beast glint in his eyes, daring her to try something.

"Fine," she growled, though her own teeth had elongated into fangs. "She comes with us as far as the edge of the Glade. But Micah's not going to be happy when he scents her so close to his court."

That was fine. Let him be pissed. Micah made them wait a week just to prove he was in charge. Lucien would rip Micah's heart out and feed it to him if he came after Jae.

❈

Maldren led them deeper into the forest, moving quickly through the increasingly dense underbrush. The dark braid of her hair, with its one white streak, hung low down her back.

Lucien had no trouble keeping up, his muscles remembering the hidden paths among the trees. He glanced back to make sure Jae wasn't getting too far behind and was pleased to see she was holding her own.

An hour later, Mal stopped where Ethan was leaning against a tree, waiting. "This is where the human waits."

"The human has a name," Jae said, setting a hand on her hip.

"A single letter is hardly a name," the shifter retorted with a grin.

Jae released a quiet huff, but she turned to Lucien. "I'll be right here."

He didn't like the idea of leaving her here. It was at least another hundred feet to the Glade, if he remembered right, and he wouldn't have line of sight through the trees.

"Ethan will take you the rest of the way," Maldren said to Lucien. "I'll stay here with your friend." Her face softened. "I won't let any harm come to her. You have my word."

Could he trust Maldren? Did he have a choice?

Ethan pushed off the tree and gestured for Lucien to follow. The Glade opened up before them just as Lucien remembered—a wide clearing within a nearly perfect circle of trees, with a throne of carved wood and antler and bone in the center.

A crescent of shifters were positioned on either side of the throne. Some were in their human forms while others sat as huge beasts, nearly as tall seated as the human-shifters were standing. Of course there was an audience. Micah had always been one for pageantry.

On the throne, a male shifter sat in human form. His long blond hair hung loose over the mantle of sable fur around his shoulders as he bent forward and rested his elbows on his knees.

"Lucien Longshadow," Micah Fogrender bellowed across the clearing. "What brings you to grace us with your presence?"

Lucien crossed the space until he stood before the throne. "I need to get to the Heart of the Forest," he said, his voice carrying through the Glade.

Laughing, Micah leaned back on the throne. "Yes, Maldren informed me. But what I'm certain she failed to convey is your reason. So tell me now, Lucien Longshadow, why do you want access to the Heart?"

Lucien inhaled deeply, breathing in the scents of the forest. The pull he'd sensed last time was still there, but now that he'd felt the corruption of the shifters through his last vision, he could sense the struggle between that invasive force and the forest's true nature. Beneath that rage-inducing pull, power thrummed through the moss-covered ground. It ran deep here, deeper even than the roots of the tree in Taernfane.

I'm here, Lucien told the forest. *I want to help you.*

That edge to the forest that had been fraying his nerves dulled just slightly. Just enough to help Lucien focus.

"Several months ago, the elemental gods returned," Lucien said. He doubted news of the battle in Taernfane had yet spread to the Red Forest. A murmur ran through the gathered shifters, confirming his suspicion. "And since that time, I've received visions of the shifters and how we used to be. We were not always these creatures. We were wolves once, living in balance with our beasts. I believe we can be so again."

Silence echoed through the Glade until Micah shattered it with a hoarse, cruel laugh. Lucien's ears burned, and he clenched his fists at his sides.

"Perhaps you can explain this a bit more," Micah said in that patronizing tone Lucien had always hated. "I'm afraid I'm at a loss for what *exactly* you mean by that."

Lucien lifted his chin and said, with all the command and authority he could muster, "I can fix us."

"And how is it that you came by this knowledge?" Micah's voice was as sharp as his claws. "Who are you to know some supposed lost history of centuries ago?"

It was now or never. Whether they believed him, or Micah ordered his execution for heresy, it was time to speak his truth. "Because I am the Chosen of the goddess Taerna. And she has charged me with this task."

The assembled shifters reacted with a mix of gasps, muttered curses, and nervous chuckles. Micah, however, snorted his disbelief. "The goddess Taerna!" He laughed harshly. "She spoke to you and wanted you to heal us poor fools, is that it? To fix that which is broken?"

"Yes. And I can prove it." The idea of parading his power in front of the shifters turned Lucien's stomach, but there was little choice. He knew his words wouldn't be enough to convince them. He needed to show them *something*.

Lucien raised his hand slowly, pulling with it a clod of earth from the ground. He held the dirt and rocks suspended before sending it flying past the throne to the far side of the Glade.

"That's your proof?" Micah laughed again, and a few of the shifters joined him. "A parlor trick. Any half-trained mageling could do the same."

The beast within Lucien growled, itching to be released and lunge for Micah, but instead, Lucien swallowed down the rage and raised his hands, palms toward the sky. The ground beneath Lucien's feet rose with the gesture, lifting him, raising him on a mound of earth seven feet across. Sweat beaded on his forehead, but he stopped only when his head passed the height of Micah's where he lounged upon his throne.

Micah stood so he was higher once more and sneered at Lucien. Lucien bared his teeth.

"Tell me," Micah said, turning now to address the crowd, conveniently ignoring Lucien's display of elemental magic. "What is it about us that needs *fixing*, Lucien? What about the shifters is *broken*? We are strong!"

A murmur of agreement rippled through the gathered shifters.

"We are powerful!"

A quiet cheer of approval.

"We are free!"

Another cheer, louder this time.

"Free to live and die by our own laws. We are not subject to human weakness. We are not subject to their whims. So please"—he spun back to Lucien and raised a hand, inviting him to address the gathered shifters—"tell us! What precisely do you mean to *fix*? What has your time among the civilized humans taught you about our sad, twisted life?"

Lucien's shoulders tensed. "You're not free," he said, still glaring at Micah. "This beast, this blind fury, this urge to kill and maim and destroy. That is our weakness."

"That is our strength," Micah countered. "That is what keeps the humans from imposing their laws on us. That is what keeps us free!"

"That is not freedom," Lucien growled. "It's a collar. It chains you to the beast inside. At best, it makes you only a tool for the beast's rage."

"And at worst?" Micah's eyes glinted with a predatory light. He was baiting him, but Lucien didn't care.

"Nothing but feral monsters."

"You think you're better than us? You are one of us, Lucien. It doesn't matter how far you run, or how many humans you surround yourself with. You are a monster, and you will always be a monster. And instead of being free, you proudly throw yourself into chains and call it progress. You come here, to our home, and tell us that we need to be fixed? That we're broken? You seek to take away that which makes us special—that which gives us our power."

The shifters were all cheering now, a cascading chorus of howls, barks, and shouts.

"Our siblings in the north know our strength as well as I do," Micah went on, addressing his court. "They know our power. That is why they prepare for war. That is why they prepare to march upon the humans' lands."

More murmurs surged through the crowd. This was new information, even for them, and Micah was taking the opportunity to use it as a rallying tactic. Lucien's claws lengthened, but he willed them back.

"Why should we be content with so little when the humans have so much?" Micah asked the shifters. "Why should we be limited in our reach and our resources? Our kin in the Wilds lay the groundwork, and I've already sent a team of scouts to offer my support. When the time is right, we will join them and take what is ours!"

Another chorus of cheers and howls erupted through the Glade. Lucien had known about the reports of shifters gathering in the Wilds—he and Jae had been headed there back when they still did odd jobs for Tanithe, before they knew who and what she was—but he hadn't realized the extent of it.

Micah silenced the Glade with a single upheld hand. He faced Lucien and shook his head, making a show of looking sorrowful. "I know you never took to your circumstances, Lucien, but I had hoped that after so many years you would have found some peace with your nature. I'm sorry, but I cannot allow you access to the Heart when you seek to destroy all that we are."

Every muscle in Lucien's body tensed as his beast strained against the chains. Before he could fully rein it in, he charged Micah. Two shifters caught him by the arms before he made it more than a few steps.

"This isn't natural!" he roared. "This isn't how it's supposed to be!" He yanked his arms free of the two shifters but held his ground. "You can't possibly enjoy living like this!"

Micah held out his arms, encompassing the Glade, the throne, and every shifter bearing witness to Lucien's failure. "What's not to enjoy?"

"You're a fucking fool," Lucien snarled. "You're dooming every person here to live in this horror just because you get off on power. But you're just a coward."

Micah went deathly still, fixing his piercing gaze on Lucien. "Say that to me again," he said, his fangs lengthening as he spoke.

Lucien's claws dug into his palms as he fought for control. "You're a fucking coward."

Micah stepped forward, coming to stand within a few inches of Lucien. "I know what I am." His eyes dragged down Lucien's body and up to his face. "Can you say the same? You smell like them. Like prey. What have you been doing all this time? Masquerading as human? Pretending to be . . . What? A family man?" He leaned in, whispering the last words so only Lucien could hear. ". . . In a little cottage on a little farm?"

Lucien froze.

"I bet your wife was quite a beauty, back in her day," Micah continued. "And that daughter of yours . . . She grew into quite the spitfire, didn't she? You've tried to walk the line between man and monster for years. Maybe it's time someone forces you to choose." He returned to his carved throne and lounged upon it as though he'd grown bored with Lucien's presence. "Once you're finally free of these humans dragging you down, perhaps you'll see your true potential." Micah gestured to one of the shifters who stood beside the throne. "See that it's done. I want nothing left. Make sure their bones are picked clean."

Lucien was sprinting out of the Glade by the time Micah finished his sentence. He shifted as he broke through the tree line, bounding forward until Jae and Mal came into view. A crash in the trees behind him signaled the pursuit. They weren't just going to kill his family. They were going to kill Jae, too.

He angled a look over his shoulder and caught a glint of metal high up in one of the trees. He couldn't shout in this form, but he barked a warning, hoping Jae would understand.

Jae spun behind a tree as an arrow ricocheted off the trunk.

"Hold!" Maldren shouted in the direction the arrow had come from, but another one loosed, embedding itself into the bark of the tree Jae hid behind. "*Hold!*" she yelled again.

Lucien swung wide around Mal, heading for Jae. He slowed just enough for her to grab a fistful of his fur and swing herself onto his back. He counterbalanced her weight, jerking a shoulder up to keep her from flying clear off his other side with the extra momentum.

"I take it that didn't go well," Jae shouted in his ear as she pressed herself along the length of his back and shoulders.

Another arrow sailed over them, and another, before one landed in Lucien's side, just below his shoulder. He stumbled but kept to his feet, and Jae's grip on his fur tightened, her legs squeezing around his ribs so she didn't fall.

Jae grabbed the shaft of the arrow and yanked it out of his side. "Sorry."

Lucien grunted, but it was all he could manage. His focus was on getting them out of the forest alive and back to Ethriel and Faith.

Lucien bolted along the too-familiar paths in the woods. He didn't slow, even after they cleared the edge of the Red Forest and all sounds of pursuit faded from his heightened senses.

"Slow down," Jae said, patting his shoulder. "They're not following."

Lucien ran.

"Lucien! Stop for a minute. Let me check the arrow wound; I can hear you wheezing."

He slowed and skidded to a stop in the open plains. He didn't like being in his beast form out in the open like this, but time was not on his side. Once Jae hopped down from his back, Lucien continued padding a circle in the tall grass.

Jae set her hands on her hips. "Lucien, what the fuck is going on? And don't just growl and yip at me. Shift back so I can talk to you."

Lucien growled anyway, but shifted back into his human form. "Ethriel," he blurted out as soon as his mouth was human enough for speech. He took a heaving breath through the burning in his side. "He's going after Ethriel and Faith."

"Fuck!" Jae circled him, checking him over for any other wounds. "Are you hurt?"

Lucien lifted his arm, trying to get his eyes on where the arrow had landed between his ribs. "That arrow," he said. He could hear the wheeze in his breathing now that he'd stopped running. "It still stings."

Jae's brows furrowed as she came to his side. "That should have healed by now," she muttered, leaning in for a closer look. A wound that small shouldn't have taken hardly any time to close up once the arrow was removed. Jae lifted his shirt, peering at the damage. "The whole area's inflamed," she said, her voice softening in a way Lucien didn't like at all. "And the veins around it are dark purple. Lucien . . ."

"It's fine," he said gruffly, pulling his shirt back down. "It's dart thistle. A poison the shifters use." He had to take another deep breath. "It slows down our healing."

"Slows down?" Jae asked, studying his face.

"Just *slows down*," he reassured her. "The longer the poison has to seep in"—another breath—"the worse it is." That damn arrow must have hit his lung. "I'll be fine in an hour." Another breath. *Maybe two . . .*

"You should rest," Jae started, but Lucien was already shaking his head.

"They're going after Ethriel. He knows where they are . . . He must have . . . had someone follow us when . . . we left the last time. Jae . . . we led the shifters right to them . . ."

Jae drew her bottom lip between her teeth. "Alright, we need to move, but just don't kill yourself trying to get there. I don't want to have to explain to your wife that I let you literally run yourself to death."

CHAPTER 45

IT WAS RAINING, BUT Corvin Crosse didn't mind. The weather never bothered him much, even as a recruit when they were forced to train in all conditions. While other soldiers always griped about the cold or the damp, Corvin put his head down and did what needed to be done.

Today, weeding the western field was what needed to be done. And a small sapling had taken root near the western wall. He'd been meaning to chop that down for the last few weeks. Ethriel told him it could wait until the weather cleared, and Faith shook her head at him, making sure to be out of her mother's earshot before calling him a kiss-ass. Corvin simply smiled, picked up the hatchet and the bucket where Ethriel kept her gardening tools, and set out into the rain.

Lucien and Jae had been gone for a couple of days, though they hadn't told him much about where they were going. Ethriel was sad to see them leave, and Faith seemed angry, which had been fairly constant since the two had shown up. Corvin thought he could understand why, though his relationship with his own parents had been much more straightforward. At least as far as Westholden military households had been concerned. His father had been an officer, as had his three older brothers. Corvin had followed after them in rank and file, as expected, though he had always hoped he'd make a name for himself, something that would distinguish his military career from those of the other men in his family.

Well, he'd certainly accomplished that.

The rain varied from steady to misting and everything in between while Corvin worked. It was on the heavier side of things as it neared lunch. Corvin caught movement out of the corner of his eye by the cottage and . . . was that a shout beneath the drumming of the rain? Corvin grabbed the hatchet and took off at a jog, his boots squelching in the mud of the garden.

A few steps in and he heard it again. His name carried on the wind.

"Corvin!"

He picked up his pace, and as he rounded the crumbling wall heading toward the cottage, Faith appeared from the small building on the other side where Ethriel had given him a bed and a place to stay. Through the rain, he could make out that she was carrying something that was taller than she was—

His sword.

"Corvin!" she shouted again just as a crash came from inside the cottage. "Help!" As soon as he was close enough, Faith tossed his sword. He caught it with a firm grip around the sheath and lobbed the hatchet toward her in the same motion. She caught it by the handle and spun it once in her hand before they both swung toward the front of the cottage.

"Who?" Corvin asked, his voice dropping into the tones of command. "How many?" The front door was open, one of the hinges broken. Were they thieves? Assassins from Westhold?

"I don't know. I only saw two."

Corvin took the cottage steps at once, keeping his sword sheathed. The two-handed sword was far too long to be of any use inside—except for hopefully intimidating whoever had come to call.

A man and a woman stood in Ethriel's cottage. They were clothed in shades of brown and leather armor, and both had jagged, curved knives drawn.

The man had a meaty hand around Ethriel's throat and was threatening her with his knife while the woman made a mess of the place, sweeping a stack of plates off the table to shatter on the floor.

Corvin stepped toward the man holding Ethriel, though he was careful to keep the woman where he could see her. He pointed at the man with the hilt of his massive sword. "Let go of her!" he snapped. Both of the intruders turned at his command, though the man made no other move to obey.

"Mind your own business," the man said as he pressed the tip of his blade to the side of Ethriel's neck. She was leaning back against the table, her hands flat behind her to keep herself from falling. Her eyes were wide and red, but she seemed unharmed.

Faith stepped in beside Corvin, the hatchet raised. "Get the fuck out of here!"

The woman laughed as she advanced a step toward Faith. Corvin positioned himself to where he could intercede if necessary, but he didn't want to move too far from Ethriel just yet.

"Oh look," the woman said, her eyes wild. "The pup's got fangs."

Faith's grip tightened on the hatchet and she cocked her arm, ready to throw it. "Call me that again," she ground out between clenched teeth.

Ethriel's hand inched along the top of the table, reaching for a paring knife that lay just beyond her reach. Corvin moved a step closer.

"I said you've got fangs, *pup*." The woman bared her own sharpened fangs at Faith. Shifters. "But I bet you're all bark and no bite, just like your old m—"

The woman didn't have a chance to finish the sentence before Faith's hatchet was buried in her shoulder. She roared and staggered toward the hearth.

The man howled in pain as Ethriel stabbed him in the side with her knife. He reared back, his own blade sliding down as he stumbled. It sliced a thin line of red across the front of Ethriel's dress. With a startled cry, she spun away from him so she was no longer stuck between him and the table.

"Get out of my house!" Ethriel shouted, grabbing a large carving knife from the wooden block beside the wash basin.

Corvin advanced on the man. "You heard them. Get out before I throw you out."

The man charged him with a feral growl, but Corvin dropped his shoulder and stood into the shifter, flipping him up and through the open door.

The woman tore the hatchet out of her shoulder with a shriek and hurled it back at Faith, who ducked out of its path. The small axe embedded itself inches deep into the cottage wall.

The wound in the woman's shoulder began to slowly stitch together. Corvin had seen such healing from the shifters in the Red Forest, but it was still startling to witness. He hardly had the time to wonder at it before the woman launched herself forward.

Faith was ready for her. She dropped to the ground and rolled into the woman's legs, tripping her up. Corvin caught the shifter, sidestepped, and flung her outside. She collided with the other shifter, who was getting to his feet.

As Corvin stalked to the door, Faith was up and yanking the hatchet out of the wall, primed to follow him.

He turned and set a firm hand on her shoulder. "Stay inside," he said sharply.

"You don't get to tell me—"

"Protect your mother," Corvin ordered. "Don't let them get back in."

Resolve fell over Faith's features as she gripped the hatchet and moved toward Ethriel.

Rain pelted Corvin as he stepped outside to meet the two shifters. He shoved the sheath off his blade and gripped the sword hilt until his knuckles turned white. He hadn't wielded it since he'd been attacked in Southport, but the weight of it felt right in his hands. Corvin had trained with this sword since he was a teen, and his muscles remembered how to handle its weight, with or without Ainam's power.

The woman was getting to her feet, but the man had already changed into a beast of black fur and gleaming fangs. He prowled toward Corvin, who moved from the doorway, leading the beast away from the cottage. Behind the monster, the woman dropped to all fours with sickening crunches and pops as she shifted. In this bestial shape, her shoulders were nearly as high as Corvin's. She roared and charged.

Corvin feinted to her left before bringing the sword around and slashing to her right. He hit the same front leg, a little lower down from Faith's initial strike, and the shifter gave a high-pitched yowl.

The other was starting to circle around behind him. Corvin dashed backward. He couldn't let them flank him.

The beast leapt, and Corvin instinctively reached for his power—*Ainam's* power. He found nothing but a heavy, weighted silence. Without a shield to deflect the attack, he dove out of the way, but his hesitation—his mistake—cost him. The beast's massive claws raked across Corvin's calf. He rolled and landed on his feet, though fire tore up his leg as he put weight on it.

The shifter stalked forward again, his fangs dripping with spit as his large tongue flicked across his lips. He lunged. Corvin dodged, deflecting the attack with the honed edge of his blade. The beast yelped as the sword carved a line down his side, all the way to his flank, though it wouldn't slow the shifter down for long.

The woman—wait, where had she—?

Corvin spun, getting her back into his field of vision, but she'd nearly made it all the way behind him. He thrust forward with his sword, driving her back a few more steps so he could get out from between them. His leg buckled as he lunged, and he nearly fell to the mud. Regaining his balance, he backed toward the southern edge of the clearing.

The female shifter growled at him, teeth bared, and swiped with her massive paw. Corvin sidestepped, swinging his sword over his head to bring it crashing down on her outstretched front leg. The blade slid through the fur and sinew and bone. The massive paw fell to the ground in a bloody mess.

The creature roared. She stumbled back, hobbling on three legs. Blood poured from the stump of the fourth. She turned tail and ran east into the forest.

Corvin turned as the male shifter leapt again. He tried to push himself out of the way, but his leg gave out, dropping him to one knee. So he raised his sword.

The beast slammed into Corvin. Claws dug into the soft flesh of his side. Corvin twisted as they fell, setting the pommel of his sword against the ground. He hoped it wouldn't sink too far into the mud, but it seemed luck was on his side. The pommel—followed by Corvin's shoulder—struck the line of rocks that marked the edge of the southern garden.

Pain shot through Corvin's shoulder, and there was a crunch of bone. His sword drove through the underside of the beast's maw and pierced the top of its skull. The shifter twitched, paws sliding in the mud, scrambling for a moment as though trying to pry himself from the blade. But then he fell still. The body shifted back into the human form of the man who had held a knife to Ethriel's throat.

Corvin rolled the shifter and the sword off to the side. The rain was coming in torrents now, splattering against his face. His left arm was numb. He tried to twist to the right so he could push himself up, but his side screamed with the movement. He touched his right hand to the tear in his shirt, just beneath his ribs, and caught the bright crimson of blood before the rain washed it from his fingers. He pressed his hand to his side, sending a wave of pain and nausea over him and tearing a yell from deep in his chest. Keeping pressure on the wound, Corvin used his elbow against the raised stones to lever himself up.

Each step toward the cottage shot burning pain through his leg and through the gash in his side. His left arm hung limp, useless. He couldn't carry his sword, so he left it embedded in the dead shifter's head. He'd have to retrieve it later.

Corvin hadn't realized how far the southern garden was from the cottage. He knew it shouldn't be taking him this long to get back, but the world was swaying. He stared at his feet, making sure to put one foot in front of the other. Just as he had the day he'd stumbled back here from Southport, dazed and bleeding. Dying. He hadn't made it to the cottage that time. He'd staggered and fallen almost as soon as he'd made it to the clearing. But soon he'd heard the chiding voice of his savior.

"Taerna's blessings, what trouble have you gotten yourself into this time, Soldier?" Her tone had been light, teasing, but there was a tightness beneath it. The worry, or perhaps even a certainty, that he was going to die.

But he hadn't died. She'd stitched him up and bandaged his wounds, and when he could do nothing but lie still in a half-conscious delirium, he would listen to her soft humming as she moved through the cottage.

Savior, he'd called her the very first time she patched up his wounds after the battle at Taernfane—the burns and broken ribs from the Warden's magic that had shattered his shield and crashed into him. Corvin had refused to give his name and had asked she not give hers. And so she had called him *Soldier*, and he had called her *Savior*. Though it was only that second time when she had truly saved his life.

Corvin stumbled in the mud but kept to his feet with a groan, knowing that if he fell now he might not get back up.

"Corvin!" Faith's voice reached him through the roar of the rain.

The world tilted when he lifted his head, and Corvin dropped to his knees, fighting to keep himself upright through the dizziness and blood loss. But Faith was there, just ahead of him, Ethriel running close behind. They were both drenched.

Faith slid on her knees in the mud when she reached him. Then Ethriel was on his other side, and he found himself looking up into the shining eyes of his savior once again.

"Let's get you inside," she said. She crouched in front of him, looking him over.

Faith gripped his good arm and hauled him to his feet. "Come on," she urged. "We've got you."

Corvin was quite proud that he made it all the way inside and to a chair before he collapsed, hand still pressed firmly to his side. Ainam's glory, every breath was like fire. "Are you two alright?" he asked.

Ethriel raised a brow at him as she tore open the side of his shirt and moved his hand to get a better look at the wound, which was bleeding freely and dripping onto the floor. "You're asking us if *we're* alright?" She scoffed quietly, shaking her head. "Keep pressure here." She pressed his hand back against his side, forcing a sharp inhale. "Faith, get some water in the basin please." She stepped away and returned a few moments later with some cloths, bandages, and a small box.

Ethriel moved Corvin's hand again, just long enough this time to press the cloth against the wound, then she returned his hand to hold it in place. "I'll need to clean and stitch these wounds," she said. She took a small strip of something from the box. It looked like a small piece of bark. "Here, chew on this. It'll dull the pain."

Corvin did as she instructed. Bitterness coated his tongue. "You didn't have this the last time," he mused as Ethriel set to work cleaning and stitching Corvin's wounds.

"Yes, well, after the last time, I thought I'd better keep some on hand, just in case." She hummed while she worked, and Faith busied herself with fixing their front door.

"Between the blood loss and the witchwood, you might feel a little light-headed," Ethriel said when Corvin was sewn together and bandaged. "You need to get some sleep, but first, let's fix that shoulder."

Corvin nodded, finding his thoughts were muddled and weighed down with exhaustion.

Ethriel grabbed his left hand in hers. She set her other hand along his bicep. "On three. One—" Before she even got to *two*, Ethriel yanked hard on his arm and twisted.

The bones of his shoulder ground together. The sudden, sharp pain pulled a yelp from him, even through the dulling effects of the witchwood. Feeling rushed back into his arm. Corvin leaned back in the chair, letting his head hang as he took a moment to simply breathe. He wiggled his fingers, happy to see they responded.

"You've done that before," he said, pulling his hand up to rest in his lap and taking some of the pressure off his shoulder. The stabbing pain had abated nearly as quickly as it had come on, but it left behind a deep ache. He knew from experience that his shoulder would be sore for a while.

"Get some rest," Ethriel said gently. Faith appeared beside him, and again the two women hauled him to his feet. Sleep sounded like an incredible idea. "And you're staying in here tonight," Ethriel added as Corvin registered that they were leading him toward one of the cottage rooms.

He wanted to protest, to say that he'd put them out enough and that he could sleep in his own bed, but he was having trouble putting the thought to words.

"Before you try to argue about it," Ethriel continued, "I need to keep an eye on you to make sure those wounds don't become infected. That'll be easier to do if you're here."

He couldn't argue with that.

They guided him to the bed, and Faith arranged some pillows while Ethriel helped him lie back. "Thank you for what you did, Corvin." Her voice was even, but there was a shimmer of tears in her eyes. "Thank you for protecting us."

Corvin's eyes were closing on their own, and he was asleep before he could ask why anyone would've done anything else.

CHAPTER 46

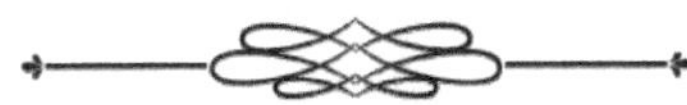

DARE LAY AWAKE FOR a long while after Verity left. The trial was set to start in the morning. He'd tried. Gods fucking dammit, he'd tried a dozen times to explain to someone—anyone—what had happened. He'd tried everything he could think of to get out of the oath, but it was no use. It shackled him down better than any chains.

A faint zing of magic skittered across his skin. Dare propped himself up on his elbows. On the desk, which he'd left bare after helping Verity with her repairs, sat a small strip of paper. His stomach sank as he rose to get a better look.

The note, in Tanithe's fine script, read, *Last chance, my dear. Yes or no?*

Fuck this and fuck Tanithe Ash. Dare snatched the quill from its holder, dipped it in ink, and scrawled across the bottom of the paper, *Go fuck yourself.*

The paper disappeared with another little puff of magic before Dare could consider whether that had been the wisest response. But he was out of patience and out of time, and the only thing he knew for certain was that he'd sooner die than help Tanithe.

But it wasn't *his* life he was gambling with. It was Gregor's. Thankfully, Gregor was safe at the embassy; Finn and Verity had seen to that. Tanithe wouldn't be able to get close to him.

Right?

Of course, Tanithe had the power to travel through shadows. Could she use that to sneak through the defenses they'd constructed?

Perhaps, but if he knew anything about Tanithe, it was that she kept her promises, and while she had promised to kill Gregor, she'd also promised that

Dare would be there to watch. As horrifying a thought as that was, it meant Gregor was safe, at least for now. The trial would have too many witnesses, so she wouldn't try anything there. And after the trial, well . . . Dare doubted Gregor would even be speaking to him after that.

Another thought struck Dare then, like a hammer.

He could run.

No. Dare refused to give up. He'd wasted too many hours—too many days—in self-pity. As hopeless as it seemed, his friends were counting on him. King Dominic was counting on him. The families of the people Tanithe killed in Taernfane were counting on him.

By the time the sixth chime echoed across the base, Dare pushed himself up from where he'd spent the last few hours hunched over his desk. A few ideas had percolated in the predawn hours, the most promising of which revolved around guiding the questions he was asked. If he could steer the conversation, perhaps he could skirt around his oath while still implying that Tanithe was responsible. If that proved infeasible, the next best thing might be to refuse to answer entirely. Surely no testimony from him would be better for Drahkonia's case than what he'd otherwise have to say?

It could work. This could still work.

Dare dressed for the day in the formal gray attire of the Wardens. It was important to look the part today, Verity had said when she had the clothes sent over a few days earlier. He splashed some water on his face, hoping to make it look like he hadn't been awake all night, and pulled his hair back at the temples. Then he set his hand on his chest. At this angle, his fingers brushed the Warden's brand while his palm rested against the scar from where Solace had saved his life. And over the center of that scar, the key from Gregor hung on its chain.

This life you lead, it isn't yours, the strange old man in Southport had said. *You stole it.*

Maybe he had. But Verity had believed in him enough to make him a Warden. Solace had believed in him enough to save his life and to trust Dare with his own. And Gregor—shit, Gregor had been the first to believe in him.

Verity's words from their first full day in Whitehollow—when she'd defended him to Commander Cairn—echoed in Dare's mind.

The world is a better place, a safer place, because he walks in it.

He could do this. He could make things right.

✸

Dare arrived at the large meeting space that had been designated for the hearing a little early. He wasn't surprised to find Verity already there, as well as Gregor, Lorekeeper Harrow, and Chancellor Caelan.

Caelan spotted Dare first and crossed to him, clapping him on the back. "Ah, glad to see you, my friend."

Dare smiled, forcing his nerves down into the pit of his stomach. "Of course." He hoped he sounded confident. "Wouldn't miss it."

"I know." Caelan guided him toward the center of the room. Several long tables were arranged in an open square.

Gregor sat on the side nearest the door, his shoulders hunched, head bowed as he read over a few documents spread out on the table in front of him.

"Honestly," Caelan continued, stopping beside Gregor, "I was hoping we'd find something in all the files that Valda sent over—something that would nail them down and make all of your testimonies redundant and unnecessary." He sat on the edge of the table, one leg braced against the floor. "Alas, though Gregor found some evidence, it's circumstantial at best. I'm afraid this still will very much come down to you and your knowledge of Tanithe's actions and connections."

A lump caught in Dare's throat, though thankfully one of the Wardens on the committee entered just then, pulling the chancellor away for introductions. Gregor looked up at Dare, and he looked even more tired than the last time Dare had seen him.

Maybe, Dare thought. *Maybe when this is all over, he'll be able to relax. Maybe once he knows Tanithe will get what she deserves, he'll feel safe.*

Even still, Gregor favored Dare with a soft smile, and the slightest hint of a dimple appeared on his cheek. "Are you ready?"

Dare swallowed hard and squeezed Gregor's shoulder before taking the seat beside him. Was he ready? He actually had a plan, so that was more than he'd expected. "Yeah," he said after a moment. "Yeah, I'm ready."

More Wardens trickled in over the next several minutes, as did Finn, and a tall, spindly man with tousled brown hair and ambassador's robes that appeared a few sizes too big on his thin frame. Dare recognized him immediately as Nathanial Jorn, the Valdane emissary. He greeted Verity and Lorekeeper Harrow, then made polite small talk with Caelan before taking a seat at the table opposite Dare and Gregor.

Finn came to sit beside Dare as Verity moved to one of the empty tables along the side of the square. "Good morning, everyone," she said, her voice easily filling the room. "I'm High Commander Verity Corallan. On behalf of the Wardens of the Flame, welcome to Whitehollow."

Watching Verity command the room was like watching a master dancer take the stage. She held everyone's attention with her grace and presence. Despite the manner in which the responsibility had fallen on her shoulders, Dare couldn't picture her doing anything else.

The door at the back of the room swung open hard, banging into the wall. Several of the Wardens who'd taken their seats stood at the interruption as Jonah entered without a word. He hurried to Verity's side and when he whispered something to her, her eyes went round before they darted to Dare, or maybe Gregor.

The door swung open again, pulling everyone's attention. "Sorry I'm late," Tanithe Ash crooned, striding into the room like she owned the place. Four Wardens flanked her. "I hope you didn't start without me."

CHAPTER 47

DARE WAS ON HIS feet, one hand reaching for the dagger tucked behind his back. A small choking sound came from Gregor as Tanithe waved at him with a little waggle of her fingers.

Caelan stood, hands pressed against the table, and the question on his lips was the same as the one painted blatantly across Nathanial Jorn's face.

"High Commander," Jorn said, waving a hand at Tanithe. "Who is this?"

Dare rolled his eyes. Of course Valda would send someone who'd never even met Tanithe Ash before.

Tanithe's eyebrows shot up in mock insult. "I would have thought that much was obvious. Or were you really planning to conduct my own trial without me?"

Verity's hands clenched into fists, but she kept her tone surprisingly neutral. "Ambassador Nathanial, Chancellor Caelan, this is Tanithe Ash."

"Nice of you to make it," Caelan said, his voice far less polite than his words.

Tanithe smiled at him, all teeth. "I wouldn't miss it for the world." She turned that smile on Dare next. "Nice to see you again, *Warden*." An upward nod acknowledged Gregor behind him. "Buttercup."

Dare's blood boiled in his veins. "Fuck you," he growled. He was sick to death of her fucking games.

"Now, now," she chided. "That kind of language hardly seems befitting of a venerable *Warden of the Flame*."

Lorekeeper Harrow cleared her throat as Dare sneered at Tanithe. "Warden Wilhaven," Harrow said. "Please take your seat." The tension in her voice was clear, but her tone was gentle.

"What are you even doing here anyway?" Dare demanded.

Tanithe swept her arm to encompass those gathered. "I already told you. I'm here for my trial. I'd be remiss not to personally address all these heinous accusations against me."

"Warden Wilhaven," Harrow said again, more forcefully this time. "Please, sit."

Dare shot a look at Verity, hoping for backup, but she only shook her head. *Not now*, was the silent message. He grudgingly sat, his hand relaxing only when Gregor's slid into it under the table and squeezed tightly.

Tanithe, still grinning like a cat, slipped into a chair opposite Verity, hands demurely resting on her crossed knee. The Wardens who'd escorted her in looked to Verity for orders.

She waved them to the back of the room. "Stay here and remain on your guard." She turned then to Jonah, who hovered nearby, uncertain, and gestured to the wall directly behind her. "You, too. Please."

Jonah nodded, a shadow falling over his young face as he took up his new post.

Verity addressed the room again. "As I was saying, welcome to Whitehollow. Before we begin . . ." She swallowed hard, hesitating for only the briefest moment before she continued. "As many of you may already have heard, it is my solemn duty to inform you all that I am a Chosen of Pyrannis."

There were a few exchanged looks among the Wardens, as though they'd perhaps heard it as a rumor but hadn't known whether it could be believed. Tanithe arched one delicate brow and leaned back in her chair.

"As such, I have it on good authority that the old superstitions of Wardens' oaths being magically binding are not superstition any longer. A formal oath made in the presence of a Warden cannot be broken by any known means." Verity held her head high as she swept her gaze across the room.

Murmurs broke out now; this was new information for most everyone. Not for Dare though. He'd figured that out the hard way already.

"I tell you this," Verity went on, "so that there is no confusion or misunderstanding regarding the proceedings here today, and it is important that everyone have a full understanding of what they are consenting to. Anyone providing testimony will be asked to swear an oath of honesty. And any attempts to lie will be both obvious and uncomfortable."

Verity paused, letting this information soak into the assembly. At the scattered nods, she sat and gestured to those along the side of the table with Caelan. "The committee gathered will make the collective decision regarding the truth of what transpired in Drahkonia's capital city of Taernfane. The committee is comprised of Chancellor Caelan Toleth, representing Drahkonia. Ambassador Nathanial Jorn will represent the city-state of Valda. Wardens Talley, Meriet, and Kirek serve on the committee as the neutral parties. Both Drahkonia and Valda have agreed to abide by the decision of the committee." Verity surveyed the room again. "If there are no questions, Chancellor Caelan may begin by presenting Drahkonia's case."

Caelan stood, setting a hand over his heart, as Lorekeeper Harrow rose and said, "Chancellor Caelan Toleth, do you swear to answer all questions and to tell the truth to the best of your knowledge and ability?"

The chancellor's voice projected through the chamber. "I swear to answer all questions and to tell the truth to the best of my knowledge and ability."

A faint warmth, so gentle Dare almost missed it, emanated outward from Caelan.

The magic of the oath.

From her seat on the other side of the room, Verity stiffened just slightly. Had she felt it too? Could she *feel* the oaths taking effect as Dare could?

There wasn't time to think on the ramifications of that now. Caelan was reading from his prepared statement, describing the devastation that Tanithe and her shadow creatures had caused through Taernfane.

Dare had been there, of course, but he'd been in the palace courtyard during the attack. He'd only seen the aftermath of what the monsters had done to the city. Hearing it described now—the terror, the innocent people who were injured or killed—was nauseating.

Next came an accounting of the evidence Drahkonia had against Valda, or more specifically Tanithe. Caelan listed off the witnesses, including Finn, Gregor, and Dare, before diving deep into some documentation that had been provided by Valda.

Dare tried to focus on what Caelan was saying—it was immensely dry, relating as best as he could follow to the accounting of asset movements within Valda, as well as beyond the city-state's borders—but Tanithe's bright eyes were fixed on Dare, sharp and intent, as though she were trying to send a message directly into his mind.

Perhaps she was. Dare was grateful, and not for the first time, for the shield that Tykaras had placed around his mind.

"The ledger dated for the time of the attack," Caelan was saying, "shows a transfer of funds to an independent bank in Finnegan's Forde, with no note as to what these funds were allocated for, or why the transfer took place. Although Finnegan's Forde is in the neighboring kingdom of Southreach, its proximity to Drahkonia, as well as the timing of the transfer, suggest it may have had something to do with the attack."

Ambassador Nathanial shook his head, his palms open on the table. "That's a bit of a stretch, Chancellor. A random transfer of funds to a private bank that's not even in Drahkonia?"

Dare's focus drifted back to Tanithe, which caused a smile to creep across her lips. As he watched, Tanithe held up three fingers just above the table. She lowered one. Then another. When only the one remained, she angled it toward Jorn. A small pulse of pain hit Dare in the temple, like the first throb of a headache.

"Although . . ." Nathanial Jorn angled his head, considering a question as though the thought had just struck him. "Who did you say discovered this problematic transfer?"

The chancellor lifted his chin. "Gregor Thalesen was the one who initially identified the line item, though I reviewed the ledger myself and completely—"

"Ah," the ambassador said, cutting him off. "Convenient that one of the witnesses most insistent on placing the blame on Valda was the one to find this issue."

A flicker of rage rolled through Dare. How dare he accuse Gregor of making it up! Across the table, Tanithe's smile stretched wider.

Of course. She was manipulating Jorn with mind magic. She must have told him what to say, or at least planted the idea. Vire's unholy shit, she was infuriating.

Caelan and Nathanial debated back and forth for a time until the committee finally insisted that they move along with Drahkonia's evidence.

"The kingdom of Drahkonia," Caelan announced, "calls Fionna Garrison to provide her testimony to the committee."

Finn stood from her seat beside Dare.

"State your name and rank or occupation for the record, please," Caelan instructed.

Finn cleared her throat. "Fionna Garrison. Full commissioned member of the Crimson Brothers."

A twinge of jealousy tightened Dare's chest as one of the Wardens stood and addressed Finn. "Do you swear to answer all questions and to tell the truth to the best of your knowledge and ability?"

"Yes," Finn said clearly, projecting her voice to be heard through the chamber. "I swear to answer all questions and to tell the truth to the best of my knowledge and ability."

Again, the little spark of warmth rushed through Dare.

"Thank you." The Warden gestured for Chancellor Caelan to continue.

Caelan referred to his notes before addressing Finn again. "You were present in Taernfane when the shadow creatures attacked?"

"Yes."

"Can you please describe what you saw?"

Finn shifted her weight from one foot to the other, her amber eyes darting briefly to Verity. "I was at the outer edge of the palace gardens," she said. There was a nervous tremble in her voice, but otherwise, she was calm and focused. "Tanithe Ash was on the parapets. She shot at my friend, Jae, and wounded her. Then Tanithe shot at me and some of the city guards who came to help. Eventually, she sprinkled something on the ground, and the shadow monsters appeared. That's when I moved away from the gardens."

"You ran away from these shadow creatures?" Nathanial asked. There was no malice in his voice at all, but rather a humble curiosity.

Finn turned her attention to him. "They were attacking the city," she bit out. "I went to see how many I could kill before they hurt anyone."

He glanced at his notes. "And how many did you kill?"

"Fourteen," Finn said. Then she shrugged. "Maybe more. I lost count."

The corner of Dare's mouth twitched with pride.

Nathanial looked suitably impressed and jotted down a note. "Going back to the events in the courtyard, you said that you were at the gates of the gardens?"

"Yes."

"And you saw Tanithe Ash on the parapets. So that would be on the opposite side of the garden from where you were? Closest to the palace?"

"Yes," Finn repeated.

He nodded, jotting another note. "And the length of the gardens, from end to end," he said, leaning forward to address Caelan on the other side of the Wardens, "is about a hundred and fifty feet, correct?"

"A hundred and eighty," Caelan said.

"With Taernfane's sacred tree in the center, yes?"

The chancellor nodded. "That's right."

"So from a hundred and eighty feet," Nathanial said to Finn, "through the branches and leaves of a massive oak tree, you could tell with absolute certainty that she"—he gestured toward Tanithe—"was the person on the parapets? The person who created monsters of shadow and shot at your friend and the guards, correct?"

Finn shifted again. "Yes. I'm an archer," she explained. "I can see a target clearly from a hell of a lot farther than that."

"Tanithe Ash was a target?" one of the Wardens asked.

"Considering what she was doing at the time? Yes."

Tanithe scoffed quietly. Finn dutifully ignored her, though the sound made Dare's fists clench.

"Had you seen her before?" Nathanial asked.

Finn blinked. "I . . . What?"

Ainam's bollocks, where was he going with this?

Nathanial set down his pen. "Before that day, had you ever seen or met Tanithe Ash before?"

"Twice before," Finn said. "The first time was a few days earlier. Tanithe had kidnapped one of our friends and was threatening to hurt him."

The ambassador checked his notes and frowned. "Which friend was this?"

Finn cleared her throat again. "Gregor Thalesen."

"Ah," he said. He circled something on the paper. "And the second time?"

"About two days after that. She attacked our camp."

Tanithe made a show of rolling her eyes, accompanied by a loud sigh.

"And," Nathanial continued, "you know Tanithe Ash's occupation?"

Finn fidgeted with her hands, her focus straight ahead on Nathanial Jorn. "She's the spymaster for the Valdane Council."

A small sound snuck out of Nathanial, sounding a little like a surprised laugh. "Well, I have to say, Miss Garrison, that's news to me."

I bet it is, Dare thought bitterly.

"How were you made aware of her employment with the Council?"

"Dare—uh, Warden Wilhaven told me."

Nathanial's eyes flicked to Dare before he made another note. "I understand. Thank you."

With no further questions for Finn, she sat back down, wiping her palms against her pants.

"Thank you, Miss Garrison," Caelan said kindly. "The kingdom of Drahkonia calls Gregor Thalesen to provide his testimony to the committee."

Gregor stood, hands clasped behind his back, which was straight as an iron rod. Dare's jaw clenched at the thought of Gregor having to recount the pain and fear he'd felt at Tanithe's hands—all while she watched the proceedings like a bored house cat.

"State your name and rank or occupation for the record, please," Caelan said.

"Gregor Thalesen. No rank or occupation at present. Former house secretary to the Duke and Duchess Wilhaven in Duchy Wilhaven, Bremmaran."

Warden Talley, who had administered Finn's oath, stood again, repeating the same words to Gregor. And just as it had with Finn, a little pulse of heat rolled through Dare.

The chancellor set his notes down and regarded Gregor with a soft smile. "I recognize that these questions may bring up some difficult memories for you. I apologize in advance if anything I ask you today is upsetting."

"I understand," Gregor said, his face and voice devoid of any emotion.

"According to provided statements, you were held hostage by Tanithe Ash prior to the events in Taernfane, is that right?"

"Yes, that's correct."

Tanithe leaned back in her chair, crossing her arms over her chest. She wasn't watching Dare anymore. She stared hungrily at Gregor.

Dare wanted nothing more than to slit her throat.

"Did she introduce herself to you at the time?" Caelan asked.

Gregor nodded. "She said I should call her *Tanithe*. She didn't provide a surname."

Caelan gestured toward Tanithe. "And to be clear, it was the woman seated there?"

Gregor turned, regarding Tanithe with as cold a gaze as Dare had ever seen. "Yes," he said flatly.

"Had you met her or seen her before that moment?"

"No, Chancellor."

"And when you were in the palace of Taernfane," Caelan continued, "you saw her again?"

"Yes." Gregor's expression didn't change as he said, "She strangled me, threw me down the hallway, and threatened to kill my friends while I watched." Dare's heart ached as Gregor spoke about what had happened in so bland a tone, but it was the role he had to play, and he would do his duty.

Nathanial leaned forward a little, clasping his hands. "If that's true, how did you escape?"

If that was true? Dare ground his teeth, but Gregor only angled his head toward Tanithe. "You should ask her."

Tanithe's predatory gaze soured, a vile hatred emanating from her as she glared at Gregor.

Warden Meriet cleared her throat. "Please answer the question," she said gently.

Gregor didn't turn away from Tanithe. Didn't blink. "I stabbed her in the side."

"Thank you," Caelan said, flipping one of the pages in his notes. "Do you know Tanithe Ash's occupation?"

While Gregor's face remained passive, his knuckles were white from where his hands were clasped. "Yes, she's the spymaster for the Valdane Council."

Nathanial didn't look up as he scribbled something down. "Did she tell you that herself?"

A muscle twitched in Gregor's jaw. "No. She didn't." As Nathanial opened his mouth, Gregor added, "Warden Darcy Wilhaven said she was the spymaster for the Valdane Council. He had indicated they had worked together in the past."

"Thank you," the ambassador said, writing that down. "I think that's everything." He glanced at Caelan, who nodded.

"Thank you, Gregor," he said.

Gregor sat, though the tension in his body didn't ease. Dare put a hand on his knee. "You did great," he whispered.

"The kingdom of Drahkonia calls—"

"Excuse me, Chancellor."

Everyone in the room turned to Tanithe, who stood gracefully.

"I apologize for interrupting." Her voice dripped with such sickly sweet sincerity that Dare's stomach turned. "Do I not get the opportunity to refute these claims?"

Caelan looked to Verity, who seemed poised to say something, but Nathanial Jorn spoke first. "That seems only fair, Miss Ash." He, too, turned to the high commander "By your leave, Commander."

Verity swallowed and looked to Dare.

With the oaths in full effect, she'd be bound to tell the truth like the rest of them. She might have the same tricks up her sleeve that Dare had up his, but he wouldn't let her skitter through any loopholes in the truth.

He nodded.

"Very well," Verity said. "Warden Talley, please administer the oath."

Yes, Dare thought. *Give her the rope to hang herself.*

CHAPTER 48

Dare didn't know what kind of bullshit Tanithe was going to try to pull under the Warden's oath, but he didn't care. There were only so many ways to dance around the truth. He knew as well as Tanithe did that she was guilty. She wouldn't get away with this.

"State your name and rank or occupation for the record, please," Warden Talley said, addressing Tanithe.

"Tanithe Ash, second lieutenant of the Night's Call."

Among the startled whispers that erupted, Caelan's head shot up from where he'd briefly hunched over his notes. "The assassins' guild?"

Tanithe smiled. "We prefer *blades for hire*."

"I bet you do," Dare murmured. That must be what she did on the side. She probably spent just enough time with the Night's Call for it to be a plausible alibi. Dare shuddered. Where the Crimson Brothers were honest mercenaries who took care of their clients and their members, the Night's Call were the dark, deceiving underbelly of the mercenary world. They were the ones who took the jobs too vile for the Brothers. Whose name only need be whispered as a threat to send a jolt of fear down most spines. Who were just as likely to kill you without a contract as with one.

"Do you swear," Warden Talley continued, "to answer all questions and to tell the truth to the best of your knowledge and ability?"

"Yes, Warden," she said. "I swear to answer all questions and to tell the truth to the best of my knowledge and ability."

Caelan eyed her, the open distrust on his face a mirror for Dare's own feelings. "So you have no problems answering our questions related to the attack on Taernfane?"

Tanithe held her hands out to her sides. "None. I'm an open book, Chancellor."

"Very well. I see no reason to dance around the heart of things. Did you attack the city of Taernfane last autumn?"

Dare held his breath, waiting to see how Tanithe would twist her answer to fit within the bounds of the truth. He didn't have to wait long.

"No."

Whispers rolled through the room.

No? How could she say *no*? Dare looked to Verity, who was already on her feet.

Caelan cleared his throat. "Did you release the shadow creatures described today into the city?"

Tanithe smiled sweetly. "No."

Hands pressed flat against the table, Caelan rose. "Are you saying that you weren't in Taernfane? You didn't attack Warden Wilhaven, Jae Aleissandra, Finn Garrison, or Gregor Thalesen?" The words came out through clenched teeth.

"That's correct," Tanithe said. "I've never been to Taernfane, though I hear it's a lovely city."

Vire's hells, she wasn't just twisting the truth. She was *lying*. But how? It shouldn't be possible. By Dare's own experience, it wasn't possible.

"She's lying!" Verity blurted out.

Beside the Warden commander, Lorekeeper Harrow stood, though her focus was on Verity. "Commander," she warned softly.

Nathanial Jorn arched a brow. "But you said yourself, Commander, she's not able to lie under the Wardens' oath. Or is that not the case?"

"I don't know how, but she's lying," Verity said, and even from Dare's side of the table, the heat radiating from her was palpable, at least to him.

Tanithe's smile never faltered.

"I'm afraid you can't have it both ways, Commander," Nathanial said. "Either the oaths are binding or they're not."

Dare wanted to jump up and defend Verity. He wanted to scream at the top of his lungs that Tanithe was a lying piece of shit who was manipulating all of them. But he couldn't. It wouldn't do any good. He needed to play this calm. He needed the committee to believe him when it came time to spin his own story.

Lorekeeper Harrow, still standing beside Verity, leaned toward her, whispering something in her ear. Verity's hands clenched into fists, but at last she sat, her lips pressed in a thin line. Harrow waved to Caelan. "Please continue, Chancellor."

With an almost apologetic nod toward Dare, Finn, and Gregor, Caelan returned to his seat as well. "I'm afraid I don't have any further questions."

"I have one," Nathanial said, consulting his notes. "Just to ensure there's no confusion on the topic, are you or have you ever been the spymaster for the Valdane Council?"

"No," Tanithe said, the lie sliding easily off her tongue. "Never."

"Do you work for the Valdane Council in any capacity?" he asked.

"No, Ambassador. I do not."

That lying sack of Vire's demon shit! Dare's finger twitched, itching to grab the dagger in his boot and end her.

"Thank you, Miss Ash," Nathanial said. "You may sit."

Dare drummed his thumb against the table. They could still do this. They could still pull this off. It wasn't over—not yet. If he could avoid speaking the truth while still convincing the committee of it, they had a chance. He didn't need them to agree that Tanithe—and by extension, Valda—was guilty. He just needed them not to dismiss the evidence and rule that she was innocent. As long as the hearing could continue another day . . . After the meeting, he could talk with Verity. Maybe they could figure out how Tanithe managed to lie with the oath. Then, they could come back before the committee and—

"The kingdom of Drahkonia calls Warden Darcy Wilhaven to provide his testimony to the committee."

Dare stood, clasping his hands behind his back in much the same manner that Gregor had, though he kept his shoulders relaxed. A soldier at ease was the impression he needed to convey. He needed the Wardens on the committee to view him as a peer.

"State your name and rank or occupation for the record, please," Warden Talley said.

"Darcy Wilhaven," he said. "Warden of the Flame and, uh . . . former commissioned member of the Crimson Brothers."

"Do you swear to answer all questions and to tell the truth to the best of your knowledge and ability?"

"Yes." Dare took a breath, swallowing hard. "I swear to answer all questions and to tell the truth to the best of my knowledge and ability."

Warmth flooded his chest, centered on his Warden's brand.

Caelan flipped through his notes, and Dare could imagine the chancellor was taking a moment to collect himself after questioning Tanithe. Dare appreciated the extra few moments as well. Finally Caelan said, "Warden Wilhaven, in your previous occupation as a commissioned member of the Crimson Brothers, you worked with Tanithe Ash, is that correct?"

"Yes," Dare said. "She sometimes gave me jobs to do."

"Did she ever ask you to do anything illegal?"

"Almost exclusively."

Nathanial scratched a few notes as Caelan continued. "In the time that you worked with Tanithe, was it your understanding that she was the spymaster for the Valdane Council?"

Dare had spent hours going over the language of his oath—the *exact* words he'd used in swearing it. He needed to be confident when the time came to spin the truth. He couldn't look like he was trying to lie, after all. And so he said, "I'd met with her several times in the Valdane Council's meeting hall. Her offices were on the lower level."

He spared a glance at Tanithe. Thankfully her exhaustive list of magical and divine abilities didn't appear to include killing someone with a look, otherwise Dare might have dropped dead in that instant. He had to admit, though, that the little glimpse of Tanithe's impotent rage gave him a bit of a thrill.

"And you were present at the attack on Taernfane, correct?" Caelan asked.

"Yes," Dare said, focusing on the chancellor again. "I was present."

"Can you tell me what you saw?"

Perfect. During their prep for the hearing, Caelan had indicated he would ask open questions like this. Dare had been hoping he wouldn't change his mind.

"When we arrived at the courtyard—"

"Who is *we*?" Nathanial interrupted.

Dare's jaw tightened. "Finn, Jae, me, and"—his voice cracked, and he swallowed—"and Solace."

"Thank you. Please, continue."

Clearing his throat, Dare pushed forward. "When we arrived at the courtyard, someone was shooting poisoned crossbow bolts at anyone who set foot in the garden. Through the trees, I could see red hair. We spoke across the courtyard."

So long as he didn't name names, he could be talking about anyone.

"After the shadow creatures appeared, I climbed the parapets, hoping to find Tanithe," Dare continued. He resisted the urge to breathe a sigh of relief that he was able to get that sentence out. It had worked in the early morning hours, but then again, he'd been alone at the time. "That's when Tanithe used her magic to speak to me directly in my mind." It was working—mind magic didn't mean she was absolutely there at the palace, but it certainly implied it.

"Why would she do that?" Caelan asked.

Dare hesitated. He hadn't expected this question, though admittedly he should have. "To taunt me," he said. "And to hurt me. I . . ." Shit. Even though more people knew now than ever before, it still wasn't something he was used to sharing. "I'm a Perceptive. I can feel magic. Tanithe figured that out and wanted to use it to hurt me."

To his right, Verity was smiling. She gave him an encouraging nod when their eyes met. To his left, Tanithe drummed her long fingers against the table, biting the inside of her cheek.

"Why?" Nathanial asked. "Why would Tanithe Ash go through such lengths to attack you?"

Dare took a deep breath. He knew this would come up, but thank Ainam's shining ass he didn't ask why Tanithe would go through such lengths to attack *Taernfane*. "Because she is a Chosen of Vire, and we had something that she wanted." And so Dare told the committee the story of Solace and how his death awakened the old gods. "Taernfane was the unfortunate arena for the battle, through no fault of its own."

The Wardens on the committee exchanged a look, two of them furiously scribbling notes while the third openly stared at Tanithe.

It was working! Despite Dare's best efforts to completely fuck everything up, he was actually pulling this off. Even Nathanial Jorn regarded Tanithe with suspicion. The *Chosen of Vire* information certainly seemed to ruffle his carefully groomed feathers.

"Why Taernfane specifically?" Nathanial asked.

"Each of the gods has a place of power," Dare explained, "where their connection to the world is strongest. Or, at least, where the distance between them and the world is thinnest." He still wasn't sure he fully understood how it worked. "We needed a place of power to destroy the weapon. And Taernfane, which is tied to Taerna, was closest."

"What are the others?" Caelan asked, leaning forward.

Dare hesitated, glancing at Verity. "Pyrannis is tied to Embercliff. Neoma belongs to Lanara, and Aetherann has the Reach."

Nathanial clasped his hands together. "Where's Ainam's place of power?"

Tanithe cackled so loud and shrill that half the chamber startled at the sound, including Gregor. Dare's hand fell on Gregor's shoulder before he could think better of the movement. Of what it would suggest.

Tanithe didn't miss it for even an instant. "What a ridiculous yarn," she said, still laughing. She favored Dare with an upward nod, her lips curling into a sneer. "He's clever, I'll give him that. But see how he comforts the one behind these allegations? His lover weaves a tale for the committee, and this so-called *Warden* goes along with it, despite being oath- and honor-bound to do the opposite."

"Take your seat," Verity barked.

"I'll admit that Gregor Thalesen and I have had a run-in in the past," Tanithe continued. "He has every right to be cross with me over how things ended. But Gregor, darling, this is a bit much, don't you think?"

Gregor's face took on a sickly pallor, his fingers shaking as they traced one of the scars around his wrist.

Tanithe focused again on Dare. "You sidestepped the questions beauti-fully." She moved around the table toward him.

He turned his back to Gregor, keeping Tanithe in front of him. If she wanted to kill Gregor, she'd have to go through Dare first. And if she wanted to kill Dare, well . . . He was done running from her.

"Clearly he truly believes his own fabricated story," Tanithe continued. "The poor dear. But you know better, don't you? Tell me, who did you really see on the battlements that day in Taernfane?"

Verity slammed her fist against the table. "Sit. Down."

Tanithe ignored her. "Who was it, Warden? Who did you see?"

No. No, fuck her. He'd come too far. He wasn't about to let her make this whole committee hearing crash and burn. He wouldn't let her put the blame on Gregor. "I heard your voice in my head," Dare repeated, though godsdammit, his voice shook. "I saw your red hair. You had every reason to be there—"

"Was. It. Me?"

Verity was moving now, her hand gripping the sword on her hip. The other Wardens who'd stayed behind as guards moved with her. Dare was vaguely aware of Gregor and Finn being pulled out of the way as the Wardens circled him and Tanithe.

"Stand down," Verity commanded. "Return to your seat. *Now.*"

Dare lifted his chin, staring down Tanithe even as the swirling, nausea-in-ducing spiral began, threatening to knock him over. He set one hand on the table to steady himself. "I don't have to say shit to you," Dare snapped. "I don't have to answer any questions from you."

Tanithe turned slowly toward her chair, but not before her answering grin spread from ear to ear.

Shit, what is she—

"But Warden Wilhaven," Nathanial said. "You do have to answer ques-tions from me."

No! They were so close. He could do this! He just needed—

"Did you see Tanithe Ash in Taernfane?"

Fuck. Dare tightened his jaw, but he felt his brand burn in warning. He had sworn to answer all questions from the committee. He couldn't simply refuse to answer. *No, no, no.*

"I saw—"

The ambassador held up a hand. "Yes or no, Warden. Was Tanithe Ash in Taernfane that day?"

Dare's heart thundered in his chest. Everyone stared at him, waiting on his answer, with only Tanithe aware of why he was desperate to stall.

With Tanithe seated again, the Wardens surrounding him dispersed, though Verity stayed close. Her brows knit as she watched him floundering.

"Ambassador," Dare tried, "I—"

"Yes or no," Nathanial repeated.

Dare closed his eyes. He couldn't bear to see the look on his friends' faces—on Gregor's face—when he said, "No."

Chapter 49

THE WORLD SEEMED TO lurch to a stop as Verity's breath caught in her throat. Beside Finn, Gregor staggered a step. Finn put a hand on his back. He looked as though he stopped breathing. Verity wanted to check on him, but—

"I'm sorry," Caelan said. "What did you say?"

Verity watched, helpless, as Dare drew a slow breath. "I said, no."

"What are you doing?" she hissed.

Caelan's fingers tightened around his notes, the paper crinkling. "Warden Wilhaven," he said, straining to keep his voice even. "Fionna Garrison and Gregor Thalesen both said they saw her in Taernfane during the attack. They were both quite certain."

Dare opened his eyes and looked only at the chancellor. "Tanithe Ash wasn't in Taernfane," he said flatly.

The door behind them slammed as Gregor rushed out of the room. Dare flinched.

Verity glared at him, her anger sparking in her chest, dancing with the little flame from Pyrannis within her. What had he done?

"Well," Nathanial said gently. "I don't think I have any further questions."

"Verity." Finn's voice was soft, pleading. "Do something."

"I can't," Verity whispered back, her heart wrenching. She hated to see the pain in Finn's eyes, but there was nothing she could do to ease it. "I didn't see her there."

"Because I wasn't," Tanithe said, tossing her arms up. "You have only the misguided word of a little girl who saw *someone* through tree branches and shadows, and a deeply troubled man who deluded himself and everyone around him into thinking I was there. You see"—she gestured toward the closed door—"he can't even face the truth."

Verity's anger flared hotter. "Stop talking," she snapped.

"I'm afraid she has a point, Commander," Nathanial said.

Caelan's face was sorrowful. "Indeed." After a moment he shook his head, as though clearing a bit of fog from his thoughts. "I suppose I don't have any more questions either." He looked across the table at Dare. "Thank you, Warden Wilhaven," he said, his words heavy with disappointment. "We appreciate your time."

Dare dropped his head.

"Perhaps we should take a brief break," the ambassador said. "We can reconvene in half an hour to make our final decision?"

Yes! Maybe Verity could try to undo some of the damage Dare had done.

Tanithe stood again with a flourish. "Well, this has been fun, but if there's nothing else you need from me, I'll be on my way."

"Don't leave the city just yet," Caelan said quickly. "The committee may have a few more questions for you."

"Of course, my dear." She smiled sweetly to the chancellor before blowing a kiss at Dare. "Always a pleasure, darling." She sauntered out of the chamber.

Gods, Gregor! If she caught up with him—

Dare took a step to follow her, as though the same thought had struck him as well.

But Verity sidestepped to block his exit, even as she turned, pointing first at Finn, then at Jonah. "You two, follow her. See that she doesn't cause any trouble or try to leave the city." The two of them dashed out of the room without a word, though Finn's hand slid along the small of Verity's back as she ran past.

The light, comforting touch grounded her. She forced herself to draw a deep breath before she faced Dare. "And you." She bit the words out through clenched teeth. "You will wait for me outside."

"Verity, I—"

"*Now.*" She would give him the space to speak his piece, but now was not the time. Right now, she needed to fix the disaster he'd just caused. Verity stepped to the side to allow Dare to pass.

He left without another word.

Verity spun toward the chancellor, who was already packing up his notes as the others spread themselves throughout the room. "Caelan—"

"It's done, High Commander," he said, glancing up as she approached. "I only wish he'd said as much in Taernfane and saved us all the trouble."

"Something must have happened," she said, her voice tight with urgency. "Dare wouldn't just *lie*—"

"Apologies, High Commander," Nathanial Jorn said, coming up alongside Caelan. "But you cannot simply ignore the Wardens' oaths that were sworn when someone's testimony doesn't align with what you want to hear." He shook his head, inclining it in such a way that he almost looked remorseful for the hearing's outcome. "I'm sorry, High Commander. What happened in Taernfane was a horrible tragedy. And I know you only want justice for the city and her people. But I think we've seen now, beyond a doubt, that that blame does not lie with Valda."

✺

An hour later, Verity stormed out of the meeting chamber. After the committee reconvened, she'd urged them to reconsider, but Nathanial was convinced, and Caelan was resigned. The best she'd managed was getting them to delay their final decision until the morning, and even that had been under a strong caution from Lorekeeper Harrow not to stray too close to interfering.

Outside the meeting hall, Dare leaned against the side of the building waiting for her as she'd instructed. His hands were stuffed in his pockets, and his head was bowed. He didn't even look up at her as she stopped beside him.

Verity needed to talk to him privately. She needed answers, but she didn't trust herself to keep her temper in check, and the last thing she needed after her little outburst during the hearing was for anyone to overhear her shouting or crying. Her office was out of the question then.

"This way," she demanded. Then she spun and headed across the base. The crunch of his boots on the gravel path let her know he was following. When they reached the building with the indoor training room she'd used for practicing her fire with Gregor and the Banishments with Dare, she yanked the door open. The handle groaned under her grip. "Get inside."

Dare slipped through the door, still avoiding looking at her. Verity paused and took a steadying breath before following him down the hall to the room at the back.

The door had just swung closed behind Dare, so it slammed hard into the wall as she stormed in.

"What was that in there?"

Spinning to face her, Dare scrambled backward, trying to put some space between them.

She didn't let him. She wasn't going to let him run from this. "Answer me, Warden," Verity ordered. "What the *fuck* was that?"

Dare met her glare, his mouth falling open as he searched for words.

"She's going to get away with it now," she said. "Because of what you said. She killed people. She hurt Finn and Jae. And Gregor—"

At the name, Dare's eyes darted to the edge of the room. Gregor sat on a bench against the wall, his elbows resting on his knees, his glasses hanging from one hand.

Verity hadn't realized Gregor was there, but it didn't matter. He deserved answers as much as anyone else. Maybe more so. "She hurt your friends, Dare," she continued. "She's going to get away with everything. And I need you to tell me why."

Dare watched Gregor, still silent.

He always had so much to say. Where were all his words now? "Why, Dare?" she asked again, and this time her voice cracked on his name.

Finally looking at Verity again, Dare spoke at last, but the voice that emerged barely sounded like his. It was only a rough, hollowed out husk. "I didn't have a choice."

That was it.

Verity's hands clenched at her sides as her fury roared within her like a bonfire. "She killed dozens of innocent people and hurt your friends, and I don't understand how or why, but you let her get away with it. Tanithe Ash will never face justice for what she did in Taernfane. Because of you." Her eyes burned. "You *had* a choice. And you made it." She couldn't look at him another second. Verity turned her back. "Get out."

Silence stretched behind her, though she managed to hold her shoulders steady until there was a quiet rustle and the click of the latch as the door opened and closed.

The silence held fast, yawning wide.

"I thought you were going to hit him," Gregor murmured.

Verity pushed out a heavy breath as her shoulders sank. "I don't understand how he could do that." When she turned to Gregor, his eyes were red and shining with tears. She imagined hers must look the same. She crossed to him and dropped onto the bench beside him. "How could he do that?"

He slid his glasses back onto his nose. "I don't know." His voice was rough and jagged. "I've never known him to do anything without a reason . . . even if his reasoning isn't always sound. But I don't understand why he would lie—"

"Or *how*." Verity tilted her head to the ceiling. "The Wardens' oaths are binding now. And I could actually feel them, Gregor." It would take some getting used to—feeling this particular brand of Pyrannis's magic the way a Perceptive might. She'd have to find time to marvel in it later. There was too much at stake now.

"You could feel them?" Gregor straightened. "And you felt it with everyone? You're sure?"

She'd thought so.

In Verity's silence, Gregor added solemnly, "Dare wasn't the only one who lied today."

Of course. "Tanithe." She'd stood there and lied through her teeth. She'd been too distracted in the moment, but now that Verity was thinking back on it . . . "I didn't feel the oath with her."

"And Dare?"

Had she felt something when Dare stood before the committee? She'd been so thrown off by Tanithe's blatant lies, had she been paying attention to Dare's oath? "I'm not sure."

They were silent a long time, sitting together on the bench in the dim light of the training room.

"There's . . . There's something else," Gregor said, hanging his head. "Something else that Dare's lied about."

Verity's chest tightened.

"I didn't want you to find out this way," he went on, speaking to the floor. "I feel like I'm somehow betraying him by telling you this." He laughed, soft and humorless. "I already betrayed him by overhearing it in the first place."

Verity angled herself toward Gregor, resting her hand on his knee. "Tell me," she said gently.

"Just after we arrived in Whitehollow, I overheard someone talking to Dare in his mind, and Dare was answering back." Gregor finally lifted his head. "Verity, I think it was a god."

Verity focused on her breathing as she and Gregor left the Warden's base. If things with Dare were as bad as she feared, she was going to need all her wits about her. She couldn't let her emotions get the better of her.

Drystan's voice echoed in her mind. *You can do this, Vee. You're strong. Stronger than you think you are.*

But was she strong enough to do what might need to be done?

Gregor had insisted on finding Dare so he could talk to him and sort out this whole mess, but Verity wasn't about to let him go alone. Gregor didn't think Dare would ever hurt him, and Verity wanted to believe that was true, but it wasn't a risk she was willing to take. The problem was, neither of them had any idea where Dare might go.

It was midafternoon, and the streets were crowded. At some point while they'd been in the training room it had begun to rain. Heavy, cold droplets pattered against the cobblestones, loud in Verity's ears. On either side of the road, the gutters turned into small rivers, rushing the rain water toward the bay.

A question weighed on her mind, even as they searched for Dare. Perhaps she could tackle this one at the same time.

Pyrannis? I need to speak with you. Please.

A warmth blossomed in Verity's chest as the little flame within her brightened. *Hello, Verity Corallan.*

I have a question for you. About oaths sworn in your name.

The flame crackled. She had his attention.

Would a Chosen of Vire be bound by your oaths?

The fire within her flared angrily. *I have no power over Vire's minions.*

Verity's steps faltered as she walked beside Gregor. *Why?*

Vire is strong. Stronger than I, and stronger than any of my siblings. Only by working together could we even hope to compare to the strength of either Vire or Ainam. And that was before we slumbered. I can only assume they have grown in power since then. But more than that, Vire is chaos incarnate. Nothing short of Ainam's limitless order can bind him. We are fortunate that neither of them has a conduit in the world. If either of them did, they would be nigh unstoppable.

A conduit? You mean a place of power, like you have in Embercliff?

Correct, Pyrannis said.

Why don't they have one? Verity asked.

Because they were not here when the world was forged.

Verity let this thought turn over in her mind, but before long, Gregor stopped short, his hands flying to his head. "Not now," he muttered through clenched teeth. "Please."

"Gregor?" Verity stopped beside him. He didn't answer. "Are you alright?" When she set her hand on his shoulder, he startled. "Is it Aetherann's power?" she asked slowly. She'd been with him a few times when it had seemed to overwhelm him all at once.

He nodded, his eyes pinching shut. "I'm fine," he ground out, moving forward again. Verity jogged to catch up, letting her connection to Pyrannis dissipate. The last thing she wanted was to add to Gregor's discomfort.

She followed Gregor until he stopped in front of an unfamiliar tavern. She peered at the sign, an otter holding a frothing tankard. "What's this place?"

"No idea," Gregor said. He glanced down at his clothes, now soaked through by the rain. "I'm freezing. I need to warm up for a minute."

Verity wasn't cold, but she was drenched, and the rain only seemed to be coming down harder. She nodded and followed Gregor inside.

The main room of the tavern was spacious, warm, and dry, with a fireplace roaring against the far wall and a set of stairs in the corner leading up to rented rooms. Unfortunately for Gregor, it was also crowded. Verity glanced his way as the door shut out the sound of the pattering rain. Gregor closed his eyes and drew a steadying breath.

Verity coaxed him toward the fire. "Come on," she said gently. "Let's warm you up."

They hadn't taken more than two steps when Gregor's head snapped up. He turned toward the bar, like he'd heard his name shouted from across the room.

"Gregor—" she started, but he was already pulling away from her.

"Over there."

Verity followed his gaze and spotted Dare through the busy tavern room. He was hunched over the bar, damp shirt clinging to his back, with a mug and a bottle of some dark liquor between his hands.

Of all the taverns in the city, what were the odds?

As she watched, Dare drained what was left in his mug and added a heavy pour from the bottle before taking another long swallow. Pyrannis's flames, had he been at this since he'd left the base?

Gregor crossed to the bar and slid onto a stool beside Dare, Verity just behind him.

"What are you doing here?" Verity asked before Gregor could say anything.

Dare didn't turn. "Are we back to this game?" He took another swig from the mug. "Drinking," he said. "What are you doing?"

"We're talking to you, I hope," Gregor said, his voice strained. He pressed his hand to his forehead again.

Dare scoffed into his mug. "What ever for?"

"Because you lied to the committee today," Gregor said.

Verity studied Dare's profile. The dark circles under his eyes were noticeable, even in the tavern's dim light, and the lines of his face were tired and worn.

"And because you've been lying to me for months," Gregor added.

That got Dare's attention. He paused in mid-drink and set the mug down hard on the bar. "I don't lie to you," he said slowly. He glanced to Verity. "Either of you."

Gregor winced, his thumb pressed against his temple. "Can we go somewhere more quiet so we can talk?" he asked. "I can hardly hear myself think in here."

Dare eyed the bustling tavern over his shoulder. He reached for the bottle, but Gregor set his hand on it. "Leave it."

"You're no fun," Dare said, his words running together.

Gregor stood. "And you're drunk enough already."

Dare sketched a half bow from his seat on the barstool. "As you wish." He hopped down, lost his footing, and stumbled. Verity caught his arm, steadying him, but not before Dare collided with the man seated on his other side.

He muttered a quiet, "Sorry, sir," before righting himself and heading toward the stairs.

Verity shot a look at Gregor. She'd never seen him in so much discomfort over his power from Aetherann. Was this what being in the city was like all the time? No wonder he couldn't sleep.

Gregor nodded solemnly as he passed her. "I'll be fine," he said. He followed Dare up the stairs, with Verity right behind him.

CHAPTER 50

DARE TRUDGED UP THE stairs. The warmth of the alcohol he'd drunk very quickly in a very short time had settled in his gut and was slowly rising through his arms and legs and into his head. He was expecting a blackout in the near future; part of him wished it would start now. He didn't want to face either of them after what had happened today.

After what he'd done.

At the top of the stairs, Dare fished a key out of his pocket, staring at the number stamped onto it. It took a moment for the small indentations marking a *4* to steady themselves in his vision, but soon he made his way to the correct door. The key found the lock on only the second try, and Dare pushed the door open to the empty room, ushering Gregor and Verity inside.

"Better?" he asked, taking a seat on the edge of the bed.

Gregor rubbed at his temples briefly before surveying the room. "Yes, thank you. I—Wait, you have a room here?"

"Oh, fuck no," Dare said. He twirled the key around his fingers. "But that drunk at the bar does."

Verity sighed deeply as Gregor's eyes widened. "How the hell did you—No, you know what, I don't want to know."

Dare couldn't help the mischievous smile from dancing across his lips as he pocketed the key. He would let himself have this one small bit of amusement before his world burned down around him.

Verity leaned against the door and crossed her arms as Gregor sat in the one chair in the room and removed his glasses. He rubbed his eyes before saying, "Let's start with what happened today at the trial. Your testimony."

Dare sighed, the grin fading. Even the whiskey wasn't dulling the ache in his chest as much as he'd hoped. "For what it's worth, I'm sorry, I never wanted to—"

Gregor held up his hand to stop him before he got any further. "I'm not interested in apologies. I want to know why."

Of course he would want to know why. And he had a right to know. They all did.

He owed them all an explanation.

But that was the one thing he couldn't do, and he couldn't bear to look at Gregor as he said, "I can't tell you."

"Dammit, Darcy!"

Dare dragged his fingers through his hair, still damp from the rain. "I can't. I want to, but I can't."

"Why not?" Verity demanded from the door.

His fingers clenched into fists in his hair as a growl tore through him. "I. *Can't.*" He dropped his hands helplessly to his sides. "I'm sure you think I'm a fucking asshole," he muttered.

"Honestly, I think you've been corrupted by Vire," Verity said flatly.

Dare snapped his focus to her, though it made the whole room wobble. He thought Gregor might give an indication of whether Verity was making some sort of cruel joke. He didn't. Though Gregor didn't look hurt any more. He looked pissed. Dare wasn't sure which was worse.

"You think . . ." Dare's mind struggled to catch up. "What?"

"You've been acting strangely since . . . after Taernfane," Verity said. "And with the testimony you gave today, it let Tanithe, a known Chosen of Vire, get away with everything she's done."

"I tried to stop her!"

"Did you?" Verity's voice was ice. "Or did you just need us to think that?"

"What the fuck? So you jumped straight to divine corruption?" He turned to Gregor, pleading. "Come on, you can't be serious."

Gregor only bowed his head. "It fits with everything, including the timing."

Dare hadn't thought his day could get any worse. "So you think I'm . . . what, Vire's puppet?" he asked Verity. The question was met with silence. He studied Gregor, but his face was unreadable. This couldn't be happening. "And what do you think?"

Gregor slid his glasses back up the bridge of his nose. He didn't flinch or waver as he said, "I don't know what to think."

Those words were a slap in the face, though one Dare knew he deserved. "Gregor," he said, trying to force down the drunken haze that was encroaching with each passing minute. This was important. "You know me. I've never lied to you. I'm not being controlled by Vire."

Verity glanced at Gregor as his frown deepened, sorrow darkening his normally soft features.

"I thought I did," Gregor said in scarcely more than a whisper. Dare's heart clenched. "But you have lied to me."

Dare shook his head, bracing his hands on his knees as the world started to sway. "No, never. I wouldn't—"

"Darcy . . ." Gregor darted a look at Verity before focusing on Dare again. "You need to know that one of the powers I was gifted from Aetherann . . ." He swallowed hard. "I can sometimes hear other people's thoughts. A couple of weeks ago, when you were in my room, I heard someone talking to you in your mind. It sounded . . . I've heard Aetherann once, and I've heard Pyrannis speak with Verity. This sounded . . . not dissimilar. Verity thinks it's Vire, but I'm not sure what it is other than I think you have a god speaking to you. You were Chosen that day in the courtyard, just like the rest of us. Weren't you?"

Every thought in Dare's head evaporated. The room was spinning, but it was even odds on whether it was because of the whiskey or everything Gregor had said.

"You . . ." The words caught in his parched throat, but another thought struck him, and that one emerged much more easily. "You told *Verity*?" He'd known since they'd left Taernfane that Gregor had been confiding in Verity. But somehow this particular seed of jealousy gave him a far stronger foothold right now. Otherwise, he might lose his balance entirely.

Verity rolled her eyes and began to pace the room, but she didn't deny it.

"Don't change the subject," Gregor pressed, his face stern. "Are you Chosen or aren't you?"

Dare clenched his jaw, then uttered a quiet, "I am."

Gregor didn't hesitate. "Who?"

Verity stopped pacing, moving closer to Dare.

"That's a long story . . ."

"It's not," Gregor snapped. "There are only so many gods. Who spoke to you that day?"

Even drunk, Dare could see the promise of violence in Verity's demeanor. She was ready to act if he were to try something. If he were to admit to being a Chosen of Vire.

Dare rubbed the back of his neck. The liquor he'd downed was steadily making it harder to think straight. He didn't want to explain it like this—Ainam's bollocks, he wasn't sure he *could* explain it like this—but it was apparent that he'd better try if he didn't want Verity's sword through his throat.

"Tykaras," he said.

Verity's brow furrowed. "Where have I heard—"

"Like from the pages?" Gregor asked. He'd always had an excellent memory, especially for things he'd read.

The recollection seemed to strike Verity then too, as she and Gregor exchanged a look. "The illuminated manuscript," she said. "The extra page with the violet eyes. Dare, I asked you if you knew what that meant—"

"And I didn't," he said, dropping his face into his hands. The gentle spin to the room was turning aggressive.

"There's a seventh god?" Gregor murmured.

"How is there a seventh god that none of us have even heard of?" Verity asked. When the silence stretched for more than a few moments, the edge returned to her voice. "That wasn't rhetorical, Dare. How is there a seventh god?"

Dare wasn't sure he knew how to answer that question even if he were in his right mind, and he was far, *far* from in his right mind.

Verity hardly gave him a chance to try. "How do we know this isn't another lie?" she demanded.

"I will tell you everything I know," Dare groaned, dropping his hands. "By the gods above and below, I will tell you everything when I am fucking sober and can explain properly. But I swear to you that it isn't Vire."

Verity crossed her arms over her chest as she glared at Dare. Clearly she wasn't buying it.

At last, Gregor blew out a long breath. The air in the room stirred. "Verity, would you give us some time alone, please?" he asked.

Her face softened as she turned to Gregor. "Are you sure?"

That question hurt more than any beating Dare had ever taken. It hurt more than Caleb's spear through his chest. She thought he might hurt Gregor.

She didn't trust him.

Gregor nodded. "I'm sure," he said. "I'll be fine. I'll come find you later."

Verity cast one last appraising look at Dare. "Alright. I have a mess I need to clean up now anyway." She turned and left.

As soon as the door was shut and silence surrounded them again, Gregor leaned forward, studying Dare. "I believe you."

The relief that flooded Dare was short-lived.

"I asked you," Gregor went on. "That day in my room. I asked you if there was something going on, and you lied."

Dare's memory raced to that day. "No," he said quickly. "No, you asked if there was anything I wanted to tell you. I definitely did *not* want to tell you about this." He hadn't been ready. Not then. And not now.

Gregor's face turned a shade of crimson Dare had not witnessed before this moment. "I refuse to argue semantics with you! You knew what I meant, and you intentionally led me to believe that nothing was going on when there was, in fact, something very important going on."

While some part of him knew he deserved Gregor's anger, that part of him was rapidly dissolving in alcohol. The rest of him—the part that had control of his mouth—didn't like being attacked. And besides, Gregor was acting like Dare was the only one keeping secrets. Like he was the only one hiding anything. "Something important? You mean like being able to hear people's thoughts? I'd say that's pretty fucking important too. And I asked you about it plenty."

Gregor stood. "I told you there was something and that I wasn't ready to talk about it yet," he seethed. "But you made me think there wasn't anything at all. *That's* the difference."

Dare squeezed his hands into fists in the blankets. He didn't trust himself to be able to stand. "But you told Verity." It was a petty bit of jealousy, but it was all he had to throw back at Gregor. Otherwise, all he had left was the growing self-loathing that had led him to the tavern in the first place, and that wasn't something he was willing—or able—to handle just now.

"She's been trying to help me control it," Gregor snapped, his voice rising. Another first. "I wanted to know how this damned power works before I burdened anyone else with it. And that was my decision to make."

"As was mine."

"Yes, but you *lied* to do it. I thought I could trust you, Darcy. I thought that no matter what else, no matter how much time had passed, that you would always be honest with me. But it seems you really have changed."

Damn him. Damn them both. "Yes, well, I'm sure *Verity* would gladly walk you through the exhaustive list of my failings. So that everyone's on the same page."

Gregor threw his hands up. "This is pointless," he muttered. "We'll talk tomorrow. When you can think straight."

As Gregor turned toward the door, Dare finally let himself flop back onto the bed. *The problem isn't thinking, you arrogant bastard*, he thought bitterly. *This fucking Warden's oath binding my tongue's what's making my life a living hell.*

Gregor stopped, the door half opened. "Dare . . ."

"Look, just go already." Dare propped himself on his elbows. He was getting sick of waiting for this damned blackout to start. The sooner Gregor could leave him to wallow, the better.

But Gregor wasn't leaving. He slammed the door closed and whirled around, rushing to the bed. "I heard you!"

"Good," Dare barked. "Then why are you still—"

"What *Warden's oath*?"

Dare could only blink at him as his mind reeled and his vision spun. "What the hells are you—"

"I *heard* you," Gregor said, his voice tight with urgency. "Think that again. What Warden's oath?"

CHAPTER 51

IT TOOK ALL GREGOR'S remaining patience to get Dare to focus his thoughts long enough to relay the details of the ill-considered oath he swore back in Valda. By the time they were done, Gregor was kneeling beside the bed, head in his hands, while Dare barely managed to remain sitting upright, eyes glazed in what was increasingly becoming a drunken stupor.

At last, the pieces seemed to fit together. Most of them, at least. Gregor had a few more questions, mostly about the god Dare called Tykaras, but he didn't think he'd get anything more out of him now.

"Are we done?" Dare groaned. He leaned back, settling onto the bed. The bed that wasn't his.

Gregor caught him by the wrist. "No, no you don't," he said, tugging him sharply back into a sitting position as he stood. "You cannot sleep here."

"I can," Dare said, trying to lie back again.

Gregor yanked harder, pulling Dare to his feet. "This isn't your room."

"Ah, but I have the key," Dare sang, twirling the key around his finger.

Gregor snatched it mid-twirl. "Which we're going to return, and then I'm taking you back to sleep it off at the Drahkonian embassy."

"You're no fun."

"I know," Gregor said tightly. "You said that already."

"Well, it bears repeating," Dare huffed.

Gods, spare me.

"Wait." Dare stopped. "I don't have a room at the embassy."

"I know, but I do."

"Oh." Something seemed to click into place in Dare's mind as a devilish smile played across his lips. "*Oh . . .*"

Gregor groaned as he opened the door and shoved Dare into the hallway. "I need to keep an eye on you."

Dare's thoughts, which had been getting more jumbled and distracted as the afternoon wore on, still tickled the back of Gregor's mind. *He can keep anything he wants on me—*

"Dare!" Gregor's cheeks burned as he moved to follow. "Focus, please."

But Dare blocked the doorway. "What?" he whined. He wrapped his arms around Gregor's waist and pulled him in. "I *am* focused." Back home, Gregor would have melted into a puddle at the desire in Darcy's voice.

But they weren't back home.

Gregor set his hand against Dare's chest, pushing space between them. "No," he said firmly. "You don't get to pretend everything's fine just because you're drunk. Now let's go."

Dare's hands fell from Gregor's hips as he took a silent step back.

Gregor moved into the hall and stopped. One of the Drahkonian guards from the embassy was standing against the wall opposite the door. She straightened to attention, despite not being in her uniform.

"Talia." Gregor smoothed the front of his shirt. "What are you doing here?"

"Commander Corallan sent me to walk you back to the embassy," she said, though her sharp eyes, close-set in her copper skin, darted between Gregor and Dare.

Gregor blew out a breath. That was one concern eased, at least.

He hadn't been looking forward to getting Dare back to the embassy alone. In truth, he didn't relish the idea of bringing Dare to the embassy at all, but realistically, he had few viable options. Bringing Dare all the way back to the Wardens' base in his current state wasn't the wisest decision, but neither was leaving Dare to flounder for himself, nor leaving him alone here or at another inn. Tanithe was likely still roaming the streets of Whitehollow. The sooner they could get somewhere safe, the better, and having Talia there to help him was one less worry.

By the time Gregor and Talia got Dare down the stairs and outside, the lanterns were lit and the rain had eased, falling in a gentle drizzle reminiscent of the mist at the bottom of the Ragebrook Falls back home.

Together, they kept Dare pointed in the right direction until the embassy came into view. Inside, Dare tried to angle toward the crystal decanters of aged Drahkonian whiskey on the sideboard in the front sitting room, but Talia grabbed him by the shoulders, steering him toward the stairs instead.

Gregor unlocked the door to his room. "I've got it from here, Talia. Thank you for your help."

Talia hesitated only a moment before she nodded. "You know where to find me if you need anything else."

As Talia left, Gregor practically dragged Dare inside. He helped Dare strip out of his wet clothes before Dare flopped onto the bed like a rag doll, moaning as he nestled into the pillows. Gregor grabbed a spare blanket from the chest at the foot of the bed and threw it over him.

"I need to talk with Verity," Gregor said, crossing to the door. "I'll be back in a couple of hours."

"Stay." Dare's voice was muffled against the blankets, but one eye watched him through his tousled brown hair. "Please."

"Dare, I really need to talk to Verity. After everything today, I need to tell her—"

Dare lifted his head, propping himself up on his elbows. "Gregor, I . . ." He winced, rubbing his chest. Where the Warden's brand was scarred into his skin. It truly did cause him pain if he tried to break the oath he swore. "I shouldn't have . . ." Another wince. The pain seemed to sober him somewhat. "Dammit, I thought I could—"

"I know," Gregor said quickly, before Dare could try to say anything more. "I know. And I'm sorry I didn't tell you about all this." He gestured vaguely to himself. He crossed to the bed and sat down beside Dare. "I wanted to be able to control it before I said anything."

"Why?"

Gregor scoffed. "What do you mean, *why*?"

"I mean, why would it matter?" Dare rolled onto his side, the lines of his face softening as he looked up at Gregor.

"Because not being able to control it terrifies me," Gregor said, speaking aloud the thought he hadn't dared voice, even to Verity. "I didn't want you looking at me like I'm some kind of monster."

Dare levered himself up, swaying a little. He took Gregor's face in his hands, pressing their foreheads together. "What am I thinking right now?"

Gregor closed his eyes and listened, but he couldn't hear anything beyond the soft pattering of rain on the window. He grimaced. "I don't know," he said. He was so tired of not having any control over this power that was supposed to be a boon. So far, it had been nothing but a burden, except for the stroke of luck that allowed him to overhear Dare's thoughts about the oath.

"I'm thinking," Dare said, slowing his speech until it was clear he was choosing each word with care. "That I could never, *ever* think you're a monster. And I will always do anything within my power to help you. No matter what."

For you, he would burn down the world. A chill ran through Gregor, and he pulled away from Dare. "I know," he said. "Thank you."

Dare's lips quirked to the side, but he didn't say anything else.

"Get some sleep, Darcy. Please."

Dare settled back onto the bed, pulling the blanket up over his bare shoulder. "Will you stay?"

Gregor glanced at the window. The rain sounded like it was picking up again. "I really do need to talk to Verity," he said, not looking at Dare. But then again, he wasn't sure he even knew where Verity was. Would she have gone back to her office at the Wardens' compound? Or did she have other matters to attend to elsewhere in the wake of the hearing? "Let me get a message to her," he said, settling on the best course of action. He could at least dry off and warm himself while he waited for word from Verity. "I'll be right back."

He stood before Dare could say anything else and headed into the hall. As he closed the door behind him, Dare's thoughts drifted to the very edge of his mind.

I think I really fucked up this time.

It seems so, the answering voice said. Gregor's steps faltered. It was the same voice he'd heard weeks ago. So this was Tykaras? Had they been listening in on their conversation? For how long?

What do I do? Dare's mental voice asked. *How do I fix it?*

The voice that must have been Tykaras sighed, deep and expansive. *I wish I knew, Child. Truly. I wish I knew.*

Gregor forced himself down the hall, even though his own thoughts were screaming with a hundred questions. He'd intruded enough.

The study on the main floor was surprisingly empty. Gregor was grateful for it; he couldn't face Caelan right now. He found the supply of enchanted parchments used for official embassy business and drafted a quick note to Verity, letting her know he needed to talk to her as soon as possible.

He couldn't have been gone more than ten minutes, but by the time Gregor returned to his room, Dare was snoring peacefully. Gregor changed out of his own damp clothes and sat in the armchair in the corner. He didn't know how long it would be until he heard from Verity, and he tried to distract himself with reading, but his mind wouldn't let go of what happened during the hearing.

Gregor ran through the day over and over, fixating on every detail for at least an hour. When he couldn't stand the thought of it anymore, he finally picked up his book again and managed to read for another hour until his stomach rumbled, calling his attention to the fact it was now well past dinner and he hadn't eaten anything since breakfast.

Gregor slipped silently into the hall in the hopes of scrounging up something to eat from the kitchens.

He was almost to the stairs when a door slammed open behind him.

"Where is he?" Finn shouted, tearing out of her room. Verity was close behind as Finn made for the stairs.

She stalked toward Gregor where he was frozen in place on the landing. "You! Where is he?" Finn was on him before he could react, pushing her finger into his chest. "Where the fuck is Dare?"

"I know you're angry," Gregor said.

"Angry? I'm not *angry*, Gregor. I'm fucking *furious*. And why the hells aren't you?"

"He is," Dare said from just outside Gregor's door. He was still fastening the tie on his pants, and one of Gregor's spare shirts was flung over his shoulder.

Finn stormed toward him, Gregor and Verity trailing behind.

"Finn . . ." Dare's gaze fell as she reached him. "I'm—"

Finn didn't slow as she cocked her arm and threw a right hook.

The punch caught Dare in the face, whipping his head to the side and spinning him into the wall. Verity caught Finn by her arms before she could throw another, and Gregor pushed past them both as he rushed to Dare's side.

Dare pressed his hand to his cheek, still leaning against the wall. He didn't say anything. He didn't look at any of them.

Finn strained against Verity's steel grip, staring daggers at Dare. "Look at me!"

Gregor held out a hand, bidding her stop. This was all moving far too quickly. "Finn, there was more happening than—"

She lunged toward him, toward Dare, though Verity still held her. She pulled so sharply, Gregor worried she might hurt herself. "I said *look at me*, you fucking coward!"

Dare lifted his eyes and met hers, though he still didn't speak. The truth of it was painted across his face, clear and raw. That punch might have caught Dare by surprise, but if Finn managed to break out of Verity's grip and throw another, Dare wouldn't even try to avoid it. Of that, Gregor was certain. He would take the hit. As many as she would give. Because he believed he deserved it.

"Finn, if there's an explanation—" Verity began.

"What possible explanation is there?" Finn roared.

Gregor stepped away from Dare, fully turning to Finn, both hands raised as he stood between them. "Let's at least take this into a room," he said sharply. "Before the guards forcibly remove us from the embassy grounds."

Finn didn't take her eyes from Dare, but she finally stopped struggling. Verity opened the door to Finn's room and ushered her back inside, though she shot a pointed look at Gregor over her shoulder. "Get him cleaned up, then we'll talk."

Gregor turned back to Dare. "What are you doing?" he asked. "Why'd you come out here?"

Dare watched the door close behind Verity. The couple hours of sleep seemed to have sobered him a bit more. "I didn't want to hide from them."

Gregor moved Dare's hand away from his face. A small cut along his cheekbone trickled blood, and there were two little red spots in the white of his eye. Gregor touched Dare's cheek gingerly, eliciting a hiss of pain as Dare jerked his head back.

"Come on," Gregor said. He stooped to pick up the shirt that had fallen, then headed back into his room. Dare followed without another word.

Dare tugged on the shirt and Gregor tossed him an extra pair of pants as well, since Dare's were still wet from the rain. The clothes were a little baggy on Dare, but they'd do. Gregor fetched a cloth and a bowl of cold water, then motioned for Dare to sit on the edge of the bed. Gregor sat beside him, dabbing at the cut under Dare's eye.

Dare dragged his hands through his hair. "Gods, Gregor," he sighed. "I fucked up."

"Yes," Gregor said, wiping the blood from Dare's cheek. "You did. Though it's not like it's the first time."

Dare breathed a laugh. "But I don't know how to fix this one." He touched his rapidly swelling eye.

"We'll figure something out."

Dare raised a brow. "We?" He studied Gregor. "You're not still pissed?"

"Of course I'm still pissed, Darcy," he snapped. He was. Gods knew, he was. He was so angry his heart hurt and he felt sick to his stomach. But he couldn't let Dare go through this alone. "We'll take this one thing at a time, yeah?" He waved a hand toward the door. "Let's go tell them what happened."

"I can't," Dare said, a hand drifting to the Warden's brand on his chest. "Remember?"

Gregor set his hand over Dare's. "Then I'll help you."

Finn was pacing in front of the window when Gregor and Dare entered her room. She froze as soon as she saw Dare, her jaw tight.

Gregor had barely closed the door when Finn moved closer and squared her shoulders. "Alright," she said, crossing her arms over her chest. "Explain it."

Gregor stepped forward. He was almost between them, and it made the hair on the back of his neck stand on end, like he was tempting lightning.

Before he could speak, Finn held up her hand to stop him. "Not you," she said. "I want to hear him say it."

"I can't," Dare said.

"Vire take you," Finn spat.

Dare flinched as if she'd taken another swing at him.

"He *can't*, Finn." Gregor took a deep breath. He'd better get this over with. "He swore an oath as a Warden that he'd say Tanithe was never in Taernfane." He turned to Verity where she sat on one of the narrow beds. "And he swore he wouldn't tell anyone about it."

Finn resumed her pacing. "Why the *fuck* would he do something so stupid?"

"Because he thought he could break it," Gregor said, still looking at Verity. "He swore the oath with every intention of breaking it."

"But with Pyrannis back," Verity said, "the oaths have power again. They're binding."

"But he swore an oath to tell the truth at the hearing," Finn said. "So what the hells?"

"That one said to tell the truth to the best of his ability," Gregor said. They'd covered that loophole in the phrasing while he was getting the story from Dare, and he'd made a mental note to tell the Wardens to update their word choice.

Dare let out a long, slow breath.

Finn wheeled on Gregor, her anger flaring. "Then how come you know about it?"

Gregor sighed. This was not how he wanted to explain any of this, but he had no options. "One of the powers I have from Aetherann is that . . . sometimes I'm able to overhear . . . thoughts."

Finn blinked, staring at him. "You're serious?"

"It's true," Verity chimed in.

"You've been hearing our thoughts this whole time?" Finn demanded. She took a step away from him.

Gregor's chest tightened. "No," he said quickly. "I . . . I didn't say anything earlier because I can't control when it happens." He pushed forward. He could explain more about his gift later, but right now he needed to get out the words that Dare couldn't say. "But I overheard Dare thinking about the oath. He can't talk about it or even write it down." He glanced quickly to Dare, who was watching him, his eyes sorrowful. Gregor's heart twinged at the pain—the remorse—on Dare's face.

Finn stepped between him and Dare. "Verity told me about the other part." She glared at Dare, her shoulders taut as a bow string. "Can you talk about *that*?"

Dare swallowed hard, and when he spoke, his voice was hoarse. "I can."

"Is it true?" she asked. "Are you Chosen?"

"I am," Dare said.

Finn laughed, but it was a low, tortured sound of disbelief. "By *Tykaras*?"

"Yes."

"That doesn't even make sense!" Finn shouted. "How is it even possible there's a seventh fucking god?"

Dare inclined his head, the gesture resembling a shrug without the raising of his shoulders. "I'm honestly still not sure."

"What is he . . ." Exasperated, Finn threw her arms up. "She . . . even the god *of*?"

"They," Dare said quietly. "They're the god of luck. And . . . fate."

A breath fluttered against the back of Gregor's mind, there and gone in the time it took Gregor to focus on it.

"You were Chosen by the god of luck?" Finn asked, incredulous. "Exactly what part of your life over the last eight months has felt like *luck* to you?"

"I survived it all." One corner of Dare's mouth curled upward. "That was pretty lucky."

Verity tensed, pulling her arms around herself. "Why didn't you tell us?" she asked. "Any of us?"

Gregor found that he desperately wanted to know that answer.

"I meant to, I just . . . I tried that day in the courtyard when everything happened, right after you all woke up. But I was so relieved you were all alive, and then the king got there, and . . ."

He let the rest of the thought go unspoken as his gaze drifted to Finn.

Gregor knew the rest, even without hearing his thoughts. *And the king was carrying Finn, who was dying.*

"And then I didn't hear anything from Tykaras for a while and I . . . I thought I'd imagined it." Dare swallowed hard. "And by the time I realized I hadn't, everyone was dealing with so much shit, I didn't want to add my own on top of it."

Finn dismissed him with a wave of her hand as she stalked toward the door. "I need to go," she said sharply. She didn't look at any of them as she left. The door slammed shut in her wake.

Verity watched Dare carefully for a long moment. "After everything we've been through," she said, her voice low, "I think of you as a brother, Dare."

Dare lifted his face toward Verity, hope sparking.

She drew in a long breath. "And yet, after *everything* we've been through, I can't believe you can still be such an idiot." The Warden followed Finn, leaving Dare and Gregor alone.

Dare's shoulders drooped. He looked ready to fall over. "Fuck, what am I going to do?"

"First, you're going to go back to sleep." Gregor held out his hand to Dare. "And then tomorrow, when you're sober, you're going to figure out a plan."

Dare took the offered hand, swaying only slightly as he followed Gregor across the hall to his room. "Plan?"

Gregor couldn't look at him as he said, "You lied to us. You broke our trust. You're going to have to work to fix the damage you've caused."

Dare sat on the edge of Gregor's bed. "I know. I just . . . I don't know how. What can I do?"

"I don't know!" Gregor snapped. "I can't do this for you, Darcy!" Then, more quietly, he voiced the thought that had been twisting his stomach since the committee meeting. "I don't even know if you can."

"Gregor—" Dare began, but Gregor was already opening the door to leave. "Where are you going?"

Gregor sighed, his hand on the latch. "I don't know," he said. "I need some time."

"Time for what?"

"To be away from you." The words slipped through too quickly to bite them back. "I just need to walk for a while," he added. He waved Dare toward the bed. "I'll see you in the morning."

Out in the hall, Gregor leaned against the door. Getting the story from Dare of *how* it happened had dulled some of the edges, but he still didn't understand *why* it had all happened the way it did.

In the end, did the *whys* matter? He would either be able to forgive Dare, or he wouldn't. But the wound was still too fresh, too sharp, for him to answer that now.

Outside, the rain was coming down hard again. He let the cold seep into him, taking root in his muscles and his bones. And his heart. He didn't care about the rain, and he didn't care that he was outside alone. He needed time to himself and as much space as he could manage.

He'd been walking for a while—though not nearly long enough to soothe the ache in his chest—when the whispering susurrus began again. Gregor gritted his teeth as every doorway he passed brought with it a collection of jumbled thoughts.

Not now, please, Gregor begged. *I can't do it tonight.*

The voices grew louder, more insistent.

I can't.

He didn't have it in him to fight the voices. He couldn't find it within himself to care about that either. So he let the voices flow over him, past him, around him. If the voices were to be there, *fine*. He wouldn't get in their way, but he'd be damned if he let them get in his either.

The rustling voices quieted, as though relegated to the background of his thoughts. They weren't gone but more easily ignored.

In the distance, thunder rumbled as if in answer.

CHAPTER 52

CORVIN DIDN'T REMEMBER GETTING out of his soaked and bloody clothes, but the next time he opened his eyes it was morning. Sun streamed in through the curtains of Faith's room. He was wearing only a pair of loose-fitting linen pants, and his left leg was propped up on several pillows, bandaged tightly. His right side was bandaged as well, and his left shoulder was wrapped, minimizing his range of motion.

Everything ached, but that seemed the worst of it. He slowly pushed himself up to sitting, careful to keep his movements slow and even until he could see how his body would react. Hushed voices and softly clinking plates in the kitchen reached him first, followed by the wafting scent of bread, bacon, and coffee. Corvin's stomach rumbled loudly.

He took his time standing and was pleased to find he could put some weight on his injured leg. He hobbled to the door and pulled it open.

Ethriel and Faith were busy in the kitchen, setting out food on the long table. Ethriel laughed at something Faith said. Faith was smiling.

"You're up," a voice said from beside the hearth.

Corvin blinked at the figure tending a pot of coffee hanging over the fire. "Jae," he said once he found his voice again. She looked . . . *happy?* . . . to see him. Or, at least, not annoyed by his presence. Her dark eyes sparkled with the light from the hearth.

The short walk from the bed had been surprisingly exhausting. Corvin leaned against the door frame for support. "When did you get back?"

Ethriel handed the stack of plates she carried to her daughter and crossed the room to Corvin's side.

"We got back yesterday," Jae said, taking the coffee pot from the fire with a cloth wrapped around the handle. She brought it to the table.

Corvin's brows drew together. "Yesterday?"

Ethriel smiled warmly and offered her shoulder. "Here. Come sit and let me have a look at you. You've been asleep for two days."

His stomach rumbled again as though to corroborate her story. Corvin put his arm around Ethriel's shoulders, and she helped him to one of the chairs at the kitchen table. She hummed quietly to herself as she checked the bandages around his calf and his side.

The scene of Ethriel and Faith busy in their little kitchen warmed his heart, and he allowed himself a moment to appreciate the simple beauty of it.

"What do you think?" he asked, a small smile tugging at his lips. "Will I live?"

Ethriel set the bandages back into place and gave him a playful swat on his knee. "Despite your best efforts, I dare say you will, Soldier."

Corvin laughed outright. She hadn't called him that since he'd finally relented and given his name after she'd patched him up the last time. When she'd offered him a place to stay in exchange for his help around her farmstead once he'd healed.

The front door swung open with a creak. Lucien entered, his yellow eyes landing immediately on Corvin, who swallowed the rest of his laugh and was suddenly painfully aware of Ethriel's hand still resting on his knee.

Ethriel rose with a smile and moved around to the other side of the table. Together, she and Faith set the pots and bowls in the center, all heaped with food.

Lucien strode through the room, and Corvin sat up straighter, though it caused his side to twinge as he stretched the stitches. It was an instinct he'd felt most often when he was in the presence of a commanding officer. Leaders had a certain air about them, and when they spoke, you listened.

"Thank you," Lucien said, his voice gruff.

Corvin stared up at him. He wasn't sure what he'd expected the man to say, but that wasn't it.

"You kept them safe," Lucien continued. "I owe you."

Corvin regained his composure. "You don't owe me anything. Anyone would have done the same." Utensils clinked against plates.

"Not anyone," Lucien said. "You could've run. Facing a shifter isn't something most people would do willingly. And you took on two to protect my family."

Faith stepped around the table and set the plate she'd been preparing in front of Corvin. His mouth watered as he took in the fresh baked-bread with red jam, bacon, eggs, and roasted potatoes.

The warmth in Corvin's chest radiated outward as he looked up at Faith and Ethriel. Was helping them such a strange thing for him to do? Would others really have turned and run, leaving them to their fate at the hands of those monsters?

Corvin eyed Lucien, guilt making his ears hot. Not monsters . . . at least, not because of what they were. Lucien was proof enough of that. He could have killed Corvin that day in front of the cottage—Corvin certainly had given him enough reason to. Being caught by surprise and without his power from Ainam, Corvin had stood little chance against the shifter. But despite what he'd done to Lucien's friends—to Jae—Lucien had spared him.

Corvin grabbed a piece of bacon and took a bite. It was cooked perfectly and had a sweet flavor he couldn't place, but it pulled a grunt of appreciation from him. "Ethriel, this is amazing," he said around a mouthful.

"Thank Jae," she said, giving a nod to the other woman.

Jae smiled and set a mug of black coffee in front of Corvin. "My father's a baker," she said, pouring herself a mug as well. "He puts sugar in everything. Especially maple sugar."

Corvin angled his head as he took another bite of bacon. "Maple *sugar*? Like from the tree?"

"You've never had maple sugar?" she asked, completely stunned. "Do you not have maple trees in Westhold?" Even Lucien's brows rose.

Corvin shifted in his chair, suddenly a little embarrassed. "We do," he said, shoving the rest of the piece into his mouth and taking another immediately. "But we don't make *sugar* out of it."

Jae leaned across the table and set a small clay jar in front of Corvin that had some sort of gooey, amber liquid inside. Corvin eyed the jar as Jae took a seat across from him. "Oh, have you been missing out!"

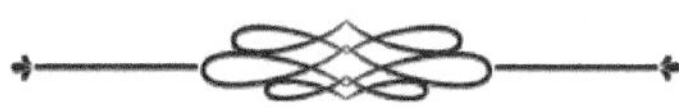

The look on Corvin's face when he tried the maple syrup was amazing, and Jae couldn't help but laugh at the way his eyes widened. He practically coated his plate with the stuff, drizzling it over everything.

Corvin mopped up some residual syrup with the last of the bread on his plate. "Do you know why the shifters came here?" he asked, glancing at Lucien. "Why they attacked?"

Lucien grabbed the last piece of bacon from the center of the table and shoved it in his mouth. "They were trying to get to me," he said. "My efforts in the Red Forest were . . . unwelcome." His yellow eyes darted to Ethriel and Faith before focusing back on Corvin. Then he explained about the shifters and their hidden society, led by Micah.

Faith kept eating, pretending like she wasn't listening even though she watched Lucien carefully. Corvin's brows rose in surprise, though Ethriel somehow looked relieved.

"They're people," she breathed. "Not monsters."

Lucien sat back in his chair. "Of course they're monsters."

"They're not," Ethriel argued. "Some of them may do monstrous things, but that doesn't mean they're all monsters, Luc." She gave him a pointed look, and Jae heard the message as clearly as if she'd spoken it aloud. *That doesn't mean* you're *a monster.*

Jae didn't need her power to know that Lucien's guilt was weighing him down—guilt that his actions had almost caused harm to come to his wife and daughter. Corvin had taken the brunt of it to keep them safe, but what horrors would she and Lucien have returned to if Ethriel had sent Corvin away like they'd wanted her to?

"Ethriel," Lucien continued. "I think you and Faith should leave. Go somewhere safe."

Ethriel stopped just as she rose to put her empty plate in the wash basin. "Excuse me?"

"Just for a little while."

"I'm not running away!" Faith said around a mouthful of bread.

Lucien gestured to the doorway. "They're still out there. I caught their scent on the wind when we were on our way back. The one that escaped must have had others nearby. I doubt they're just going to tuck tail and run back to the Red Forest. They'll be back. And there will likely be more of them next time."

Corvin tensed at the mention of the one female shifter who'd escaped, his right hand drifting absently to rub at the bandage on his side.

Ethriel crossed her arms over her chest. "Where exactly do you expect us to go?"

"Ma!" Faith practically jumped out of her chair. "You can't seriously be considering this. We can't just *leave*."

Lucien focused his attention on Ethriel. "They're not going to stop, and you were hurt last time—"

"Barely," Ethriel interjected.

But Lucien's hand swung toward Corvin. "And he was almost killed. None of you are going to be so lucky when they come back."

"So you expect us to just pack up and leave everything behind because *you* traipsed into the monsters' den and pissed them off?" Faith exclaimed.

"I need to make sure you're both safe," Lucien growled, his fingers flexing against the table.

"Then maybe you just should have stayed gone," Faith spat. "We were fine until you came back."

Ethriel turned to her daughter. "Faith, it's not—"

"Don't do that," Faith said. "Don't defend him!"

Even without focusing on her power, Jae was nearly overwhelmed by the flare of anger from Faith and heartache from Lucien. She wanted nothing more than to defend her friend, but she wasn't a part of Lucien's family. She suspected that giving in to her urge to call Faith a spoiled brat would do more harm than good, so Jae bit her tongue. Corvin had a similar look of discomfort painted across his generally stoic features.

"This is his fault!" Faith continued. "I'm not giving up my home because he fucked up!" She stormed through the door and into the morning sun.

Lucien kept his hands pressed against the table, fingers tensing against the wood. After a long silence, he opened his mouth again. "Ethriel, I . . ."

She held up one long, slender finger and he fell silent. "I'll talk to Faith. We'll take the day to consider it." She resumed the task of cleaning up the plates from breakfast. "But the question remains, where would we go, Luc?"

Lucien blew out a long breath, and his hands relaxed. "We have friends in Whitehollow," he said. "I'd like to send you to meet up with them, until things have quieted down here." He glanced at Corvin. "I have no right to ask anything more of you when you've already done so much. But would you be willing to escort them?"

Corvin sat up a little straighter, looking between Lucien and Ethriel. "I'd be honored, but . . ."

"You're a hell of a soldier," Lucien interrupted. "We already knew that. But you've proven that you're willing to protect them." A muscle ticked in his jaw before he added, "I trust you to keep them safe."

Something shone in Corvin's eyes, something bright and hopeful.

Jae cleared her throat, pulling Lucien's attention. "And what about me?" If he even suggested she stay with Ethriel and Faith, she was going to—

"I want you with me. I'm not done with Micah, and I have a feeling I'm going to need backup." Beneath his dark beard, Lucien grinned. "I can't think of anyone better."

A little swell of pride bloomed in her chest. Jae trusted Lucien with her life, and it was gratifying to know he did the same.

✹

Later that night, Ethriel spoke with Lucien and Jae. She and Faith would leave, she said. They'd allow Corvin to escort them to Whitehollow, where they could join with Verity and the others. Corvin said if they got horses, he could be ready to travel the day after next.

Jae followed Lucien outside so they could plan some of their own next steps. They still needed to update Verity about what Lucien had learned in the Red Forest, and they'd need to keep watch that night and the next day in case the shifters returned.

"I'll take first watch tonight," she told Lucien. "You take second."

"I'll take a watch as well," Corvin said, limping to where Jae and Lucien stood in the grass.

"You need to rest so you can heal," Lucien argued. "The ride to White-hollow isn't going to be an easy one."

"I'm an early riser," Corvin said. "Give me the last watch. I can wake you if anything comes."

Lucien stared out toward the forest for a long while, but finally nodded. "I don't think they'll try anything while I'm still here anyway," he grumbled. He started down the gravel path toward the woods. "I'm going to check the perimeter."

Jae watched him disappear into the trees at the edge of the clearing. She still didn't know what Lucien was planning to do about Micah. He needed access to the Heart of the Red Forest, which Micah controlled. There was no doubt in her mind that they'd soon be heading for another confrontation, but maybe she could convince Lucien to seek out other allies first. That one shifter, Maldren, seemed like she knew Lucien from before, and she'd done her best to keep her word about not letting any harm come to Jae while Lucien was in the Glade.

They'd had a bit of time to talk, Mal keeping up a steady stream of chatter that Jae'd had trouble ignoring. She seemed . . . nice. Sympathetic, even. And her intentions had seemed honest, as far as Jae could tell. Maybe Lucien could start by talking to her . . .

"Jae, I . . ."

She startled as Corvin spoke. She'd forgotten he was there.

"Sorry," he added quietly. It was dark, but Jae could have sworn that was a blush darkening the former captain's olive skin. It must have been from the exertion of being on his feet. He needed to rest.

"It's fine," Jae said, a little more softly than she intended. She cleared her throat. "You should get some sleep."

"I will," he said. But instead of heading toward his cabin, he turned to face her. "But first, I want to apologize."

Jae arched an eyebrow. "Apologize?"

Corvin might have proved that he could be trusted with Ethriel and Faith, but that didn't change what he'd done last autumn. Memories rushed into her. Solace's scream right before his face went slack and he attacked Jae with volleys of elemental magic. Being swept up by a shadow monster, only to be dropped by Corvin's stasis. Crashing into Lucien as she fell, and the nauseating *cracks* as several of his bones broke on impact, along with her arm.

Jae had allowed herself to relax around him—she'd let her guard down because he'd been helpful with Lucien's family—but she couldn't let herself forget that everything that had happened was because of the man standing beside her.

And he had the audacity to apologize for it? As though that could fix anything? Her anger swelled, rising like the tide. "What could you possibly have to apologize for?"

His eyes widened and his hands fidgeted for a moment before he clasped them sharply behind his back. "Well, I—"

"I'm afraid you might've misunderstood me," Jae interrupted, stepping closer. How dare he try to undo what he'd done. "What I meant was, after everything you did, what do you think you could actually atone for with a fucking apology? It's not going to erase you hunting Verity and Dare and Solace across the whole godsdamned continent, or kidnapping Solace and binding him. It's not going to erase you shattering the wall that kept him safe. It's not going to erase the fact that he's dead."

Her eyes were stinging but she clenched her fists. She would not cry in front of Corvin Crosse. "So what," she spat, "could you possibly think you can apologize for?"

Corvin swallowed, his scarred throat bobbing. "I . . . want to apologize for what I did to you," he said slowly. "When I shot that demon out of the sky, I shot you down too. And I . . . I can't close my eyes without seeing you falling, without wishing I could take it back. I'm sorry for hurting you, Jae. And for what it's worth, I promise I won't hurt you again. I'm grateful Lucien was there to catch you. I don't think I've ever known anyone who would do something like that for me."

"Probably because you're willing to murder innocent people in the name of your asshole god," she snapped.

Corvin reeled back like she'd slapped him.

It didn't matter that he'd only ever helped Faith and Ethriel. That couldn't make up for everything that came before.

Could it?

Of course it couldn't. Even if it was easier than she wanted it to be to ignore the past when she looked into his gray eyes, when she caught glimpses of the guilt that racked him.

He wanted it back, she reminded herself. Corvin was trying to get his old life back—to be the Chosen of Ainam again. How guilty could he truly feel if he was willing to go back to that? How much could he have truly changed in only a few short months?

Corvin nodded once, stiffly, as though it would have been a bow if it weren't for his injuries. "I'll see you in the morning." The softness had left his voice, though Jae hadn't even realized it was there until it was gone. He was cold now, detached. A soldier. "Good night, Jae." He turned and limped toward his cabin without waiting for a response.

The next morning, Jae woke at dawn. No shifters had come sniffing around the cottage during the night. As she stretched on her blankets near the hearth and rubbed the sleep from her eyes, movement nearby caught her attention. She rolled over and spotted Corvin packing a few things into a bag. He looked up as she moved.

"Sorry," he whispered, quickly turning away. "Didn't mean to wake you."

Jae pushed down the urge to offer her own apology for her words the night before, but Lucien stirred beside her as Corvin moved toward the kitchen. Lucien's eyes snapped open, and a moment later, he was on his feet, sniffing the air.

"Where's Faith?" he demanded of Corvin, even as he rushed the short distance to her room.

"I don't think she's up yet."Corvin said, setting his bag on the table.

Lucien shoved the door open without warning, and it slammed into the wall.

Jae moved to follow him, but Ethriel's appearance in her own doorway stopped her. Ethriel had a light shawl over her shoulders, and her red curls fell wild and untamed down her back. "What's going on?" she asked, blinking through the haze of sleep.

Lucien emerged from Faith's room a second later, fear and rage rolling from him in equal measure. Jae was already shoving her feet into her boots when Lucien growled, "She's gone."

"Faith?" Ethriel was suddenly much more awake and moving toward her daughter's room. "Faith's *gone*?"

At the same time Corvin said, "What do you mean she's gone?"

Lucien crossed to him and grabbed the front of his shirt, shoving him back into the table. Corvin winced as he bent backward, Lucien leaning into him. "You were on watch," he roared in Corvin's face. "Where is she?"

Corvin gripped the edge of the table, fighting to keep his balance. "Lucien—"

"She was here when your watch started."

"I thought she was in there."

"Where *is* she?!" he bellowed.

"I don't know."

Lucien released his shirt with a shove, flinging Corvin harder against the table.

Ethriel looked in the empty room and turned to Lucien. "Her window's open. Luc, what's going on?"

Rage rippling from him like a pulse, Lucien stepped into his boots and slid his hunting knife into its sheath. "I'm going to find her." And then he was gone, out the door, running toward the woods.

Jae was still tying her belt as she moved to follow.

Corvin pushed off from the table. "What can I do?"

"You've done enough," Jae said, grabbing her swords from where she'd left them by the door. She looped one onto her belt as she sprinted outside. Lucien was already far down the path, heading for the trees. "I'm coming with you!" she shouted.

"Stay here, Jae." His voice rumbled as he picked up his pace.

"You need backup!" she called, strapping her other sword onto her back. "I'm not letting you do this alone. I'm coming."

Lucien shifted before he reached the tree line, the pops and cracks that accompanied the change echoing across the clearing. He turned to face her as she ran after him, his snout dripping spittle in his anger. Although this shape had frightened her at first, Jae had stopped being afraid of his beast form long ago. But the rage in his eyes gave her pause, and she slowed her approach.

She finished securing her weapons. "Lucien, let me help. Corvin can stay with Ethriel."

Lucien growled, baring his teeth.

"I don't like him any more than you do, but he's proven he won't hurt her. Let me help you find Faith. Let me help you bring her back."

Lucien snorted once, then sniffed the air. He angled his head toward the woods, though he dropped to his haunches with another snort and a shake of his massive shoulders.

Jae knew that gesture: *hop on before I leave you here*. With a quick check to make sure her swords were secured, Jae gripped Lucien's charcoal gray fur and pulled herself up onto his back. She barely settled into place before he bounded into the trees.

CHAPTER 54

LIGHT POURED IN THROUGH the window, blinding in its unchecked brightness. Dare groaned and buried his face in the pillow, grateful for the artificial darkness.

"Good morning." Gregor's voice contained none of its usual cheerfulness, and the notes echoed and reverberated through Dare's skull.

He groaned again, pulling the pillow in tighter.

"Or afternoon, I suppose," Gregor continued without concern for the volume at which he was speaking.

Dare's head felt like a hammer was striking his temples with every beat of his heart. Everything hurt. Gods above and below, Dare couldn't recall the last time he'd been this hungover. What had he even . . . ?

Slowly, the memories of the night before trickled in.

Oh . . .

When Dare pushed himself up, the room spun violently. His vision blurred. He steadied himself on the side of the bed, closing his eyes.

Gregor's footsteps sounded through the small room until he was standing beside the bed. Glasses clinked against each other on the bedside table. "It seems you kept yourself busy after I left last night."

He had. When Gregor had gone out, Dare had been left alone with his thoughts which was, frankly, the last thing he'd wanted. He'd snuck downstairs and raided the cabinet that housed a number of very old—and likely very expensive—liquors meant for dignitaries and guests of the embassy. His long-awaited blackout had finally settled in soon after.

A touch to the side of Dare's face sent a sharp pain through his cheek and around his eye, and he breathed sharply through his teeth.

"She really did a number on you," Gregor said.

With everything else throbbing or aching in equal measure, Dare had nearly forgotten about the black eye and bruised cheek he had, courtesy of Finn.

"Fuck . . ."

Gregor huffed. "That's all you've got to say for yourself today?"

Dare still hadn't looked at Gregor. He wasn't sure he could. So he set his head in his hands instead.

"What are you doing?" Gregor asked.

"Dying, it feels like." *Or at least wishing I were dead.*

"Well, you're not." His voice was sharp, leaving no room to argue. "So what are you going to do instead? Besides feeling sorry for yourself?"

Dare lifted his head slowly, trying to ignore the spin of the room. Gregor stared down at him, arms crossed. The curtains on the window behind him were thrown wide, bathing Gregor in a warm, if blinding, radiance. Dare blinked. Even that hurt.

"What do you mean?" Dare asked.

"I mean, what are you going to *do*? Because you certainly aren't going to be moping around my room for the rest of the day."

Dare let his head fall again. "What am I supposed to do? I fucked everything up, Gregor."

"Alright, so you fucked everything up."

Dare's head jerked up at the unfamiliar sound of a curse on Gregor's lips.

"What are you going to do about it?"

What *could* he do about it? About any of it? Everyone hated him, and for damn good reason. But this was why he was always better off on his own. No hurt feelings, no broken hearts.

Sighing, Gregor pushed his glasses up to sit on the top of his head. He pinched the bridge of his nose. "Stop it."

Dare's face heated. "Get out of my head," he muttered before he could bite his tongue.

"I told you, I can't control it," Gregor snapped.

Briefly, in the aching fog of his hangover, Dare wondered if that was true.

Gregor stilled, and his voice was icy as he said, "Trust me, if I could stop hearing your self-pitying thoughts, I would."

Dare kept quiet and focused on stilling his mind. If only the room would stop spinning, he might be able to get a handle on his thoughts.

Gregor set his glasses back on his nose and crossed to the door, pausing with his hand on the latch. "I have a few things I need to take care of. I need you to not be here when I get back." He glanced at Dare over his shoulder. "We've acknowledged that you fucked up, Darcy. Now I expect you to do something about it."

The door opened and slammed shut.

Dare flopped back onto the bed and closed his eyes. Gregor's voice echoed through his head.

I expect you to do something about it.

But what could he do? He was fairly certain Verity didn't even want to look at him right now. Lucien and Jae were still off roaming Southreach. And Gregor had just walked out.

He owed Finn an apology—her probably even more than the others—but he had no interest in getting punched again. He touched his face gingerly, the sting of her right hook still fresh.

But maybe if he started by talking to them . . . Maybe if he tried to explain his intentions, they'd understand. Maybe they could even forgive him.

Someday.

But that would never happen if he just lay here. So Dare pushed himself up with a groan and washed his face, careful around his eye.

In another time, another life, Dare would have cut and run. But he wanted to fix this, he realized. Dear gods, he *wanted* to fix this. He didn't want to lose them—any of them.

If he could patch things over with Finn, that might soften Verity into giving him a chance. So Dare ducked out of Gregor's room and headed into the city in search of one small blond woman who was almost as good at not being found as Dare was.

Dare searched for the rest of the afternoon and into the evening before he finally admitted that Finn was better at not being found than he was. He'd started with her room at the embassy, in its incredibly convenient spot across the hall from Gregor's, but she hadn't been there—why should it have been that easy for him?

Dare wasn't as familiar with Whitehollow as he was with Valda, so he didn't know where Finn might spend her time. There was no precariously balanced lighthouse for her to climb here. There were a few spots that overlooked the port and the bay, and there were some quiet green spaces where he thought he might find her.

But he was wrong.

Dare cast an upward glance at the sky. *You couldn't have helped me out with that one?* he asked of Tykaras.

Met with no answer, Dare heaved a sigh and headed toward the last place in the city he could think to look for Finn.

Dare stood in front of the doors that led to Verity's office. He almost hadn't made it onto the base, as the Warden manning the gate wasn't someone Dare had met before. The derisive look he'd received as he approached had set his teeth on edge, and he'd had to flash his brand to be taken seriously.

He shook off the lingering frustration and pushed the door open silently, not bothering to knock. It was getting late, but Verity was still there, as he'd expected. Several lamps and braces of candles were lit around the room, illuminating the space brightly enough to read by. The High Commander of the Wardens was hunched over one of the tables rather than the desk, quill in hand, scribbling furiously as the candlelight glimmered off the steel plates of her arms.

Dare leaned against the door frame, trying for all the world to muster his usual calm, aloof exterior. It was more difficult to summon than he was comfortable with.

"Evening, Commander."

Her eyes flicked up for an instant before darting back to the paper she was working on. "I'm busy." When he didn't leave immediately, she set the quill down with a huff and fixed a glare on him. "What do you want, Dare?"

"Were Finn and Jonah able to keep tabs on Tanithe?" he asked, his nerve starting to falter.

Verity picked up the quill again and went back to writing. "Of course not. She's in the wind again. Not that it matters. We've got nothing on her now anyway." Her hand paused as she reached for the ink. "Now why are you really here?"

"You're getting much better at reading people," Dare said, toeing the floor with his boot.

She scribbled something else across the page. "Stop wasting my time, Dare. I've got too much paperwork to deal with tonight, thanks to you."

"I just want to talk," he said, staying in the doorway. "And I was looking for Finn." He swept his gaze over the room, as though he might find the young woman perched on a chair in the corner.

Verity didn't look up.

"Do you know where she is?" he asked.

"I do."

Silence stretched between them. "Could you tell me?"

"No. She doesn't want to talk to you. And frankly, neither do I."

Dare pushed away from the door frame and crossed to her. "My lady Warden—"

Verity slammed the quill on the desk, flecks of black ink scattering across the parchments. "Don't do that," she snapped. "I'm your commander, for the time being. You will address me as such."

His stomach knotted. "For the time being?"

"You tried to break an oath that you swore on your honor as Warden." She rounded the table toward him, and he resisted the urge to retreat from her.

"But I didn't."

"You *couldn't*," she corrected, her voice strained. "I can't even be around you right now after the shit you pulled."

Dare swallowed around the tightness in his throat. "Are you sending me away to another base?" That was within her power now, if she wished.

Verity glared at him, all fire and fury, but when she spoke again, her tone was icy. "You used your status as a Warden to swear an oath that you had no intention of keeping. Our honor as Wardens is all we have. We don't get titles or legacies to hold on to. We only have our honor and our word. That's it. And you wanted to trade it away for coin."

Dare ran his fingers through his hair, letting his hands come to rest on the back of his neck as he worked up the courage to ask the other question. The one he hadn't realized had been plaguing him since yesterday. The one he hadn't known would matter so much to him until now.

"Are you expelling me from the Wardens?"

She stood in silence for a long moment, her head angled toward one of the nearby candles.

Toward the flame that danced there. Heat began to radiate from her as though she were a hearth.

It was the longest moment of Dare's life.

"No," she said at last.

He let out the breath he'd been holding. Dare was acutely aware that it had not only been *her* decision. He didn't know which side Verity had landed on herself, but Dare made a note to himself to offer up a prayer of thanks to Pyrannis later.

"But," Verity went on, "I cannot guarantee the outcome if that question needs to be asked again. *This* is your second chance, Dare. You will not get another one. Am I clear?"

He nodded.

"Good." She returned to the table and retrieved the quill from beside the ink-splattered paper. "Do me a favor and steer clear of the Drahkonian embassy."

"The embassy?"

"I had to pull some strings with Caelan to keep the Drahkonians from locking you up for collusion against the crown. I hope you appreciate the work I put in for you."

"I do." He swallowed hard. "Thank you."

"You're dismissed."

He didn't move. "My la—" He caught himself and started again. "Verity. I'm sorry. It was . . ." *More gold than I'd ever seen in my life.* The brand on his chest burned a warning as he began to stray too close to the truth of what happened. "I'm giving it away," he said. "The money. I never planned to keep it. I know that's hardly worth anything to you right now, but I wanted you to know. And about Tykaras . . ." He drew a deep breath, but Verity held up her hand.

"I never asked and you never said. As far as I'm concerned, it's your decision how much you want to share." She looked up at him again, and the fury on her face flickered out, replaced by a sadness that tore at Dare's heart. "Although I'd hoped you would have trusted me enough by now."

"I do!" he blurted out. "I do trust you."

She ignored him. "But when it comes to keeping that secret, I don't think I'm the one you need to apologize to."

"I know . . . Will you tell Finn that I was looking for her? Please."

Verity studied him for a moment before nodding. "Alright. Now would you please go? And close the door on your way out." Her attention returned to her paperwork, and she didn't look up again. Not as Dare bowed to her with a quiet farewell, nor when he turned back, lingering in the doorway before finally leaving, the heavy latch sliding home with a finality that raised the hairs on the back of his neck.

He would fix this. Somehow, he would make this right.

CHAPTER 55

Corvin sat on the front stoop of the cottage, his bandaged leg outstretched. Ethriel had been pacing Faith's room for the better part of an hour, and after Corvin's fourth apology, she had politely but firmly asked him to give her some time alone.

The sun was climbing higher, Lucien and Jae were out there looking for Faith, and Corvin was unable to do anything but wait. It was his fault. It had been his watch when Faith snuck out of the cottage and ventured into the woods alone. He hadn't heard her leave. What kind of a soldier was he, that she could sneak past him without any trouble? And with his injuries, he couldn't even help search for her.

What good was he?

Corvin bowed his head, clasping his hands. *Lord Ainam,* he prayed. *I beseech you. I am your servant.* He'd prayed every night since his power had been stripped from him, until the night Ainam had finally answered. The night Jae had found him out by the western wall.

Corvin hadn't prayed to Ainam since that night. Until now.

Lord Ainam, take me into your Light again. Allow me to be your faithful servant. Grant me your Grace and with it the power to help my friends and defeat your enemies.

The familiar but long absent intensity, like an unwavering focus, surrounded Corvin, rushing into him.

My Lord? He closed his eyes, praying harder.

You plead for my attention, the voice of Ainam boomed in his mind. *You have it. Speak.*

My Lord Ainam. Corvin's voice trembled, even in his thoughts. *Your enemies still abound.*

And you wish to defeat them in my name?

Corvin swallowed. *Yes. I wish only to serve you.*

The voice of Ainam was sharp, stabbing into all the corners of his mind. *You wish to serve yourself.* The god's presence pressed forward, stifling, smothering in its complete, all-encompassing rigidity.

Corvin braced himself against the intrusion, bowing his head. "My life is nothing," he strained to whisper, "if not in your service."

I already told you what you needed to do to prove yourself to me. I do not like having to repeat myself.

But, My Lord—

If you want to serve me, then you will do as I have commanded, Ainam said. *You will kill the shifter and the human who follows him.*

The same command he'd been given that night by the wall. And now, his answer was the same. "No."

Ainam paused—actually *hesitated*—for the briefest moment. *What did you say?*

I won't kill Lucien, Corvin said in his mind. *He's a good man—*

He is no man, Ainam roared. *He is my enemy. He and the girl both. They stopped you from obtaining the weapon.*

Jae and Lucien were good people. They had only wanted to do what was right. And Ethriel . . . she had only just gotten her husband back—and Faith, her father. He couldn't do that to them. He wouldn't.

If the farm woman and her daughter vex you, Ainam continued, sensing his thoughts, *destroy them as well.*

Corvin tried to pull back, to move away from the overwhelming presence, but his body was locked down. His muscles wouldn't respond. *But they're innocent!*

They are not. Ainam's presence seemed to almost lean into Corvin, taking up even more of the space within him. *They worship the old gods. They are of no use to me, and they serve only to distract you from your purpose. Kill them.*

They don't deserve to die. Corvin set his jaw, grinding his teeth. How many people had he killed in Ainam's name? How many had he believed deserved that fate?

And how many had truly been just as innocent as Ethriel and Faith?

But it had always been to make the world better. Safer. It had always been in the name of justice, of light . . . of *good*.

. . . Hadn't it?

He'd thought so. He'd been certain of it . . .

Jae's words from the night before echoed in his mind. *You're willing to murder innocent people in the name of your asshole god . . .*

If Ainam were truly the god of good, He wouldn't demand that Corvin murder innocents. *I won't kill them,* Corvin said. Determination flowed through him.

Ainam's voice was heavy in his mind. *You were the most powerful mortal I have ever Chosen. You were my favored warrior. Your devotion was unmatched.*

It still is, My Lord, Corvin said through the crushing weight of Ainam's glory. *But I won't kill innocent people. Good people. I won't do it.*

If you cannot demonstrate your loyalty, then you will never be worthy of my power or my attention again. You will be to me as an ant on a blade of grass.

Ainam's hold on Corvin's mind and body relaxed, leaving in its wake only a devastating emptiness. An overwhelming sense of loss—one final parting blow from Ainam.

That sudden, gaping emptiness sucked the breath out of his chest with the weight of it, leaving him doubled over on the steps of the cottage, gasping for air.

"Corvin?"

Ethriel sounded so far away. He tried to respond, but he couldn't get a breath in around the crushing loss in his chest. Someone was shaking him, and a sudden pain shot through his shoulder, forcing a sharp inhale.

Corvin's eyes snapped open. Ethriel knelt in front of him. She gripped him tightly, taking no care at all with his injured shoulder.

She set her hand against his forehead. "Corvin—gods, what's wrong?"

"I . . . I'm alright," he choked out. He focused on taking one breath at a time.

"Can you stand? We should get you inside so you can lie down. I should check your wounds again in case there's an infection. You don't have a fever, but—"

"Water," Corvin managed hoarsely. "Can you get me some water, please?"

"Of course!" She gathered her skirts and stepped around him into the cottage.

Corvin tilted his face toward the sky. He'd believed that Ainam was a god of justice, of honor. But there was nothing honorable in murdering innocent people. There was no justice in killing people solely because they worshiped the old gods, or because they had once stood on opposite sides of the battlefield. Not when Corvin's side, he was learning, had very likely been the wrong one.

Ethriel returned a moment later with a fired clay mug filled with cool water and offered it to him.

Corvin took the mug and drank, coughing once as he swallowed too quickly. "Thank you."

Ethriel crouched in front of him again. "We really should get you inside."

Corvin set the mug down and bowed his head, letting it rest in his hands. "I just need a moment, Ethriel." He was pleased to find his voice was steady. "I'm fine. Truly." He was far from fine, but the last thing he wanted was for Ethriel to spend any of her time worrying over him.

Although Corvin's world had crashed down around him a few months ago, he had been holding on to the hope that he could redeem himself and earn his way back into Ainam's good graces. But this . . .

The things Ainam was asking him to do . . . No god of justice would demand such a demonstration of devotion. Corvin wiped his face with a trembling hand, and his fingers came away wet.

"What was that about?" Ethriel asked gently. She sat beside him on the step.

He swallowed and forced down another lungful of air. "It was . . . a crisis of faith, I suppose," he said, his voice hollow.

"Do you want to talk about it?"

He shook his head. He wasn't sure he could articulate it even if he wanted to.

Ethriel watched him for another moment before turning her gaze south along the path that led into the forest. "I won't pretend to understand anything about it," she said. "I can't imagine what it must be like to hear the voice of a god in your head, let alone any of the rest of it. Or what it must have been like to lose that connection." She inhaled deeply. "I've always taken comfort in the idea of the old gods. The elements are all around us all the time, so it just made sense to me. I know you've always been a devout of Ainam, and I'm not at all, but . . . But you're a good man, Corvin. You don't need Ainam, or anyone else, to deem you worthy of that. You do it all on your own."

It was a nice sentiment, but it wasn't so simple. Not for him. "Ethriel," he said, his voice hushed. "The things I've done . . . I thought . . . I thought He was the god of good. Of . . . hope."

"And now?"

The question hung between them like smoke from a bonfire, stinging his eyes and tightening his chest.

Corvin swallowed hard, rubbing his neck and the rough scar etched into it. "I don't know. But I think I still need him to be."

"Why?" she asked, all gentle curiosity.

"Because . . . Because of what I've done. Everything I did, I did for Him. If He's not *just* . . . If He's not *good* . . ." He couldn't look at Ethriel as the last question passed his lips. "What does that make me?"

Ethriel seemed to truly consider his words. "It sounds like you were misled," she said after a long silence. "It sounds like perhaps Ainam used your faith to serve his own purposes. Being tricked by promises and lies doesn't make you evil, Corvin."

"But a person doing monstrous things, even for the right reasons, is still a monster. And I knew." He clenched his hands and sighed. "I knew the things I did were horrible. But I thought . . . sometimes horrible things have to happen for the greater good. I thought that if I was Ainam's hand in the world, then I could do the horrible things that needed to be done. I could do them so others wouldn't have to. That I would help make a better world, even if in the end I was too tainted by my actions to live there." He'd never given voice to those thoughts before, those fears. His shoulders sagged.

"You thought you were doing what was right," Ethriel said, her voice steady. "That doesn't make you a monster. At worst, it makes you a fool, but an honest one. The true measure is what you do once you learn the truth."

He bowed his head again. "Thank you" was all he could think to say.

"I should be thanking you. I don't think I said it the other night, but you saved my life when those shifters attacked us. They'd have killed Faith and me both just to get to Luc. You almost died protecting us."

Corvin stared at the gravel path just beyond his outstretched leg, the bandage tight around his calf where a hint of crimson was seeping through. "I owe you so much. But more than that, it was the right thing to do."

"You're a good man, Corvin," Ethriel said again. She picked up the empty mug at Corvin's side and moved to stand, but she paused, her gaze snagging on the trees at the southern end of the path again.

"She'll be alright," Corvin said, guessing at her worry.

Ethriel's brow furrowed as her thumb ran along the smooth handle of the mug. "Why do you think she left?" she asked. "You don't . . . That shifter you wounded . . . You don't think Faith went after her, do you?"

Corvin inhaled a sharp breath through his nose. Ethriel missed nothing. Knowing what he knew about Faith, it wasn't a far stretch, though it was reckless, even for her. He wanted to offer Ethriel comfort. He wanted to tell her that surely that wasn't where Faith went, she was just angry and left to clear her head. But he couldn't bear the thought of lying to her. And in any case, he didn't think she'd believe him.

"I worry she did," he said honestly. "But Lucien will be able to track her. He'll find her. And he and Jae will bring her home."

Ethriel fiddled with the mug, never taking her eyes from the path. "Do you really believe that?" she asked.

"I do."

Ethriel nodded slowly and finally stood. "Come inside," she said. She extended a hand down to Corvin. "I still want to check your bandages."

Corvin took Ethriel's hand with his good arm and let her leverage him to his feet. "Yes, ma'am."

CHAPTER 56

LUCIEN FOLLOWED FAITH'S SCENT east. She was alone, at least when she left the cottage. Good. That was good. Maybe she was just hunting before the journey.

He picked up his speed, the extra weight of Jae on his back hardly anything at all in this form. The beast clawed and raged to be let out fully, but Lucien held it back. He needed to focus if he wanted to find his daughter and bring her home.

The fairy tale he'd been trying to spin himself dissolved as he picked up two shifter scents suddenly appearing alongside Faith's.

Fuck! His rage came out as a guttural growl. Thankfully, there was no blood on the ground or on the wind, but—

On his back, Jae tightened her grip and leaned down against him. "We'll find her," she said into his ear. "And if they've hurt her, we'll kill every last one of them."

Lucien bared his teeth in a feral sneer. Yes, they would.

Lucien only slowed his pace when the scents grew stronger. He picked his way through the trees, moving quietly through the underbrush despite his massive size. His wide paws cushioned his weight, silencing his approach.

The trees opened ahead to a small clearing. Four scents—no, five—plus Faith's mingled in the air. Lucien moved around the outer edge of the clearing hoping to stay downwind.

"We can smell you!" a deep voice called from the clearing. "You and the human both. Come out."

Dammit. Lucien's sigh rumbled through him, but Jae scratched at the fur behind his ear. "It's alright," she whispered. She slid down from his back, landing in the underbrush with a quiet crunch of leaves. She checked the draw on her swords and nodded to him. "Let's go."

Lucien and Jae stepped into the open side by side. Morning sunlight broke through the trees in a few places, illuminating the clearing.

Two shifters stood in their beast forms, one gray and one dark brown. They stood on either side of the three others who were in their human shape. One was a woman who was clutching her right arm to her chest, her hand missing. Lucien guessed she was the one Corvin had wounded back at the farmstead. The other two were men, and Lucien's rage flared even more as he recognized the one in the middle.

"Welcome, Lucien," Micah called.

Faith stood between him and the other male, who had a tight grip on her bicep. Her hands were bound together in front of her with a length of rope. There was a bruise on her cheek, and the fear radiating from her reached Lucien even at the edge of the clearing.

When Faith saw him, her eyes widened. Lucien's heart stalled. Faith had never seen him in his bestial form before this moment. Vire's hells, she would be just as terrified of him as she was of the others.

Lucien braced himself, but as recognition dawned on her face, she took a step forward, as though she wanted to run to him. "Lucien!" The male held her firmly in place.

Mother Taerna, he wanted to run to her too. But for her sake, he needed to keep his movements slow and even. He dug his claws into the earth with each step.

"Human form, if you please," Micah said. He held one of his jagged-toothed daggers casually in his hand, but he didn't need that blade to kill Faith before Lucien could close the distance to them.

At Lucien's brief hesitation, Micah waved the dagger in Faith's direction. "Now."

Lucien shifted, standing upright as the fur and muscles withered from him. He kept his hands neutral at his sides, although he had to flex them several times to get them to relax.

"Your issue is with me," Lucien called across to the group. "She has nothing to do with this."

Micah smiled, the corners of his lips twisting. "See, I disagree." He tapped the tip of the dagger against Faith's collarbone, a drop of blood appearing where it scraped her skin.

She whimpered and closed her eyes. "Please . . ."

Lucien's heart lurched.

"*She* came looking for *us*," Micah said, tapping his blade against his open palm. "And she's *your* kin, right? I think that makes her as much a part of this as you."

"I wasn't!" Faith blurted out. "I swear!"

The male with a grip on her arm yanked her back, silencing her.

Lucien flexed his hands again. Beside him, Jae balanced on the balls of her feet, ready to move if he gave her the signal.

"I'm thinking," Micah continued, "that you lot need to be taught a lesson."

Lucien took a step toward him, but Micah's dagger pressed to Faith's throat, and the two shifters in their beast forms growled, raising their hackles. Lucien froze.

"Let her go, Micah," Lucien said, his voice low and even. "You and I can come to some kind of agreement." His eyes darted among the shifters threatening his daughter. He'd rip all their throats out if given half a chance. "This doesn't have to get messy."

Micah laughed, his fangs elongating as he threw his head back. "Now that's where you're wrong," he said. "It's about to get very messy."

One of the massive beasts bounded forward, turning its body to serve as a barrier between Lucien and Jae and the rest of the group. With Lucien's path blocked, Micah circled around behind Faith.

"You know what makes a shifter, don't you?" he asked.

Lucien bit the inside of his cheek to keep from charging him. Within, the beast tore at its chains, wanting nothing more than to charge and sink its fangs into the flesh of every shifter there and watch the life bleed from their fallen bodies. Lucien had never agreed with his inner monster more than he did in that moment. But Faith was still in danger. He needed to wait, even though it killed him. He needed patience.

Micah set a hand on Faith's trembling shoulders. "You know, don't you, sweetheart?"

Faith's eyes met Lucien's as she nodded. "A bite." Her voice was almost too quiet to be heard.

"Ah, but not just a bite," Micah said. "You need the bite to mix with that shifter's blood. That's the only way to do it."

With feral swiftness, Micah leaned forward and bit down on Faith's shoulder.

She screamed, blood welling from the wound and coloring the front of her shirt.

Lucien barely felt the shift as he changed, the beast breaking through the chains. He lunged, but was blocked by the shifter in front of him, who turned and swiped a massive paw to push him back.

But it wasn't the shifter's strike that made his blood run cold. Micah held the edge of his dagger against his own forearm.

"Ah, ah," Micah chided. "None of that, or I'll turn her right here."

Faith shook, the other shifter holding her arms in a bruising grip, keeping her upright in front of Micah. Her eyes locked on Lucien's, pleading. "Da!"

Lucien snarled but didn't move an inch.

Micah tsked him, moving his arm a little closer to Faith. "Shift back."

Faith closed her eyes again. "Da," she whispered, but his keen ears heard it even over the pounding of his own heart and the rush of blood in his ears. "Da, please help me. Please. I'm sorry."

Lucien rolled his shoulders, forcing the beast back. It bucked and howled in protest, but he wouldn't let its rage hurt his daughter. Lucien roared as he forced himself to shift back into his human form. His clothes stuck to him with sweat, and his knees shook with the effort of controlling the change.

Micah grinned at Lucien as he fought to keep control. "Here's how this is going to work." He still held the knife to his own forearm over Faith's bleeding wound. "You're going to come with us. And so long as you don't give us any trouble, we'll let your little humans run along home."

Jae's shoulders tensed. Her hand tightened around the hilt of the sword on her hip. "What are you going to do with him?" she demanded.

Micah angled his head toward her, shock flashing across his features. "Was I talking to you?"

"Did I give the impression that I give a fuck?" Jae shot back. "What are you going to do with him?"

Micah laughed. "He'll be dealt with as per the den's laws."

Lucien didn't know what that meant, but he was certain it wasn't good. He expected death was high on the list of likely possibilities. Publicly, if he had to guess. They'd want to make an example of him. Otherwise, they'd just do it here. Lucien wasn't sure he'd be able to take them all.

Judging by the upward tick of Jae's fear, she must have assumed the same.

Lucien raised his hands, open, palms out. "Alright," he said. "Just let her go." He swallowed. "Let them both go."

Jae slid her sword about an inch out of its scabbard. Under her breath she said, "Lucien, you can't . . ."

"I can," he said quietly, never taking his eyes from Micah. From the blade threatening to turn Faith into a monster. This was not a fate he would wish on anyone, least of all anyone he cared about. He'd sooner die than see his daughter suffer through this tortured existence.

Micah watched him with interest, a grin creeping across his lips. "Kneel, if you don't mind."

Lucien dropped to his knees in the grass.

Micah gave an upward nod to the shifter beside him, who yanked Faith by the arm, pulling her forward until she was standing only a few feet away.

She was breathing hard, panicked. "Da, I'm—"

"It's alright," he said quickly, his heart squeezing in his chest. "Jae will take you back home."

She tried to run the last few steps to him, but the shifter held her arm fast, tugging her back to his side.

"It's alright," Lucien said again, as much to himself as to her. "Everything's alright." He chanced a quick look at Jae, who was ready to murder every person in that clearing, likely including him for going along with it. "Jae, see that she makes it home. Please."

Jae's jaw clenched as she sized up the shifters, weighing her odds.

"Jae," he said more forcefully. She turned to look at him. "Please. Make sure my family is safe." He left the rest of the plea unspoken. *Go with them to Whitehollow. Don't you dare try to follow me.*

Her shoulders sagged as the hardness in her eyes softened. "I will. I promise."

They'd be safe. Jae and Corvin would be with them. Then they'd join Verity and Dare . . . Lucien could think of no safer place for Faith and Ethriel to be. Whatever else happened to him, at least they would be safe.

Micah slid the dagger back into his belt. "Outstanding," he said. "You were right, Lucien. We were able to come to an agreement." With another nod from him, the shifter holding Faith untied the rope binding her wrists and then flung her at Jae, who caught her, keeping her from falling.

Jae put a comforting arm around Faith's waist. "Come on, let's get you home," she said, her voice low and soothing. "And we'll get your shoulder cleaned up too. That doesn't hardly look like anything."

Lucien suspected that last part was for his benefit as much as Faith's.

Jae looked at Lucien as she turned to lead Faith toward the edge of the trees, away from the shifters.

He hadn't realized how much he would want to say to Jae until this moment. He'd always thought they'd have more time, though that was a foolish thought. It had always been likely that one or both of them would die a bloody death with little warning. It was the life they led. But they'd led it together for the last ten years.

Right now—this moment—was likely the last time he'd see her. His eyes burned, his vision going blurry. For all that Jae was a pain in his ass, she was like a little sister . . .

Or perhaps more like a daughter.

There had been a hole in his life when he'd left his world behind, and Jae had filled part of what was missing. She couldn't replace Faith—no one could—but she had become like a daughter to him all the same, somehow without him even realizing it until now.

There were too many things he wanted to say, but he was out of time. He always thought he'd have more. They were almost to the trees, though both women kept turning back to look at him.

Gods above, he thought he'd have more time.

Lucien opened his mouth as they reached the edge of the clearing. His throat tightened around the words. Jae and Faith didn't look back again.

And then they were gone.

Micah crossed the clearing to where Lucien remained on his knees. "If you cause me even the slightest bit of trouble," he said as he grabbed a fist full of Lucien's hair and yanked his head back, forcing his gaze to where Micah now towered over him. "Any trouble at all, and I will track them down and personally eat their hearts. Do you understand?"

A guttural growl tore from Lucien's chest.

Micah tightened his grip, giving Lucien's head a violent shake. "Do. You. Understand."

Lucien gritted his teeth. "Yes."

"Good." Micah released his hair, wiping his hand on the front of his pants. "Now, just one more thing." He reached into the pouch on his belt and removed a small vial. The liquid inside was an unnatural shade of pink. He unstoppered the vial and held it out to Lucien. "Drink this."

Lucien eyed the liquid. He didn't have much choice, but not knowing what it was irked him.

Micah rolled his eyes and sighed, long and loud. "Do I need to send someone after them already?" He pushed the vial into Lucien's face. "Drink it."

Lucien tipped the contents into his mouth. It was sharp and bitter, and it had a thick, oily consistency that burned on the way down. He fought to hold back a cough but couldn't manage it, which only made the liquid burn more.

Micah's grin spread wide across his face as Lucien's stomach cramped horribly, doubling him over. He dug his hands into the dirt, claws extending as the beast thrashed. But then the beast withdrew, falling silent. Lucien's claws retracted. His arms buckled and he fell into the grass, the world spinning.

Micah appeared over him, still grinning, as Lucien's vision faded into darkness. "Nighty night."

CHAPTER 57

JAE PULLED FAITH—PULLED *HERSELF*—AWAY from the clearing. She wanted nothing more than to go back and cut all of those godsdamned shifters' heads from their bodies. But Faith . . .

But *Lucien* . . .

While Lucien had been tracking Faith's scent, Jae had focused on strengthening the levee around her mind, fortifying it against emotional intrusions. She'd had to. Lucien's anger and fear had been nearly overwhelming in the small cottage. She couldn't even imagine what he would be feeling if something happened to Faith. So she'd worked on her levee, the way Lanara had shown her, building it higher and higher until finally Lucien's feelings had faded from her perception.

And it'd held true, guarding her from Lucien's rage and Faith's panic throughout the dangerous confrontation, but now, as she led Faith away from the clearing, Lucien's emotions crashed up and over her wall.

Yet it wasn't rage that tightened her chest to the point where she could hardly breathe. It wasn't even fear. Her heart was breaking—*Lucien's* heart was breaking. It was love that rolled from him in great waves.

A father's love for his daughter.

Jae had to focus. She had a job to do. She couldn't let Lucien down any more than she already had. So she pushed that heartache down and away until only her own frustration, anger, and sorrow simmered beneath the surface.

Faith stumbled a little as they moved. The shock must have started to wear off about half a mile from the clearing, because she finally spoke. "We . . . we can't leave him."

"We have to," Jae said through clenched teeth. "There were too many of them."

"But Lucien—"

"I promised him I'd get you back home. I'm sure your mother's worried."

"I'm not a child," Faith grumbled.

"You're not?" Jae rounded on Faith with a suddenness that made the other woman take a step back. "You sure as shit have been acting like one! What the *fuck* did you think you were doing?"

Faith planted her feet, squaring her shoulders with Jae in a move that was entirely Lucien. "I didn't go after them!"

"You left without telling anyone where you were going," Jae shot back.

"Because I'm *not a child!* You all were about to drag me away from my life, remember? I was going to say goodbye to my friends."

Jae scoffed. So Faith was only immature and selfish instead of a complete idiot. "Alone? When you *knew* the shifters were still out there." Faith remained silent, so she pressed on. "You saw what they did to Corvin. *Corvin.* A highly skilled and expertly trained soldier and swordsman." She pointed back in the direction of the clearing. "Do you realize how dangerous they are?"

"I didn't think—"

"Obviously," Jae snapped, her anger surging. "You didn't think." She turned and started walking again. "And now they have him."

Faith's footsteps crunched in the underbrush. "What are they going to do to him?" she asked in a small voice.

Jae didn't answer. She couldn't. She couldn't think about the hell the shifters were about to put Lucien through. Jae shoved her own emotions down deep. She could deal with them later, once she fulfilled her promise to Lucien.

"Jae." Faith's voice grew firmer. "What are they going to do?"

A jumble of emotions lapped at Jae's mental levee. She ignored them, though she turned back. Faith was so much like Lucien, even though she'd really only met him a few days ago.

It was amazing how that worked.

Jae studied her for a moment. She was barely twenty and just had her whole world turned upside down. She hadn't meant for any of this to happen. Jae knew that. Thinking back to some of the decisions *she'd* made at twenty years old, Jae could guess at how Faith was feeling right now.

She eyed the blood drying on Faith's shoulder. "Come on," Jae said, the fight sinking away from her. It left behind a quiet, tense exhaustion. "We should get that cleaned up."

"Are they going to kill him?"

Jae swallowed against the tightness building in her throat. "They're probably going to try. But if there's one thing I know about Lucien, it's that he's not going to make it easy for them."

Faith looked back the way they'd come. "Isn't there anything we can do to help him?"

"We can patch your shoulder so you don't keep bleeding all the way back home," Jae said. "And then I can get you and your mother safely to our friends in Whitehollow."

And then? Could she really leave Lucien and not even consider going back for him? Whitehollow was a long way from the Red Forest, but more importantly, she promised him. By the time she delivered Ethriel and Faith to Verity and made it all the way back south . . . whatever was going to happen—whatever the shifters were going to do—would almost certainly be done by then.

Jae removed the cloth that held back the coiled curls of her hair. She didn't have any gear on her besides her swords and was regretting not grabbing a skin of water on her way out the door. She tied the cloth tight around Faith's shoulder. It was the best she could do under the circumstances. Ethriel would be able to clean it properly when they got back.

It was a few more hours before the clearing with Ethriel's farmstead came into view through the trees. The sun angled across the fields to the west, nearly touching the forest canopy.

"Would you . . . tell me about him?" Faith asked, pausing before they cleared the trees. "About Lucien? I've only ever heard things from my mother and she . . . I think she just really missed him. And that was all from before, through her happy memories of him. I want to know what he's like now."

Jae considered for a moment. Should she tell Faith about the hard days? How hard Lucien fought to keep the beast within him in check? Or should she focus on the good days?

"Lucien is very brave," Jae said, deciding for something in between. "I've seen him charge into a fight outnumbered because someone needed help. He struggles sometimes. But he's never given up, no matter how hopeless it seems. And he's a stubborn, curmudgeonly old bastard, but he's had my back through everything. I trust him with my life."

Faith nodded, her gaze turning slowly toward the clearing. Toward where her mother was waiting.

"Lucien is the toughest son of a bitch I know," Jae said. "If anyone can deal with whatever those bastards have planned and come out the other side, it's him."

As Jae and Faith stepped out of the forest and onto the path, a figure was sitting on the cottage steps. The late afternoon sun shone on Ethriel's fire-red curls as she stood and called something over her shoulder. Corvin's tall frame appeared in the doorway a moment later, but Ethriel was already hurrying down the path toward her daughter.

She took Faith into her arms and pressed her cheek to her daughter's dark hair. "Faith, gods, are you hurt?" Ethriel's crystal blue eyes landed on the cloth wrapped around her shoulder, the blood staining the front of her shirt.

"I'm alright," Faith said. "But . . ."

Corvin limped down the path to join them.

Ethriel held Faith close, though her gaze was fixed on the trees at the end of the path. Looking for him.

It was all too easy to imagine Ethriel, twenty years younger, holding an infant Faith and staring at the line of trees. Waiting for him.

Jae pushed her sorrow down deeper as Corvin finally reached them. "Ethriel, there were shifters," she said. "Five of them. They threatened to hurt Faith if Lucien didn't agree to go with them."

Ethriel closed her eyes as she hugged her daughter.

"Go with them?" Corvin asked. "Where? Why?"

"Back to the Red Forest," Jae said. Then she lied and said, "I don't know why." She swallowed hard, stepping closer to Ethriel and Faith. "There wasn't anything either of us could do without risking Faith's life. I'm sorry."

"He's not coming back," Ethriel said softly.

"He asked me to help Corvin get the two of you to Whitehollow," Jae went on, pushing through the tightness in her throat. "And I promised him I would."

Ethriel tilted her face to the sky. She whispered something under her breath that sounded like "As long as he has breath in his lungs . . ." but Jae wasn't sure what that meant.

Her chest and throat were painfully tight. "I'm sorry I couldn't do more."

"You helped save my daughter," Ethriel said, her voice strained but even. "That's more than I could ask for. And I know we'll be that much safer traveling with you."

"Ma," Faith said, face still pressed against Ethriel's shoulder. "It's my fault. I'm sorry."

Ethriel leaned her head against Faith's hair and rubbed soothing strokes along her back. Her voice quavered as she said, "It'll be alright."

Corvin stood nearby, discomfort painted across his face as though he was afraid of intruding.

Ethriel turned toward the cottage, guiding Faith along with her. Corvin hung back, his gait a little slower from his wounded leg. Jae kept pace with him as her mind wandered. With this first small goal done and the next not due to start until they left for Whitehollow, it was harder not to let her emotions bubble back to the surface.

"What really happened?" Corvin asked, his voice low.

Jae's shoulders tensed.

"I don't think you were being untruthful," he continued quietly, "but I can't help but feel there were some details you omitted."

"They weren't just going to hurt Faith," Jae admitted. "They were going to *turn* her if Lucien didn't agree to go with them. They're taking him back to the Red Forest so they can make an example out of him." Her hand rested on the hilt of her sword, and she opened and closed her fingers around it uselessly. "They're going to kill him, and I can't do anything to stop it."

Ahead, Ethriel and Faith made it to the cottage and stepped inside. Corvin paused, taking a moment to rub his injured leg. Then he nodded toward the crumbling stone wall halfway across the fields. "Walk with me."

Jae looked toward the quiet cottage. She wasn't sure she could face Lucien's wife right now. Jae had dragged him back into her life and now failed to keep him there. With a quiet sigh and a kick at a stone on the path, she followed Corvin.

They walked in silence until they reached the old wall. He sat on the edge, much as he had the first day she'd followed him, though this time she sat too.

"Are you alright?" he asked.

"There wasn't a fight—"

"That's not what I mean, Jae."

"I know!" It came out sharper than she meant it to, as all the emotions she'd submerged were threatening to explode back to the surface. She tried to tighten her grip on them, but they poured up and out—everything she couldn't say to Faith, everything she couldn't let herself feel on the long walk back to the farmstead. "I'm not alright! I couldn't *do* anything, Corvin. They made him kneel in the dirt, and I had to walk away. I had to leave him there, and I fucking hate it. It's like I'm giving up."

The same ache in her chest from when she'd had to walk away from that clearing was back, but this time she wasn't sensing anyone else's emotions. It was her own heart that was cracked in two.

"They're going to kill him," she choked out. "And there is exactly *nothing* I can do about it. And I didn't—" Her throat constricted around the words.

I didn't say goodbye.

Jae turned her face away as the tears streamed down her cheeks, no matter how hard she tried to hold them in. She didn't want Crosse to see her cry.

Corvin inhaled deeply before he said, "My first year as a lieutenant I led my men into an ambush. It wasn't directly my fault—our scouts had missed it somehow—but the end result was the same. Three soldiers were killed outright and another ten were captured. I wanted nothing more than to charge in there and pull them out, get them back home to their families. I had twenty-seven soldiers still with me, some wounded. I thought we could do it. I thought if I pushed hard enough, fought hard enough, I could save the rest of my men. I saved six of the ones who'd been captured, but I lost another twelve in the fight."

He was silent long enough that Jae's tears slowed. When he spoke again, his voice was rough. "I refused to leave ten of my soldiers to die, so I sacrificed sixteen of them instead. Sometimes we're faced with terrible decisions, and the best we can do is cut our losses and walk away."

Jae looked toward the cottage, watching the smoke gently curling from the chimney. "This wasn't a soldier in some war," she said, and she hated how weak she sounded. She scratched at a bit of moss growing between the stones. "This was Ethriel's husband. Faith's father."

My friend.

"All the soldiers I lost that day were someone's father, someone's wife, someone's child," Corvin said. "I remember their names still. Every single one of them."

"You remember all sixteen of them?" She turned to watch his expression, checking for the lie.

Corvin nodded as he stared out toward the trees. "I do. I remember the names of all the soldiers who served under me."

Jae's lips twitched with a thought, but she pressed her lips together, biting it back. She shouldn't be worried about the past when the future was so uncertain.

"What?" he asked. Jae hadn't noticed him turn his attention to her. "Whatever question you have, just ask."

"You remember *all* your soldiers?" Jae asked.

"I do."

She bit her lip before she said, "So you remember Solace? From before, I mean. Before he became the weapon."

Corvin drew a deep breath, tucking his hands between his knees. "He was a private first class. He'd been in the army almost three years and served in my company for two of them. He was a good soldier, eager to learn. I could see an officership in his future, if he wanted it."

Corvin stared at the ground, a wave of guilt pushing from him, even without Jae reaching for it.

"For what it's worth, I am sorry. I know it's not worth much. And I know it doesn't erase what I did. Nothing can change what I did to your friends. To you. But I'm sorry. I thought—" He shook his head. "It doesn't matter what I thought. I was wrong."

Jae watched him, unsure what to say or how to feel. Overhead, a bird flew by, squawking angrily.

"And I'm not looking for your forgiveness," Corvin added. "I just wanted you to know. I wanted you to know that I regret all of it." At last he lifted his chin, clearing his throat as he focused on Jae again. "Sorry, this isn't about me. The point I was trying to make is that you did the right thing, Jae. You did what you needed to do. You got Faith out of there, and you're going to get her and Ethriel somewhere safe."

Corvin lifted one hand a few inches, but it hovered there in the space between them, like he wasn't sure what he'd meant to do with it. After a moment, it fell to rest along the wall as he blew out a long breath. "Sometimes surviving is all we can do."

Chapter 58

It was a long, tense journey from Southreach to Whitehollow. Corvin suspected the others were weighed down with the guilt of leaving Lucien behind. He certainly was. Even though Faith hadn't gone after the shifters as he'd feared she had, she'd still snuck out during Corvin's watch. It was his fault, more than anyone else's, that Lucien was a prisoner, being marched alone into enemy territory.

He didn't know why they weren't able to see that.

Corvin couldn't travel as fast as he wanted to, even on horseback. The healing wounds on his leg and side forced him to stop frequently. Whenever he would try to push himself farther, Ethriel would ask for a break, claiming she wasn't as young as she used to be. But he knew from her gentle, knowing smile that she was doing it for his benefit as well as her own.

Whitehollow was farther than either Ethriel or Faith had ever traveled, but they held up admirably. Jae served as their scout in addition to sharing the nighttime watches with Corvin while the others slept. Her poise and grace were impressive, but so was her intensity, especially under the circumstances. He was beginning to see why Lucien had such a connection with her.

After weeks on the road, the city of Whitehollow opened before them at last.

"Do you know where your friends will be?" Ethriel asked as they entered the city gates in the midmorning.

Jae slowed her horse to ride beside Ethriel. "Verity gave me some Sending parchment before we went our separate ways," she said. "I messaged a week ago to let her know we were coming."

Dread settled in Corvin's stomach. "Did you mention . . . me?"

Jae favored him with an amused glance, her notched eyebrow rising. "Well, yeah. Unless you wanted to take the chance of running into one of my friends, unexpected and unannounced?"

That seemed decidedly worse than facing them head-on, considering they would very likely kill him on sight otherwise.

They still might.

"Verity should be at the Wardens' compound," Jae went on, returning her attention to Ethriel. "We'll start there."

From just behind them, Faith spoke up. "What are you going to say to them?"

Corvin glanced over his shoulder and realized she was speaking to him. After Lucien and Jae had left on their journey to the Red Forest, Corvin had felt it best to tell Faith his own story, including everything that had happened in Taernfane. And, like Ethriel, she had seemed willing to accept him as he was.

He swallowed against the icy chill seeping into his chest. He wished he could say he hadn't thought about what he would say to the Warden when he saw her again, but he had. He'd been thinking about it since Lucien asked him to escort his family to Whitehollow. "I'm not sure," he said.

"Maybe let me start," Jae said with a soft chuckle.

Something lightened in Corvin's chest at the sound, and he had to agree that was probably a very good idea.

❋

Jae sent another message to Verity to let her know they'd arrived, and she received a swift response asking to meet at the Wardens' base in an hour. It was hard to miss the compound, sprawling as it was at the edge of Whitehollow. They found a stable nearby, and when a young man came to tend to their horses, Corvin handed him an extra gold coin to keep an eye on his sword. He didn't want to give the Wardens the wrong impression by going in armed.

At the gate to the compound, Jae informed the Wardens on guard duty that they were there to see Warden Verity Corallan.

"High Commander Corallan said to escort you to her office," one of them said.

Corvin's brow furrowed. Last he'd heard, the Warden commander at White-hollow was a man by the name of Joseph Cairn.

Jae seemed equally surprised by the news, her eyes widening. "High Commander? Since when?"

The guards exchanged a look. "That may be best for her to explain," the first one said.

One of the Wardens escorted the four of them across the courtyard to a long, low building. As they approached a large set of doors, Corvin counted no less than six Wardens loitering in the hall and four stationed prominently by the door.

"Is there something going on?" Jae asked their guide.

"No, miss," the Warden said.

But Corvin caught the way their attention shifted when he passed by them, trailing behind Ethriel and Faith. They were there for *him*.

Their guide looked pointedly at Corvin and gestured to the bench along the wall opposite the doors. "Commander Corallan has asked that you wait here a moment while she speaks with the others. She'll let you know when she's ready for you."

Corvin eyed the Wardens standing guard. His stomach felt as though he'd swallowed a lead weight.

This is fine.

Jae nodded to Corvin before opening the door and heading inside. Ethriel started to follow, but she turned back and gave Corvin a gentle hug. He stooped, returning it.

"Thank you for getting us here," she said. Then she added, more quietly, "I'll put in a good word for you."

He couldn't help but smile as she stepped back and followed Jae and Faith into the Warden commander's office.

A fluttering feeling was building in Corvin's gut, and he didn't like it. He considered waiting outside but suspected that the Wardens set to guard him—guard *against* him—wouldn't appreciate him trying to leave the building.

Or perhaps he could leave entirely? He could leave Whitehollow and head back to the farmstead. He could look after things there until it was safe for Ethriel and Faith to return.

He wiped his damp palms on his thighs. No, he needed to face the consequences of his actions—his choices. Besides, he'd promised Lucien he would protect his family. That promise didn't end just because they'd arrived at their destination.

And he didn't *want* to leave. Corvin leaned his head against the wall at the realization.

Why did it feel like his heart wanted to pound out of his chest?

Half an hour later, the door swung open again. Ethriel and Faith stepped into the hallway.

"They're ready for you," Ethriel said gently. "We'll be waiting out here."

Corvin's nerves steadied somewhat as he spotted Jae holding the door open for him. He drew a slow, deep breath and stepped across the threshold.

The large room was filled with bookshelves, a desk and two wide tables, and all the surfaces were covered with maps and parchments of various sizes. Three people were already in the room with Jae. Corvin recognized the Warden, Verity, immediately. He remembered her well from their previous encounters. Her dark auburn hair was pulled back in a braid, and her metal arms were crossed over her chest as she leaned back against the wider, center-most table.

At the edge of the table, nearer to the window, a man stood. Corvin recognized him from King Dominic's throne room. He'd been with Verity before the fight broke out. His ice-blue eyes watched Corvin cautiously from behind wire-framed glasses, regarding him with more curiosity than distrust.

Lastly, behind Verity and slightly to her right was another young woman. She was shorter, with golden blond hair that curled and swirled in little wisps around her face. Corvin didn't recognize her, but she watched him with a skepticism that was only slightly more veiled than Verity's.

Jae closed the door and moved toward the man with glasses. "You said Dare was coming too, right?" she asked. "Where is he?"

"Late, of course, but he'll be here," he said.

Jae chuckled softly, shaking her head. Her tight curls bounced with the motion. "Of course."

Verity stared at Corvin with such profound distrust that it sent a chill through him. But he knew why she looked at him that way. And he couldn't blame her in the slightest. If their positions had been reversed—he'd had plenty of time on their trek to torture himself with that particular thought exercise—he wouldn't be acting much different. He set his feet in a neutral stance, shoulder-width apart, and clasped his hands behind his back to keep from fidgeting with them.

Jae turned to him, though she gestured to the man beside her. "Corvin, this is Gregor." Her hand moved to acknowledge the woman on Verity's other side. "And that's Finn. And . . ." She paused awkwardly as she searched for a decent way to address the discomfort in the air. "And I think you know Verity."

Corvin nodded to all three of them but kept silent. He would let Jae take the lead, or Verity, if the Warden commander preferred it. But he could be the patient soldier and wait.

Verity stared at him for a long moment, letting the silence stretch and fill the room. Finally she said, "You're no longer the Chosen of Ainam?"

Corvin's jaw ticked, but he worked to keep his face even. He'd expected this question. "I am not," he said, his voice flat. "Though I understand if you may not believe me."

Verity held up her hand to stop him. "We'll verify it."

He wasn't sure how she planned to *verify* something like that, but he wouldn't question it yet.

"Are you seeking a way to return to Ainam's favor?" Verity asked.

Jae set a hand on her hip, watching him carefully. She'd asked him that question weeks ago. He hadn't had an answer for her then.

"I was," he said, looking at Jae as he spoke. "But I believe my path no longer aligns with Ainam's will."

"Jae informed us that you've been helping Lucien's family since the events in Taernfane," Verity continued, pulling his attention.

Corvin nodded. "Yes, High Commander. I stumbled across a farm in Southreach, owned by Ethriel Zamorra, your friend Lucien's wife. She patched me up twice—once after our fight in Taernfane, and again after my general ordered my assassination because of my failures."

Verity's brows rose, the only sign of her surprise.

"I had nowhere to go and no allies. Ethriel offered me a place to stay in exchange for some help around her farm. I'm sure she told you that just now. I didn't know of her connection to Lucien until some time later." Corvin swallowed reflexively, remembering Lucien's hand on his throat when he'd recognized Corvin.

Verity opened her mouth to say something else, but the door behind Corvin swung open. Another man entered with a swift wave and a mumbled "Sorry I'm late." He circled around Corvin and paused just ahead of him. He was a little shorter and thinner than Corvin, and his clothes were plain and slightly worn. The man's brown hair fell to his shoulders, and Corvin was somewhat surprised that he recognized him as the man he'd met in the library in the Reach before he'd gotten into his first fight with Verity. Though now the man was sporting the remnants of a black eye.

The newcomer regarded Corvin, moving a step closer to him before giving a quiet "huh" and moving further into the room. To Corvin's surprise, the tension in the room seemed to increase. Verity watched him, arms still crossed, but the other two looked away. Only Jae brightened a little at his entrance, though she too seemed to notice how the others reacted.

The man gave a solemn nod to Verity and moved to stand a bit away from everyone.

Verity sighed. "Where were you, Dare?"

He swept his gaze over her, taking in her posture and tone. "Don't ask me questions when you don't want to know the answer," he muttered.

The Warden sighed again and pinched the bridge of her nose before turning her attention back to Corvin. "Why should we trust you? You tried to kill half the people in this room."

"Directly," the newcomer, Dare, said. He kept his tone light, though his fists clenched before he shoved them into his pockets. "And the other half you tried to kill *indirectly*."

Verity gave him a sidelong look but didn't comment.

Corvin raised his chin, hands still clasped behind his back. He could understand their distrust. He certainly didn't blame them for it. But if Ethriel and Faith trusted him—if Lucien and Jae had come to trust him, at least a little—perhaps he wasn't as irredeemable as he feared.

"Have you ever believed in something, Commander?" he asked.

Her brows rose slightly, but she nodded.

"Have you ever believed in something so strongly that you knew without a doubt in your mind or your heart that it was right? Or fair? Have you believed in something strongly enough that you would do anything that was asked of you because you *knew* it would make the world better?"

Slowly, Verity nodded again.

Corvin drew a breath. "I believed," he said. "I believed in Ainam with all my heart. Even before I was His Chosen. I believed. And . . ."

His throat tightened as he thought back to the joy that had filled his heart the first time Ainam had spoken to him. Now the memory filled him with shame.

"And when He Chose me to serve Him, He told me of the weapon forged by the elemental gods, and He told me He needed me to find it for Him. That it was a danger to the world, and only He would be able to keep the world safe." Despite his efforts to stand tall in the face of his failures, Corvin's chin dipped as he said, "And I believed Him."

Verity watched him, her face a passive mask.

"And what of Solace?" Dare asked, hands still pressed tight into his pockets. "You practically tortured him."

"Dare." Verity breathed the warning but didn't turn to him.

He was undeterred. "You neglected him. Bound him. And then you took *everything* from him."

Corvin focused on Dare, on the tension wound through his shoulders and his stance—the false impression of casual when really he was approaching his breaking point. Did none of the others see it?

"I did," Corvin said to Dare. "I did all of those things. I believed the weapon was dangerous and that *he* was a danger to the world because of it." His voice remained steady as he said, "So yes, I bound him, and I treated him like an inanimate object instead of a person, instead of like one of my men, because I *knew* him. My soldiers *knew* him. And I knew that if we just continued thinking of him as . . ." He hesitated, watching as the face of every person fixed on him, their attention hanging on his words.

They hadn't known him before the weapon took him over.

Corvin darted a quick look at Jae before he forced himself to continue. ". . . As Bastian . . . Private Bastian Sayle, who had a strategic mind and liked to hum while he was on duty and would sing drinking songs with the men around the campfire when we were on the road. When he touched the weapon . . ."

He swallowed hard. How could he tell them that his heart had splintered at the loss of one of his men because he knew the fires would be quiet without him? How could he tell them that the only way he'd been able to deal with it and carry on with his duty was to convince himself it wasn't *him*?

"So yes," Corvin said, unable to keep the sorrow out of his voice. "I bound him for what I thought was the safety of my soldiers and the cities we traveled through, and I told the men that Bastian Sayle died the moment he touched that weapon, and that it was nothing but an alien power walking around in his skin. And that's how I treated him."

The room was silent for a long while after Corvin finished speaking.

Verity uncrossed her arms with a heavy exhale and set her metal hands on the table behind her. She angled her head toward Gregor, who gave as noncommittal a head tilt as Corvin had ever seen. On her other side, Dare apparently gave up his calm pretense and began to pace the room.

"Would you excuse us for a few minutes so we can discuss your story?" Verity asked, though it was quite clear it wasn't a request.

Corvin nodded, standing up a little straighter. "But didn't you want to confirm that I'm no longer Ainam's Chosen?"

"We have," she replied swiftly. "We believe that part of your tale is true."

He blinked. When had they had the chance? They'd only been talking here for a few minutes, and certainly no one had studied him, observed him, or performed any sort of Sight ritual on him.

In the wake of his stunned silence, Verity held her hand out toward the door. "Please wait outside, Captain."

"Certainly, High Commander. Though you can call me Corvin. I'm not a captain anymore."

"Thank you," Verity said, "for what you did to help Lucien's wife and daughter."

"Of course," he said, not looking back. "There was no choice to be made."

When he reached the door, he paused. This could be his only chance, he realized. If they dismissed him, he might not have another opportunity to ask for their help with the task that weighed on his mind.

"I know I have no right to ask anything of you," he said from the door. "But I've wanted to get a message to Private Sayle's family, to let them know what happened and to . . . to ask for their forgiveness. They live in the capital, Goeth, on the western coast, but I've been banished from all of Westhold, and if I even try to get a message in, the army will come looking for me. Could you get a message to his family for me? Please? I don't want them to continue on without knowing what happened to their son."

Verity was quiet for a moment before she nodded slowly. "On my honor," she said. "I'll see that they're told of their son's fate. And if you have a missive to include, I'll see that it reaches them."

"Thank you, High Commander." Corvin's chest tightened as he left the room, though he wasn't sure if it was from relief or shame.

CHAPTER 59

DARE WATCHED CORVIN DEPART as though he'd been dismissed by a superior officer. Once the door was latched behind him, Dare's hands finally unclenched, though he kept pacing. It had been a challenge not to hurl a dagger at Corvin Crosse the moment he'd walked into the room.

In the week since the hearing, Dare had barely seen any of the others. Every time he tried to talk to them, every gift he bought to try to show he was sorry, it was all turned away. Until today, when Verity asked him to meet them in her office because Jae was in Whitehollow and had brought Corvin Crosse with her. They needed him, Verity said, and so he had come.

Verity whirled on Dare. "What in Vire's hells was that?"

Dare stopped pacing just long enough to thrust an angry finger toward the door. "You can't honestly be considering keeping him around after what he did to Solace!"

Bastian . . . Vire's fucking hells, his name was Bastian.

Verity rolled her neck and it popped audibly. "But you felt nothing of Ainam on him, correct?" she demanded. "He wasn't lying?"

Dare dragged his hand through his hair, pushing it out of his face. Of course. Gods above and be-*fucking*-low, he'd been such a fool. Of course they hadn't needed *him*. They'd only needed what he could do. "No," Dare said sharply. The suffocating, rigid *wrongness* that he'd always felt around Corvin Crosse was strangely absent. "He wasn't lying about *that*."

Finn leaned against the far wall, playing with a lock of her honey blond hair. She twirled the end in her fingers, spinning it until it folded up on itself, before tugging it straight again. Dare could have sworn there was a shimmer lining her eyes.

"I don't think he's lying about any of it," Jae interjected. She looked almost apologetic, hands open at her sides. "Crosse did horrible things, but as shitty as his actions were—and I can't believe I'm saying this—I think he believed he was doing them for the right reasons. I . . . I think he was manipulated into doing terrible things, and he feels genuinely remorseful about it."

Verity nodded, shooting a pointed look at Dare. "Who here can't say the same?"

Dare's face heated, his shoulders tightening as he resumed his pacing. "So he tortured and killed our friend and that's it? We're just going to forgive him?" He threw his hands out to his sides. "Sure, he can hang around. Why the hells not? Let's replace Solace with his murderer."

Finn pushed off the wall and rushed out of the room. One hand covered her mouth, but Dare still caught the stifled sob she was trying to hold in as she left.

Fuck.

Verity took a step after her but stopped short. Her ire returned to Dare full force. "*Corvin* didn't kill Solace."

"No." Dare met Verity's rage with his own. If this was the game she wanted to play, fine. "You're right. Crosse didn't kill him. We did. You and me, Verity." He pointed toward the door. "But he may as well have. Have you forgotten what he did? If he hadn't forced Solace into unleashing the magic of the weapon, we could have—"

"We could have *what*? Saved him? Unmade the weapon without killing him? We literally don't know what would have happened. All we had to go on was a cryptic passage about a blood sacrifice." Verity steadied her breath and met Dare's gaze, voicing the thought that had been haunting Dare since that afternoon beneath Taerna's tree. "For all we know, we would have had to kill him anyway."

Dare moved toward her, stepping into her space and meeting her eye to eye. "Are you sure this is a wise decision? *High Commander.*"

"Are you really one to be talking about wise decisions right now?"

His eyes narrowed. "Why are we even talking about this? We all know you're going to do what you always do." He waved an encompassing gesture at Verity, his voice going cold. He was sick of her high-and-mighty attitude, like she'd never made any mistakes. "You're going to pretend like you want everyone's opinions, but then you'll make the decision you wanted to make in the first place. And we'll all have to live with the consequences."

"Darcy—" Gregor tried, but Dare turned away, stalking toward the door. Whatever Gregor was going to say now, Dare didn't want to hear it. If Gregor was going to side with him, then it was too little, too late, but he didn't think that was likely, and he definitely couldn't handle the alternative.

"Good luck with that." Dare slammed the door shut behind him. He didn't look up as he trudged past Corvin and the two women who'd been there when he'd arrived—he could only assume they were Lucien's wife and daughter. No one tried to stop him.

He'd spent the last week trying to patch things over with Verity, and with Finn and Gregor, but none of them wanted anything to do with him. How was he supposed to fix things if they wouldn't give him a chance? Even today, they only wanted him there because he'd always been able to sense Ainam's power in Corvin. He had no doubt they wouldn't have bothered asking him to meet if he wasn't of use.

Dare stopped at the compound gates. He breathed deep, pushing some of his anger out on the exhale. The city of Whitehollow was open ahead of him.

Maybe the problem was that he was trying too hard. Maybe he needed to give them some space first. If he let them calm down, let their anger at him subside, maybe he'd be able to explain later. Maybe he had to let them be pissed before he could try to fix it.

There were a few things in Valda he needed to sort out, and now that the hearing was done—and irrevocably fucked—the danger had mostly passed. Tanithe was still likely to be a pain in his ass, but he no longer felt like he had a giant target on his back. Because of him, she was free and clear of any responsibility or ties to the events in Taernfane, so she had no further reason to want him dead. Neither did the Valdane Council.

Dare could make the journey to Valda and take care of a few things, like making sure Matron Nora got the money for the orphanage. Getting it had certainly cost him enough. He wanted to at least make sure it ended up where it was needed.

Where it could do something good.

That would give him a week away from Whitehollow, minimum. And maybe by the time he got back he could start trying to make things right. He needed to be able to fix this.

He didn't want to think about what it would mean if he couldn't.

Dare turned and crossed the courtyard toward the barracks. In his room, he lit the small lamp on his desk, the little flame flaring to life. He took his knapsack out of the trunk at the foot of his bed and set it beside his desk. He could pack and be out of Whitehollow—and out of everyone's hair—by midafternoon.

Pausing before he'd packed more than a spare shirt, Dare looked over his room, at his meager belongings that had started taking up space beside Drystan's. He was building a life here, he realized. He *wanted* to build a life here. He was a Warden of the Flame, at least until Verity decided she was sick of his bullshit.

He tugged the iron key Gregor had given him out from under his shirt. It hung on its chain, the key warm from where it laid against the scar in the center of his chest. Dare swallowed against the tightness building in his throat.

This key is to remind you not to look back, Gregor had told him, *because no one can chain you down again.*

He wouldn't leave for long, he was certain, and he wouldn't leave without telling his friends. He wouldn't run again.

Dare sat at the desk and took out a few pieces of parchment, a stylus, and ink. Then he pulled his well-worn flask from where he'd taken to keeping it in the desk drawer and took a long swig.

High Commander: I have a few loose ends I need to tie up in Valda. Consider this me asking for forgiveness for leaving Whitehollow without talking to you first, but I think you and I both know that my face is the last one you'd want to see right now.

He hesitated, the stylus suspended above the paper. There was more he wanted to say, but he needed to find the right words. He took another sip from his flask. He wanted to tell her that he hoped they could talk when he got back—because he *would* be coming back. He wasn't about to leave this behind. He wasn't about to leave them behind. And he wanted to apologize for what he said earlier.

He hoped that his fears were wrong and that things would work out with having Captain Corvin in town. But honestly, that was probably another reason it would be best if Dare was out of the city for a little while so they could sort all that out.

Dare took another swallow of liquor and, as he set the flask on his desk, the cold edge of a blade pressed against the side of his neck. Dare tensed, his heart nearly jumping out of his chest as one hand reached for the dagger on his belt.

"Ah ah, now," Tanithe Ash cooed in his ear, stilling his hand. "Try it and I'll slit your throat right here."

Dare's mind raced, but he needed to buy himself some time to catch up. "What are you doing here, Tanithe?"

And how had she gotten in? In answer, the lantern on his desk flickered, as though Tanithe's very presence dimmed the light.

The shadows. She must have used her shadow travel to get in, but when? Even with her consciously muting her dizzying aura as she'd done when they'd met at the café, Dare would have felt her step through the shadows.

Tanithe wrapped her arms around his neck, as though giving him a warm embrace, though the blade still sat against his throat, threatening to slice into his veins at any moment.

"Oh, sweetheart," she said, sounding so much like a lover that Dare's stomach churned. "I'm here to get you to work for me."

"I told you last time," Dare said, feeling the edge of the blade scratch against his throat as he swallowed. "I'll never work with you."

Tanithe laughed as she stepped around his chair, shoving the papers to the side so she could perch on his desk. One boot lifted, coming to rest on the chair between his legs.

"You really aren't terribly bright, are you?" She brandished the knife about an inch from his eyes as she leaned her elbow on her raised knee. "You're referring to the time when I offered you a job. And your exact words were, *Tell me what in your twisted fucking mind makes you think I would ever willingly work with you.*" She smiled, teeth flashing. "What I said just now was, *I'm here to get you to work for me.*" She tapped the point of the dagger against the tip of his nose. "*For me* was the operative part of that sentence. And I never said anything about it being willingly."

Dare's blood turned to ice.

"I gave you the chance to do this the easy way, little lordling." Tanithe slid the dagger under the chain around his neck and pulled, breaking it. The key to his parents' dungeon clattered to the floor. "You declined. And quite rudely, I might add. So now we get to do things the fun way."

"You won't make it very far," Dare said, hoping to sound a good deal more confident than he was, but his head was swimming. "Verity—"

"*Verity,*" Tanithe mocked as she picked up the note he'd been in the process of writing. "*Verity* is going to find this lovely message from you, slipped neatly under her door, explaining exactly where you went."

Tanithe hopped down from his desk, taking the parchment with her. She folded it as she walked toward the door.

If ever Dare was going to have a chance at killing her, it was now. Her back was to him. He only had a moment. He had to act.

Dare reached for the dagger on his belt and launched out of the chair. The blood rushed to his head as he stood and his knees buckled, sending him sprawling on the floor. A fog settled into his mind, blurring the edges of his vision, and his limbs felt like little more than jelly. He struggled to push himself up and failed.

"Now, now, Darcy," Tanithe said, crouching over him. One boot balanced precariously on his hand. "I'd like to give you points for trying, but that was just sloppy." She stood, putting just enough pressure on his fingers that he knew she could break them with hardly a second thought. A moment later, his flask hit the floor in front of him. "At least you're nothing if not predictable."

She'd been waiting for him . . . Vire's fucking demons, she'd drugged his flask and he'd walked right into it . . .

The room was gently rocking, and his head was heavy as he managed to pull himself up until he was slouched against his desk. "They'll come looking for me." Dare forced the words past his sluggish tongue. "They'll find me."

"My dear, at your current level of fuck-up, who exactly do you think is going to come looking for you? Your dear Warden? Your lover? Please. They'll be thrilled just to have the silence for a while."

She crouched again, her smile seeming to take up his entire field of vision. "How many days do you think it will take them to start worrying about you?" She waved the note he'd written in front of his face. "A week? Two? What do you think I could do to you in fourteen *uninterrupted* days?"

The panic he'd been trying to keep at bay clutched at his heart and turned his guts inside out. She was right. He'd fucked up so thoroughly no one even wanted to look at him. How many days *would* it take them to care that he was gone? Hells, even the note said he'd be in Valda for a while.

Dare was well and truly fucked.

"Don't worry, darling," Tanithe continued, tracing a fingernail along the line of his jaw. "I've got lots of plans for you, but the real fun will start once we get back."

Even Dare's thoughts were unsteady. *Tykaras?*

The god didn't answer.

He swallowed thickly. "How do you plan on getting me out of here?" She had her shadows, he knew. It would probably be nothing for her to drag him along that way, but he needed to stall for time. Maybe Verity would come back to her room soon—

"The gods have power, Darcy," Tanithe said, all flirtatious cooing dropping from her voice until only cold brutality remained. "And anyone connected to them has power. I have plans for how to use that power, but I need to test it first. I need to know if it's enough. Whitehollow is the perfect playground."

"Enough?" Dare wasn't sure he wanted to know, but he needed to. "Enough for what?"

Holding Dare's half-finished note in one hand, Tanithe grabbed the front of his shirt with the other. The shadows that had pooled in the corners of the room surged forward.

Whatever protection Tykaras had given Dare from Tanithe and her mind magic clearly didn't extend to her shadows. As they swirled over his shoulders, the biting chill they brought with them was the least of Dare's concerns. Reality twisted and warped, his body at the epicenter. Every nerve felt as though it were being folded, snapped, and torqued.

He might have screamed.

There was a lurching stop and then a second violently spiraling start before they stopped again. The cold faded. Dare collapsed onto the ground, retching as the immense, contorting pain slowly lessened.

"Well, that was fun," Tanithe teased. Her arm slithered around his neck, and she hauled him to his feet, holding him up by his throat. "Look at it," she said, her other hand gesturing to the expanse of Whitehollow before them.

They were up on the city's walls. Dare tried to pull her forearm away from his throat, but his arms barely had any strength at all. He struggled just to breathe.

As they stood above the city, a howl went up from somewhere within the walls. Then another, a few streets over. And another, and another, until at least a dozen had erupted across the city.

The screaming started next. Dare couldn't see what was happening, but he could hear it—the monstrous roars and terrified screams, the panic that was overwhelming the city below. Bells rang out.

"What . . ." Dare choked out, "did you . . . do?"

"I told you, darling, I have plans. And they require magic. Both arcane and divine." She tightened her arm under his chin, pulling him into her. "You, my dear, have a surfeit of both. But I need to make sure it works before I tap into you. So then the question becomes, how does one find smaller amounts of divine power to draw on while channeling arcane magic?" She waved her hand at the city as another set of howling snarls echoed.

Whatever she was trying to do, only one thing was certain: Tanithe Ash was fucking insane.

Tanithe released her grip, throwing Dare to the stones at her feet. He coughed and sputtered, unable to do anything beyond stare up at her. The bright blue sky shone behind her as she closed her eyes, raising her hands.

Swords clanging, shouting, and yowling reached the top of the wall. Tanithe's voice was soft as she began an incantation. Dare had heard the words before, the day Verity channeled through him to wake Solace from the Binding spell.

Magic washed over Dare, sending needles prickling across his skin. But there was another sensation with it too—strong, solid, enduring. He tried to focus on that undercurrent of strength, familiar somehow, but wave after wave of magic crashed into him until his awareness was reduced to those thousands of stabbing needles.

He didn't know how long he lay sprawled on the walls surrounding White-hollow, but eventually the prickling needles combined with the twisting, spiraling magic of Tanithe's shadows. It crashed into his consciousness as Dare felt himself hauled off the ground, and he had enough wherewithal left to recognize, as his vision faded to black, the familiar skyline of Valda.

Chapter 60

Verity bowed her head as Dare stormed out of her office. Near the window, Gregor sighed deeply, like he needed the breath to bolster himself.

"Jae, do you really think we can trust Corvin Crosse?" Gregor asked.

"I honestly don't know," she said. "And I can't tell you whether or not you should. That'll be up to each of you. But you heard Ethriel and Faith's side of things. How he's helped them. How he almost died protecting them from shifters. I don't particularly trust him, and I sure as hells haven't forgiven him for what he did. I don't know whether we should count him as an ally, but certainly not having another enemy to deal with would be a boon."

Verity pushed off from the table she'd been leaning against. She couldn't let herself be distracted by Dare right now. "What do you think?" she asked Gregor.

He slid his glasses off and cleaned one of the lenses with the hem of his shirt. "Thinking practically, Jae's right. Between Valda, Tanithe, and whatever the shifters are up to, we have enough enemies right now." He replaced his glasses and crossed his arms tightly. "Not to mention that I hardly knew Solace, so I don't have the deeply personal connection to him—to his memory—that the rest of you have. Though regardless of how well I knew him, he was a person and didn't deserve what Corvin did to him."

Verity frowned. "I think we shouldn't make any brash decisions one way or the other," she said, her metal fingers tapping against her leg. Crosse was a dangerous enemy. But if he wasn't Ainam's Chosen anymore, and if he was remorseful about his actions, did he deserve a second chance? "I don't think we should leap into trusting him, but I also don't think we should turn him over to Westhold. Or Drahkonia, for that matter."

Regardless of any of their personal feelings about Corvin, he'd wreaked havoc in Taernfane. They had a responsibility to King Dominic. It was why they were in Whitehollow in the first place. But in this case, it could complicate matters. There were a lot of moving pieces to consider, but any way she looked at it, they would all need some time to sort through what it meant that Corvin Crosse might be an ally. Or, at least, not an enemy.

Gregor's lips pressed into a thin line. "You think we should keep his presence here a secret from Chancellor Caelan," he said.

Verity didn't like it either, but she nodded. "For now. Only until we can ascertain his intentions here."

"Alright," he mumbled, biting the nail on his thumb. "We won't say anything yet."

"Good. Thank you." Verity turned back to her desk. "I'm sorry about Lucien," she said to Jae. "Do you think there's anything we can do for him?"

Jae sank into a chair like all the wind—all the fight—had been pulled out of her. "I don't know. I worry there isn't. He made me promise to make sure his family made it here, but now . . . I don't know what to do, or if it's already too late."

Gregor crossed to her and perched on the arm of her chair. "If there's anyone on this continent that can survive whatever the shifters have planned for him, I have no doubt it's Lucien."

Jae leaned her head into Gregor's side, and he draped his arm around her, rubbing her shoulder as he gave her a reassuring smile. A pang of jealousy struck Verity. If only Drystan were here with her. Gods, she missed him so much. What would he say about this new development with Corvin Crosse?

She knew what he would say. *Give him a chance, Vee. Keep your eyes open and your guard up, but give him a chance.*

Verity sat on the edge of her desk. "Jae, we'll find Lucien's family and Corvin a place to stay in the city not far from the base. Once they get settled, I'd be very interested in hearing more about how the shifters aren't all monsters."

Jae nodded. "And you got our message about the ones in the Red Forest allying with the ones in the Wilds?"

"I did." Not to mention the news that the shifters mobilizing was about waging war and expanding their territory. Verity had shared that news with Lorekeeper Harrow and Whitehollow's magistrates, as well as sent missives to the Valdane Council and the Wardens stationed in Lostward. So far she'd received no response from any of them.

"Good," Jae said. "And *I'd* like to hear more about this *High Commander of the Wardens* thing because honestly, when the fuck did that happen?"

Despite everything, Verity laughed, and Gregor smiled a little wider. It was good to have Jae back.

"And you also need to tell me about whatever the hells happened with Dare," Jae continued. "What did I miss?"

Gregor and Verity both groaned.

"It's a long story," he said, his shoulders sagging.

"He's an asshole and an idiot." Verity crossed her arms. Her blood still felt hot in her veins when she thought about what he tried to pull.

Jae looked between the two of them, then pleadingly up at Gregor. "Neither of those things is new information," she said, causing a quiet snort of laughter from Gregor. "But that's not what I saw when he showed up. The both of you *and* Finn looked like you were about ready to walk out, stopped only by virtue of our guest." She gave Gregor a pointed look. "All *three* of you. One, sure, that's any day. Two of you, fine, he made some smart-ass comment. I'd buy that. But all three of you?" She looked between them for a moment, and when neither of them spoke up she added, "Come on, please tell me what happened."

Gregor pushed his glasses into his hair and rubbed his eyes with his thumb and forefinger.

"Let's get Ethriel and Faith settled in first," Verity said with a heavy sigh. "Then we'll tell you everything. Bring them to the Snapdragon. It's close by and will do until we can find them something more permanent."

"Alright, fine," Jae said, pushing out of the chair. "But I want *all* the details." She hurried into the hall.

"I hate to ask you this," Verity said to Gregor once Jae had left. "But did you hear anything? From Crosse?"

Gregor shook his head, gazing at the ceiling. "Unfortunately no. It's been quiet all day today. I'm sorry."

Verity dismissed his apology with a quick wave. "It's fine," she said. "Don't worry, Gregor. Honestly, I'm glad it's been a quiet day for you."

Outside, a bell clamored. Verity's breath caught in her chest for only a moment before she grabbed her sword and rushed to the door as other bells joined the first from beyond the outer walls of the base.

Gregor moved to follow. "What is that?"

"The alarm. Something's happened." Verity sprinted down the hall. That alarm was only used for natural disasters or if the city was under siege. Civilians were to lock themselves in their homes until given the all-clear. "Stay here!" she shouted over her shoulder, leaving Gregor standing in the middle of the hallway.

✳

Outside, Wardens rushed across the base toward the city gates. Jae had barely made it out of the building with Corvin, Ethriel, and Faith, let alone into the city. Good, that was one less worry Verity had to deal with.

Verity grabbed a key out of her pocket and tossed it at Corvin. "That building there," she said, pointing across the base to the commander's quarters. "The brick one. The three of you go there and lock yourselves inside. Jae, you're with me." She prepared herself to snap at Corvin if he started to argue about staying behind.

"Yes, Commander," he said, before ushering Ethriel and Faith toward the building she'd indicated. He didn't hesitate or look back.

Verity charged toward the gates as Jae fell into step beside her. "You trust him alone?" Jae asked.

"No, but they do. And he seems to care about them, so I trust he'll stay put until it's safe." When they reached the compound's gates, Verity glanced over her shoulder. A handful of Wardens were still heading for the city. "Once those Wardens are through, close the gates!" Verity ordered the two Wardens standing guard. She pushed her scabbard through the loop on her belt and hurried into the city.

"What's that alarm for?" Jae asked.

"Nothing good."

A few people stood around, confused, inquiring after the alarms. But a moment later, screams rang out to the south.

Shit, the market! It was bound to be crowded. Verity took off running, Jae right beside her.

The market district was only a few blocks away, and the closer they got, the louder the commotion became. On the final half-block, dozens of people rounded the corner in terror.

Jae stumbled, her hand clutching her chest.

Verity slowed. She reached to steady her.

"I'm alright," Jae gasped as she regained her stride. "Their panic—I wasn't ready for it."

Before Verity could respond, they rounded the final corner to the edge of the market district and were confronted with the source of the terror.

A massive beast, all snarling fangs and black fur, stood in the center of the market square. Several bodies littered the ground around it.

"Vire's demons," Jae muttered. One hand still rested on her heart, though the other reached for the sword on her back. "A shifter?"

"If you need to go back," Verity said, "then go. Don't put yourself in a bad spot, alright?" Verity had enough to worry about right now. If shifters were attacking Whitehollow—she wouldn't be so foolhardy as to assume there was only one—then a lot of people were going to die.

Where were Dare and Finn? The image of Finn bleeding out, pale and dying, bombarded Verity's mind. What if something like that happened again, and Verity wasn't there to heal her?

"I'll be fine," Jae said, snapping Verity out of her spiraling thoughts. She drew her swords.

Verity slid her broken blade out of her scabbard as the shifter reared back on its hind legs, its head stretching at least ten feet in the air. Two people were in its path as they tried to run for safety.

The spark of Pyrannis that flickered in her heart flared to life. She'd learned quickly to heed that spark when it called for her attention. She raised her left hand toward the towering shifter. A bolt of fire shot from her palm, striking the shifter in the shoulder. It staggered back, returning to all fours out of range of its human targets. Embers singed its fur, sending up little wisps of smoke. The beast turned toward Verity and roared.

"You don't have to do this," Verity tried, circling slowly around the front of the shifter. In her periphery, Jae circled the other way. The shifter cocked its head, as though surprised someone was speaking to it calmly. "You can shift back," Verity continued. She stepped closer. "We can talk."

The shifter lashed out with bloodied claws. Verity threw her arm out, and the massive paw slammed into her wall of force. Behind the beast, Jae slashed at its hind quarters. When it tried to spin out from between them, Verity threw another force wall in its path, corralling it away from the remaining people.

Realizing what she was trying to do, the shifter lunged at Verity. The heat of its breath hit the back of Verity's neck as she dove out of the way. Several howls erupted across the city, more shouts and screams following. How many were there? Above the line of buildings surrounding the market square, black smoke billowed into the blue sky. A second plume joined it moments later.

The shifter spun toward Jae. She ducked a swipe of its claws and slashed upward as she stood. Blood splattered the cobblestones as the beast roared. Jae roared back and brought her other sword crashing down.

The shifter glared at Jae with wild, murderous eyes. It brought its paw around again, slamming into Jae on the back swing. She flew backward into the brick wall of a nearby building.

Verity took advantage of the beast's distraction. She drew on the power from Pyrannis. Her heart thundered in her chest knowing what she was about to try. But she needed to do something quickly. The shifters were attacking—burning—her city. She couldn't allow that to happen. Not when she could do something to stop it.

She gathered her breath, imagining a steadying hand on each shoulder.

She could almost hear Drystan's voice in her ear. *You've got this, Vee.*

You're not alone. Gregor's voice, calm and sure in her memory. *You're alright, Verity. You can do this.*

Verity pulled on Pyrannis's power and launched a wall of fire at the shifter.

It roared and tried to leap out of the flames, but its fur and its flesh had been set alight. She pulled on those flames, willing them to burn hotter. There was a person somewhere within the beast, she reminded herself. Although they were her enemy, she didn't want them to suffer. She needed this to be over quickly.

The shifter was dead before they hit the ground.

Verity's stomach turned, but she pushed it back. Chaos was still erupting across Whitehollow. She needed to focus. She needed to move.

Jae.

Verity spun, finding Jae still against the wall, though she was on her feet now, and a familiar figure stood beside her, bow in hand.

"Finn!" Verity ran to her side, throwing her arms around her before her mind had a moment to catch up. Finn returned the embrace, one arm pressing hard against Verity's back, holding her close for an instant. Verity's chest tightened.

"Where do you need us?" Finn asked, nocking an arrow.

Verity was about to check on Jae, but Jae dismissed her question before she could ask it. "I'm good," Jae said. "Where to?"

Black smoke darkened the sky and screams filled the streets.

"Jae, can you try to do something about the fires?" Verity asked. "Finn, help with the wounded. Any who can walk, take them back to the base. Tell the Wardens guarding the gates to open them for any civilians who need help."

Both women nodded and took off into the streets. Verity turned toward the mostly empty market square. She needed to help drive the shifters out of the city, but—

Nearby, a woman lay on the ground, crying, her hands clutching at a wound on her side. Verity ran to her, calling on Pyrannis's fire again.

A deep gash above the woman's hip bled freely, and her dark skin was ashen. Verity set her hands on the wound and let Pyrannis's power flow through her, searing the wound closed from the inside out. The woman gritted her teeth, a choking sob escaping her, though she relaxed as soon as Verity removed her hands. Only a knot of scar tissue remained.

"You'll be alright," Verity said quickly. When she pushed herself to her feet, the captain of the city guard, along with several other soldiers, stood nearby. They were fully armed and armored, though they stared at her with open astonishment.

"H-High Commander," the captain said. "How did y—"

"Now is not the time, Captain," Verity said, grabbing her sword from where she'd dropped it beside the injured woman. "Get your archers on the walls and as many rooftops as you can manage. We need to know how many shifters there are."

The captain snapped his attention to Verity, shaking the wonder from his face. "My men have already felled three. The attacks seem isolated for now. We may be dealing with as few as ten citywide."

As though corroborating the captain's theory, several howls rose up, but there were far fewer than before. They seemed spread out across the city. Even the shouts seemed to lessen.

Still, even ten shifters left unchecked could slaughter hundreds. "We need reports from all districts," Verity ordered. "We need to know where they are, and we need to clear any remaining civilians out of areas where shifters have been spotted. The Wardens will take any survivors who are displaced or need medical care."

The guards saluted her and dispersed. Verity followed the captain. She had more work to do.

Chapter 61

ALONE. GREGOR WAS ALONE.

A chill ran through him as the memories of another hallway in another city haunted him. The last time he'd been left behind, alone in a long hall, Tanithe had found him. She'd nearly killed him.

With the trial finished, could Tanithe still be in Whitehollow? Could she find him here, in the safety of the Wardens' base?

He was safe here. He tried to convince himself, but his pulse doubled. He was safe here.

He was safe.

Yet he couldn't stop picturing Tanithe dangling him over a set of marble stairs. He could still feel her nails digging into his throat.

Gregor breathed deep, trying to steady his mind the way Verity had shown him. He was safe.

Alarms clanged across the base—across the city. *He* might be safe, but others weren't. If he followed Verity, what could he hope to do? What help could a house secretary be in a citywide emergency?

But he wasn't Gregor Thalesen, House Secretary to Duke Wilhaven anymore.

He was Gregor Thalesen, Chosen of Aetherann.

With one more steadying breath, he sprinted down the hall after Verity.

Gregor squeezed through the compound's gates just before they closed. People ran by, a couple city guards ushering them toward their homes. Echoes of shouts rose up from all directions. No sign of Verity.

Or Dare. Gods, where would he have gone after he left Verity's office? Would he have left the base? Gregor didn't even know where to begin to look.

He turned north and ran toward what he knew to be one of the residential parts of the city. Once he lost sight of the Wardens' base, the streets were empty. A door slammed shut somewhere ahead of him, but no one was outside at all. Gregor's heart thundered in the eerie stillness.

A small group of guards stepped into view from one of the nearby side streets. Gregor started toward them; perhaps he could ask what had happened and whether there was anything he could do to help.

Confused shouts echoed through the empty streets, summoning the guards' attention, but before they could take more than a couple of steps toward the sound, a shriek rang out. A mass of people flooded the road, running, frantic, heading for the guards. The guards tried to move past them, toward where another scream pierced the air, but the panicked crowd swarmed them. Gregor bolted around the corner they'd come from.

And froze.

A monster with brown fur and slobbering jaws blocked the way. The shifter didn't seem to notice him as the focus of the beast's attention screamed again. A girl with dark, braided hair and pale skin pressed herself back against a wall. She couldn't have been older than fifteen, and she was bleeding freely from a wound on her forearm. A little boy, similar enough in his complexion that he must have been the girl's brother, hid behind her, clinging to her skirt and sobbing.

Before Gregor could think, he hurled a gust of wind at the shifter, concentrated to a narrow focal point. The beast's long claws scraped the cobblestones as it slid a few feet away from Gregor and, more importantly, away from the children.

The girl grabbed her brother by the hand and sprinted from where they'd been trapped, running to Gregor. He turned to lead her toward the soldiers around the corner; they would know what to do. The shifter leapt. Its dark shadow passed over Gregor's head to land in front of them, blocking their path. Icy fear gripped him.

The little boy screamed. Gregor picked him up and took the girl's hand, pulling her into a narrow gap between two buildings. The shifter was too wide in its bestial state to fit easily.

The little boy buried his face in Gregor's shoulder, his arms wrapped tight around his neck as they ran. A roar behind them shook the alley. Gregor didn't know where he was going. He only knew they needed to find someplace safe.

They bolted out of the alley and into a wider thoroughfare. It was empty—no people, no guards, and, thankfully, no shifters. Black smoke drifted through the air, obscuring other nearby streets from view.

Gods, there were shifters in Whitehollow!

The girl stumbled, and Gregor stopped. "Are you alright?" he asked. He considered putting the little boy down so he could go to his sister, but the child's legs were wrapped tightly around Gregor's waist.

The girl covered the gash on her arm, holding it tight to her chest. She was breathing hard, but she nodded.

"What's your name?" Gregor asked.

"Reverie," the girl said. She gestured to the boy clinging to Gregor. "That's Haven."

"I'm Gregor," he said. "I have friends in the Wardens. If we can get to the base, you'll be safe."

In his arms, Haven lifted his head and screamed. Reverie's eyes widened in terror. Gregor spun, arms tightening around the little boy. The brown-furred shifter was there, charging him. He couldn't run. There was no time.

Gregor turned his back on the shifter, pulling Haven in front of him, shielding him. Gregor's eyes pinched shut as he pulled on the trickle of Aetherann's power that flowed through him and pushed it into a sphere of wind. It whipped around Gregor, Haven, and Reverie. If he was lucky, it might deflect the worst of the shifter's charge.

Shouts and a snarl rose from behind him where he'd expected only to be ripped apart. He spared a glance over his shoulder to see a dozen city guards surrounding the shifter. Gregor let the wind fade as another guard rushed toward them.

"This way!" she shouted, sword out and aimed at the beast. "The Wardens opened the gates."

"Reverie, go!" Gregor said. "I'm right behind you."

He ran, following the guard until the Wardens' base came into view. A throng of people filed through the gates, some wounded, others crying. Gregor and Reverie joined the crowd funneling inside.

Within the compound walls, Gregor's mind was blank. He looked for his friends but otherwise let himself be ushered along with the other survivors. He saw no one he recognized as one of the Wardens separated the crowd into those with children and those without. He stayed with the children, following others to one of the long buildings off the training rings. Medics tended the wounded, though most people here seemed only shaken.

Gregor sat with Reverie and Haven. Reverie watched Gregor curiously while one of the medics bandaged her arm. Gregor leaned his head against the wall. Panic threatened to take over as the full weight of what had just happened set in, but the little boy still clung to him like a life raft. He couldn't lose his composure now. Not while these two were still relying on him. So Gregor closed his eyes and took a few deep breaths, letting the weight of the child in his arms be a kind of comfort.

"How did you do that?" Reverie asked.

Gregor opened his eyes. They were alone again, or at least as alone as they could be in the crowded space. The Warden who had bandaged Reverie's arm had moved on to help someone else.

Reverie tucked a strand of her brown hair behind her ear from where it had fallen out of her braids. "Before, I mean. Are you a mage?"

He could hardly recall what he'd done in the moment. His brain had stopped working and some instinct seemed to have taken over. Gregor opened his mouth to say *no*, but thought better of trying to explain the idea of being a Chosen of the old gods. "Something like that," he opted for instead.

It took a few minutes for Haven to loosen his grip on Gregor, but he finally unwound himself enough to look around.

"Do you want to go to Reverie?" Gregor asked gently, but the boy didn't turn.

"He can't hear," Reverie said. She tapped the little boy on the shoulder and signed something with her hands. Haven shook his head and signed something back before his little hand gripped the front of Gregor's shirt.

"He said you feel safe," Reverie said.

Gregor's heart squeezed as he held Haven. "He's your brother?" Gregor asked.

Reverie nodded.

"How old are you both?"

"I'm fourteen," the girl said. "Haven's five."

They sat in silence for a few minutes. Tension wove through the room, several children and some of the adults crying quietly. Where were the others? Verity and Jae, Finn, Dare? Were they alright? Had Jae been able to get Lucien's family somewhere safe? Was Corvin still with them? What about Finn and Dare? They'd left Verity's office ahead of anyone else. Could they have gotten caught up in the attack on the city?

"Thank you for helping us," Reverie said.

"Of course." Gregor's lips curved gently. "I'm glad I could help."

The girl gestured to her brother. "I can take him," she said, "if you need to go."

Gregor looked down at the little boy who still gripped his shirt like a lifeline. His friends would be alright. Except for Finn, they were all Chosen, like him. And Finn was tough enough that demons hadn't stopped her in Taernfane. He doubted a shifter would be able to do it now.

"That's alright," he said softly, tightening his arms around Haven. "I don't have anywhere else I need to be."

✺

"Gregor?"

He wasn't sure when—or even *how*—he'd fallen asleep, but Gregor opened his eyes. A bone-deep weariness had settled into him at some point over the last several hours since he'd brought the children to the Wardens' base. Haven was still sitting on him, snuggled up and asleep against Gregor's chest. Reverie was out too, her head resting on Gregor's shoulder.

Jae crossed the room of frightened people, rushing to Gregor's side. "Are you alright?"

He nodded, unable to do much else without waking either child.

Jae breathed a sigh of relief as she crouched. "Verity said she'd left you in her office. I nearly lost my mind when we got back and you weren't there."

"Sorry," Gregor whispered. He hadn't meant to cause any worry.

"What happened?"

"He saved us," Reverie said in a sleepy voice. She lifted her head and told Jae about how Gregor had found them and knocked one of the monsters aside with his magic, and how he had shielded Haven. How he had protected them when everyone else had run away.

Hearing his own actions told from this young girl's perspective was so strange. She made him sound like some kind of hero.

Even Jae's eyes widened at the tale. "Wow. That sounds pretty incredible."

Reverie nodded.

"Do you live around here?" Jae asked.

"We live with our aunt," Reverie said. "We were heading back there when the monsters came."

"We'll make sure you get back to her, alright?" Jae gestured to Gregor. "I need to take him with me now. Is that alright?"

Reverie looked up at Gregor like she wasn't sure she wanted to let him leave, and his heart broke in two for these children. He hated to leave them alone, but if Jae needed him . . .

"Alright," Reverie said, her voice tight.

"I'll check in with you as soon as I can," he said, handing off the still-sleeping Haven to Reverie. He made sure to get their aunt's name, as well as where she lived. "I'll see that you make it home. I promise."

"Thank you," Reverie said.

With one last look over his shoulder at the children, Gregor followed Jae outside. "Do you have any idea what happened?" he asked once they were clear of the civilians. "How are there shifters in Whitehollow?"

"I don't know everything yet," Jae said, "but early reports sound like it was about a dozen shifters who infiltrated the city in their human forms and attacked different districts at the same time. We don't know why yet. We all thought they were targeting Valda, not Whitehollow."

Gregor shook his head, trying to wrap his mind around everything that had happened. "Why were there so few of them?" he asked. "You said the shifters were planning war. Expansion. If that's their goal, and their target was Whitehollow all along, why only send a dozen?"

"Great question," Jae said. "I think that's what Verity's trying to answer now."

"Are the Wardens coordinating aid?"

Jae's nose scrunched up. "So, that's the problem. Most of the Wardens are either up north helping along the border of the Wilds, or they're out on other missions. The ones that were on base are helping, and Verity's conscripted a few of the city guards to bolster their numbers, but they're still missing someone to coordinate it." She gave him a pointed look.

"Oh." Gregor looked back toward the low building where Reverie and Haven were among the other survivors.

"If you're up for it, Verity said to talk with her and she'll get you started."

The children would be taken care of, and he'd check on them when he could, just like he promised. But this was something Verity was trusting him with. This was something he knew he could do to help. "Where can I find Verity?"

Chapter 62

Lucien's world was drowning in a sea of darkness and burning pain. Every time he came up for air, he would reach for the beast. He could use its strength to break free. But whenever he looked, all that was there was a silent shadow, like a wraith, formless and intangible. Fear shot through him before something was poured down his throat and he was drowning again, spiraling into the abyss.

Lucien opened his eyes. It was dark, and a thick canopy of leaves blocked out the sky. In the darkness, Lucien couldn't tell if the leaves were green or red, but the power of this place thrummed against his skin where it touched the dirt, and he knew where he was.

He rolled onto his side. His hands and feet were bound with iron chains, and his wrists were chafed and bleeding from the manacles. Bleeding.

He was *bleeding*.

But why hadn't he healed yet? Something that small should take hardly more than a few seconds. His pulse quickened. His head was pounding, and his throat burned. He could sense the beast within him, as he always did, but it seemed farther away somehow, like he was looking at its shape through frosted glass. Lucien reached for it, reached for the power he'd always tried to push away. If he shifted, he could snap the chains like they were twigs.

But the beast didn't rise to the surface.

"Good, you're awake," a voice said from somewhere in the darkness. Maldren Thorn stepped out of the shadows to crouch over him, a wooden bowl in her hands. She pushed it toward him. "Drink this."

Lucien jerked away. He tried to speak, but his throat was too parched and raw for words to form.

"It's water, you nitwit," she said. She grabbed his elbow and yanked him up until he was sitting, then held the bowl to his lips.

He gulped down the cool water, though it did little to ease the soreness in his throat. "Why can't I shift?" He swallowed, tasting blood. "Or heal?"

Mal's lips twisted. "Ashroot and dart thistle," she said. "The ashroot blocks the connection to the beast for a while. Burns all the way down and it'll gnaw up your gut. Vile shit. And dart thistle—"

"I remember." He'd experienced that one more than once, including the arrow that had struck him when he and Jae escaped the Red Forest the last time.

Mal continued. "Micah mixed them in with whatever he gave you when he brought you back here. I think he remembers what happened the last time he tried to bring you in." A shadow of a grin flickered across her face, there and gone in an instant.

"Ashroot." Lucien searched his memory. "That's new."

"Barrick's apothecary discovered it a few years back. He didn't want to use it, but Micah convinced him it would be useful for securing his power. Once you stop getting dosed with it regularly, your shifting should come back in a day or so."

Lucien twisted against the chains binding his wrists. "When did I get it last?"

"About two hours ago." She set the bowl down on the ground. "I was supposed to mix it in with the water I just gave you."

The poison may have tamped down the beast and made its power unreachable, but Taerna's power was still there, calling to him. He had that much at least. Even if he wasn't as familiar with it. Even if he hadn't practiced wielding the goddess's magic, it would come when he called for it. He was certain of it.

Lucien eyed the bowl. "And the dart thistle?"

She held up a small vial between two fingers. "That too."

"Why didn't you?"

Maldren leaned in closer, lowering her voice. "Rumors are flying about what you said in the Glade. Did you really tell Micah you can fix us?"

Lucien nodded, watching Mal for any flicker of movement—for any threat.

"Did you mean it?" She searched his face. "You really believe that?"

Believe? It wasn't a question of believing or not. It was something he had to do. It was his task to complete. Taerna trusted him with this. He had to figure out a way.

But how could he explain that to Mal? So instead, he simply said, "I do."

She studied him for a long while. "And then, what?" she asked at last. "Is the beast just . . . gone?"

Lucien shook his head. "No, not gone. But it was never meant to be this way. Taerna . . . She showed me how it used to be. It was . . ." Words failed him. In his visions, the shifters still had their beasts, but they seemed to work together rather than be at odds. It was like nothing he'd ever experienced. "I don't know how to describe it."

Mal fiddled with the vial in her hand. "Try."

He swallowed down the uncertainty and met her gaze again. "Peaceful."

She inhaled, blinking rapidly before turning away from him. "And you were really blessed by Taerna?"

"I'm her Chosen," Lucien said. The trees seemed to sing in answer.

Mal must have felt it too. She looked to the forest around them for a moment before focusing on him again. She held out the dart thistle.

"I need to dose you with this." She nodded to his wrists. "If the others see you heal, they'll figure out something's going on before we're ready." She unstoppered the vial.

"*We*?" he asked.

"Micah doesn't speak for all the shifters," she snarled. A bit of her beast showed through. "Some of us are sick of his bullshit and the brutality he disguises as leadership."

Could he trust her?

Lucien tilted his head back, exposing his throat to her. If she wanted him dead, she'd had more than enough opportunity. He opened his mouth, and she poured a splash of the poison in. It was flowery and bitter, stinging the back of his throat, but he resisted the urge to spit it out.

"I need some time to set things in motion," she whispered as she stood. "Be ready. Don't do anything stupid in the meantime."

Lucien waited, biding his time and biting his tongue. Although his ability to shift had come back by the next evening—the beast now furious and thrashing in its chains—he couldn't let anyone know. Maldren came to him a few times each day with the same wooden bowl of water, the dart thistle mixed in to stop him from healing. The second time she came, a couple of other shifters were within ear shot, so Mal instructed him to act like he'd just been dosed with the ashroot as well.

Other shifters came by where he was being held and laughed or jeered at him, or spit on him. One shifter even sent a solid kick into his ribs as he lay on the ground, his hands still bound. Lucien saw it coming and rolled with the kick just enough to lessen the impact and avoid breaking any ribs. With the dart thistle, he wouldn't be able to heal, and he'd have to deal with any injuries until the poison wore off.

How much time had passed since Micah had dragged him back here? It had to have been at least a few days, given the distance to cover, but with the canopy of leaves hiding the moon, he hadn't been able to judge exactly how long it had been. He prayed that Jae made it back to the farmstead with Faith, that she and Corvin were guiding his family to Whitehollow now.

After a few days, Lucien was barely containing his fury at Micah and the shifters. But if he cut the beast loose and changed now, if he tried to fight his way through, he'd never make it to the Heart alive. And even if he did, he'd never make it out of the Red Forest, and Micah would spend as much time as it took to hunt down Ethriel and Faith. Lucien needed to be smart about this. He needed to bide his time and wait. He needed *patience*.

Maldren arrived one night, just after full dark. She moved to him silently and crouched, unlocking the manacles around his wrists, then his ankles. "It's time."

"Why are you doing this?" Lucien asked. He'd been puzzling over the question since she'd stopped dosing him with the ashroot as she'd been ordered to. "Why are you helping me?"

"I was changed on my twenty-fourth birthday. I've lived with this"—she set her hand on her chest—"for damn near thirty years. And every day I have to fight just to be myself and not some slobbering monster. Micah doesn't want us to have more control than we do, because he knows then he'd have to fight us for the power he holds over us. But this can't be all there is. This can't be what we were meant to be."

"It isn't." Lucien's blood pulsed with Taerna's power, the Heart beckoning him.

"I'm helping you because I need to believe we can be more than what we are."

Lucien stood. He held his hand out to Mal, who clasped his forearm and hauled herself to her feet.

"Now keep your head down," Mal said. "We're going to have one shot at this." She whistled a light bird trill. Lucien spun at the rustle of leaves behind him.

Ethan crept out of the shadows, his human footfalls surprisingly light. He carried a bucket full of some foul-smelling muck.

"He's with us," Mal said to Lucien.

Lucien eyed the bucket. "Is that mud?"

Mal gave half a shrug. "Among other things." At his raised brows, she added, "It'll mask your scent. Micah set some of those loyal to him to guard the Heart. If they smell you coming, you're dead."

"How do you know all this?" Lucien asked.

She waved a hand at the bucket. "It's not a difficult problem."

"Not about the mud. About Micah. About everything he's doing."

Ethan cleared his throat, giving Mal a shake of his head in warning, but she held up her hand, cutting off his silent protest.

"Because I'm his second-in-command" she said. "When Micah overthrew Barrick and took the throne, he brought me with him. So you see . . ." She glanced over her shoulder, peering into the darkness. "I have an awful lot to lose by helping you, Lucien."

Ethan and Mal helped cover Lucien in the mud. Its pungent stench singed the inside of his nose, but once it dried, it smelled like little more than the decomposing leaves deep in the underbrush. Then Mal covered Ethan in the same stuff.

"Once we get to the edge of the Heart, he'll lead you the rest of the way while I distract the guards. I'll join you as soon as I can, but don't wait for me. Do what needs to be done, understand?"

Lucien nodded. "I understand."

"I'm trusting you. Don't fuck this up, Longshadow."

Chapter 63

Dare was only vaguely aware of sounds around him. More distinct and prevalent was the sharp, wrenching pain in his shoulders. He shifted to try to alleviate the pressure but met resistance against his wrists and another searing jolt through his arms.

When he opened his eyes, shadows surrounded him, though a diffuse light provided just enough of a glow to see the outline of nearby shapes. His hands were bound and pulled tight above his head with iron chains bolted to the wall. He could stand, which eased the pressure in his shoulders slightly.

His breath quickened. *What the fuck?* Dare pulled against the chains, but all it did was torque his shoulders further.

Tykaras?

There was no answer.

Tykaras!

Panic swelled in his chest. "Fuck!" Dare pulled against the chains again and forced himself to think back. His head was foggy, his thoughts slow and dulled. It was almost like being drunk, but it was distinct and seemed to cling to the edges of his thoughts. How did he get here? He'd been in his room, writing a note to Verity, but then . . . Tanithe had drugged him . . . and . . .

He tried to brush the cobwebs away. Maybe whatever drug she'd used was affecting his connection to Tykaras somehow. The channel had to be open in both directions, after all, and if he wasn't in control of his side . . .

Dare steadied his mind. *Tykaras,* he tried again.

Child, Tykaras replied after a moment, the words accompanied by the familiar, expansive presence of the god.

Relief flooded through Dare, and he leaned his head against the stone wall. *What happened?*

I don't know, Tykaras said. *My attention was needed elsewhere. But . . .* The last of the fogginess in Dare's mind dissipated, as though Tykaras had waved it away with a sweep of their hand. *I do not like the look of this.*

Cold dread wove through him. Tykaras hadn't seemed one to exaggerate or give false impressions. *You mean, it's worse than just the fact that I've been drugged and chained to a wall?*

I'm afraid so.

Dare tugged instinctively on his bindings again, though it changed nothing. *Lovely. Where am I?* He vaguely remembered a city skyline . . . *Am I in Valda?*

Yes. She used the power from the dying shifters to open a portal.

Dare's thoughts snagged. *She . . . fucking wha—*

The shifters are tied to Taerna, even now. There's power here, and Vire's Chosen lurks nearby. Something's not right. I need to strengthen the shield.

The shield? What shield?

I will return, Child.

Tykaras, wait—

But the presence lifted, leaving Dare alone with his startlingly clear thoughts.

Tanithe had opened a portal. But that was impossible. That was *supposed* to be impossible. And she'd said it had been a test. A test for what? Dare shook his head. That was a problem for another day. Now that he could think straight, he needed to figure out how to get out of this mess.

The ground and walls were rough and uneven, though some places had clearly been sculpted and decorated once but worn over time, while others appeared purely functional. He was underground somewhere. Perhaps some old catacomb or sewer beneath Valda, but given the expansiveness of the city, that could be literally anywhere.

The already deep shadows near the room's entryway darkened further. Dare squinted and strained, trying to see or hear anything, but as the shadow flowed closer, a spiraling dizziness washed over Dare, turning his stomach.

"What the fuck are you doing now, Tanithe?" he asked, leaning his head against the wall again. "In case you didn't notice, you won. You're free to go on dicking about Valda and making whatever fucking power play you're after. You won." He was so sick of Tanithe fucking Ash fucking with his fucking life. Dare jerked his hands forward, rattling the chains so loud the clangs echoed. "You fucking *won*, Tanithe."

Tanithe fucking Ash emerged from the shadows at the edge of the room, a sinister smile pulling at her lips just a bit too far. "Aw, thank you," she cooed. "It's so nice to hear you admit it."

"What the fuck do you even still need me for?"

"There are seven gods in this world," Tanithe said, her voice low and soft. "Four of them have places of power that bind their influence to the mortal world. Surrounding those places of power, the god's influence flows like water, worshipers flock to their calling, and their power grows." Her eyes narrowed on him. "Do you know who *doesn't* have a place of power connecting them to the mortal realm?"

"Ainam?" Dare knew that wasn't the answer she wanted, but he couldn't help himself.

And yet she nodded once before tapping him in the chest. "Also Tykaras and"—she pointed to herself—"Vire." She stepped back, gesturing to the space around her. "And Valda is primed to receive Vire's power. His influence is everywhere already. All he needs is enough power to break through into the mortal world."

"Break through?"

Slowly, the pieces snapped into place. *Break through . . . Like a portal . . .*

"It needs a large amount of magic to accomplish. Divine and otherwise. But my test yesterday afternoon proved it's possible."

Yesterday? He'd already lost a day.

Tanithe's eyes locked on Dare's as her smile widened. "Lucky for me, I've got a direct connection to a god right here and a powerful Channel on top of it."

"What's the matter?" Dare baited. "You're not strong enough to do it so you need my sorry ass?"

Tanithe laughed again, loud and slightly unhinged. "Oh, my sweet little lordling. This requires far too much power to accomplish on my own. Divine power pulled through a god's Chosen to pierce the fabric of the world, and arcane magic to hold it open and bind it to this plane." She cupped his chin. "If you'd only agreed to help me, we could have split the work. But instead, I'll simply take what I need from you and save myself the effort."

Dare swallowed hard. She meant to bleed him dry. "You can't channel that kind of power," he tried. Maybe he could hit on her logical side. "You'll just kill me, and then where will you be?"

"Oh, it'll take days." She cracked her knuckles, though she never took her eyes from Dare. And never stopped grinning wildly. "Possibly weeks. It'll be like charging a very large periapt. We'll have to take our time, darling, and do this right. Lucky for us, we have plenty of time."

Fuck fuck fuck. This was very bad. *Tykaras, please . . . Help me.*

But there was no answer save Tanithe's voice echoing in his ears. Between one blink and the next, a dagger was in her hand, the tip pressed against the soft flesh of his tricep. She drew a line down his arm, pain blossoming at the slow, methodical—but shallow—cut. "I can't wait to see what goodies you have for me in here."

Panic settled into Dare's chest. He'd fucked up so completely that no one would even know he was missing. And if he never came back? Would they think he just ran away? Would Verity realize she made a mistake in swearing him into the Wardens? Would Gregor worry about him, as he'd claimed he'd done when Dare had left Brookshire? Or would he take Dare's disappearance and add it to the lies, the deceit—to everything Dare had worried he'd despise—and decide he was better off without Dare in his life after all?

And even if they somehow discovered that Tanithe was holding him captive in Valda . . .

Would they care?

Two people in dark clothes and black masks over the bottom halves of their faces came into the room. A symbol was etched into the cheek of each of their masks, like a teardrop.

No, not a tear. An eight-pointed star.

Tanithe licked her lips as they unchained him and shoved him through the tunnel toward a large chamber where other black-clad people stood in a circle. At the center of that circle was a tall stone pillar with an iron loop bolted to it. The two who brought him in pulled him to the pillar and chained his manacles to it, locking his arms above his head again. His bindings secure, they joined the others around the circle.

"I didn't realize we were going to have an audience," Dare said, his voice steady even as his mind reached frantically out for Tykaras again.

The twinkle in Tanithe's eye sent a shiver through his core. "Oh, they're not the audience, my dear." A sweep of her arm encompassed the room. "They're the crew."

Chapter 64

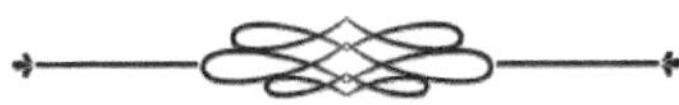

The Heart of the Red Forest was in a deep ravine, bordered on three sides by steep cliffs. The only trail leading into it by foot was blocked by four shifters, all in their bestial forms. Mal approached from the wooded path, as they'd discussed, while Lucien and Ethan circled around. Even with Mal distracting them, they were going to have to scale down the cliff face into the ravine.

If Lucien had thought Taerna's tree in the center of Taernfane was a strong connection to the goddess's power, standing at the edge of the ravine, so close to the Heart, was something else entirely. It was as though the crystal core within himself stretched down into the earth beneath his feet. Taerna's power hummed within him. Each stone he touched seemed to resonate, amplifying the song in his blood. The crimson leaves above rustled in a breeze that wasn't there. They were calling to him. They wanted him to bring his magic forward, to relax into that power and let it become part of him.

But terrible things always happened when he relaxed. If he loosened his control, the beast would emerge on its own and cause nothing but destruction.

And yet the power sang in his veins, thrumming in tune with the stones and crystals of the ravine, the leaves overhead, until he was certain every shifter within a mile of the Heart would feel it.

Lucien signaled for Ethan to pause. The other shifter angled his head toward where Mal was distracting the sentries, his warning clear. They didn't have much time.

Lucien held up one finger. He would only need a moment. He hoped.

If there was ever a time that he needed to trust in Taerna's power, this was it. She had brought him this far. She had trusted this task to him. To bring the shifters back from Vire's corruption to the warriors they once were. If Taerna wanted him to let go, he would trust her.

Lucien closed his eyes and let go.

The power within him flowed through the crystal at his core and split like light cast through a prism, illuminating the world around him in shades of gray behind his eyelids. The earth and stones, trees and plants all opened to him, as though he could reach out and pull each of them to him with a command.

Lucien reached with that humming power toward the trees around him. Vines unfurled from the trees, unwinding toward Lucien and Ethan. Following his thoughts, the vines trailed through the underbrush, over the edge of the ravine, and down the cliff face.

"Longshadow . . . ?" Ethan's voice was soft but wary.

Lucien grabbed two of the vines, holding one out to Ethan. "It'll be faster than climbing down."

"Yeah," Ethan replied, taking the offered vine. "Especially if we fall."

They wouldn't fall. Thin though they were, the vines would hold strong. Lucien knew their strength as surely as he knew his own.

Lucien and Ethan belayed down the cliff until they stood at the bottom of the ravine. Within the Heart, the canopy was even more dense than in other parts of the forest, and yet the light from the stars seemed to reflect off the leaves overhead, lighting their way. He could sense the shifters on the outer edge of the ravine. Five of them. Mal must still be up there.

Energy flowed through the earth, and Lucien followed the pull as it led him deeper toward a crystal-clear pool in the very center of the ravine. The pool was open to the sky and perfectly still, the moon and stars mirrored in its surface.

Lucien knelt at the water's edge. Here. He'd seen this lake before, in his visions from Taerna. Here was where the shifters were made with Taerna's power. But now what? He'd hoped for a sign about what to do next. Maldren and Ethan were counting on him. Ethriel and Faith were counting on him.

He sank his hands into the mud at the edge of the water, sending a gentle ripple floating across the surface and disturbing the perfect reflection of the sky. *Taerna, what do I do? What do you need of me?*

Lucien closed his hands into fists, and a sharpened stone stabbed against his palm. He withdrew his hands. The center of his right palm was bleeding. He waited for the wound to heal over, but it didn't. He'd been dosed with dart thistle for days; it was going to take longer than a couple of hours for his healing to return.

The red blood mixed with the mud and silt from the lake's edge. It swirled together, tan and crimson. Earth and blood. His blood, which held the power of a goddess. The earth, from which the goddess had, eons ago, spawned the shifters.

Lucien brought his cupped hand to his lips, his eyes closing. *Mother Taerna,* he prayed, *may my blood and your earth break the curse and free your warriors. Grant your children peace.*

Lucien drank the mixture of blood and earth from his palm. Warmth spread down his throat and settled into the deepest parts of him. The gentle heat built until it was a heaviness in his chest, a crushing weight that pulled him in on himself. He struggled to stay upright.

You are as a stone of the earth, little wolf, Taerna had told him once. *Pressure does not break you. It only serves to strengthen you.*

Lucien imagined himself as a stone of the earth, letting the building pressure compress him into something harder, something stronger. If this would be his crucible, he would not break. He would find his strength in the crushing pain, and he would come out more than what he'd been.

In the darkness behind his closed eyes, Lucien saw his beast held fast in its chains. It thrashed, as though it felt that same crushing pressure. Lucien gritted his teeth, and so did his beast. As the weight, the pain became too much—as it crossed the line from what he thought he could survive into what he knew he couldn't—the beast collapsed, and so did he.

"Lucien?"

A voice, distant.

"We have to go."

Somewhere in his mind, Ethriel's voice reached him. *Get up, Luc.*

"Lucien, get up!"

Luc, you promised.

"Can you hear me?"

As long as you have breath in your lungs . . .

Deep within the pitch dark, the beast lay with its chin resting flat against the ground, looking up at him.

. . . And legs to carry you.

As though sensing Lucien's attention, the beast lifted its head and cocked it to the side. *Run?*

No, Lucien said, and the beast settled back down.

You promised, Luc. Come back to me.

As though hearing it too, the beast's ears pricked up. Yet it still lay contentedly on the ground, its tail thumping in a slow rhythm.

You promised.

"Lucien!"

He opened his eyes to find Maldren standing over him. Ethan crouched nearby, his dark eyes staring warily at Lucien.

"I distracted the sentries, but someone must have realized you were missing and raised the alarm. It won't be long before they figure out what we're up to." Mal looked him over where he lay in the mud and sand of the shore. "Well?"

Lucien stood slowly on shaking legs. He could scarcely find the words. The near-blinding rage, the urge to tear apart anything with a pulse . . . They were simply *gone.* He felt like a version of himself he hadn't known for twenty years.

Lucien called on the beast within him. In his mind, he unlocked the chains holding it at bay.

The caked-on mud and grime flaked away, and the shift happened so smoothly, so perfectly, Lucien had to check his reflection in the lake to ensure that it had happened at all. There, staring back at him, was a massive wolf with dark gray fur, golden eyes, and a scar cutting from his temple down his jaw.

Not a monster. Not a beast.

A wolf.

Lucien wasn't sure if he wanted to leap for joy or fall to the ground weeping, but he had time for neither. Remembering the other two with him, he turned to find Maldren and Ethan gaping at him.

Lucien shifted back to his human form. There was no pain, no cracking of joints and bones. It was swift and natural, as easy as breathing. He beckoned Ethan closer as he held a hand out to Mal. "I know what we need to do."

At the water's edge, Lucien took a handful of silt and water, swirling them together with the blood from his still-bleeding palm. He offered his cupped hands to Maldren.

She hesitated only a moment before she drank. Her eyes rolled back in her head, and Ethan caught her as she fell.

A howl pierced the night. Another sounded after, closer. They were running out of time.

"You next," Lucien said to Ethan. But the shifter didn't move from Mal's side. "I'll watch over you both until you come to. You have my word."

Ethan still crouched beside Maldren.

"How long was I out?" Lucien asked.

Ethan looked up at him. "About three minutes."

Another howl cut through the silence of the ravine.

"We don't have time to wait until after she wakes up," Lucien said. At the edge of his awareness, he could feel the shifters moving through the trees toward the Heart. "We have to do this now."

Ethan nodded.

Lucien repeated the process, and Ethan drank. His eyes fluttered closed, and he began to collapse where he knelt beside Mal. Lucien caught him and lowered him the rest of the way to the ground.

The trees along the edge of the Heart alerted him to the four shifters sprinting toward the ravine. Those must be the sentries Mal had distracted. They'd be at the Heart before either Maldren or Ethan would be awake. He scooped Maldren up in his arms and brought her to the edge of the clearing. He did the same with Ethan, laying them side by side. Stretching out his hand, he willed the ferns and bushes to drape over them both, hiding them from view. It wouldn't stop the shifters from sniffing out Mal—Ethan's scent was still blocked by the mud covering him—but it should buy them some time at least.

A howl ripped through the night, coming from the bottom of the ravine. *Intruders*, it said. Another howl. *Betrayal*.

So they'd figured out about Mal. Dammit.

Other barks and snarls joined it from farther away. They echoed through the clear night. *Coming*, some of them said. *Attack*, others said. *Maul*.

Then a series of howls shattered the night. They boomed through the Red Forest, silencing every other shifter.

Only Micah Fogrender would have that kind of power.

The howls were an order. A promise.

Kill. Them. All.

Lucien ran toward the path that came into the ravine. He'd meet them there, keep them away from the pond. He didn't want to taint this purest place of Taerna's power.

As he stepped through the trees, the four shifters came into view ahead, lumbering toward him in their beast forms. Lucien raised his arms, palms out. Words had never been a strength of his. But where he'd failed in the Glade, maybe he could convince them now, here.

"Give me a chance to explain what I'm trying to do," he said.

He'd hardly finished his sentence when the shifters roared and charged ahead. *Fine.* If they wouldn't listen, he would show them.

Lucien dove out of their way, letting his wolf out. He landed on all fours, growling a warning at the four shifters. He didn't want to kill them, but he needed to hold them off long enough for Maldren and Ethan to wake. Then they needed to get the hells out before every shifter in the Red Forest arrived to stop them.

They hesitated a moment at the sight of the wolf standing before them, but it didn't last long. They moved to circle him, though thankfully they had to work around the dense trees, which gave him some protection. As a mottled gray and brown shifter charged, Lucien stayed low. He pushed up under the shifter, closing his jaws around their throat as he flipped them onto their back in the underbrush. He held his teeth against their throat without breaking the skin.

The shifter beneath him froze, but the others closed in.

Lucien backed off from the one on the ground. He needed to give them one more chance before he killed any of them. He pulled the wolf back, and it withdrew without a fight. In his human form again, Lucien took a few steps back from the shifters.

"You don't have to do this," he tried again. "You don't have to follow Micah. There's another way."

The shifters slowed their approach but didn't stop. He only had another moment to try.

"Let us go. Give me a chance to challenge Micah."

One of the shifters was directly in front of him, snarling.

Lucien stared them down. "We're meant to be wolves, not monsters. You've seen—"

The shifter opened its maw and lunged. Lucien raised his forearm as the shifter's jaws snapped shut. Their fangs clamped down, and stabbing pain flared through his arm. Lucien reached for Taerna's power and pushed it forward. Vines descended from the trees and wrapped around the shifters legs, torso, throat. The beast roared and released Lucien as the vines lifted them from the ground, holding them aloft.

His arm throbbed, bleeding freely. He'd forgotten about the dart thistle; his healing still hadn't returned. He needed to be more careful.

The other three shifters were closing in. As one moved to launch itself at Lucien, another creature leapt through the trees and slammed into their side. The massive wolf had had silvery, pale gray fur.

Maldren.

She didn't show the shifters the same mercy Lucien had tried to. She closed her jaws around the throat of the shifter she'd barreled into and tore her head back. Blood splattered the nearby trees. When she turned to Lucien, her muzzle dripped red.

Seeing another wolf gave the remaining two shifters pause. No doubt they recognized Maldren, even in this new form. She barked a warning at them. *Back off.*

One of the shifters lifted their head toward Lucien and snarled back. *Betrayer.*

Maldren growled low in her chest. *Champion.* A quiet yip followed. *Friend.*

Another series of howls reverberated through the ravine, much closer than earlier. Dozens of shifters were about to descend on them.

"Mal, I think we're out of time." Lucien pulled his wolf forward. The ease with which he could shift between forms was going to take some getting used to. He moved to stand beside Maldren and growled one last warning to the remaining shifters.

Last chance.

They charged with a bellowing roar.

Lucien dodged, bounding to the side. The ground thrummed where the shifter landed. Lucien pulled on Taerna's magic, willing the earth to move. A pit opened beneath the shifter, dropping them into the earth fast enough that their chin slammed against the edge of the hole.

As the shifter hurried to climb out, Lucien pushed the dirt forward again, filling in the pit as though it had never been. One paw scratched at the ground, the shifter's head thrashing as they tried to free themselves, but the rest of their body was buried in the packed earth of the ravine.

Lucien turned to Maldren, who circled the last shifter. She slashed at them with her claws, driving them back. Lucien snapped a sharp bark. The shifter glanced his way, and Mal took advantage of the split-second distraction. She leapt on the shifter, slamming them into the ground. They tumbled together, Mal clawing them with everything she had.

The shifter managed to get to their feet, blood dripping from at least a dozen wounds, staining its pale fur. They scrambled backward, putting as much space between themselves and Maldren's wolf as they could.

Mal reined the wolf in, shifting back into her human form. Blood stained her lips and chin. "Tell Micah what happened here," she sneered. "Tell him what you witnessed."

The shifter turned tail and ran. Lucien and Maldren bolted back to the lake where they'd left Ethan. He was just climbing out from the hiding place Lucien had created when they reached him. He looked like he'd seen a ghost.

Lucien shifted back to his human form. "We need to get out of here. Are you both alright?"

Mal dropped her hands onto her knees, breathing hard. "Holy shit, Long-shadow." She straightened again and tilted her head to the sky. She set a shaking hand on her chest. "It's . . ."

"Quiet," Ethan said, touching his chest as well. "It's *quiet*."

"I had no idea," Mal whispered. A tear slid down her cheek.

"Me neither." Lucien wished he could give them all the time in the world to marvel at their new situation, but they needed to go. "Follow me. As quick and silent as you can."

Lucien shifted and took off around the far side of the pond, trusting that Mal and Ethan were behind him. His foreleg throbbed as he ran, the bite still painful and bleeding, but he would have time to worry about that later.

The underbrush was thicker on this side of the water. Lucien stretched his awareness out in all directions. The shifters were storming the ravine from the footpath as he'd expected. He willed the plants to part before them and tighten up behind them, becoming denser and harder to navigate while also covering their tracks.

When they reached the steep walls that marked the edge of the ravine, Lucien shifted to human again. Mal and Ethan trotted up beside him and did the same.

"Got any more of those vines?" Ethan asked.

Before Maldren could get a word in, Lucien asked the trees at the top of the ravine for their help. The vines lowered as before, strengthening at his touch. They each grabbed hold of one, and Lucien asked the vines to retract, pulling them swiftly and silently up the cliff face.

He'd never had the gift for magic, and he'd hardly tested his powers before this. But somehow, here at Taerna's Heart, at the birthplace of the shifters, the magic of the earth flowed into him from every direction. It was so easy, so simple here. And it seemed to just make sense the way little else did.

At the top of the ravine, they shifted into wolves again and ran. Lucien continued clearing their path and, with every bounding step, closed it behind them. In some cases, he grew brambles to make the way more difficult, though he was careful not to leave a trail of obstructions that would be just as easy to follow.

Lucien, Mal, and Ethan burst through the tree line at the northern edge of the Red Forest and headed straight into the foothills of the Mistvale Mountains. Only when the pink rays of dawn crested the hills in the east did they slow.

Staggering a few steps, Lucien returned to his human form. His limbs felt like they were made of stone with how they weighed him down. The further he got from the Heart, the harder he had to work to call on Taerna's magic to move the earth and plants in their path. He hadn't let that slow him down, but now the exhaustion closed in.

"You should sit," Mal said, moving to his side.

He sat unceremoniously on the cold ground, breathing hard. About an hour ago, his arm had stopped throbbing, and he was pleased to find that the bite wound had healed over at last. It seemed the dart thistle was finally out of his system.

"Thank you for your help," he said to Mal and Ethan. "I don't think I could have pulled that off without you both."

"Thank you for this," Mal said, holding her arms out to the side as though to encompass herself and everything around them.

Ethan nodded his agreement.

"But now what do we do?" she asked.

Lucien's chest heaved as he lay back. "We break the curse for the rest of the shifters."

"How?" Mal crouched beside him. "We can't help them if we can't get back to the Heart."

"I don't know," Lucien admitted. They'd figure something out. They'd find a way to save them from the curse. But for now, he needed to rest. And they needed to regroup.

"Where do we go?" Ethan asked, his focus on the path behind them, as though he expected Micah to appear at any moment.

"Whitehollow." Lucien's eyes closed as he breathed in the fresh air of the mountains, sleep pulling at his tired and aching muscles. "We're going to White-hollow."

Chapter 65

Two days passed. Two days of Gregor coordinating care for those who'd been impacted by the shifter attack. Thankfully, it had been a small assault, all things considered, and the shifters had been taken down remarkably quickly by the city guard and the Wardens who were still in Whitehollow. Verity was still trying to sort out the *why* of it, as well as whether this was related to the shifters mobilizing north of Valda.

That first night after the attack, Gregor hadn't gotten back to the Drahkonian embassy until well after midnight. After updating Chancellor Caelan, he'd been about to collapse into bed when Verity had shown up with a note from Dare.

He'd left.

Part of Gregor was grateful Dare had somehow managed to get out of Whitehollow before the attack, but . . .

But he'd left.

Gregor had pushed everything down so he could focus on the work to be done, but he saw the way Jae watched him, as though she knew he was only fooling himself.

After a couple of days, the relief efforts were running largely on their own with minimal direct oversight from Gregor. Unfortunately, that meant his worries had room to creep back in. He hadn't checked on Reverie and Haven yet, but the guard he'd assigned directly to them had said he returned them to their aunt's house. Gregor would check on them soon, but there was something else he needed to do first.

Gregor stopped in the hallway in front of Verity's office. Was he making something out of nothing? Verity was so busy, Gregor didn't want to waste her time if he were being foolish. But the more he thought about it, the more his worry settled into his stomach and refused to let go. *Something* was wrong.

Gregor swallowed his uncertainty and knocked on the door.

"Come in," Verity called. The High Commander of the Wardens was leaning over her desk, though she smiled warmly at him when he entered. "Gregor! It's nice to see you."

Finn looked up from where she was reclining in one of the chairs reserved for visitors, her feet up on the other chair. She jumped up and ran over, giving him a tight hug.

He'd hardly seen either of them for the last couple of days, and he smiled despite his gnawing anxiety. "I'm glad you're here," he said, returning Finn's hug. "I actually wanted to speak with both of you."

Finn's face turned serious as she guided Gregor to one of the chairs.

Verity set her quill on the desk and clasped her hands, her paperwork forgotten. "What's wrong?"

He slid his glasses off and cleaned the lenses with the hem of his shirt. "It's Dare," he said after a deep breath. "I haven't seen him since . . . Well, since we all saw him right before the attack on the city." It had only been two and a half days. Was he being foolish?

Finn leaned back in the chair, crossing her legs at the ankles. "He said he'd leave us alone for a while." She glanced at Verity, who nodded. "He left that note for Vee about going back to Valda."

Verity scoffed quietly but otherwise said nothing.

"I know," Gregor said. "But . . . I think something's wrong. This isn't like him."

"Which part?" Verity asked. "The part where he does something stupid and selfish, or the part where he disappears without a trace?"

Gregor flinched even as Verity caught her words and inhaled sharply.

"I'm sorry," she added. "That was unfair of me. I just mean that this doesn't seem entirely out of character for him."

She wasn't wrong, and yet how had Dare managed to get out before the attack? There'd hardly been enough time for him to pack his things.

"This feels different," Gregor said. "I'm not sure I can explain it. Even when he left years ago, he told me he was leaving. He didn't just—" He thought of Jae and bit off the rest of his sentence.

Verity's face softened. "I'm sure he'll be back, Gregor. He probably just needs some time."

"Could I see his room?" he asked. "I need to see what he took with him and what he . . . what he left behind."

"Alright. If it will help you." Verity stood, stacking a few papers neatly on her desk.

Gregor followed Verity and Finn out of the office and across the base to the barracks, past the ever-burning brazier to Pyrannis. Verity kissed her fingers and set them on top of the low stone wall surrounding the brazier as they passed.

They stopped to grab the extra key from the older man in the office at the front of the building, and Verity led them to the room. She opened the door and stepped aside for Gregor to enter.

Dare's room was messy by what he'd come to expect from the Wardens but neater than what he'd come to expect from Dare. The bed was unmade, and a few books and papers were scattered across the desk. Beside it, Dare's knapsack lay empty save for a few small articles.

"If he was leaving," Gregor said, pointing at the abandoned pack, "wouldn't he have taken that?"

Verity shrugged. "Normally I'd say yes, but he was heading to Valda. He has a home there and money that he's saved. I don't know that he'd bother with any of the meager belongings he had here. Especially if he was in a hurry."

"Still," Finn said quietly. "Isn't it about a three-day ride from here? Seems like he would've taken something."

"It's less than a day by ship." Verity set her hand on Gregor's shoulder. "I'm sorry, Gregor. I'm sure he'll be back when he's ready. In the meantime, I'll send word to the Wardens in Valda to see if he's checked in with them. I can't promise he would've done that, but it's one thing I can do. Alright?"

He nodded slowly. "Yes, thank you, Verity."

She watched him for a moment before she stepped toward the door. "I need to get back," she said gently. "Stay as long as you need to." She handed Finn the key before she turned and left, her boots clicking down the stone hall.

"I'm sure everything's fine," Finn said, moving to sit on the edge of the bed.

Gregor sat in Dare's chair, looking over the desk and the papers strewn over its surface, the quill with ink dried onto the tip. When he moved, his foot kicked something metal that skittered across the floor. He stooped to pick it up.

Finn leaned in a little closer. "What's that?"

"Something I gave him," Gregor murmured. He ran his thumb over the iron key, its chain broken.

It had meant so much to Dare. Would he have left it behind? Would he have left Gregor behind?

Again?

The corners of his eyes burned.

"Finn," he said after a long moment, once he was certain he could keep his voice steady. "I need your help with something."

She tore her attention away from the key. "Anything. What do you need?"

"I know what you think," Gregor said. "And I know what Verity said. And I know you don't want to see him right now—Vire's hells, I'm not sure *I* want to see him right now, but I think something's very wrong." He paused. He was rambling. "I need you to find him for me."

Finn traced her fingers along the rough blanket bunched up beside her. "I may be pissed as hell with him right now, but that doesn't mean I want something bad to happen to him. It might take me a while, though. Especially if he went back to Valda. I know most of his usual haunts there, but if he doesn't want to be found . . ."

A memory surfaced, unbidden. Gregor was standing on the parapets in Taernfane with Dare.

You're hard to find when you don't want to be found, Gregor had said to him that night.

Dare had given his usual smirk. *A useful skill in my line of work.*

If Dare truly didn't want to be found, would even Finn be able to find him?

"I know," Gregor said. "But we have to try." His voice trembled. "Find him, Finn. Please?"

"I will," she said as she stood. "I promise."

499

EPILOGUE

HOW MANY DAYS HAS it been? I've lost count of the times I've been dragged to that standing stone. When the channeling started, I thought briefly to compare it to when Verity channeled through me to banish the Binding spell on Solace.

But that was one mage trying very hard to draw enough power to do a job without hurting me. This is a dozen mages trying very hard to pull every ounce of power they can without allowing me to die.

There is no comparison.

Tykaras tried to shield me from it at first, but their power is what Tanithe is after. The more Tykaras tries to protect me, the more of their power Tanithe gets.

I block them out as best I can. The connection has to be open on both sides. I can't always focus enough to keep it closed, especially once the channeling starts, but I do the best I can. Just because I can't stop Tanithe doesn't mean I have to make it easy for her.

My world is agony and stabbing magic. Screams echo around me—*my* screams. It's more magic than I've ever felt in one place, and no amount of training from Verity can help me. It's like a part of me is being stripped away. They need blood to do it, and I'm certain my back and chest and arms are a patchwork of cuts. Eventually, I pass out.

When I wake up, my body feels as though I've been wrapped up tight in a blanket of nails. But I'm back in the dungeon, chained to the wall. It's hard to think. I can't find Tykaras in the cold, empty dark.

One of Tanithe's minions, their face covered with a black mask, comes into my cell sometimes to bring me water. At least, I think it's supposed to be water. But it tastes like shit and makes me retch half the time. They force it down my throat.

The only relief I get is in the moments when they drag me to that damned standing stone. That's when Tanithe mutters a few words and the needling cocoon dissipates. Once the pain fades away and I can remember how to think again, there's just enough time before the channeling starts for me to think of you.

Then the pattern repeats.

I wish she would just fucking kill me. But I regret the thought almost as quickly as it strikes me. If I die here, I'll never see you again. But it's *that* thought—the thought of losing you forever—that makes me want to die. I'm not afraid of death. Not this time. Everything dies.

All stories end.

I picture your face for as long as I can. You'd always been such a crucial part of my life before I left home. And it's funny—I hadn't seen you in eleven years, and yet . . . and yet that flutter in my heart when I see you . . . That warmth that you bring to my life . . . It didn't fade. Not a bit.

Maybe not everything can die after all.

If this is to be the end of my story, I'll hold that picture of you in my mind. I'll hold on to the feeling of your arms around me, your chest pressed against my back.

The next time I wake, the masked minion is there, pressing the cup of water to my lips. How long have I been here?

"Vire's demons," she mutters, but the rest of her words trail off. My vision darkens around the edges until all I can see are the whiskey-colored eyes staring at me over the mask.

"Stay with me," the voice says, sharp.

But I can't. Not when a hundred thousand shards of magic are pushing me in on myself. Not when the darkness promises peace.

So I let myself fall.

ACKNOWLEDGEMENTS

This book simply wouldn't exist without all the people who have been cheering me on through book one and much, much, *much* earlier than that.

Thank you to YOU — my readers. Thank you for coming with me on this wild journey, for messaging me with reactions and incoherent screaming, for creating ships and head canons and theories, and for loving these characters as much as I do.

My husband has been my partner and champion through publishing two books (during the most stressful time in our lives, I might add), and I'm so grateful for his continued love and support. The number of times I've started a conversation with "Can I just talk out a book thing?" is truly staggering, as is the fact that he's somehow not tired of it yet. Thank you, love.

Thank you to my son for being the strongest person I know, and for making sure I take time to play. I'm not yet ready to admit that you can beat me in Super Smash Bros. Ultimate . . . You're amazing and I love you. You can read this when you're older.

I would not be the person or the writer I am today without the unconditional love (and blank notebook purchases) of my parents. They've been cheering me on since *literally* the beginning. Thank you for everything. Extra thanks to my mom for helping with proofreading. You definitely saved me from a couple of embarrassing typos!

Many thanks to Gina for always being up for hearing my newest wild idea for adding more angst to the series. Her friendship, encouragement, and support through all of this nonsense has been a balm, a cozy blanket, a warm cup of mulled cider, a comforting hand on my shoulder. Thank you, bestie.

Thank you to my editor, Hannah. Working with her has been such a pleasure! She has no shortage of thoughtful suggestions that have made the series stronger and have helped make me a better writer. Thank you!

Thank you to my amazing beta readers: Alyssa, Dana, Gina, JodiMarie, Jon, Lauren, Nancy, and Paul. Thank you for taking the time and effort to provide feedback. Your insights and suggestions are magic.

Thank you to my ARC readers for spending time on this book before it's even been released. I appreciate you all so much!

Special thanks go to Jon D., Alyssa H., Veronica R., Hayley T., Kim D., Becca M., and Kelley H. You know what you did. And I'm eternally grateful.

ABOUT THE AUTHOR

Lindsey Brounstein worked in the publishing industry for fifteen years and now spends her days as a freelance editor and author in New Hampshire. For as long as she can remember, Lindsey has had a crazy cast of characters kicking around inside her head. Sometimes, she likes to put two of them in the same room to see what happens. When Lindsey's not writing, she loves immersing herself in both board and video games, knitting and — of course — reading.

You can follow Lindsey on Instagram or Threads as @writerlindsey or you can email her at lins@lindseybrounstein.com. You can also sign up for her newsletter or find Five Fates merch at www.lindseybrounstein.com.

THANK YOU FOR READING

Thank you for reading *Earth's Blood, Fate's Folly*.
If you enjoyed it, please consider leaving a review. Your ratings and comments
help indie authors like me reach wider audiences, and they help other readers find
books they might love.
Scan the QR code below to connect to various reviewing platforms.